DEVIL HUNTERS

TALES OF THE CRYPTO-HUNTER - 2

R. GUALTIERI

DEDICATION & ACKNOWLEDGEMENTS

For all of those awesome readers who have shown infinite patience to me with regards to this book, and J.G. — You continue to inspire me.

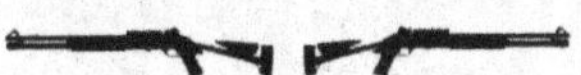

Special thanks to my awesome beta team: Jeffrey, David, Jeanette, Nora, Evelyn, Stephanie, Jonno, Eric, Phil, Jill, and Kyle. Tearing this story apart gave me the insight I needed to build it up again stronger than ever.

PROLOGUE

"Is this going to take much longer?" Sophie Guiterrez asked, breaking the silence permeating the dense forest. It amazed her that such a primal wilderness could exist here, barely an hour's drive from Atlantic City. There, crowds gathered upon the boardwalks and traffic snarled the streets. Desolate was the last word anyone would use to describe it. Yet, despite its close proximity, Sophie felt as if she was on a different planet altogether. She wondered if her husband, John, felt the same way, but decided against asking anything that didn't have to do with them getting back on the road.

"I just have to take a few more samples," John called over his shoulder. He was kneeling next to a small creek, gathering water into a container. Once done, he would seal it, mark it, and then place it with the half dozen or so other samples he'd already collected.

Grunting unhappily to herself, Sophie found a stump to sit down on. She knew her husband was passionate about his job, but that passion was supposed to be focused on her this weekend. A suite at the *Borgata* awaited them, as well as three days away from both their jobs. It was their first real vacation since getting married nearly a year ago. At the time, money had been tight, so they'd forgone a proper honeymoon. Fortunately, their finances had improved in recent months. Atlantic City might not have been an exotic getaway, but the accommodations were more than adequate.

Not like we plan on going out much anyway.

For the past few months, she and John had been trying to conceive. So far, their efforts had been unsuccessful. He claimed it was probably just stress from their jobs – he an employee for the New Jersey Agency for Environmental Protection, NJAEP for short, she an elementary school teacher in Jackson Township. She couldn't entirely disagree. He worked endless hours, while she had a long commute and unruly students on the best of days.

Still, it had begun to worry her nevertheless. They both wanted children. There was no disagreement on that subject. In the back of her mind, though, Sophie was starting to wonder if they should consider other options. They hadn't discussed it much, but fertility problems ran in her family. Her mother had gone through menopause early in life and her sister, Julia, had undergone a hysterectomy a few years back due to complications with ovarian cysts.

Sophie took a deep breath and tried to think of other things. Now was not the time for those concerns. She was determined to have some fun this weekend. Besides, maybe John had a point. If the mood was right and there was no stress to worry about, who was to say they might not return home a threesome in the making? That was a thought worth hanging onto.

Of course, they could have already gotten started had he simply told his superiors *no* like she had asked. He was originally scheduled for a half day so they could beat the weekend traffic down to the shore. But then he'd gone and agreed to this last minute *field trip*.

"It's not gonna take me long," he'd told her the night prior. "And it's on the way. By the time I'm finished, we'll already be most of the way there."

"I don't understand why they need to send you to begin with. You're not a field tech."

"I already told you, Charlie's out sick and nobody else is available."

He had then gone on to explain, much to her chagrin, why this couldn't wait. The sensor readings being shared in his office had crossed the minimum safe thresholds by a wide margin. An investigation was needed to ensure there wasn't a potential environmental situation in the making. That's how he always phrased it – a *situation*. His bosses at the NJAEP heavily frowned upon any use of the word *disaster*. The last thing they wanted was someone slipping up in a conversation, especially since most people were only a button push from Facebook these days.

Every year, reports came in from local hikers and fishermen regarding mutations – three-eyed fish or frogs with no legs. Generally speaking, this happened in any ecosystem from time to time. However, certain thresholds were maintained depending on the location. These data points were especially important for sanctuaries and protected areas. According to John, the threshold for toxins in this section of the reserve had been exceeded by a substantial margin as of late. The higher-ups wanted everything retested ASAP, before anything leaked to the local press.

"Afraid they'll start running stories about monsters in the Pine Barrens?" she'd joked.

John hadn't laughed. "That's exactly what I'm afraid of. Most people couldn't care less when it comes to ecological impact. But if the papers start talking about Bigfoot or the Jersey Devil, we'll have every yahoo in the tri-state area converging on this place. Then, if it turns out there actually is a problem with the water or soil, we'll find ourselves knee deep in a PR situation."

Sophie had cringed at his use of situation – his own personal *S word* – again. Such politically correct nonsense. She'd grown to despise it as their relationship had progressed. That ended the conversation for her, and she immediately changed the subject before it devolved into an argument.

Her curiosity had been piqued, though.

On the ride over, she found herself bringing it up again. By then, she had no choice but to come along, so she figured a little enthusiasm might put her husband in a good mood for the weekend ahead.

"What do you think is causing the problem?"

"Who can say?" he'd replied from his spot behind the wheel. "Could be illegal dumping, or it might be something leaking from one of the old mills."

"Old mills?"

"Yeah. It's all protected area now, but there used to be all sorts of efforts to develop this land. Lumber, paper mills – hell, there was even a moderately successful bog iron industry in the Barrens back in the day."

"Back in the day?" she'd asked, giving him her first grin of the morning. He was only twenty-five.

"Well, maybe a little further back. We're talking birth of a nation here. Industrial Revolution and all that."

"How could something so old affect anything?"

John had smiled back, seemingly encouraged by her show of support. "All those places closed up shop a long time ago, but a lot of the old buildings are still around, albeit they're all husks now, long taken back by the forest."

"How is that dangerous?"

"You have to realize this was before much thought was given to the environment. Back when they were still in operation, these mills produced tons of toxins, most of which were dumped wherever it was convenient."

"And?"

"*And* these guys weren't exactly big on cleaning up after themselves when they shut down. It was cheaper to just lock the doors and walk away. Over time, machinery rusts, storage tanks rot, you know the deal. When that happens where people live, we have a major cleanup on our hands. Out here, though..."

"Let me guess," she had replied, looking out the window of the state-owned SUV they were conveniently borrowing for the weekend. "Out here it's a massive pain in the ass."

"Exactly. Finding the source of the spill is hard enough. Getting a cleanup operation running, well, that's a whole other level of *fun* right there."

Upon their arrival, John offered to let her wait in the car while he collected samples. Sophie had refused. She knew he had a tendency to get lost in his work. Although she wasn't particularly fond of spending an afternoon in some godforsaken wilderness, she figured that continually reminding him of her presence could mean the difference of a few hours.

Now she was beginning to regret her decision. Though the temperature was cool, the effort of hiking through the woods had left her sweaty, dirty, and feeling a little gross. Forget about the casino – the first order of business upon arriving at the hotel was going to be a nice, long shower. The possibility that she wouldn't be taking it alone was small comfort to her at the moment. "I'm bored."

"I don't see how," he replied cheerfully. "Isn't this place great? Makes me wish I got out of the office more often."

Sophie ignored him as she stood and stretched. She felt wetness on her behind, reached back, and discovered that the seat of her pants was now sticky.

Just great! These are brand new jeans. Hopefully it was only morning dew or sap from the stump. The possibility that she may have accidentally sat in something else threatened to darken her mood further.

She was just about to complain again when she heard a chuffing noise from a few yards off. Thinking nothing of it, she said, "Bless you."

"For what?" John called back from where he was still organizing his pack.

"Didn't you sneeze?"

"Wasn't me. You probably just heard a bir..." The sound came again, catching his attention this time.

"What was that?" she asked. Whatever it was, it had originated from somewhere close by, the source hidden by the thick growth surrounding them. There was a heavy wheezing quality to it. One of Sophie's childhood play-mates had been asthmatic. This didn't sound entirely unlike her friend whilst in the grip of an attack. "Is someone there?" she called out, scanning the brush.

John chuckled in response. "You spook easily."

"That didn't sound like a person to you?"

"There's a lot of wildlife around us."

"A bear maybe?" she asked, a note of concern in her voice.

John didn't appear perturbed in the least. "Doubt it.

Even if there is one in the area, it'll just be a black bear. They won't bother us."

"Are you s...?"

Before Sophie could finish the question, something launched itself from the brush near John. Whatever it was, it was large and quick. It tackled her husband before he even knew what hit him. Together they went down in a tangle of arms and legs.

Heavy snarls replaced the chuffing, but those were quickly drowned out by the sound of John's screams.

Sophie stepped forward on instinct alone, but before she could reach her downed husband, his cries became a thick gurgle. There came the sound of something wet being torn and then a warm liquid splashed across her face.

In the space of an instant, she came to two realizations: she'd just been sprayed with her husband's blood, and the thing tearing into John was like nothing she had ever seen.

Her mind had just enough time to register the thick bumpy hide across its back, almost like a snake's scales. Then her nerve broke. Without another thought, Sophie turned and fled through the forest.

A bellowing cry followed her, almost human sounding, but that must have been her imagination. Whatever was out there wasn't human, not even close. Then another thought hit her, one that caused her to slow down ever so slightly. What if it had come from John? What if he was still alive, screaming out for her help ... help that wasn't coming?

Tears obscured her vision, but still she ran. Whatever it was that had attacked him, she knew in her heart that she would be ineffective against it. It had been larger than her husband and obviously far more powerful. Her panicked mind assured her there was nothing she could have done to help him. Disgust and sorrow welled up in her simultaneously. It threatened to drive her to her knees, but still she kept moving. The fear was too strong to let her stop. She tried to rationalize it by telling herself that if she could make it back to the car, she could find help, she could...

Sophie realized too late she had no idea if she was even fleeing in the right direction. For all she knew, she was racing deeper into the seemingly endless forest surrounding her. Suddenly, she was certain she'd been right earlier. Atlantic City *was* a world away, a world that she and her husband would never see again.

She tried to push that thought away and concentrate on running. The direction didn't even really matter. Getting hopelessly lost was better than standing there. Better than letting that thing catch her.

Her mind was still aflutter when she spied a break in the trees ahead. She ran into a small clearing and cried out in relief. There was someone standing near the far edge, facing away from her. She had made the right choice after all. There was still a chance. If he was armed or had friends nearby, maybe they could still save John.

"Please!" she cried out, racing forward. "Please! I need help. My husband..."

The figure turned to face her and she slid to a halt, the words dying in her throat.

Sophie thought she had found another person.

She was wrong.

1

The golden eagle soared effortlessly above the frozen landscape, its wings barely moving, held aloft by the updraft that preceded the storm front. A clap of thunder sounded in the distance, but the mighty bird paid it no mind. It was far too preoccupied searching for prey.

Something on the snow-covered ground caught its sharp eyes and it banked its impressive six-foot wingspan to investigate. It moved with the easy grace of a super predator, certain in the mastery of its domain. Soon, it spotted the fresh kill. It was likely that wolves or maybe a bear had brought down the great antlered beast below, but none of that mattered to the eagle. It had few qualms about facing down either opponent over meat. It knew it had little to fear from even the largest of land predators.

In the fading sunlight, as the storm's approach quickened, it began to circle, slowly descending toward the appetizing prize.

All at once, movement registered in its vision from down below – a flash of yellow hair, followed by something stepping from the brush near the kill. Like many predators, the eagle did not outright fear a lone human. However, its instincts commanded it to be wary. It continued circling, waiting to see if the intruder would move off. That was when something else caught its eye.

The eagle had no fear of any creature that walked the land, but what came from the sky was a different matter entirely. Though it realized the newcomer was still far above it, the shadow it cast on the ground dwarfed its own.

Banking its wings, the eagle made a sharp turn. The prize on the ground wasn't worth it. The creature that had entered its airspace was an enemy against which it could not win. With one last shriek, the eagle headed west, hoping to try its luck elsewhere.

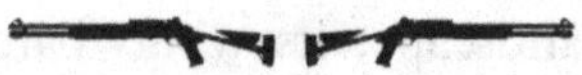

"What are you doing?" the voice from the Bluetooth headset demanded.

"My job," Daniella Kent – Danni to her friends – replied, stepping out of the hunting blind and approaching the dead moose.

"That's why we set the bait."

"This thing's already taken two kids from that village and it's started going after the adults, too. It's a man-eater and you know it, Derek. The bait isn't going to attract anything more than the usual scavengers." Danni rolled her eyes. It had been nearly a year since she'd joined the team and he *still* acted like she was a kid.

"We just need to be patient..." Derek began when another voice over the radio drowned him out.

"I see it!"

Danni was tempted to reply, "Told ya so!" but knew it would be childish. Besides, if the creature really was approaching, it would be unwise to engage in unnecessary banter.

"Can you get a shot, Frank?" Derek asked.

"No good," came the answer. "Still too far away, and the goddamned wind is picking up."

"They don't call them Thunderbirds for nothing," Danni said under her breath. She pushed an errant strand of blonde hair from her face, then lifted her rifle and scanned the sky through the scope.

"Danni..." Derek's voice warned.

"Where is it?" She lowered the rifle just as the oncoming clouds blotted out the sun. The dazzling brightness was immediately replaced by a shape much darker than the clouds above it.

The creature had been using the glare of the sun to mask its approach. With its cover gone, Danni could see the monstrous bird in all its glory. It was huge, with an eighteen-foot wingspan and a curved beak that looked like it could shatter bone. Worse, it was coming at her fast ... too fast.

Shit!

There wasn't time to line up a shot. Her training taking over, Danni threw herself into a hard dive, losing her grip on the gun in the process. Fortunately, big as the creature was, it was incapable of making a quick turn to compensate for her movement.

She had just enough time to think, *Where the hell are the others?* when the reports from multiple rifle shots reached her ears.

Danni hit the ground and rolled onto her back, hoping for the best. A splay of feathers fell from one of the creature's massive wings, but the monstrous bird remained airborne. *Damn it!*

It had been Derek's idea to split the team up at

multiple bait sites so as to cover more ground, but still remain close enough to provide cover for each other. Not a bad plan, really. Unfortunately, the storm was moving in faster than expected and the erratic wind gusts were playing havoc with their ability to hit a moving target. *Even one as big as a Cessna*, Danni mused, getting back to her feet in time to see the creature bank for another pass at her.

Not afraid of people. That's gonna cost you, you ugly son of a bitch. Despite the danger, a small smile played out across her lips. She must have been hanging out with Francis too much. His attitude was obviously starting to rub off on her. It probably wasn't the healthiest mindset for living a long life, but it was better than running scared.

Speaking of running... "Danni, lead it toward me so I can get a head-on shot."

She didn't need to be told twice. Despite its size, the bird was more maneuverable than she would have given it credit for. It was already positioned and building up speed for another run. Danni spotted her discarded rifle, determined there wasn't time to retrieve it, then turned and dashed toward Derek's position.

Thunder crashed overhead and suddenly the storm was upon them. The wind picked up and pinpricks of frozen rain began to pelt her.

"Just a little more," Derek said from over the headset.

A shriek from behind told her she didn't have a little more.

Screw this! She reached into her jacket and drew the semi-automatic pistol from the holster inside. Throwing herself into a dive, she spun, landed hard on her back, and took aim. There was almost no chance of missing at this range. The bird took up nearly her entire field of vision.

She squeezed the trigger over and over, unleashing a small volley of hellfire upon the beast. But then Danni realized she had a new problem. Regardless of whether she killed it, the small caliber bullets weren't going to stop the monster bird's momentum. Alive or dead, it was going to slam into her. Between its massive beak and outstretched talons, she was about to be impaled...

The creature's side exploded in a spray of blood just before the roar of a powerful rifle reached Danni's ears. The impact pinwheeled the bird off course just enough. It slammed into the ground a few feet to the right of where she lay, just as her gun clicked dry. As the mighty teratorn, king of the skies, came to rest, one of its massive wings fell upon her as one might put a blanket over a sleeping child.

"Danni!" came Derek's worried voice over the headset. "Are you okay?"

"Roger that, chief." She turned her head and coughed. "Damn, this thing stinks," she added, more to herself than to anyone listening.

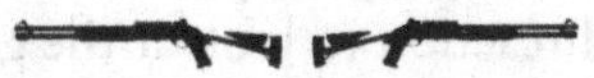

As Danni waited for Derek and Francis to join her, she studied the creature. It took her mind off the fact that she was probably going to get chewed out when they arrived. *Deservedly, too*, a small voice in the back of her head added.

Looking at the bird was like staring through some portal into the past. The creature rivaled some pterodactyls in size, dwarfing even the largest of modern raptors. At one point in history they'd been fairly common. It was a scary concept, but a little sad, too. This creature, like many others her team worked to keep off the general populace's radar, was highly endangered. To kill it was almost a crime in itself, but it was a necessary evil. This one had developed a taste for human flesh. Culling it saved lives. It probably also saved the few remaining members of its species. If this beast's existence was made public knowledge, every moron with a gun would want to bag one for their trophy room ... all in the guise of keeping people safe from *monsters*.

She tried to not let its death get her down. This thing had been plaguing a local Inuit village for months. The women, children, and elders were afraid to go outside, and their hunters weren't numerous enough to protect everyone at all times and still keep the village fed. Now they could get back to their lives and let the Thunderbird return to the legends where it belonged.

"You're going to give me a heart attack before my time. You know that, right?" Dr. Derek Jenner, her team's leader, asked from behind her, dragging her out of her reverie.

"I know. That was stupid."

"*Very* stupid. And unnecessarily risky."

We hunt monsters, Danni thought. *Technically, everything we do is unnecessarily risky.* She turned to face him. Despite an initial reaction to look at the ground, like some chastised child, she forced herself to meet his gaze. "Are you mad?"

Derek glanced down at the dead bird. "More worried than angry."

"Good because..."

"That doesn't mean I'm happy about it. We're going to have a little talk about teamwork later on..."

Before he could say more, the team's *cameraman*, Francis "Frank" LaCroix, joined them. "Holy shit! I should send this sucker home to my wife, tell her to stuff it in the freezer for Thanksgiving dinner." His gruffly jovial manner immediately cut through the tension.

No doubt realizing the moment was over, Derek's tone lightened up. "That's right, Frank. Give the poor woman one more reason to divorce your ugly ass."

"Aw, Shakti's a sweetheart," Danni playfully chided,

sensing it was safe to join in the banter. "She'd never leave him."

"Don't be too sure," Francis replied. "Hell, if this thing showed up in a box at my doorstep, even I'd leave me."

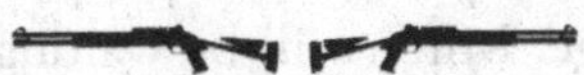

"What are you doing?" Danni asked. She and Francis had been preparing to burn the body so as to destroy any lingering evidence of the giant bird's existence.

"Threat or not, these creatures are sacred to the village," Derek replied from where he knelt over the corpse, hacksaw and pliers in hand. He rose a few moments later, holding a severed talon.

Francis raised an eyebrow. "Gift for the elders?"

"Something like that. It'll also prove to them the threat is over."

Danni glanced at it sidelong, then echoed Derek's earlier concern. "Isn't that unnecessarily risky?"

"Shouldn't be." He grinned back at her. "This will hold some pretty heavy spiritual significance for them. They won't let anyone else near it. Besides," he added with a wink, "it's a fake. We sent it to a lab in New York and they declared it to be made of whale bone."

Francis chuckled. "Did they now?"

"Our audience will be *so* disappointed," she said with mock concern.

Derek shrugged. "Fortunately for them, we'll leave just enough room for them to wonder ... like always."

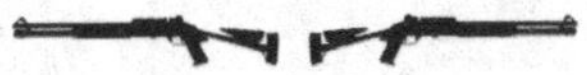

"...and thus for now, the Thunderbird will remain in the realm of myth and legend. But I remain ever vigilant. Should this creature decide to step from the shadows and once more claim dominion over the skies, my team will be there. The truth cannot hide from ... the Crypto Hunter."

"Cut!" Francis lowered the camera. "I believe that's a wrap for the field footage."

"Great," Derek replied. "Let's get packed up and head back to the village. Mitch will be waiting. Wouldn't want him thinking we ended up as bird food." He turned to Danni. "Speaking of which, we have a long walk back. Let's have a little chat about trying a bit harder to not end up on the menu of the things we hunt."

2

Mitchell Harkness, the team medic, was waiting when they arrived back at the small village some fifty miles northwest of Nome. Though not usually pleased with the concept of splitting up the team during a hunt, he'd found upon their arrival that many of the villagers were in need of medical assistance – some because of the creature they'd come to kill. Being that the nearest doctor only flew in once every few weeks, Mitchell had volunteered to stay behind to tend to the patients. However, that didn't mean he hadn't been getting increasingly antsy as the hours passed.

Despite the cold, he had kept one window cracked open so as to listen for gunfire. With the impending storm, he knew it was foolish but couldn't help it. The incident in Colorado a year earlier had left its mark on all of them, so he indulged himself the best he could while patching up those who needed it.

Once finished, he was tempted to head out to join his teammates, but that was an even worse idea than letting the three of them trek off without him. Knowing his luck, he'd find them at the exact wrong moment and end up getting his head blown off. Besides, it was only their second day in the village. If nothing was found, he could join them for tomorrow's hunt.

To keep his mind occupied, he'd grabbed one of Francis's spare cameras from the Snowcat and proceeded to question the elders about the legend of the Thunderbird, figuring a little extra footage wouldn't go unappreciated.

He was just finishing his second interview when there came a commotion from the far side of the lodge. People were gathering and talking excitedly. He excused himself from the elder and turned toward the door just as his friends entered, Francis in the lead.

The burly, bearded man took one look at him and crossed his arms reproachfully. "Stealing my job, eh? The union's gonna hear about this one."

"You should've seen that thing chasing Danni. It was like something out of *One Million Years BC*, minus the fur bikini."

"Thank God for small favors," Danni muttered, causing Francis to laugh.

"Let's keep that one on the down-low," Derek said. "If our producer hears about it, he's liable to ship one up here."

Danni made an exaggerated gagging sound, eliciting more chuckles from the group. She hadn't been shy about sharing her misgivings regarding the wardrobe choices offered to her.

Her motives for joining the team had been to help people. For the most part, it had been a rewarding experience. Being on the team, though, had meant joining the TV show that was their cover – *The Crypto Hunter*. Danni didn't mind being in front of the camera. Unfortunately for her, their core demographic *appreciated* her presence a bit more than she'd expected.

As a result, the executives at the Adventure Channel had tried at every turn to find excuses to stuff her into the skimpiest outfits possible. At twenty years old and in excellent shape, she wasn't above admitting she pulled it off well. Still, sometimes she felt her billing in the credits amounted to little more than the letters T and A.

"Get used to it," warned Francis. "AdventureCon is next month and rumor has it they're printing up extra posters. I have a feeling your autograph line is going to be a wee bit longer than the rest of ours."

Danni sighed, wondering for perhaps the thousandth time what she'd been thinking. A few months back, as part of a promo for the new season, she had agreed to a photo-shoot. One shot in particular, her in a green bikini posed somewhat salaciously across a statue of Chessie – the monster said to inhabit the Chesapeake Bay estuary – had proven exceptionally popular. Much to her chagrin, it had quickly become the top seller at the Adventure Channel's online store.

As part of their cover, the team made appearances at various conventions throughout the year. Danni had little doubt she'd be spending hours signing half-naked pictures of herself for lonely guys, all while feeling like a piece of meat.

"I can see why Chuck hated those things," she said.

"Yes he did," Mitchell replied, his voice taking on a respectful tone for their deceased comrade.

"Why don't we focus on something he didn't hate, then?" Derek waved over the waitress of the small tavern, little more than a converted supply shed. She brought over shot glasses and a mason jar full of a clear liquid. "I'm told the local hooch has quite the kick."

Derek poured out three shots then hesitated. Danni was technically underage, but he sometimes made an exception for their customary post-mission toast. He was still annoyed by her earlier actions but, after a moment, decided to focus on the fact that it had all worked out in their favor ... this time anyway.

He poured a fourth and passed it over.

The glasses distributed, all took theirs and held them up.

"To Chuck," Derek said.

"To Harrison," Danni added next.

"To all of those who fell at Bonanza Creek," Mitchell said.

"May they rest in peace," Francis finished.

There was a momentary beat while all of them let this sink in, then they simultaneously downed the contents of their shot glasses.

The solemn moment was cut short as both Mitchell and Danni started coughing. "Holy crap!" she gagged. "What is that, whale piss?"

"Smooth, just how I like it," Francis replied, reaching to refill his glass.

"I've degreased engines with less potent stuff," Mitchell said, right before holding his glass out for more.

Derek turned to Danni. "That's enough brain cells killed for one night. I believe you have work to do anyway." He was curious to see if she was going to raise a protest, especially after dressing her down during the hike back about the difference between taking initiative and being reckless. However, she appeared to understand that what she'd done was wrong. Besides, the look on her face echoed what his taste buds were already screaming. Whatever was in that jar was nigh undrinkable.

"You're right." She stood up. "I'm going to see if I can grab a signal and sign on."

"No cheating," Derek admonished as she walked away.

"Yes, *Dad*," came the reply back.

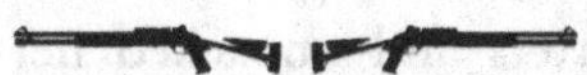

Though she rankled a little at Derek's parental tone, deep down, Danni had to admit it wasn't bad to have a surrogate father figure around. Under different circumstances, being the lone female in a group of guys – more often than not far from civilization – could have been a daunting prospect. Fortunately, she had lucked out. Francis was happily married to his high school sweetheart. Mitchell was single but also a stringent workaholic – far more interested in their case files than his social life.

That left Derek. Though sixteen years her senior, he was smart, brave, and good-looking. Had he acted any differently toward her, she wasn't entirely certain she would have been turned off by the prospect. Certainly many of the female fans of their show thought the same way, based on the opinions left in online forums.

However, he had quickly nipped any such thoughts in the bud, taking on a decisively parental attitude with her from the very start.

Danni understood. Though Derek didn't talk about it much, and usually tried his best to keep an upbeat tone, he still felt guilty over the events that had led to her joining the team. It was a feeling she shared. After all, her beloved brother Harrison had saved both their lives from the rabid beasts which had threatened them all, only to then be taken away from her forever.

Though Derek had offered her a spot on the team afterward, he had never quite gotten used to exposing her to the dangers the job entailed ... something her actions today didn't help. Still, there was no way around it. They all answered to a higher power, the U.S. government, and in doing so had signed on to put themselves at risk for the good of others.

She pushed those thoughts from her head once she reached her quarters and unpacked her laptop. Though stable internet access wasn't exactly common this far north, the risks of her job also came with some perks – such as the portable high-gain satellite dish currently mounted on top of the building.

As the computer booted up and established a connection, Danni turned to the framed photograph of her brother that she brought along on every mission. "We got another one, Harrison. Wherever you are, I hope I'm making you proud." She said a quick prayer, then turned to her work. Though she would eternally love her brother, she also realized he'd be pissed if she spent her days moping around because of him. She had a life to live and planned on doing so ... even while facing creatures that mostly wanted to end it.

Living that life, however, meant dealing with the more mundane aspects of it. In joining Derek's crew, Danni had accepted that she'd be leaving her college career behind. A life on the road wouldn't leave a lot of time for pursuing her degree ... or so she had thought.

Not so. Danni's parents, still grieving over her brother, had absolutely flipped out at the thought. Unbeknownst to her at the time, they had approached Derek about it. The end result: in addition to all the work she put in for the show and their missions, she also had to take online classes to keep up with her courses. Derek had made that a non-negotiable condition of staying on the team.

Oh, well. As much as the extra work could suck at times, at least Uncle Sam was now footing the bill. All in all, things could have been far worse.

Derek excused himself earlier than usual. Danni had been right about the local swill tasting like fermented whale urine. A few shots in and he was pretty certain he'd be regretting it come morning. Not that it mattered to him much. A slight hangover was pretty light penance for this type of work.

He stepped outside to make the short walk back to the bunkhouse he, Francis, and Mitchell were sharing, but quickly scanned the skies first. His right hand came up and checked for the reassuring weight of the shoulder holster and snub-nosed Ruger it held. These were the moments, the lull following a mission, that haunted his dreams. Though the Bonanza Creek massacre had been an extreme aberration, he never again wanted to make the same mistake. He'd let his guard down and, as a result, a lot of good people had died. Though he knew the chances of a flock of teratorns swooping down upon the village to avenge their fallen comrade were as close to zero as statistically possible, that didn't mean he wanted to be caught unawares.

Derek looked skyward for one more moment then blew out a sigh. He knew he needed to stop torturing himself. The past year had been busy, but mostly successful. They'd completed several missions without a single hitch, even with one of their team being a *rookie*.

He considered that. Danni had definitely made a rookie mistake earlier, one that had nearly scared him to death. But the truth of the matter was she'd been right. There was a good chance they'd have missed their window of opportunity had she not offered herself up as live bait, something he couldn't pretend to have never done. Calculated risk was a part of the job, and it wasn't like she was just some kid in off the streets.

After recruiting her, he'd called in some favors and sent her to Fort Bragg for several weeks of intense training. Since then, she had more than proven her worth. What she lacked in experience, she made up for with hard work and bravado. Despite her age, their backers had granted her a badge and a sufficient clearance rating for field work – albeit she was still considered an agent-in-training.

There was also the fact that she got along well with the others, fitting right in. Heck, Frank's wife had practically adopted her.

They'd gotten lucky in that the show's producers loved her, too. She was personable and worked well on camera. It also didn't hurt that she hadn't punched out any of their fans, as Chuck Wayans, their former tracker, had been known to do on occasion.

All of that aside, though, Derek couldn't help shake the feeling that his actions had pulled her away from the life she'd been meant to live – a life where she could see her friends on the weekend and indulge in a steady boyfriend. One in which she didn't have to worry about nightmare creatures constantly trying to disembowel her.

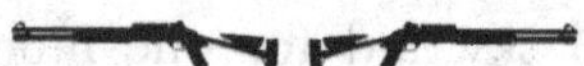

Derek reached the bunkhouse, took one last look at the empty sky, and stepped in. Tomorrow, they'd pack up their things and take their leave of the elders – who'd been exceptionally pleased at the gift of the creature's claw. After that, it was time to move on to their next assignment.

Fortunately, official missions didn't always coincide with their production schedule. Cryptids weren't always running amuck and killing people. As a result, a good portion of their travels involved little more than shooting wilderness footage, interviewing locals, and making sure to steer clear of any conclusive evidence.

They planned on flying down to Wisconsin next to film an episode on the monster of Bray Road, the scene of purported werewolf sightings. Derek had studied the evidence and concluded it had all the hallmarks of misidentification. A couple of people had been spooked by something, probably a bear, and from there the story had taken on a life of its own. Then, years later, a cleverly hoaxed film had reignited interest in the subject. All in all, it was a cakewalk. They'd do a night hunt and then reanalyze the evidence, leaving just enough doubt for the next group of investigators who wanted to come along and give it some attention.

Or at least, that's what he assumed they'd be doing.

Derek entered his room with the intent of sacking out, but instead saw the blinking light on their satellite phone, indicating a message had been left. The phone was government issued. His producers neither had its number nor knew of its existence. That wasn't good. His contacts typically didn't call to shoot the breeze.

"What now?" he mumbled to himself as he picked it up and started dialing.

3

"Hello, Derek." There was some interference – this far north, the aurora borealis could make even satellite connections a bit flakey – but the smooth voice at the other end was unmistakable.

"Calling a little late, aren't you, Norah?"

"Not really. It's not even dusk down here in D.C., and can we please keep this professional?"

Derek inwardly sighed. "Sorry, *Agent Caseman*."

"Thank you. Now, Derek, we have a..."

"Dr. Jenner."

"Excuse me?"

"You just said to keep this professional. Derek sounds so informal. Almost like ... you were my best friend's wife."

"Ex-wife," she snapped.

"I thought the papers hadn't been signed yet."

"I didn't call to talk about Jacob. Oh, and just for the record, that's none of your business."

Derek allowed himself a momentary smirk. He had always liked Norah, but now with the split happening, he could sense some strain. Unfortunately, couples tended to divide their friends up the same way they did their belongings when they went their separate ways. That she had been recently reassigned as his team's liaison within the labyrinthine bureaucracy of the U.S. government, well, that had to have been someone's idea of a karmic joke. "Sorry. I officially rescind the statement."

"Accepted," she said, then hesitated a beat. "You haven't spoken to him, have you?"

"Didn't you just say it was none of my business?"

"You're right ... I..."

"Although, for the record, no. I've been too busy hunting Thunderbirds. The cell service kind of sucks up here anyway."

There was another pause on the line, then Norah quietly said, "Thank you," before resuming her official tone. "How goes the hunt?"

"Fragged and bagged."

"Evidence?"

"Nothing but ash."

"Good. I'm sure the villagers are relieved."

"It's definitely a weight off their shoulders. By the way, who exactly are we mollifying by keeping this one quiet? Don't tell me the Audubon Society has a powerful lobby."

"You know I'm not at liberty to say."

"Of course not," Derek replied, unsurprised. The government paid them to cull cryptids – creatures not formally recognized by science – that became a threat to humans. However, they were always mum about their reasons why it needed to be covered up, leading his team to eternally speculate as to the motives behind their work. Their theories ranged from the mundane to the far-out. Francis in particular favored some outlandish ideas about government cover-ups – but that's all they were, theories. Unfortunately, that information was always on a need to know basis, and Derek apparently didn't have that need. "Shall I assume this isn't a social call?"

"You assume correct. I'm sorry to dump another case on you so soon after finishing one."

"No you're not."

Norah allowed herself a small chuckle. "Normally you'd be right, but this one is ... political."

"Political?" Derek asked warily. That was new.

"Yes. The request came directly from Governor Jonas Yarlberg himself."

Derek thought for a moment. "Yarlberg ... isn't he from..."

"New Jersey."

"And he asked for us by name?"

"Yes."

"You're sure this isn't about a convention appearance? Or maybe he wants us there for the opening of some mall?"

"Trust me, it's not that. This is strictly business."

"How the hell does some bureaucrat from the Garden State know what we really do?"

"Relax..."

"Don't tell me to relax, Norah. I was under the impression that this was all classified."

"It is. Yarlberg has connections. One of his former aides is now a director in the Bureau."

"Great. Nice to know that nepotism is alive and well in D.C."

"As if it ever wasn't, but that's neither here nor there as far as either of us are concerned."

"Sorry," he replied, trying to push down his annoyance. *It was only a matter of time*, he told himself. So far, most of their dealings with the government had the end result of helping people, but Derek wasn't stupid. He knew that sooner or later they'd end up getting their hands dirty in the game of politics. "So what's it about? Far as I know, the only real activity in Jersey is that small squatch clan in the southwest. Last I heard, they'd never bothered anybody. Are they...?"

"This has nothing to do with them. They've been quiet as usual."

"So what then?"

"Apparently they're trying to control a potential media firestorm."

"Go on," Derek replied, caught unawares. Usually they were given a location, suspected creature, a casualty list, and that was it. That Norah had offered up the actual motivation behind a mission was definitely odd.

"I don't have many more details, except that one of their agencies is trying to control a situation before it gets out of hand. From what I've heard, they've already lost a few people and folks are starting to talk."

That was more to the point. Derek couldn't have cared less about some politician saving face, but if innocent lives were involved... "What's been going after their people?"

There was another pause from Norah, then she replied, "They think it was the Jersey Devil."

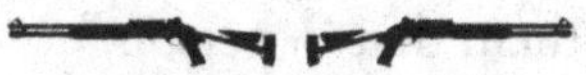

"It's not funny, Derek."

"You're kidding, right?" he asked, trying to get his laughter under control.

"No, they're dead serious."

"C'mon, Norah. If they want us to come in and do an investigation, they should call up the Adventure Channel and schedule something for next season."

"It's not like that. They want you guys there to scare off the real press."

"Ouch."

"You know what I mean. Do what you have to, so it all seems like a load of BS."

"That shouldn't be hard," he muttered under his breath.

"Then, you're to head into the woods to find and kill this creature so that the affected agency can get back to work."

"That should be easy, too, since it doesn't exist."

"Skepticism coming from you?"

"Oh, please. You have access to the same ... hell, *more* records than I do. You know about squatches, teratorns, extant zeuglodons, and all the rest."

"Obviously."

"Then tell me how many legit case files exist on the Jersey Devil." There was silence on the other end, as he knew there would be. "Exactly. Even in my circles the whole thing is mostly considered a crank. Hell, the stories can't even get their facts straight. There's a different description for the damn thing for almost every eyewitness present. You know what that says to me?"

"Do tell."

"It says that maybe the folks who live there should limit their drinking to after ten in the morning."

"You can tell them that in person."

"Really? You can't possibly convince me, based on everything you know, that you think..."

"What we *think* is irrelevant in this case," she interrupted. "If you refuse, I'm ... authorized to cut ties with your group."

Now it was Derek's turn to hesitate. There had been disagreements in the past. Heck, he had even turned down some assignments because the evidence was too sketchy to draw proper conclusions. Never had they threatened to pull the plug, though. Was this some scheme by Norah to use him to get back at her ex?

Derek quickly pushed that thought aside. He knew she could be opinionated, but he'd never known her to be petty. "Why the ultimatum?"

"It's not my doing. Yarlberg pulled some strings. Apparently his former…"

"Lackeys?"

"*Associates*," she corrected, "are still loyal. They put assurances in place to make sure this gets done."

"So they're willing to screw this whole project over, all the innocent lives we save, just to keep their asshole buddy happy?"

"Isn't that the way politics works?"

"This is the exact thing I told Jake I didn't want to deal with when I signed up for this." He knew it was low to bring up Norah's estranged husband, but this conversation was beginning to leave a bad taste in his mouth.

She took a deep breath, no doubt, Derek surmised, debating whether to take the bait. "I'm sorry. I did my best to tell them this is a one-time deal. They try this crap again and I'll register a full complaint."

"And that will do what?"

"Nothing, but it'll at least put us on record as objecting."

Derek mentally counted to ten as he weighed his options. He knew his team did a lot of good. Even if the government gave them the boot, they could potentially keep doing it. Of course, that assumed the Adventure Channel didn't pull the plug, too. They were currently riding fairly high in the ratings. But if the feds decided to be spiteful, which they probably would… And then there was the added fact that they wouldn't have the protection of the law on their side.

Yeah, we're screwed. "Fine," Derek said at last. "You have our nuts in a vice and you know it."

"Not how I would put it."

"What happens if we don't find anything or come to the conclusion that it's some whackjob running around in the woods?"

"You guys hunt cryptids. If there isn't a cryptid to blame, then your job is done."

"Fair enough. Just make sure this guy keeps his minions out of our way."

"No promises."

"Why am I not surprised to hear that?"

"Because you're too smart to not expect it."

"But still not smart enough to say no?"

"You never were," she replied, adding a little levity to her voice. This was the Norah that Derek knew and liked.

"Shoot me the details, okay?"

"Already on their way."

"All right, then. Circumstances aside, it was nice talking to you, Norah."

"You too. Take care."

Derek ended the call. He had been planning on getting some rest, but instead decided to unpack his computer. The team had to be briefed and, from the sound of things, it needed to be done soon.

Guess the werewolf of Bray Road will have to wait for the next full moon.

4

Mitchell poured himself another cup of the viscous black liquid masquerading as coffee. "You're kidding, right?"

"You mind not yelling?" Francis replied from his place at the table, a heaping pile of scrambled eggs untouched in front of him.

"I told you we should've stopped at that second bottle."

"Can we focus here?" Derek interrupted. He knew it was unfair to drop this in their laps with the previous mission barely cold yet, but it had to be done.

"So the Jersey Devil is real?" Despite her previous night's coursework, Danni appeared to be in a far better mood than her two sullen-faced teammates, but then, she obviously wasn't hungover either.

"No," Mitchell replied morosely, taking a sip. "It's a crank."

"The governor of New Jersey begs to disagree," Derek said.

Francis snorted laughter. "Maybe he should host our show, then."

Danni tried to steer them back on track. "Isn't it kind of our job to keep an open mind?"

Though Derek knew cryptozoology wasn't one of her passions, she was always interested in learning about a new creature. He could understand that. It was hard to not be excited in the face of the unknown.

"Keeping an open mind doesn't mean automatically believing every fairy tale that comes along," he explained. "Mitch and I have spent a lot of time in the archives. Every creature we go after has either documented proof of its existence or enough of a case file to warrant serious consideration."

"Then maybe we just need to go through them more carefully..."

"Been there, done that," Mitchell said. "When I was a kid, I lived in Jersey for a couple of years. My father was stationed at Fort Monmouth and I used to go camping down south with my friends. We would scare ourselves silly all night with stories about the devil skulking about in the woods. Heck, every time we heard a branch break, we'd just about pee our pants."

"Thanks for the imagery," Francis replied.

Mitchell casually flipped him the finger. "When I was first brought on board and learned about all the goodies Uncle Sam has under wraps, I couldn't read through it all fast enough. Trust me, monsters in the Pine Barrens were high on that list."

"And?"

"And, there simply isn't much there, Danni. Random sightings over the years. Very little consistency between them."

Derek jumped in. "There's also the fossil record to take into account. Even if we didn't have the evidence we do, we could potentially surmise that a creature like, say, the Oreng Pendek is real because we have fossils of *Homo flore-*

siensis to back it up. Same with most of the other cryptids we keep in check. Not so with the devil. Hell, you'd need half a dozen aberrant evolutionary throwbacks to explain it. There's just too much inconsistency with the sightings."

"There's also one very damning fact," Mitchell added. "Devil sightings can only be traced back to the eighteen hundreds, late seventeen hundreds at the earliest, long after the colonists had settled in the area."

"What about Native American legends?" Francis asked, grabbing himself a mug of coffee. "I've heard a couple of doozies about winged monsters and such."

"There's a difference. Traditional stories usually make a pretty good distinction between spiritual creatures and physical monsters. Think about Okanagan Lake up in Canada. The natives there had been telling tales of something strange living in the lake for hundreds of years before the Europeans came."

"So what then?" Danni asked. "People there have been seeing *something*."

"Maybe," Derek replied. "Even the name itself, Jersey Devil, implies Judeo-Christian beliefs. Personally, I think the whole thing is a combination of hysteria, local tall tales, and maybe a little misidentification along the way."

"In short ... bullshit," Francis concluded.

Derek nodded. "In a nutshell, but we still have to go."

"Bullshit Hunters it is, then," Francis said, eliciting a laugh from the rest.

When Mitchell questioned him as to the purpose of hunting this particular boogeyman, as he called it, Derek went into further detail about what Norah had told him, including their personal *invitation* by the governor of the Garden State.

He explained that the plan was to pack up and head out first thing tomorrow for Nome. From there, they'd catch a flight to Anchorage and then a commercial connection to Newark Liberty International Airport. Norah had assured him their vehicles would be waiting for them there. At that point, they'd head west to Trenton for a quick briefing.

"And then?" Danni asked.

"That's all I have. They'll give us the rest in person. There's some political paranoia at play, so they didn't send too many details."

"Gotta love politicians," Mitchell commented.

"That doesn't give us much to go on," Danni pointed out.

Derek shrugged. "I'm well aware. But that doesn't mean we can't do our due diligence. We'll use today for some fact finding. Read up on the area, the local fauna, et cetera. Make sure there are no surprises. I'll forward each of you what Norah sent me last night."

"I'd like to see the archive files on the devil," Danni said.

Derek considered this for a moment. Her clearance was limited due to her in-training status, but there was nothing overly classified in those records. Though it would be breaking rules, he decided to give her unsupervised access. *That'll teach them to threaten us over a snipe hunt.* "You got it. But be forewarned, kid, it's dry stuff and I guarantee it won't be all that useful."

Danni grinned in return. "That's okay. If it really is that boring, that'll just mean I sleep well tonight."

It wasn't quite as dull as Derek had warned, but it was close. Danni had been given access to other files in months past. Many of them included firsthand accounts of the creatures to which they pertained. She'd particularly enjoyed reading about a Navy diver's encounter down in the Bahamas with what he claimed to be a monstrous octopus. He had managed to escape not only with his life, but a piece of tentacle as well. The scientists who examined it had postulated that the creature it had come from was enormous – maybe even a possible contender for the ancient legend of the kraken.

Sadly, the files on the screen before her now weren't nearly as interesting. It was mostly old retellings of sightings – a dubious source of veracity in any situation – a few crackpot theories, and some unconvincing photos of footprints. While there had been some serious investigations over the years, any "evidence" found was inconclusive at best.

She smiled at that last thought. Over the past year, she had gotten some exposure to the cryptozoology community at large. While there were some truly dedicated researchers in the field, for every one of them, there were at least three shysters more concerned with a quick buck than anything else. That worked for their purposes. The less respectable types were sloppy and pretty obvious about it. The result was that anyone connected to this type of research was cast in a dim light, as far as the mainstream press was concerned. Traditional media treated them like a bad joke, which had the unintended consequence of making her team's cover all that more effective. Once they showed up, reporters would quickly pack their bags and move on, not wanting to risk giving them any sort of legitimacy. It was perfect. The press never had a clue as to how well they were being played.

Danni yawned, stretched, then went back to the files – hoping to find something that might be useful for their investigation. The one good thing about still being an undergraduate was that her note-taking skills were fresh and up to the task. She quickly glanced at them to take stock of the pertinent *facts* she had recorded.

Jersey Devil:

Legends:

- Most popular: 13th child of Mother Leeds — supernatural origin, mid 1700's

- Leeds Point attributed birth place of devil — potential tourist trap. Also half a state away from the recent disappearances, i.e. a dead end.

- Also attributed to the Shroud family name — less well known in popular culture, but still fairly well researched.

- Possibly predated by Native Americans. Lenape tribe legends account for some strange spirit activity in the Pine Barrens region. Nothing concrete, probably coincidence.

Sightings:

- Mostly sporadic. Several years pass between sightings. Possibly due to low population in region — also possibly due to it all being bullshit!

- Overly high percentage of group sightings compared to other cryptids. Odd outlier, probably one of the few reasons the entire thing isn't written off as crap. Group hysteria? Possible. This is New Jersey we're talking about.

Years of notable sightings:

1819

1840

1878

1937 — Longest gap ... why?

1960

2007 onward — related to our case?

Theories:

- Sandhill Crane. A large bird but uncommon to the area. But seriously, how many people really mistake a bird for a monster ... except for maybe Thunderbirds?

- Giant fruit bat. Possible, but not native to the region. Also, giant is a bit of an exaggeration. They're not that big.

- Undiscovered cryptid? Troublesome. No fossil record to support that theory.

- The actual devil. Hah! Note to self, bring holy water.

- Too many locals drinking wood alcohol – favorite theory so far!

Danni looked up, unimpressed. That was all she had transcribed so far. Hell, she could have gotten better information off of Wikipedia. Derek and the others were right. This was most likely a waste of effort.

She flipped through the files one last time to see if anything had escaped her attention, not expecting to find much. She was just about to call it a night when a picture near the back of one report caught her eye. It was an old black and white photo of some kind of prayer service, one with a distinct fire and brimstone feel to it. A short newspaper clipping accompanied the photo.

Local Priest Exorcises Devil back to Hell

Burlington Bugle – August 5th 1879

Reverend Jedediah Lesterfield and his wife Sarah are seen here leading the faithful in a group exorcism of the creature known as the Leeds Devil. The ungodly beast is said to be responsible for the slaughter of livestock in the area, as well as the possible abduction of three local women of goodly upbringing.

There was a brief summary in the report which gave some further insight. If it was to be believed, the creature had caused a panic amongst the citizens of Shilough, a small town bordering part of the Pine Barrens. Numerous sightings in the prior year, some disappearances – possibly unrelated – and general hysteria had put the town into a near state of emergency. Families had taken to locking themselves inside and holding all night prayer sessions to stave off the creature's wrath.

Rumors had begun to circulate that the residents finally had enough and were discussing drastic means, such as burning down the forest, in the hopes of ending their torment.

It was Jedediah Lesterfield, a local clergyman with a bit of a shady past himself – the records didn't elaborate – who suggested the ceremony. He obviously wasn't the fount of sanity the town needed, Danni considered, but his solution was far better than the disaster that could have occurred had the townsfolk gone ahead with their original plan. She looked more closely at the photo, and at the man she assumed was Lesterfield up front, waving his hands in the air like he was DJing a modern rave.

Ugly sucker, she remarked to herself. Though tall and lanky, his face had a brutish sort of bent to it. *In another time and place, this guy would probably be breaking kneecaps for the mob.*

Over the course of a grandiose day-long ceremony, he'd whipped the townsfolk into a religious froth of prayer and singing. Finally, he symbolically cast the devil out, declaring a large swath of the woods to be an unholy place – forevermore to be shunned, lest the creature return from the depths of Hell. Amazingly enough, Danni read, the exorcism appeared to have worked. The people avoided the cursed woods, and sightings died down to almost nothing for several years.

Danni chuckled to herself. It was incredible what the power of suggestion could accomplish. Nevertheless, something about it nagged her. She called up Google Maps on her laptop and quickly searched for the town. A few mouse clicks later and she saw the connection. Shilough was located close to the area where they would be investigating. Probably little more than a coincidence, but maybe worth mentioning to Derek.

5

A sigh of contentment slipped from Abigail Linton's lips as her boyfriend's hand slid beneath her bra. She had initially balked at the prospect of parking all the way out on Swamp Forge Road, but her protests gradually subsided as Mike's expert hands began to win her over. Besides, their other options were pretty limited.

Mike's parents were staying in tonight, so there was no chance of privacy there, and he wasn't welcome at her house thanks to Abby's mother coming home early the week before and catching them half-dressed. Stupidly, Mike had gotten his car detailed two days earlier, ensuring he didn't have enough cash for even a cheap motel room.

The forge, as it was commonly called, was a known make-out spot. As a result, it was on the patrol routes of the local cops. Many a friend had been caught in the act by the accusing glare of a Maglite shining through their windows. Abby was already on thin ice with her parents, so the prospect of being dropped off at home by the police wasn't particularly high on her priority list.

Mike wasn't to be dissuaded, though. His father was

an ex-State Trooper. According to him, some careful questioning on his part had given rise to a bit of insight. The patrols out on the forge took place at random intervals so as to catch any kids thinking they'd figured out a pattern, but they were staggered and somewhat inconsistent. Shilough, only a few miles to the north, didn't have much of a police force. Hammonton did, but the route was outside of their usual jurisdiction. Once a patrol car made its rounds on the forge, it would be at least two hours before another would retrace that route.

"That's more than enough time," he had told her with a sly grin.

"Yeah, an hour and fifty-eight minutes longer than you usually need," she'd replied.

Swamp Forge Road lived up to its name for the most part. It wove through marshlands with scrub brush on either side of it, the closest main road being Route 206 several miles to the west. The lack of street lights and surrounding dense vegetation made it feel even more dark and claustrophobic. Missing a turn on the narrow road was an ideal way to end up stuck in a bog.

Fortunately, Mike had that covered, too. In addition to pumping his father for information, some of his buddies knew the road well. There were dry spots, back and hidden from the road, if one knew where to find them. A person just had to be smart about where they pulled off and make sure to kill the lights once they were parked.

Mike and Abby had cruised the length of the road a few times, all while keeping an eye out for the patrol they knew would eventually drive past them. Finally, they spotted a plainly marked police car. They passed it, then headed out to grab a bite at McDonald's so as to kill a half-hour or so – lest they be overzealous, park, and the cop end up doubling back to check on them.

Now, at last, parked far back from the road and alone in the back seat of Mike's car, he was able to resume what he'd started the week before. His hands unsnapped her bra, then went back to work on her breasts.

"Stop playing around and get to it," she demanded, removing his hands from her chest and moving them down to her still-clasped jeans.

"I love it when you're aggressive."

"I just don't want to get caught, so let's go."

"You want it that badly, do you?"

She threw out a sigh. "If you can still talk, maybe your mouth isn't busy enough."

"I'll take that as a challenge," he replied, sliding his way down her body.

Abby indulged him as he stopped long enough to suckle on her nipples. Damn, he was good with his tongue. Mike could be a bit of a jerk when he wanted to be. Everything was a goddamned joke to him. But, damn, did he know his way around her body. She could tolerate his asshole humor as long as he put his mouth to better use. They got on well enough and had plenty in common, but the fact that he nearly always brought her to orgasm didn't hurt their relationship in the slightest.

Gotta have priorities, she considered as he unbuckled her pants with his teeth.

Abby felt a shudder beneath her and found herself momentarily confused. Mike hadn't even removed her pants yet.

"Like that, huh?" He chuckled.

"Wait, Mike..."

The car again jolted around them.

"What the fuck, babe?" he asked, raising his head. "I know I'm good, but..."

"Just shut up for a second. I swear, if one of your asshole friends followed us out here..." Her voice trailed off as she saw that he wasn't paying her any attention. Even in the darkness of the car, she could see that his eyes were open wide and staring past her.

Before she could turn to follow his gaze, the window behind her exploded, showering her with safety glass. The outside world no longer muffled, the sound of the window breaking gave way to a frenetic chuffing as if someone was struggling for breath but was too excited to calm down.

She barely had time to witness Mike's anguished cry as his hands moved to protect his face, having been directly in the path of the broken glass, when a massive arm came through the window. Abby couldn't discern any color in the gloom except to note that it was large and dark. Claws raked across the naked flesh of her torso and she felt the sting of her skin giving way. Then the hand pushed past her, reaching toward her boyfriend.

It grabbed hold of the front of his shirt and pulled. Whatever it was, it was deathly strong, and it dragged her boyfriend over her. Mike's head impacted with the top of the door frame, halting his progress but only momentarily. Another yank from their attacker, and his head pushed back with a sickly snap, then he was dragged through the now open window.

All of it happened so quickly that Abby barely had time to comprehend that her boyfriend was, in all likelihood, beyond help. She sat up and looked out the window, only to see a dark shape pounce upon the unmoving form of her lover. Snarls quickly replaced the tortured wheezing.

Adrenaline raced through her body, already awash in a stew of hormones, and – beyond all good sense – she found herself fumbling with the handle.

"Get off him!" She pushed the door open and into the creature, hoping to drive it off. It was like hitting concrete.

The metal slapped against the beast, causing it to grunt in surprise. Unhurt, it turned to face her.

Abby couldn't see much in the dark, but she saw enough to make her rethink her plan. It bared its teeth, housed in a misshapen head, and let loose a hiss of rage. The stench of its breath washed over her. It smelled of decay – the marshes and endless bogs of this accursed place.

She immediately abandoned her course of action, pulling the door shut in the process. Scrambling into the front seat as the abomination turned its attention back toward Mike, Abby hopped behind the wheel. She might not be able to drive it away herself, but perhaps she could scare it off or even run it over.

Realization hit as she found the ignition switch empty. Mike must've pocketed the key when they parked.

"Goddamn it!" She punched the wheel, inadvertently striking the horn. It let out a long blast and the creature screeched in surprise before launching itself at the driver's side door.

Her bravery all but spent, Abby quickly scooted to the other side and fumbled with the latch. The driver's side window shattered beneath the creature's assault and within moments, its grasping talons were seeking her.

Abby let out a shriek but managed to open the door behind her, falling to the ground.

She scooted backward from the car and managed to scramble to her feet. She turned to run but then stopped, well aware that any delay could potentially be a costly one.

The road! She couldn't afford to run deeper into the woods. That would be the end of it. If she could get to the road, maybe she could get lucky and flag down a car. Hell, maybe tonight was the one night the cops decided to double-down on their patrols.

Remembering that Mike had pulled in and then

turned around, she oriented herself with the front of the car just as the creature was extricating itself from the window.

It was a couple dozen yards at most to the road from where they were parked. Abby wasn't much of a sprinter, but considering the labored breathing of the creature, she felt her chances had to be better than even.

She ran no more than ten paces before daring to glance behind her, certain she'd see the creature's nightmare face just inches away. But there was nothing save the darkness of the forest. She might as well have had her eyes shut for all the good it did. That thing might be right behind her or it could have bounded off into the night unseen.

She didn't dare let hope slow her steps. She'd seen enough monster movies sitting by Mike's side to know that letting down her guard was a death sentence.

Abigail turned back toward the road, intent on winning this race, when she slammed into something. Dazed, she stumbled back. Sadly, all thought that she might have hit nothing more than a tree was erased as strong hands grasped her shoulders, digging into her skin.

Fetid breath washed down upon her as whatever it was leaned in closer.

"Hello, Sarah."

6

If there was one downside to their job, Derek considered – aside from the possibility of being mauled to death – it was that their government connections almost never afforded them any perks when it came to flying. The flight down from Anchorage was fine in itself, but the connection they caught in Denver was overcrowded and turbulent. Flying through a storm somewhere over Ohio, Francis had nervously joked about incurring the wrath of the Thunderbird, eliciting recognition from some fans of the show that happened to be aboard. A flurry of questions and several autograph requests didn't make the flight any more comfortable.

By the time the plane touched down in Newark, Derek was seriously tempted to blow their cover and present his badge just to get people to leave them alone. Fortunately, they were able to regain some level of obscurity again in the crowded terminal. Their gear, being of a slightly more *sensitive* nature, was being shipped by special courier. They only needed to grab a few bags before making their escape.

Fortunately, Norah was good to her word, as Derek

knew she would be. Off in a special VIP section of the long-term lot sat their rides – two gleaming black SUVs. Behind one was a trailer, in which rested two similarly colored ATVs. The vehicles were unmarked. About two years back, Francis had suggested having them detailed with the show's logo so as to make them look less ominous, but Derek had shot it down. Doing so ran the risk of fans spotting them and trying to take a closer look. Though the windows were fully tinted and the locks military grade, there was always the chance that someone would get more of an eyeful than they should and see that his team were carrying cargo slightly more lethal than camera equipment.

As usual, Mitchell groused when they came to the vehicles. Their small fleet had once included a van formerly used for FBI surveillance, but converted to a highly capable mobile lab. It had been damaged beyond repair during the Bonanza Creek debacle. Government budget cuts hadn't yet allowed for a replacement, and no more hand-me-downs had come their way.

"I'm told Rutgers has a lab less than an hour away from the site we're investigating and we'll have full access to it," Derek mentioned in passing.

"Just as long as it has doors that lock," Mitchell grumbled before climbing into one of the SUVs with Francis. Derek took the other with Danni, tossing her the keys.

"Napping or research?" she asked as she climbed behind the wheel of the massive vehicle.

"We have at least an hour and a half to the capital ... probably longer if we hit some of that famous Jersey traffic, so maybe a little of both."

"I'm gonna go grab something to eat. You in?"

Arthur Killian, a chem-bio major in his junior year, looked up from his notes. "Can't. I have a test tomorrow in molecular biology. I want to get my studying done early so I don't have to call off work later."

His roommate Leo Kelsey shrugged. "Hard to pass a test if you pass out from hunger first."

"Even harder to pass if you haven't picked up your textbook in over a month." Arthur pointed at the unopened physics book lying atop a pile of his roommate's clothes.

"I've picked it up."

"Dropping it doesn't count."

"Baby steps, bro." Leo opened the door. "Later."

"Later," Arthur replied absentmindedly, his focus already back on his notes.

His roommate walked out with an unconcerned chuckle that didn't surprise Arthur. Introduction to Physics was nothing more than an elective to fill Leo's graduation requirements. He didn't much care what grade he got as long as he passed. And, considering he had a roommate he could hit up for advice right before the final, he probably would pass, even if it was by the skin of his teeth.

Truth be told, it didn't bother Arthur much, even though Leo was pretty much using him as a means to avoid doing any real coursework. Besides, being quizzed on the basics wasn't a bad thing. It kept his mind sharp.

And he needed his wits about him assisting Dr. Reingold in the lab. The cellular biology professor was a stickler for detail. Arthur normally wouldn't have even gotten his foot in the door, except there was a shortage of graduate TAs this year due to recent tuition increases for the master's program. Their misfortune, however, had been his gain.

Now it was on him to hold up his end of the work

while maintaining the GPA which had gotten him the position to begin with.

His phone rang and he was once more interrupted from his studies.

Speak of the devil, he thought as he saw who was calling. "Hey, Dr. Reingold," he answered cheerfully, despite being slightly annoyed. Reingold wasn't one to call unless there was a good reason, though, so Arthur pushed those feelings aside so he could pay attention.

"Extra shifts?" he replied after the professor was finished. "Yeah, I'm available, but how many do you need? I have a test coming up in..."

He stopped talking as the voice on the other end continued.

"Are you serious?! Sorry, professor. I mean, yes ... I've heard of them. No, no! It's not a bother at all. I just double-checked my schedule and I'm definitely free. Yes. However long they ... I mean, *you* need me. Thank you, sir!"

Arthur hung up, the notes in front of him all but forgotten. A knot of nervous anticipation was beginning to worm its way through his guts. The call had been quick and to the point, Reingold's style, but it wasn't the conversation itself that had him all flustered as much as the subject.

He glanced up at the wall above his bed and the poster that hung there. A blonde, bikini-clad goddess stared down at him from it. She was stretched across a statue of a sea monster, her bright smile infinitely more appealing than the dour scowls that seemed to be all the rage for fashion models these days. Printed in the lower right-hand corner was the logo for her TV show – *The Crypto Hunter.*

Arthur had just been told that the entire cast was on their way to his school. Not only that, but they needed access to one of the labs too, for whatever reason. Reingold had called to see if he'd be interested in assisting them for however long they'd be there. The professor obviously considered this an assignment more worthy of a lowly assistant, and Arthur wasn't about to correct him.

In all reality, it might very well be nothing more than a babysitting assignment. After all, as far as he was concerned, the show had about as much basis in reality as professional wrestling. But it was entertaining nevertheless, so what did it really matter?

He glanced down at his notes and considered things. He knew the subject matter fairly well. The odds were still in his favor. And, even if they weren't, getting to meet the show's newest costar was well worth failing one stupid test.

Eric Zeist waited for his boss to finish his call. He knew better than to interrupt. It didn't take long to discover that working for Governor Jonas Yarlberg entailed very little leeway. You either did what he wanted you to do, the way he wanted it done, or your tenure on his staff would be a short one. There wasn't much room for discussion to the contrary, aside from maybe asking when your last paycheck would be mailed out.

As the chief of Yarlberg's personal security detail, Eric had to deal with more than his fair share of the man's quirks. Eric was a pragmatic man, though. The pay for his position was good and the prestige was even better. It was worth the aggravation or uncertainty of knowing what his next assignment might be.

"Just do your damn job, Reg." The governor hung up the phone and stared sourly at it for several seconds, as if daring it to ring again. Finally, he turned his pudgy face toward Eric, his way of letting his subordinates know it was okay to speak.

"Everything on the up and up, sir?"

Yarlberg scoffed. "Tell me, Eric, what's the point in having a fucking press secretary if I have to hold the man's hand every step of the way?"

It was a rhetorical question, but Eric knew better than to stand there silently. Obviously his boss had a point he was trying to make. "I'm not sure I can answer that, sir."

"It's all about deflection." The governor reached into his desk, pulled out a candy bar, and began tearing the wrapper off. "Lord knows the assholes in the press aren't stupid enough to expect honest answers these days, so why bother trying to give them one? Just tell them an investigation is underway and no details are forthcoming. Gives them something to hand to their editors. Makes them all happy so they can go home, fuck their wives, and bother me about something else tomorrow. This isn't rocket science."

"If you say so."

"And that pussy Donald is no better. I swear, he'd crack like an egg if he so much as saw a microphone pointed his way."

Eric nodded. Now it was making sense. Donald Krychech was the head of the agency in charge of environmental protection. His group was currently in the hot seat – something to do with a toxic spill on protected land. Eric didn't really care about the details. The only reason his agency wasn't being roasted alive on the airwaves was because the press was busy focusing on what they were trying to spin as a new serial killer on the loose. Problem was, this alleged killer's hunting ground seemed to coincide with the area that Krychech's people were busy trying to keep everyone's eyes off of. In short, it was only a matter of time before the shit hit the fan and Yarlberg went through the roof.

Fortunately, that was the reason for Eric interrupting the governor's day. "Hopefully that won't be the case, sir."

"You have news?"

"I do," Eric replied, still standing. The governor almost never invited his staff to sit. "That ... *team* you requested. They're on the ground and heading here."

"It's about goddamned time."

"If I may be so bold as to ask, sir, what exactly are a bunch of D-rate actors going to do to help this situation?"

The governor sat back in his chair, a satisfied grin appearing on his face as he munched on the chocolate bar. Eric knew that look well. It was probably a good thing his boss didn't have a gambling addiction in addition to his other vices. He had a terrible poker face.

"Appearances can be deceiving. Fortunately, I am in a position where I have friends who are able to help me see more clearly than most."

"I'm not following."

Yarlberg opened a different drawer in his desk. Eric assumed it would be to pull out another snack, but he instead produced a file folder which he held out. "Here. Read through this. It'll make it all clear."

Eric took the file and opened it. He immediately noticed the security classification stamped on the first page. "Um, sir, I'm not sure I should be..."

"Hogwash. *I'll* determine who has a need to know and I say you do."

Suddenly, Eric found himself wishing he'd thought to record this conversation. "If you say so."

"I do. After you read through that, you'll know what I mean. By inviting them here, they'll throw off the scent of those press hounds. But the best part is, they might actually be of use in solving this mess before it turns into a full-blown shit storm."

Eric nodded, not entirely sure what the governor was

talking about. However, he planned to make good use of the two hours he had to bring himself up to speed. "So you want me to roll out the red carpet, treat them like VIPs?"

"Quite the contrary." Yarlberg crumbled up the candy wrapper and tossed it toward the trash can, missing it completely. "I've dealt with these types before. Give them an inch, they'll take a mile and ask for more. No. I want you and your team to make it crystal clear to them who's in charge here. They're to be kept on a very short leash. They step out of line, you smack them back into it."

"But..."

"But nothing. Do as I've told you and let me worry about the rest. I have it handled."

Eric debated questioning his boss, but then thought better of it. He had no love of the feds anyway, having been turned down several years earlier when he tried to apply to the FBI straight out of school. He knew it was petty to take that out on people he'd never met, but the governor was pretty clear on his marching orders. He figured he might as well have some fun with it.

"Any more questions?"

Eric hesitated for a moment, then shook his head.

"Good." Yarlberg picked up the phone and dialed. "Reggie? It's me again. I want you to arrange a press conference. Yeah. For today. Yes, I know it's short notice..."

Eric knew he'd been dismissed. He turned and walked from the governor's office, glancing down at the folder in his hands.

He had some reading to do, and apparently he needed to be quick about it.

7

Route 1 proved to be closer, in actual practice, to a parking lot than a major highway, but at least it gave the team plenty of time to compare notes. Derek patched in the other vehicle via cell phone, although he knew it would mostly be Mitchell doing the talking. Francis was typically more interested in shooting than research, whether it was with a camera or a gun.

Derek went over the basic details of the case. He knew everyone had read the briefing beforehand, but he always liked to make sure they were all on the same page, especially since they had a meet and greet scheduled at the state capital before being allowed to do their jobs.

"Probably want to make sure we dance like good monkeys," Francis commented.

After Derek was done, Danni recounted her notes from the archive files.

"See what I mean about it being a dead end?" Derek remarked when she had finished.

"Yeah, I guess so," she replied, still inching along with the traffic. "Although that whole town-wide exorcism was a little freaky."

"Leave that stuff to the ghost hunters," Mitchell said from over the speaker.

"Mitch is right," Derek replied. "I'm not quite ready to chalk this up to the metaphysical. Besides, if there is a devil, I'm sure there are far more interesting places for him than some unoccupied marshlands."

Danni shrugged. "I know. I'm not trying to suggest there's anything supernatural here. It's just weird. That priest put on a show for everyone and *voila*, the Jersey Devil mysteriously stayed quiet for sixty years."

"Coincidence," Francis said.

"More likely it was power of suggestion," Mitchell offered. "The locals believed their personal boogeyman was banished, so he was. They told their kids and so on. Fast forward a couple of generations, people start to forget the stories. Tensions are running high. The U.S. is just pulling out of the Great Depression, and suddenly Germany is beating the war drums again. People needed a distraction so, much like magic, the devil showed up again."

"And then people got distracted in a whole other direction by World War Two," Danni surmised.

"Exactly."

"I guess that makes sense."

"Nothing about this cryptid makes a lot of sense," Derek replied. "That's why nobody takes it seriously. It has all the hallmarks of an urban legend that just won't die."

"Isn't that why we're here?" joked Francis, making a *kapow* noise.

"I doubt it. My guess would be those people simply got lost."

Mitchell chimed in to agree. "The Barrens are half forest, half swamp. They could have easily fallen in a sinkhole or stepped in some quicksand."

"Not a pleasant way to go," Danni said.

Derek chuckled. "Contrary to popular belief, outside of dying in my sleep of extreme old age, I can't think of too many ways to go that I *would* classify as pleasant."

"Death by snu-snu comes to mind," Francis replied from the speaker.

"What's that?" Danni asked.

"You don't watch much TV, do you?"

"Never have."

"Your loss. It's a damn funny show."

Derek sighed. "Can we stay on topic, please?"

"Yes, Mom," Francis replied with a laugh.

"The other possibility, as I see it," Mitchell said, steering the conversation back toward being serious, "is human-related."

"Murder?" Danni asked.

"Maybe."

"What do we do if that's the case?"

"Call America's Most Wanted," Francis replied. "That's more their line of work."

Derek nodded toward the speaker and said, "We call in the authorities and bow out gracefully. I don't care who's pulling the strings – we're not anyone's private police force."

The rest of the trip was spent discussing the flora and fauna of the Pine Barrens and considering whether any native species might be responsible for the disappearances. Alas, there weren't many top predators to point the finger at. Black bears were known in the area, but encounters with them were usually easily avoided. Everything else was either too small or a prey animal. More and more, Derek began to suspect the true culprit was simply human error.

People got lost in the woods and died. It was something that, unfortunately, happened. One didn't need a swamp monster or living dinosaur to blame for ninety-nine percent of such happenings.

At last, they entered the Trenton city limits. Francis commented, "Lovely. Reminds me of Detroit," right before Derek disconnected the call. It was time to focus on finding their destination amidst the winding streets.

A few minutes later, having been guided by GPS, Derek informed Danni, "Pull into that garage."

"This the place?"

"We're a couple of blocks south of the capitol building – close enough to meet with whoever wants to talk to us, but far enough away so that nobody sees us coming in."

She turned on the lights so as to navigate the parking garage. "So we're their dirty little secret?"

"Aren't we always?"

They drove the SUVs to the top floor. There, standing in front of an elevator, were two men in suits. Upon seeing the vehicles, they waved them over and directed them to park.

Derek wasn't looking forward to this. He just barely tolerated their producers back west. Politicians were often far more than he could stomach. That the governor of New Jersey had pulled strings and not been shy with his threats told him there was a better than average chance he was going to loathe the man.

The team parked and stepped from their vehicles. With Derek in the lead, they approached the suited men.

One of the duo stepped forward and addressed them. "Dr. Derek Jenner?"

"Yes. And this is my team."

"I'm Eric Zeist, Governor Yarlberg's personal security director."

"A pleasure to meet you, Mr. Zeist. Now if you could just tell us where..."

"All in good time. For now, I must ask that you leave your possessions locked in your vehicles."

Derek chuckled at what he presumed to be a joke. "We haven't unpacked the cameras. Not much point looking for monsters in the middle of the city."

"I meant whatever armaments you might be carrying. We're aware of what you really do."

"They told you?!" Francis cried from the rear.

Derek turned and gave him a warning glance before continuing. "That's highly unusual. If you know what we do, then you know we're considered undercover federal agents reporting to the Department of..."

"We are also well aware of that," Eric interrupted. "You can rest assured that the governor has the proper clearance and has only informed those on his staff who can be trusted."

Those who can be trusted? Derek was tempted to inform the man that this wasn't the way items of a sensitive nature were handled. For all he knew, the good governor also included his drinking buddies as those he trusted. Derek made a mental note to discuss this in depth with Norah once he had a moment. Elected officials, including the one who'd summoned them, weren't the only ones with friends in high places.

"Now, if you'll please raise your arms, this will only take a moment," Eric continued. He motioned to the other man, who produced a portable metal detector.

"Do you think we came all this way just to shoot your boss?" Danni asked.

"We don't joke about those types of things, miss," he replied emotionlessly. "Now, kindly do as you're told."

Derek spoke up before anyone else on his team could

say something that would only make the situation worse. "It's okay. When in Rome..." He lifted his arms and stepped forward to let the man scan him.

He finished the rest of his thought silently, reminding himself that just before the fall of the empire, Rome had become little more than a stinking cesspool.

8

After ensuring the team wasn't a *threat*, the two men led them into the elevator of the garage. They went down several floors until Danni was certain they must be below ground level. The doors opened into a nondescript passageway lit by fluorescent bulbs.

"Follow us and please keep up," Eric said, marching forward. The team followed, flanked at the rear by the other man on Zeist's detail. Danni glanced at Derek questioningly. He gave her a small shake of his head, which she took as indication to keep her questions to herself for now.

She wondered whether this sort of thing was typical. Aside from an eight-week survival training course at Fort Bragg, Danni's association with the government-related portion of the job had been limited. She had been to a few offices in D.C., had logins to some systems, and had been given a thorough background check. Not that she had much of a background to check; she was still technically only a sophomore after all.

But this? It felt as if she had stepped into a cheap rip-off of those *Jason Bourne* movies. Then again, maybe that was the point: to try to intimidate them.

If so, they were falling a bit short. The suits that the governor's men wore didn't match. If anything, they'd probably been purchased off the rack. The metal detector wand they had used was no different than those found at the entrance of any amusement park.

Zeist himself also showed the same kind of inconsistency. He was a big man with close-cropped, black hair, almost a crew cut. His bent nose suggested he'd seen his fair share of fights. Yet the way he carried himself didn't strike her as ex-military for some reason. She had seen plenty of soldiers during her training. They all carried themselves with a certain bit of ... it was hard to explain ... *precision* that Zeist lacked.

The only question was, where were they being led? Danni imagined some faux Oval Office type setup was the most likely candidate. There, the governor could keep them out of sight from the general public while also putting on whatever dog and pony show he had planned for them.

Eventually, after walking for what seemed like blocks, they came to another elevator. This one took them up a few floors to an office building of sorts.

"Please wait here for a moment." Eric stepped away and pulled a cell phone from his jacket pocket. A few moments later, he rejoined the group. "We're right on time. The governor will appreciate that."

"Right on time for what?" Mitchell asked, but the security director ignored him. Turning again, he beckoned the group to follow.

Derek gave each of them a quick glance and then

shrugged. The meaning was hopefully clear: what else were they going to do? They followed Zeist out into the lobby of the building. Suited men lined the room – obviously more security.

Derek looked beyond them to the doors leading outside and stopped in his tracks. "You've got to be fucking kidding me."

A small crowd was gathered at the bottom of the steps. Judging from the cameras and notepads present, it wasn't hard to guess their purpose. At the top of the stairs, behind an ornate podium, a stout man stood facing the reporters.

Derek turned to the security director. "Is this what I think it is?"

Eric simply replied, "This way, please, and be sure to smile for the cameras."

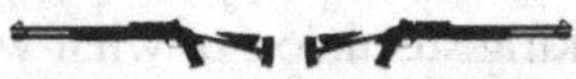

"As fellow New Jerseyan, we should take pride in our great state. Pride in its people, its resources, and especially in its storied history," the man – Governor Yarlberg, based on photos the group had seen of him – said into the microphones atop the podium. "That history includes the legends passed down from our Native American brothers to the first settlers of this fine land. While some might argue that these legends are little more than silly superstition..." Chuckles and guffaws could be heard from the crowd. "There are those who take these things seriously. Who are we to judge? If these tall tales are true, though, then my guests today will be the ones to drag them kicking and screaming into the limelight. I am pleased to welcome to our great state the cast of *The Crypto Hunters!*"

"Idiot can't even get the name of the show right," Francis mumbled.

"Not now," Derek warned, trying to keep a smile on his face as they were herded out in front of the press.

There came a mix of cheers, mingled with some more laughter, as they made their way to Yarlberg. Flashbulbs went off and a few catcalls could be heard as Danni appeared by Derek's side.

Yarlberg sandwiched himself between them for a photo op, taking the opportunity to put one meaty arm around Danni. Derek wondered for a moment whether she would slug him. A part of him hoped she did. At least that way they could end this charade and get to work. Unfortunately, punching out elected officials probably wouldn't endear them to the folks in Washington.

Playing along, at least until they could get the governor alone to explain himself, the group smiled and waved as pictures were taken. Eventually, Yarlberg peeled himself off of Danni and stepped back to the podium. Derek had a sneaking suspicion of what was coming next.

"Ladies and gentlemen, I present esteemed cryptozoologist..." A few snickers were heard from the crowd. "...and host of *The Crypto Hunters*, Dr. Derek..." He paused for a moment to look down at his notes. "Jenner!"

Derek inwardly sighed, but stepped forward anyway. If they had to play this game, so be it. Over the past several seasons, he had gotten used to both being in the spotlight and adlibbing for the camera. As leader of the team, it was sometimes his job to play the part of the dancing monkey.

Time to dance. "Good afternoon, everyone. How are you doing on this fine day? I know I speak for my team and the wonderful folks at the Adventure Channel when I say I hope nobody ran into any Chupacabras on the way over."

That elicited a few laughs, as Derek knew it would. Nothing like a softball joke to win the crowd over. "I'm happy to take any questions you might have."

A woman near the front raised her hand. She was a tall brunette with intense eyes. Derek nodded in acknowledgement and she said, "So, Mr. Jenner, why exactly are you here in the Garden State?"

He ignored the bait. Most people tended to assume his title was bullshit, added to make his credentials seem more legitimate. Of course, five minutes of actual research would have proven that assumption wrong, but then, Derek had never known the mainstream press to bother with details when good old-fashioned muckraking was so much easier. Instead, he replied, "We're here searching for the most elusive creature of them all ... an honest politician."

That brought the desired result, including some decisively overplayed guffaws from Yarlberg himself.

"Seriously, folks, we're here to do our job, which is searching for the truth."

"So you're telling us that the Jersey Devil is real?" the same woman asked.

"I'm telling you that my team and I keep open minds. We're here to evaluate the evidence, conduct an investigation, and form conclusions based upon them."

"You don't have any preconceived notions?"

"Just one ... avoid the parkway at rush hour."

More laughter ensued, except from the reporter. She kept at it, straight-faced.

"Is there any truth to allegations that you're here at the request of the governor to investigate alleged victims of the beast?"

So much for winning over the crowd. "And you are again?"

"Julia Wilhelm, WGXP News."

"Well, Miss Wilhelm, I wouldn't know anything about that or who might be making those allegations. I would expect the authorities to deal with any missing persons so as to conduct a proper investigation. My team and I are here to do some research with perhaps a little entertainment value thrown in."

"What about the rumors that your so-called *research* led to several deaths last year in Colorado?"

Shit! "Excuse me?"

"I have a sworn affidavit from one Katherine Barrows that you were directly involved in a series of events..."

Derek cut her off before she could continue. "I'm aware of Miss Barrows and her claims. Sadly, she is a troubled woman. I feel bad for her, but her accusations are nothing more than the delusions of a disturbed mind. If I recall correctly, her claims include mention of a pack of sasquatches invading her town."

People laughed again, this time not kindly. The reporter, Julia Wilhelm, narrowed her eyes at Derek. She knew she had lost any credibility with the crowd.

Wishing to both spare her any undue ridicule, as well as change the subject, Derek quickly asked, "How about any other questions?"

"Yeah!" a male voice from the back yelled. "When is Danni's new calendar coming out?"

The crowd, once again, responded with laughter.

9

Yarlberg was spirited away at the conclusion of the press conference. Derek and his team eventually found themselves in the antechamber of his office where they were informed that he would speak with them shortly.

That was fine. They had more than enough to talk about.

"She actually spoke with Kate?" Danni asked.

Derek had to give her and the others credit – they'd kept their cool earlier when the question was asked. If any of them had reacted the wrong way, it wouldn't have been disastrous per se, but some of the more intrepid members of the audience might have taken it upon themselves to dig deeper.

"It would seem so," he replied after a moment.

Mitchell nodded. "That poor woman."

"She didn't deserve what she got," Francis added.

Following the events of the Bonanza Creek massacre, during which her father and many of her friends were killed, Kate Barrows had been taken to a psychiatric hospital in Denver for observation. Unfortunately, she'd been driven over the edge by the ordeal. Derek had tried to intervene on her behalf, but had been ordered to stand down by his superiors and disavow any knowledge of her. With no one willing or able to come forward and back up her claims, she was declared mentally unstable and committed.

But apparently word of her story had leaked and at least some were willing to hear her out. That Wilhelm woman had done her homework and, in doing so, come dangerously close to the truth. Derek added that to the growing list of items he was going to have to talk with Norah about.

Danni momentarily averted her eyes from the rest of the group. "Nobody at Bonanza Creek did."

Derek stepped over and put a hand on her shoulder. She had suffered every bit as much as Kate Barrows had, but he knew that, in the end, Danni had been made of sterner stuff. Where others had crumbled, she had risen to the occasion. Without her, Derek – and most likely the others, too – wouldn't have made it out alive.

He gave the group a moment to mull that over, then pulled them back to the present. "What's done is done. For now, it would seem we have at least one nosy reporter who hopefully isn't smart enough to realize just how close she is to the real story."

"I'd say we have more pressing concerns, pardon the pun," Francis replied, indicating the door to the governor's office. It was open and Eric Zeist was standing in the doorway, looking expectantly at them all.

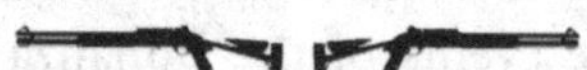

"I ask this with all due respect to your office and title, governor, but are you out of your mind?"

"Watch your tone," Eric snapped.

"Or what?" Francis shot back. "Anytime you want to go, buddy..."

"Relax, Frank." Derek said before turning back to Yarlberg. "I take it you're unaware that what we do is best done without announcing it to the world."

Yarlberg merely stared back at him, an arrogant grin on his wide face. "I am well aware of everything you do, Dr. Jenner." He reached into his desk and produced a thick file. "You've had a number of fascinating adventures, if I might say so."

Derek didn't take the bait. He already knew Yarlberg had cronies in the fed. Responding with threats or histrionics would only give the man the reaction he obviously wanted. "As I am well aware. However, if you've read through that file, you'll know that we typically don't announce our presence beforehand."

"This situation is somewhat different than those others."

"I'll say," Mitchell muttered under his breath.

"Let me see if I can summarize," Derek said, his attention on the governor. "You see, I read a lot, too. I know you're up for reelection this fall. I also know that your approval ratings have been ... how do I say it ... less than stellar."

Yarlberg's face reddened, but he quickly composed himself. "It's been a difficult few years here in the Garden State. We all do the best with what we have to work with."

"Of course."

"Fortunately, my main opponent in this year's campaign isn't exactly universally beloved. Still, I'm looking at a close race. I would prefer to not make it any closer."

"We're listening."

"I'm sitting atop a potentially embarrassing situation.

Not fatal in itself, but combined with all the smear campaigns being aimed at me..." Derek raised an eyebrow, but Yarlberg ignored it. "...It could have a snowball effect."

"The disappearances?"

"Hardly," Yarlberg replied, catching Derek by surprise.

"But I thought..."

"People disappear all the time, Dr. Jenner. That by itself is of little consequence. What concerns me is where it's happening and the unwanted attention it could bring my administration."

Derek turned and surveyed his team. They appeared as confused as he was.

Yarlberg paused for a moment. He seemed pleased to have his guests at a disadvantage. Derek had come into this with a preconceived notion of dislike for the man. He was almost relieved to find it being confirmed in spades. It saved him from having to spare any thoughts toward rethinking his position.

"I think it's safe to say, governor, that you have our rapt attention. Do go on."

"What do you know about the Pine Barrens?"

"We did our homework. We know the layout of the land, the fauna and flora to be expected, the..."

"Fascinating, I'm sure, but what do you know of the *history* of the Barrens?"

"The history of the sightings?"

"Forget the bloody devil!" Yarlberg snapped. "I'm talking real issues here, not fairy tales."

Derek remained silent, which the governor seemed to take as a sign to continue. "People have been trying to develop the Barrens all the way back to before the American Revolution. At first it was just farmers, but that didn't pan out. Damn soil is too acidic to support most food crops. Then the industries started moving in: lumber, paper, gristmills, steel..."

"Steel?" Danni asked.

Yarlberg glanced toward her, taking far too eager of a look in Derek's opinion. "Yes, bog iron to be precise. Actually managed to get a decent toehold before the boom in Pittsburgh killed it."

"So what happened?"

"They all failed, is what happened. Hell, the only business still going strong out there are the cranberry farmers, thanks to all the damn marshes."

"If I'm not mistaken," Mitchell said, "all of those industries, minus the cranberries of course, were renowned for being major sources of pollution."

"I see at least one of you reads up on things other than what bigfoot shit smells like," Yarlberg replied.

"I think I get where you're going," Francis said. "You think the Jersey Devil is some sort of east coast Toxic Avenger. Some kind of mutant running around who..."

"Tell me something, son," Yarlberg commented. "When you're not lugging around that camera, do they keep you locked in a dog crate?"

"What?! Listen, you pork rind eating son of a..."

"Frank," Derek warned, cutting him off. "Let's save the political discussion for later please."

Francis glared at him for a moment, but then gave a quick nod.

Derek once more turned to Yarlberg. "Thank you for the history lesson, governor. Your point, though?"

"My point was, all of those industries shut down years ago, in some cases well over a century. It didn't take the forest nearly that long to reclaim most of it. There's just one problem." He pushed a button on the intercom. "Myra, please send Mr. Krychech in."

Donald Krychech could have been the Stan Laurel to Yarlberg's Oliver Hardy. Where the governor was large, dark haired, and had an aggressive attitude, Donald was thin, balding, and of seemingly nervous demeanor.

Upon introduction, he gave each of the team a limp handshake before moving to an empty seat.

"Mr. Krychech is the current director of the NJAEP."

"Agency for Environmental Protection," Donald clarified before going quiet again.

"I assumed as such," Derek replied. "And does Mr. Krychech..."

"Yes, he knows all about what you and your lot do."

"Wonderful. And, if I may ask, who else have you told?"

"Whoever I thought needed to know," Yarlberg said, locking eyes with Derek – the two in a standoff of wills, each practically daring the other to say the wrong thing.

Finally, Derek said, in as judicial a tone as he could muster, "If I may, I'd like to request a full list of all the people who have been made aware of our *undercover* operative status."

"I'm not sure I appreciate your tone, Dr. Jenner. You may have grandiose ideas about being some sort of secret agent, but I'm sure some could argue that you're little more than a poacher on the government payroll."

"Some?"

"No one I'm associated with, of course."

"Of course not, governor, and I apologize for my tone. However, there is still the fact that our status is not public knowledge and, in fact, requires a security clearance of at least..."

"I'm a publically elected leader, Dr. Jenner, with powerful friends. In four years I'll most likely be running for a seat in the Senate, which I fully expect to win. After that, who can say? It would behoove you to not worry about what clearance I might or might not have. Know that, should I ever obtain the seat which I truly have my heart set upon, I will be sure to remember those who played ball with me."

"As well as those who didn't?"

"Precisely."

As far as Derek was concerned, this conversation was rapidly crossing the line from annoying to maddening. He was a conservationist when he could afford to be, and a hunter when he needed to be. This crap held no interest for him. That didn't mean he liked being dicked around, though, which was exactly what Yarlberg was doing. The man was a skilled politician, so Derek wasn't going to win a war of words. The fact that he was also a spoiled asshole, obviously used to getting his way, was merely exacerbating the situation. It wasn't enough to bring his team in to do whatever job he wanted done – he had to pound it into their heads who was in charge.

Fortunately, Mitchell, the consummate researcher, spoke up before Derek could voice his opinion. "Mr. Krychech, the governor was telling us of some sort of problem related to the area's history. What kind of problem are we talking about?"

Derek gave him a small glance of gratitude for steering the conversation back to business. They could always sort out the pissing match later.

"Donald, please," the man replied meekly. "We have a potential ... situation in the Pine Barrens."

"Situation?"

"Yes," he replied. "Six months ago, we started getting disturbing readings from one grid deep in the Wharton State Forest. Nothing conclusive, mind you."

"What kind of readings?"

"Concerning toxicity levels in the groundwater. That area has been a problem on and off. Seems every twenty or thirty years..."

"So what you're telling us," Derek said, "is that you have an environmental disaster in the making. Is that correct?"

"I prefer not to use that word, Dr. Jenner."

Derek ignored him. Turning back to Yarlberg, he asked, "Exactly why are we here, governor?"

"Very well, I'll be frank with you. However, be warned that this doesn't leave this room. I don't need to remind you of the consequences."

Derek somehow bit his tongue. He was happy to see the rest of his team do likewise, Francis especially. The big man didn't suffer bullshit artists lightly. If not for Derek's earlier intervention, he would have most likely told the good governor to kiss their collective asses.

No doubt taking their silence as agreement, Yarlberg said, "To put it concisely, the good ole boys who used to do business out that way were some pretty big players in those days. When they closed up shop, they did a shit job cleaning up after themselves, and their pockets were deep enough to ensure that nobody made any stink about it."

Donald nodded and added, "There are at least a dozen major abandoned facilities scattered throughout the region, that we know of anyway."

"That you know of?" Mitchell asked.

"You have to understand, some of these go back centuries. Many of the original business entities no longer exist, and those that do aren't particularly eager to air their dirty laundry. Once something is reclaimed by the forest, oftentimes you wouldn't even know it's there unless the floor rotted out beneath you and dropped you into a subbasement."

"And, hypothetically speaking, what would one find in such a subbasement?" Derek asked.

At this, Donald looked highly uncomfortable. Finally, he answered, "That's the problem. We don't really know."

10

"So let me see if I have this straight," Derek said after the AEP director had finished. "A section of the Pine Barrens might be teeming with toxic waste..."

Donald shook his head. "I didn't say that!"

"Sorry. Has become a potential environmental situation. Better? And you're trying to keep it out of the press?"

"The Pine Barrens is a federal reserve," Yarlberg explained. "If people learn it's been compromised in this way, it could become ... uncomfortable for me."

"I don't get it," Francis said. "Why wasn't all this crap cleaned up years ago? I mean, you knew about it, right?"

"Money," Danni replied, ending her silence. "A cleanup of that scale wouldn't be cheap."

"Smart girl." Yarlberg once again gave her an appraising glance. "The costs are simply prohibitive for this or previous administrations. As a result, we have adopted an unofficial policy of cleaning things up as issues are discovered."

"Reactive instead of proactive," Derek surmised.

"Budget conscious," Yarlberg corrected.

"So this whole thing is a smokescreen, I get that," Derek countered. "But why us? Why bother with this Jersey Devil garbage when you could have just made up any excuse to keep the public out while your people clean up? I assume this isn't the first time this has happened."

"You assume correct. Nor do I think it'll be the last."

"So what makes this different?"

"Mr. Krychech?"

Donald looked at the governor. At his nod, he began to speak. "That's just the problem, Dr. Jenner. We're not entirely sure it is garbage anymore."

"Go on."

"A few months ago, one of my men and his wife went missing. It wasn't until he failed to report back in at the office the following week that we realized something was amiss."

"What was this man doing out there?"

"He works ... worked for me in data analysis. We were short on field techs, so he was asked to go out and take samples from the affected area."

"He wasn't a field specialist?"

"I know what you're getting at." Donald folded his arms across his chest, looking more the petulant child than a government official. "Maybe he just got lost. That was our assumption, too."

"He wasn't lost, though, was he?" Danni asked, suddenly showing interest.

Donald shook his head. "No, at least we don't think so. When he didn't turn up, I sent a man to his house, then..."

"At what point did you call the police?" Mitchell interrupted.

"Well..."

"Mr. Krychech handled this as an internal investigation," Yarlberg replied, "at my personal request."

Mitchell looked like he wanted to say something else, but Derek cut him off. "Let Mr. Krychech finish his story, please."

Donald, looking more nervous than ever, waited a moment to see if there were any more interruptions. When none came, he continued. "We then remembered that John, the man who went missing, had borrowed a state vehicle for the weekend. When we remotely activated the built-in GPS, we saw it was parked out in the Barrens. Naturally, I sent a man out to investigate."

"And...?"

"He found the vehicle, but there was no sign of John or his wife."

"Did he look for them?"

"No, and that's where things started to get odd. I sent out Charlie Halstead. He's worked for the department for twenty years, one of our senior field techs. This man has been in and out of those woods dozens of times, not to mention in half the sewers of the state."

"I'm not following you."

"I'm trying to tell you, he's not a skittish fellow. But he hightailed it right out of there rather than grab his gear and look for John. The man was spooked. Said he felt like he was being watched the whole time. Heard some weird noises, too."

"That's not exactly..."

"I'm not finished, Dr. Jenner!"

Derek could see he was worked up. He just wasn't sure why. "Sorry. Please go on."

"I sent out a search team after that. Five men, all of them experienced in the field. They left in the morning. By mid-afternoon, one of them found John's discarded pack. Not too far from there he found ... well, he wasn't sure at the time, but it was John. It was hard to tell. The man was literally torn apart."

Danni let out a small gasp. Derek turned to her for a moment, but she nodded to let him know she was okay.

"His wife?"

"No sign of her, but that wasn't all. The man who found John phoned it in and then returned to the vehicles. A short while later, two of the others arrived there in a state near panic."

"Panic?"

"Yes. One reported the same thing that Charlie had. A feeling of being watched and some strange noises off in the brush."

"The other?"

"He saw ... something. He didn't stick around to find out what, but I know this man. He doesn't spook easily."

"You said there were five."

Krychech paused and then looked toward Yarlberg, who again nodded for him to continue. "We don't know what happened to the other two. They never returned to the rendezvous point."

Derek could have gladly throttled them all. "So let me get this straight," he said through gritted teeth. "You have three missing people, and one dead..."

"Five," Yarlberg said.

"Excuse me?"

"We're assuming five at the moment. The State Police got a report a few weeks back that a couple of college students disappeared during a camping trip around there. Both had a history of drugs, so we've been able to keep it under wraps, but one of their mothers has been making a stink about it."

"And that's when you finally decided to call us in?"

"More or less. That's when I put some feelers out

amongst my contacts. I'd heard rumors about the existence of your little group. You're not nearly as discreet as you think."

"Apparently not."

"Imagine my surprise when you ... what you do, I mean ... turned out to be real. Of course, this all assumes it actually *is* real. You wouldn't be the first bunch to defraud the U.S. government."

"I can assure you what we do is very serious," Derek replied. "I assume you got a peek into the Forest Service's cryptid archives."

The governor raised his eyebrows. "I'm privy to no such information."

"Nice to see some things are still a secret."

"Your point, Dr. Jenner?"

"My point, governor, is that you know what we do, but do you know how or even why we do it?"

Yarlberg quickly glanced at his people before turning back to Derek. "No, I'm afraid I do not, but I'm sure you'll be happy to explain it to me."

"Quite happy," Derek replied blithely. "We don't just pack up our bags when someone has a bigfoot sighting. The government has a relatively expansive archive of cryptid activity, including: species, territory, and even estimated populations."

"Excuse me," Donald interrupted. "The government is aware of these things, but keeps them quiet? Why would..."

"I don't know, Mr. Krychech. That knowledge goes deeper down the rabbit hole than I have access to. What I do know is that, for whatever reason, they wish it to remain a secret. Sometimes the territory of these cryptids overlaps with populated locations. When that happens, we get a call. It's a mutually beneficial arrangement. The government gets to keep things under wraps, and we get to save a few lives in the process. Everybody's happy that way."

"Okay, I see your point," the governor replied. "That's exactly the sort of..."

"No, it's not," Derek said. "You have a few vague legends, even vaguer sightings, and absolutely no archive data or even fossil records to back it up. What you do have is a fairly significant missing persons list. That's a job for the cops, not us."

"Under normal circumstances I would agree, but this is a sensitive issue and police involvement would..."

"Leak to the press?" Danni surmised.

Yarlberg narrowed his eyes at her. "Something like that."

"It's not all vague," Donald piped in.

"Excuse me?"

"Exactly that, Dr. Jenner. We have reason to suspect there's something out there, and it's not just based on what a few of my men saw."

"Go on."

"When we found John Guiterrez's remains, we also found something else."

"What?" Mitchell asked, perking up.

"We're not sure. Some sort of secretion ... mucus, maybe saliva."

Derek replied, "You yourself said that the area was potentially a hotbed of toxins."

"It's nothing like that. The chemical composition is all wrong. We don't know exactly what it is, but we're pretty sure of one thing."

"Which is?"

"Whatever it is, it's biological."

11

The meeting broke up soon after. Eric Zeist was assigned as the team's personal liaison to the governor, although Derek didn't buy that excuse. He knew exactly what Zeist's job was – to babysit them.

The team was taken back to their vehicles. They pulled out, followed closely by the security director and a few of his men. Their first stop was the Burlington campus of Rutgers University. The plan was to assess the lab being loaned to them and make any additional equipment requests if necessary. Once they were set up, Donald Krychech would send over the samples he had collected. Mitchell and Derek would perform the initial analysis – the hope being there was recoverable DNA in the sample. If so, it could be run against the vast species database maintained by the Fish and Wildlife Service, including several species that weren't publically known.

Of course, that all assumed the sample was viable – a big if.

"We're being played like grade-A chumps," Francis complained through the Bluetooth speaker. They were government grade and heavily encrypted. Considering that most of Zeist's equipment appeared to be over-the-counter, it seemed a safe bet that they weren't eavesdropping.

"I'd rather be a chump than a piece of meat," Danni said from the driver's seat. "That guy Yarlberg is a creep. Felt like he has tentacles for eyes."

"He lays a finger on you..." Francis warned, but Danni cut him off.

"He lays a finger on me and *I'll* rearrange his fat face."

Derek and the others laughed. Danni had once gone up against an enraged bigfoot alpha male and lived to tell the tale. Yarlberg didn't stand a chance.

"Watching that would be worth getting fired over," Derek replied.

"Speak for yourself," Francis said with a chuckle. "My wife is looking for a bigger house. I need that second paycheck."

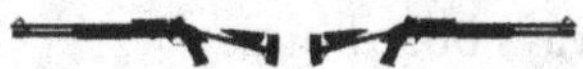

"Not bad," Mitchell said upon their initial tour of the lab. "Is everything networked?"

"Direct fiber connection to our main network. Separated by redundant firewalls, of course," Dr. Reingold, the chairman of the campus biology department, said. "We normally have full-time VPNs running to our other campuses for data sharing, but those have been disabled for the time being."

"Good to hear," Mitchell replied.

"We did some work for DARPA a few years back. At the time, everything was upgraded to government standards. You should be able to connect to whatever systems you need to."

"Network logs?"

"Disabled as well."

"And the equipment itself?"

"All of the machines with local memory have been backed up and wiped as per your instructions, Dr. Harkness."

"Mister," Mitchell corrected. "And you can call me Mitch."

"Very well, Mitch. As for the master passwords, I'll be sending one of our lab techs up with them later. I've taken the liberty of freeing up his schedule. Make use of him as you will."

"That's very kind of you, doctor. I can definitely use the help. I appreciate your foresight."

The rest of the team stood back and let Mitchell take charge. Though Derek was every bit at home in the lab as his friend, he knew Mitch really had a knack for it. Though a medic and field researcher, Mitchell's organizational skills far exceeded his own. Truth be told, Derek was happy to let him run the show. Lab work, though necessary, had always bored him.

As for the rest, Francis's eyes glazed over the moment they stepped foot into the place, whereas Danni's interest was marginal at best even though, as junior member of the team, if Mitchell needed help she was first on deck for the job. She was still a student, and as such, a little extra learning wasn't a bad thing as far as Derek was concerned ... whether she liked it or not.

A short while later, one of Zeist's men arrived with the samples Donald Krychech had promised. By then, Derek and Francis had returned to the vehicles to begin correlating the disappearances with both the recent sightings and historical data, leaving their remaining two teammates in the lab to begin the analysis.

"What the heck is this gunk?" Danni asked, eying the sealed plastic container.

Her question was met with silence.

"I believe my teammate asked you something," Mitchell said, looking up from where he was preparing slides of the secretions.

"Mr. Krychech told you his thoughts. I have nothing further to add," Eric replied crisply, ignoring Danni.

She could have gladly slugged the asshole. First Yarlberg had practically mounted her with his eyes. Now this sexist jackass was barely giving her the time of day.

Mitchell seemed to sense the tension as he was quick to add, "If that's the extent of what you have to offer, you're free to leave."

"The governor sent us to make sure the sample isn't compromised."

"Compromised?"

"They probably think we're going to put it up for sale on eBay," Danni replied, causing Eric to glower at her from behind his mirrored sunglasses. The guy was a major creep, as far as she was concerned.

"Jar of monster snot," Mitchell said. "I'm sure we could get at least three-hundred for it."

"At the very least. Is that what it is, by the way?"

"Could be," he admitted. "Until we're up and running, your guess is as good as mine. Could be snot. Could be mucus. Could be an anal secretion for all I know."

Danni backed up a step. "Glad I let you touch it first."

"Bottom line is I'm not sure." Mitchell lifted his arms and stretched. "I'll start prepping the samples for a deeper analysis." He turned toward the security director. "Under what circumstances were these collected? If they're contaminated..."

"You'll have to discuss that with Mr. Krychech," Eric answered sharply.

"Well, he's not here and I don't have his phone number."

"He's a busy man. I'll pass your question on to him."

"Thanks," Mitchell replied dryly before turning back to Danni. "Let's get to work. Hopefully, by the time we're ready, that lab tech will be here."

"Want me to give Dr. Reingold a call?" Danni asked.

Before Mitchell could reply, though, the door opened. Zeist and his men visibly tensed as a young man entered. He was in his early twenties at the latest and of average height. He had short brown hair, a medium build, and wore glasses. Overall there was nothing overly remarkable about his appearance.

The newcomer stopped just inside the door. He nervously glanced around, taking stock of them all. Danni couldn't help but notice his eyes momentarily widen with recognition as they settled on her and Mitchell, although he was quick to avert his gaze.

What are the odds he watches the show? Danni pondered, inwardly smirking.

"Mr. Harkness?" the newcomer asked, then quickly added, "Ms. Kent." Mitchell nodded and he continued, "I'm Arthur Killian. I work with ... for ... Dr. Reingold. I'm here to, well, help you in any way I can."

"Glad you could make it," Mitchell replied. "Although we can drop the formality, unless you'd prefer us to call you Mr. Killian, that is."

"No, sir."

"Relax, son. I'm Mitch. This is Danni."

"I know. I watch your show. I just wanted to let you both know that..."

"It's nice to meet you, Arthur." Danni offered her hand to him. After a moment, he took it and gave a quick shake with a slightly sweaty palm before pulling back as if she were hot to the touch.

Hopefully he'd get over his nervousness quickly. The show wasn't that big of a deal, as far as Danni was concerned. It's not like her and Mitch were Hollywood stars. Besides, it would be nice to talk with someone her own age. Heck, this was a college campus. She wouldn't have minded being given the tour and maybe checking the local hangouts. The past year had been busy for just about everything except her social life. She could barely remember the last time she'd done something simple like sit down to chill with some friends over a burger.

Of course, this wasn't a social outing, she reminded herself. They were here to work. Still, it's not like there wouldn't be some downtime. Hell, there was a good chance the whole thing was just a crock to begin with, a smokescreen to keep the governor from getting any bad press.

"Here, mister ... err, Mitch," Arthur said, handing him a printout. "It's a list of all the master passwords, as well as some instructions for navigating our network. I'd be more than happy to show you how to work anything in here."

"Thanks. I'm good for now, just stay close," Mitchell replied, opening the paper and walking over to the nearest terminal. He logged in, then headed over to the centrifuge.

Danni had seen this before. Once Mitchell was on the case, he tended to tune out everyone else. Oftentimes, her assistance came down to little more than reminding him to occasionally take a lunch break. Not that she minded, though. Most of this stuff was of little interest to her. She could always devote the time to her own studies or, at worst, listen to some music on her phone. Of course, with Zeist and his goons around, she wasn't likely to let her guard down enough to relax.

She noticed Arthur standing there, a look of helplessness on his face, and smirked. If he was waiting for Mitchell's input, he might be waiting for a while.

"Don't worry," she said, stepping alongside him and causing him to jump ever so slightly. "He gets like this."

"U-um," Arthur stammered, "is there anything we should be doing to help?"

"Not really. If he needs it, he'll ask ... and he almost never asks."

"Oh."

Almost as if on cue, Mitchell turned to them. "This is going to take a while. I'm afraid there won't be much for either of you to do until it's finished. So ... if either of you have somewhere to be, now's the time." Just as quickly, he focused on his work again.

As I thought. "I have an idea," Danni said to Arthur. "He's going to be busy for a couple of hours, and I doubt the others will want to bother him while he's working. Why don't you show me around campus?"

"Well..."

"We won't go far. I have my cell if he needs us."

"I guess..."

"Awesome!" she said. "Mitch, we're gonna go grab some fresh air. Call me if you need anything."

"Sure thing," he absentmindedly replied, tuning the electron microscope.

"Come on." She grabbed Arthur by the hand, noticing how he flinched at her touch.

Danni rolled her eyes. She had almost forgotten how shy some guys could be. Arthur kind of reminded her of Rob, her brother's old roommate. He'd also been...

She quickly pushed that thought away. She didn't need to be reminded of that right now. Bonanza Creek could stay buried in the past for at least today.

"Why don't you show me what passes for the local roach coach?" she said as they approached the door. Eric and one of his men stood flanking it. "Are furloughs allowed, or should I stay in my cell?"

He glowered down at her for a moment, but then shrugged dismissively.

Dickhead. She stepped out the door and Arthur followed a moment later.

"This way, I guess," he said, taking the lead.

After they had rounded a corner and were out of earshot, he turned and asked, "What's up with that one guy? He's kind of creepy."

"Nothing," she replied offhandedly. "Just your typical run-of-the-mill asshole."

12

B ob Hernandez scanned the empty street in front of them, wondering how such an easy gig could go south so quickly. "Where the fuck did they go?"

"I told you to take that left."

"Nobody likes a backseat driver, man," Bob replied to Chris Hopper, his partner for this assignment. It was shit duty like this that made him hate his job some days. The fact that Eric had seemingly gone out of his way to piss off their *guests* earlier certainly hadn't helped matters. As a result, they hadn't even waited to reach the city limits to make a run for it.

Hopper placed the copy of *Field & Stream* he'd been reading onto the dashboard. "You gotta admit, it's pretty impressive. Can't be easy to pull a Houdini with a ride like that."

"It is when your ass is busy planning your next fishing trip instead of acting as lookout."

"Not my fault they went squirrelly on us. Maybe next time the boss should actually say 'hi' first before he pulls out his dick and has a pissing match with the people we're supposed to babysit."

"I don't see you telling him that."

"That's because I enjoy getting a paycheck."

Bob shook his head, then turned down Myrtle Street, hoping to catch sight of the jet black boat of a SUV. Unfortunately, the numerous side streets and turn-offs made it nearly impossible to tell where they'd gone without getting lucky. "So what do we do now?"

"Not sure there's much that needs doing," Hopper replied. "They didn't do anything wrong. We were just asked to keep an eye on them."

"Which we fucked up."

"True, but do you want to radio that in?"

"We kinda have to."

"I know, but that doesn't mean we have to do it right away. It's not like these guys are under arrest."

Bob considered this. "I suppose being bitched out can wait until after lunch." He turned to Hopper. "There's a new Mexican place up on Fourth. What do you say?"

"Now you're talking."

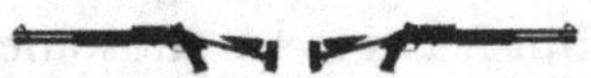

It took Francis all of five minutes to ditch their government-issued escort.

With Mitch and Danni occupied and Zeist overseeing things, Derek realized there was no time like the present to head over to Shilough and get a lay of the land.

He knew that Zeist's personal goon squad could probably track them down if they took a few minutes to figure it out. But he was willing to bet these guys were probably more closely related to mall cops than any sort of actual trained security detail.

"That was pathetically easy," Francis said from the driver's seat of the SUV, almost sounding disappointed. "I mean, hell, we're pretty hard to miss in this boat."

"Better to ask forgiveness than permission," Derek replied, scanning his phone for any messages. So far, it was clear. Apparently Zeist's men weren't too keen on phoning their boss to let him know how quickly their assignment had turned to shit.

"Think our new *masters* are going to be in a forgiving mood?"

"Ask me if I care."

Roughly forty minutes later, they took the exit from 206 as directed by the GPS and turned southeast toward Shilough. After a few more miles, when the device got confused and tried to get them to make a U-turn in a bog, Derek turned it off. "Just keep following this road."

"You sure?"

Derek shrugged, noting to himself how much difference a couple of miles made, even in such a densely packed state. The road they were on had narrowed greatly. Now there was barely enough space for two cars to pass each other going in opposite directions. There wasn't much room for error, as the shoulder gave way to a ditch on both sides. "No, but it has to let out somewhere."

"If you say so," Francis said, "but I'm not seeing any signs for Shilough. Just for the record, the Atlantic City Expressway is only a few miles back the way we came. Personally, I think we'll have a better shot at the craps table than with this turd hunt."

"Don't tempt me." Derek sat up straight in the passenger seat and pointed. "Over there. I do believe we've hit paydirt."

"Dirt anyway," Francis replied as they passed a tiny sign which read 'Shilough: Established 1813.'"

As it turned out, the sign was a fitting precursor for the town itself.

Francis scowled as they drove past a beaten-down bait

shop. "We really should make a game of road bingo for shit-holes like this."

"It's not that bad. It's kind of quaint."

"Quaint, huh?" Francis pointed to an old church with a sign outside proclaiming that homosexuals were damned to burn in the fires of hell. "Why don't cryptids ever haunt anywhere nice?"

"There's that reptoid population living beneath Los Angeles."

"Beneath, and Los Angeles are the keywords there."

"What about last year when we were down in Australia for that rogue Yowie? That was nice."

"If you call being bitten by a dingo nice. I mean, seriously. Would it really hurt one of these things to, say, show up in Bermuda or maybe Saint Martin?"

"There's no pleasing some people," Derek said with a smile before turning serious again. "Hello, what's this?"

Near the far end of the dingy little town, tucked back from the road, Derek spied a small, one story structure. It didn't seem any more remarkable than anything else they'd seen so far. What caught his eye, however, was the old hand-painted sign out in front of it. It depicted a faded image of a winged creature and had the words "Devil Museum" printed above it.

"Even the worst dung heap on the planet is going to have at least one tourist trap." Despite his complaints, Francis pulled in to the gravel lot and parked the large SUV. "Think they'll have anything useful in there?"

"Doubt it," Derek replied as the other man shut off the engine. "From the look of the place, I'm half surprised it isn't condemned. But you never know. Blind squirrel theory and all. Grab the gear. Worst case, maybe we can get some usable footage. It sure as hell looks like they could use whatever publicity we can give them."

Francis took a few minutes to film the nearly empty street. If not for the working traffic lights and a few small stores displaying neon "Open" signs, one might have thought they were in an abandoned ghost town.

"Kinda creepy."

"It's the middle of the day," Derek said. "Kids are in school and their parents are at work. I bet this place is hopping on the weekends." He smiled and added, "Or at least limping. How's it look?"

"I think that's good for now. Let me get a shot of that sign and then we can go in."

Derek waited for him to do so, then they both walked toward the front entrance. "And now for the moment of discovery." He turned the handle of the door, firmly expecting to find it locked. It wasn't. A bell jingled overhead as it opened.

"Think the Smithsonian should be worried?" Francis whispered.

They found themselves in a large, open space. A modest number of display cases and photos lined the walls. Before they could do much in the way of examining them, a man stepped in from a back room and approached them.

"My apologies for the delay," he replied in a slightly guarded voice. "The museum also functions as my home. I was in the back enjoying some afternoon TV."

"That's ... no problem at all," Derek replied, forcing himself not to stare.

The proprietor was tall, thin, and appeared to be middle-aged, but it was his face that caught Derek's attention. He had a crooked nose, a protruding brow, and an overly pronounced underbite which gave his face a decisively off-balance appearance.

The man walked up to them. "Admission is two dollars per person."

"Not a problem." Derek pulled out his wallet and extracted a bill. "Sorry. I only have a twenty."

"I'm a little short on change," the man replied. "However, donations are both welcome and tax deductible."

Derek smiled and handed the money over. "Of course. Always happy to help out a local business."

"Much appreciated." The admissions fee quickly disappeared into the man's pocket, almost as if he were afraid Derek might change his mind. He made to turn toward the displays, but then stopped and glanced toward Francis, who was preparing to turn his camera on again.

The man held up a hand. "I am afraid there is no photography allowed. Video, too. Some of the artifacts here are unique, and we would prefer visitors come see them in person rather than on some website."

"We?" Derek asked.

"My wife, Sarah, and I."

"I can do a wide shot," Francis offered. "Nothing zoomed in. Just enough to tantalize people. Our audience would probably like it. We're from..."

"I know who you are," the man replied. "Dr. ... Jenner and his crew, was it?" Derek raised an eyebrow, but the man quickly added, "I saw the governor's press conference. We have a satellite dish on the roof."

"Ah. Then you know we're here to do some research for our show."

"Yes," the man replied. "Although I can't lie and say I actually watch it."

"No offense taken."

"However, if I can be of any service in helping you fine gentlemen educate yourselves, I am happy to."

"Excellent. Then..."

"But I am afraid the no photography rule is non-negotiable."

Derek paused for a moment, then turned to Francis and nodded. The big man powered down the camera and lowered it to his side.

"Thank you kindly," the man replied, then held out a hand. "My name is Ezekiel Lesterfield. I'm the proprietor of this establishment dedicated to the history of our fine town."

"A pleasure, Mr. Lesterfield." Derek shook his hand, noting the man's grip was slick and clammy. He quickly dismissed that, though, as another detail caught his attention. *Lesterfield?* For some reason that sounded familiar. "This is my cameraman, Frank LaCroix."

"Is that French?" Ezekiel asked.

"Canadian," the big man replied. "Got Canuck blood in my veins, especially during hockey season."

If Ezekiel found Francis's joke to be funny, he didn't show it. "Will the rest of your colleagues be joining us? I seem to recall there being four. A man and a young woman."

There was something about his tone Derek didn't like, but he pushed it aside. It was most likely a combination of his over-protectiveness of Danni, combined with their host's somewhat ungainly appearance. He mentally chided himself for it. It wasn't fair of him to be judgmental. "Not today. They're busy with other aspects of the investigation."

"I see."

"But they'll be with us for our night hunt," Francis added.

"Night hunt?"

"Yeah, it's for the show. We go out and conduct a full field investigation once it gets dark. Set up trap cameras, sound lures, that sort of thing."

"And you'll be doing this investigation in the woods around Shilough?"

"We usually don't divulge that in advance," Derek said, throwing a look Francis's way. "It can be dangerous for anyone who doesn't know what they're doing and could also compromise any evidence we find."

"Of course. I merely asked out of curiosity. Be forewarned, though. The woods can be a treacherous place at night."

"Like we don't already know..." Francis began.

"As we're well aware," Derek interrupted his teammate. No point in being overly snippy with the locals. "But we're still scouting potential locations. After this, we're going to drive down to Leeds Point and consider..."

Now it was Ezekiel's turn to interrupt. "A waste of time, I can assure you. A tourist trap, nothing more."

"Oh?" Derek asked, inwardly amused at the irony.

"The story of Mother Leeds is the most popular telling of the legend, but it is little more than an old wives' tale. Sadly, it is a myth that allows the greedy merchants at Leeds Point to profit while we sit here in relative obscurity."

"We typically don't take legends like that at face value, anyway."

"That is not to say the so-called devil was not real, but as with so many things, the true story has been perverted over the years. One might go so far as to claim it was stolen by them."

"Do tell," Derek replied, letting the proprietor lead them into the museum.

"As you can see, the legend of the Jersey Devil originated much closer to Shilough than Leeds Point."

To say that Derek was less than impressed by the old newsprint within the museum's few glass cases was an understatement. Yellow journalism at its best, proclaiming the fantastical, no doubt while ignoring the real issues of the day.

"So then how did Leeds Point get all the credit?" Francis asked, looking at an old flyer offering a reward for the devil's capture.

"Simple. Shilough has always been a relatively close-knit community. We keep to ourselves and do not seek to profit off our legends."

"Says the guy running the museum."

Ezekiel grinned, showing crooked yellow teeth. "This museum's purpose is merely to preserve the truth, as well as provide a modest income for my family. You'll note the lack of a gift shop, which we would certainly have if we were willing to compromise our ethics."

Derek chuckled. "He's got a point, Frank."

"Besides," Ezekiel said, "after my ancestor exorcised the beast, there was little need for us to seek publicity. Let the folks over in Leeds keep their silly legends."

Derek finally remembered what Danni had told them on the way down. That's why this guy's name sounded so familiar. "So the exorcism actually happened?"

That seemed to perk Ezekiel's interest. "You've heard of it?"

"We would be remiss in our jobs if we didn't conduct proper research."

"I'm impressed. Most who come this way purporting to be so-called devil hunters are nothing of the sort. All they know about the Barrens is what anyone who performs five minutes of cursory research would, and most of that are lies. The Leeds legend, the Kallikak family, the Philadelphia hoax."

"They used an actual painted kangaroo for that one, didn't they?" Derek asked.

"Yes," Ezekiel replied, the humor draining from his face. "Made quite the killing before anyone thought to take a closer look. We don't have much use for those types around here." He led them to a series of framed photos on the wall. "Here he is. My great-great grandfather, Jedediah."

Derek stared at the first picture. It depicted a mature, stern-looking man standing in the center. A world-weary woman was by his side. Surrounding them was a large group of boys and young men. However, it wasn't so much the image itself that stood out, but the appearance of all those in it.

"So, is this his ... flock?"

"No," Ezekiel said. "That's his family. The woman next to him is his wife, Sarah. All the rest are their children. My ancestor was blessed with a large family – eighteen sons and a daughter."

"That's a lot of boys."

"As it has always been with my family. At least nine out of ten of the children born to my bloodline are male, perhaps more."

Derek looked closer and spied the lone girl. She was a tiny, frightened-looking thing surrounded on either side by a pair of hulking brothers who had their arms around her. He supposed it was meant to be a protective, brotherly gesture, but in the image captured, it appeared more like jealous hoarding on their part.

Again, that could have been due to the unpleasant appearance of those captured in the image. *Damned ugly family. I can see where our host gets it from.*

He glanced toward Francis and could see the big man was probably thinking the same thing.

Derek immediately felt guilty about it. He wasn't

normally one to judge by looks alone. Still, there was something off about the photo, something he couldn't quite put his finger on.

"Seventeen," Francis said, drawing Derek's thoughts back to the present.

Ezekiel turned to him. "Excuse me?"

"There's only seventeen kids, sons anyway, in the photo."

Ezekiel smiled, but it didn't quite reach his eyes. "So there is. I am told that one of his children, Abram, was quite sickly. He was often bed-ridden, under the care of his sister, Sarah. No doubt this photo was taken during such a time."

"Sarah?" Derek asked, remembering what the man had said about his wife. "Seems to be a lot of that going around lately."

He'd meant it as a joke, but Ezekiel's gaze held little humor in it. "It's a fine name for a woman. A good, God-fearing name. There are far too many strumpets in this world. Whores of Babylon, all of them. Doesn't seem anyone remembers a woman's rightful place anymore."

Derek was suddenly glad he'd left Danni behind. Not only was Ezekiel's comment sure to infuriate her, but he was getting a strange vibe from the man. Not to mention, something about Jedediah's picture was still nagging at him.

"So, about that exorcism," Francis said after a beat.

The intensity left Ezekiel's eyes as if he suddenly remembered he was their guide. "Ah, yes. I'm happy to tell you all about it."

13

Ezekiel's tale of the exorcism matched fairly closely with what Danni's research had revealed, but there were additional details that had apparently been left out of the official account.

According to his story, the creature known as the Jersey Devil had rampaged the area in the years leading up to the exorcism, but the number of those affected appeared higher than that officially reported.

Whether it was true or the man was simply exaggerating to make the story seem more dramatic, though, Derek didn't ask.

The creature had struck some of the other towns bordering the forest, enough so that outside police help began to arrive in Shilough, something the small, close-knit community apparently did not appreciate. To Derek it sounded like something out of a cliché drifter story, in which a luckless hitchhiker wandered into a town that didn't care much for strangers.

Aside from that, it appeared the two stories matched fairly closely. The exorcism itself was more of a day-long party of religious fervor by the townsfolk. When it was over, the sightings and disappearances died down.

Definitely a case of power of suggestion if ever he'd heard one, albeit it was a temporary balm, as devil sightings began to rise again in the decades that followed.

As for the missing persons, there was no way of knowing what had actually happened to them. But the preacher's warning to stay away from the more dangerous sections of the Pine Barrens almost certainly contributed to a decline in such mysterious disappearances.

In short, there wasn't anything to convince him the devil was any more real than when they'd first arrived. Still, Derek couldn't shake a strange feeling in the back of his mind as he and Francis excused themselves from the museum and turned to leave. They walked out the door, thanking Ezekiel for his time and letting it close behind them.

"What do you think, Frank?"

"I would've handed over that twenty just to get away from that guy."

"Not going to argue with you there."

"You can't tell me," the bigger man joked, "that he doesn't have a van parked around back with a sign on it reading 'Free Candy.'"

"Be nice. I can't imagine business is brisk even on the best of..."

"Son of a bitch."

"Huh?" Derek turned to find his cameraman pointing.

"Looks like we have company."

Derek glanced toward the direction of their SUV. He'd been expecting to find that their security detail had finally caught up to them. Instead, he saw a somewhat familiar-looking woman leaning against the side of their vehicle, apparently waiting for their return. "Is that...?"

"The reporter who gave you shit earlier. Looks like it."

"Well, isn't that just grand?"

Francis laughed. "Maybe the governor should hire her as our babysitter instead. She did a hell of a better job tracking us down than Zeist's guys."

There was no way to avoid the confrontation, so the two men simply walked toward their vehicle. This wouldn't be the first time, Derek noted, that they'd had to give someone the runaround. Albeit people in the press could be a lot harder to shake loose once they set their minds to something.

As they approached, the woman stood away from their SUV and smiled in their direction. "Dr. Jenner, Mr. LaCroix."

Derek returned the smile. At least she'd gotten his title right this time. "Ms..."

"Wilhelm. Julia, please." She held out a hand which both men shook in turn.

"A pleasure to see you again," Derek replied neutrally. "Although I have to admit, I am a bit surprised."

"Let me guess. You thought I just popped by your press conference to harass you so I could return home and write a story about conspiracies and cover-ups?"

Francis snorted laughter. "If I was a betting man, that's where my money would be."

Derek glanced sidelong at him before turning toward Julia again. "I'm forced to agree. No offense, but usually the only people who bother stalking us are overeager fans. I mean, if this is all for an autograph..."

"I can stop you right there, Dr. Jenner."

"Derek."

"Thank you, Derek. But up until a few months ago,

I'd never even heard of your show. I mostly stick to network television."

"Mind-numbing sitcoms and teen angst, quite the combo," Francis said.

Derek folded his arms in front of him. "And yet you had some wild claims back there at the press conference. Pretty damning for someone who has no idea who we are."

"Had," she corrected. "I did my research, brought myself up to speed ... particularly about the rumors surrounding your show. Then, when I heard you were coming here at Governor Yarlberg's request, I had to wonder whether it was just a coincidence."

"Rumors?" Derek asked, despite being well aware they existed. Even with all the threats and signed affidavits in the world, some people just couldn't keep their mouths shut. Fortunately for them, chatter like this was mostly confined to half-baked websites run by conspiracy nuts.

"Yes. Taken by themselves, they're easily dismissed. But when you begin to look at the bigger picture, it fits together like the pieces of a jigsaw puzzle."

"I hear they sell those at Target," Francis replied. "Although theirs tend to come with a lot less crazy."

"Be that as it may," Derek said, ignoring his teammate's barb, "such ridiculous hearsay doesn't strike me as something that would make for a front page story, even on a slow news day. Except for maybe the tabloids. And I wouldn't expect one of their reporters to bother stalking us."

"I'm not stalking you."

"Oh, so you just happened to turn up here in the middle of nowhere, same as us?"

"It's called research. That, and this truck ... not the most inconspicuous thing on the road."

"She has a point there, Derek."

"Next time," she said with a smile, "consider renting something a bit more low key, or just call Uber."

Derek let out a sigh and turned to Francis. "Mind stowing the equipment? We need to get back on the road."

"You got it, boss." He walked to the other side of the SUV where he opened the rear passenger door to put his camera away.

"Got something in there you don't want me to see?" Julia asked.

Derek smirked at her. "Just a couple of bigfoot corpses. At least, according to your sources."

The assuredness dropped off Julia's face after a moment. Derek assumed her next move would be to walk off angrily, shouting back at them that they couldn't hide forever from the free press or some other such bullshit.

Instead, she took a deep breath and said, "My apologies. This isn't going how I envisioned it."

"I'm not really sure what you envisioned. Some tearful confession that we're part of a global conspiracy, perhaps?"

"No. That's not what I meant. When I first heard about you guys, what some people say you do, I thought it was crazy, too. But the more I dug, the more it started to make sense. Then, when I heard you were coming here, after what's happened, I thought it had to be related. But the truth is, it was probably more wishful thinking on my part than anything."

Derek found himself intrigued. Though his better judgment told him they should get in the car and drive off without any further comment, he found himself asking, "So why the sudden interest in us? What happened to turn me and my crew from non-entities to this?" He waved his hand to indicate the area. "Off the record, of course."

She appeared to consider this for a moment before looking around, as if making sure nobody else was within earshot. "Fine. I guess if the rumors aren't true, then the worst I'll be doing is making a fool of myself."

"Nothing ventured, nothing gained."

"You've heard of the disappearances?"

Derek wasn't about to take the bait so easily. "It might have been mentioned in talks with our producer. Makes for good drama."

"Not for all of us. My sister Sophie and her husband John, they disappeared a couple of months back. No trace of them. John worked for the AEP. That's the Agency of..."

"I know who they are," Derek replied, indicating she go on.

"They were supposed to be heading down to Atlantic City for the weekend, but John had to make a stop in those damned woods first."

"And you know this how?"

"My sister. She and I talked the day before. It was all she could complain about, how his boss was taking advantage of him. Well, they never arrived. I called the hotel. They never checked in."

Derek raised an eyebrow, but was careful not to say anything. This had to be the same John that Donald Krychech had told them about, the one whose body had been found and whose wife was still missing. He couldn't tip his hand, though, as much as he wanted to. Julia was the missing woman's sister, but she was also a reporter. There was no way he could confide in her and feel confident she wouldn't try to blow things wide open. All the signed affidavits in the world wouldn't mean shit if she was on a mission.

He considered this for the briefest of moments. Maybe that wouldn't be such a bad thing in this case. The cover-up by Yarlberg left a bad taste in his mouth. Seeing the governor dragged out in front of the press to explain not only the environmental issues, but also why he'd taken the law into his own hands, would be immensely satisfying. But there would be ramifications for his team. Though he sometimes hated the secrecy that their dealings with the government required, there was one major aspect that kept him focused: they helped people, saved lives. He wasn't about to jeopardize that for something as petty as shoving Yarlberg's crap back in his own face.

He forced his voice to maintain a careful measure of neutrality as he asked, "Have you tried the police?"

She narrowed her eyes as if she wanted to scream at him, but remained calm. "Of course I did. I filed a missing person's report as soon as I could."

"And?"

"And nothing! It's like they couldn't have cared less. All they do is keep giving me the runaround."

Francis had stowed the camera and was looking over the top of the SUV toward Derek. He saw the anger in the big man's eyes and felt it himself. The AEP's people had found John. Krychech had said so himself. And yet this poor woman had apparently been told nothing.

He was well aware that certain facts surrounding a death sometimes needed to be kept under wraps – had been forced to do so himself more than he wanted to admit. The truth wouldn't bring the dead back, but that didn't mean families didn't deserve a body to bury or a memory to mourn. That was one line he refused to cross – leaving people with the torture of never knowing.

That Yarlberg and his lackeys were doing so, and all for something so petty as political gain, was almost impossible to believe.

"And I don't think it stops there," Julia continued, caught up in her tale. "I have friends in this business. Hell, my editor and I went to school together. At first, they were all happy to help spread the story. Promised me that Sophie and John's pictures would be plastered everywhere.

But then something changed. They all went from supporting me to nothing but excuses. Whenever I ask anyone about it, they're quick to change the subject. Someone doesn't want this getting out and I don't know why." She looked at the two men. "I know how I sound – probably like some crazed conspiracy nut – but all I want is to find my sister. She's a good person. She doesn't deserve this."

Derek placed a hand on her shoulder. "Believe me, I understand. I really do. Listen, we're going to be conducting our night investigation in the woods. Despite what you might think of our show, my people are well-trained and know what they're doing. I can't promise you that we'll find anything, but I will promise that if we do, we'll tell you. You have my word on that."

Julia's expression softened. "Thank you. And, sorry if I came across as a nut."

Derek smiled at her. "In this business we run into a lot of them. Believe me, you really don't fit the mold."

14

Following Derek's promise to do what they could in the course of filming their show, Julia offered him her personal cell number. He accepted on the condition that she refrain from tailing them throughout the state.

Finally, he climbed into the SUV with Francis and they drove out of Shilough.

"Slick."

"What?" Derek asked.

"Got yourself a fine lady's digits. Is it high five time yet?" Francis let out a laugh as he guided the vehicle back through the narrow road they'd used to enter the town.

"It's not like that and you know it."

After a few moments, Francis said, "I can't believe those assholes haven't told her they've found that poor guy's body."

Derek shrugged. "I'm not surprised. Confirms what I suspected about this bunch. Let's make it a point to not let our guard down around any of them if we can help it."

"You don't have to tell me twice." Francis checked the

rearview mirror, no doubt mindful they'd been followed once already.

"Paranoid?"

"Getting there. Think her sister is still alive?"

Derek found himself looking at the side mirror, too, finding nothing but an empty road staring back at them. "I don't care to speculate, but it doesn't look good. I will tell you one thing, though. That asshole can threaten us all he likes, but if we find anything concrete, I'm letting her know."

"See. I knew you were soft for her."

"Don't start."

"Come on, you have to admit your dating life hasn't been worth dick as of late."

"I work odd hours."

"Trust me, I know. Shakti reminds me every chance she gets."

Derek smiled at the mention of Francis's wife. They couldn't have been a bigger contrast if they tried. He was a large lumberjack-looking man, an avowed atheist, and could close down a bar with the best of them. She, on the other hand, was a petite woman of Hindi descent who came across as decisively meek – that is, until you managed to tick her off. So far as he was aware, there was nobody on the team who would have put money on Francis in a confrontation between the two. "She giving you a hard time?"

"Nothing major. She's fine so long as the feds keep sending us to out of the way dumps. I gotta warn you, though, another Australia trip like the last one and she's already told me you'd better be prepared to shoot her with a tranq dart to keep her from coming along."

Both men shared a laugh until Derek said, "You know I wouldn't actually do that, right?"

"Yeah, I figured you wanted to live."

That set them off again.

Finally Derek said, "All right, let's get back to Burlington. Mitch is going to be waiting."

"So is that Zeist guy."

"Don't remind me."

"Think they'll try to tag along with us on the hunt?"

Derek looked at him out of the corner of his eye. "They can try."

"What do you think?"

Danni had to admit she'd been a bit worried about the seemingly random and excessive ingredients that had been stuffed into the *fat* sandwich Arthur had recommended for lunch. It wasn't that she disliked any of it, but typically she expected to get her sides on ... well, the side, not all together on the same roll. One bite, however, had proven her wrong. "This is ... pretty awesome."

"See? Told you not everything about Jersey sucks." Arthur swallowed a bite of his own. "Believe me, there is no finer way to cram for a final. Throw in a couple of Red Bulls and you're good to go until sun up."

"I bet," Danni said with a laugh. "Although I think the name is spot-on. Pretty sure I'd look like a beached whale after a couple of these."

"I don't think you have anything to worry about." As soon as the words left Arthur's mouth, he turned bright red. He took another bite, swallowed too quickly, and started coughing.

Danni gave his back a couple of smacks until he got it under control. She smiled to herself but decided to go easy on him.

"I'm sorry," he said after a few moments. "I didn't mean..."

"It's okay. Really, it is."

"Cool," he said uncertainly. Then, as if to cut the ice, he reached for his back with an exaggerated wince. "Ow. Yeah, you really don't need to worry."

"What can I say? Derek runs a tight ship. We can't do our jobs without staying in shape."

"Hah. I don't think the guys on *Monster Chasers* have the same philosophy." He held up his sandwich. "Most of them look like they live on these things."

Danni let out a bark of laughter. *Monster Chasers* was a series on a rival network. She'd seen a few episodes. Basically, it involved a bunch of good ol' boys from America's heartland, running around the forest with guns and typically making so much noise as to make their obviously edited cryptid run-ins near laughable. Even if her team's true mission hadn't been so very different, she wouldn't have worried much about the competition.

"Sorry, but I have a confession to make," Arthur said, growing solemn for a moment. "I do occasionally cheat on you guys with that other show."

Danni blew out a sigh. "I don't know how I'll go on. Here we are, enjoying some time together, and now this bombshell. It might be too much for me to handle."

"If it helps, you guys have a higher priority on my DVR."

She took another bite and appeared to consider this. "Well, I suppose I can forgive you ... just this once. I mean, you *did* introduce me to these. It would be heartless of me to walk away now. Seriously, though, this is good. They didn't have anything like this at my school."

"Your school?"

"Yeah. I mean, we have grease trucks, but they're kind of a last resort. I'm pretty sure their cheesesteaks are just some moldy roast beef with a slice of American tossed on it."

"Um, what college?"

"South Dakota State," she replied nonchalantly, "but I've been taking online courses lately."

"What's your major?"

"Forestry and Conservation."

"Really?"

"Why do you sound surprised?"

"It's ... nothing."

"Spill."

"No, really."

"Say it, or so help me, I'll beat you unconscious with the rest of this sandwich."

"Okay," he replied, holding up his hands in surrender. "This is going to sound kind of douchey, but when you joined the show, I kind of figured..."

"That I was some airhead added for T&A value only?"

Arthur looked deeply embarrassed, but she nudged him to continue. "Well, yeah. I mean, some of us figured they fired Woodchuck so they could replace him with a spokesmodel."

Danni dropped her gaze to the ground, the flavors of the sandwich immediately forgotten. The "official" story was that Chuck "Woodchuck" Wayans, the team's former tracker, had abruptly quit and retired from public life. Some debate had arisen on their online boards over whether he'd been fired, which was exactly the type of misinformation their true bosses wanted. Only a few knew the truth: that he'd been a victim of the Bonanza Creek massacre.

Arthur, apparently misinterpreting her sudden solemn-ness, asked, "You're mad at me, aren't you?"

Danni looked up at him and quickly covered her thoughts with a smile. Now was not the time to wallow in the past. "Not at all. I mean, I definitely get that vibe from some of our fans. It used to tick me off, but I guess I should be flattered. I mean, I never really considered myself the glamourous type."

"You could have fooled me. I have your poster hanging in my room and..." He stopped when she raised an eyebrow. "That's TMI, isn't it?"

"Just a bit."

"So, um, how did it happen?"

"The poster?"

"No. How'd you join the team? I mean, no offense, but forestry doesn't seem like something that would get a bunch of network suits knocking down your door."

Danni stood up and stretched – not wanting to let her lunch cause any malaise to set in. "Come on, let's walk off these sandwiches."

Arthur's awkwardness aside, she was enjoying herself. Back when she'd been a freshman, before her life had completely changed, she'd taken little things like this for granted. Now, a bit of normalcy, just a little thing like walking around campus with a guy, was a luxury, one that wouldn't last for long. Depending on how things went, they'd either soon be deep in the Pine Barrens or hopping on a plane toward Wisconsin.

She realized she hadn't answered Arthur's question. The truth was out of the question, but that didn't mean she couldn't offer a version of it. "I helped them out on one of their hunts."

"How so?"

"It was kind of a right place, right time sort of thing." It had been, but more the opposite of right. "I was vacationing where they were filming and ended up helping them with some research. The next thing I knew, they offered me a chance to try out. The rest is history."

"Talk about a lucky break."

Lucky wasn't quite the word she'd use. Still, it was the life she had chosen. No one had forced her to do this.

There were also the benefits to take into account – all those they helped. "Yeah, I guess it was, in a way."

"Fame and fortune are hard to beat when you're a starving college student."

"I wouldn't go that far on either," she replied with a laugh. "The Adventure Channel isn't exactly HBO and we're not *Game of Thrones*, but I get what you're saying. As far as first jobs out of college go, one could do worse. Not to mention, there's the people factor."

"I can imagine. You probably meet a lot of guys."

Danni had to suppress a sigh. Awkward Arthur might be, but he wasn't afraid to cast his lure on a fishing expedition. She wasn't really in the market for a boyfriend, but he was kind of cute in a dorky sort of way and seemed really nice. If she had to spend a few days on this campus, she could do far worse. Rather than shooting him down outright, as was her initial inclination, she decided to leave the door ajar. Who knew? Stranger things had happened. "I meet a lot of folks period, young and old," she replied. "But that's not what I meant. I meant helping people." He glanced at her with eyebrows raised, which was not entirely unexpected. "I'm serious."

"Okay. So how?"

"All right, I have a good example. About four months back, we were in Ohio filming a segment. There was this nice old lady who was scared out of her mind. Kept hearing screams coming from the woods near her home. She was terrified to step foot into her own backyard after dark. Turns out it was nothing more than some owls who'd nested nearby. They made a hell of a racket, but were far more interested in field mice than her. You have no idea how awesome it was to see the relief on her face when we showed her. Mind you, that part got cut for TV."

Arthur laughed. "Sounds just like something a network would do. You know, I never considered that ...

the stuff that goes on behind the scenes. I guess you have a good point about that. For all of us watching at home, chuckling when nothing is found, I guess I never considered the people who are relieved to know it was just their imagination."

"Trust me, it can be annoying some days. To fit the show into an hour, lots of stuff has to be cut, and sometimes what's left makes us look like morons who can't tell a deer in the woods from sasquatch. Sometimes I just want to..."

Danni stopped mid-sentence as the phone in her pocket vibrated. She pulled it out and checked her texts. "Looks like we're back on the clock. Derek and Frank are pulling in now. Time to head back and see what's next on the agenda."

Arthur nodded. "We can cut through the commons and get there faster."

"Sounds good. Let's go."

"Thanks, by the way."

She turned to him. "For what?"

"For ... actually being a cool person."

She smiled back. "Likewise."

"I'm still going to ask you to autograph my poster before you leave, though."

15

Danni could tell Derek was back from way down the hall, as she could quite clearly hear Eric Zeist yelling at him. She grinned as she approached the lab. Based on what was being said, he and Francis had managed to ditch Eric's men.

"You're here at the governor's say so, nothing more!"

"Last I checked," Derek was saying as she and Arthur stepped in, "this is a free country. We're not under arrest, and even if you tried, I'm pretty sure you don't have the badge to back that up."

"One call is all it'll take to..."

"To what?" Francis shot back. "Embarrass yourself? Feel free. Your buddy can pull whatever strings he wants, but all that's going to do is get us fired, and you know what? If that happens, we're out of here and your boss gets to go on *Face the Press* and explain why he's okay with his state being a toxic cesspool."

Danni looked off into the corner where Mitchell was sitting staring at a computer monitor and ignoring what was going on around him. She could tell he wasn't completely zoned out, though, by the look of amusement on his face.

Before she could so much as say a word of greeting, Eric rounded on her and Arthur. "You ever think about knocking? That kid isn't authorized to hear this."

Danni narrowed her eyes, practically daring the larger man to step into her personal space. "That might be a better argument if you hadn't been screaming so loud as to be heard from down the hall."

"Authorized?" Arthur asked. "What are you guys talking about?"

Danni shared a glance with Derek. His eyes said it all. The governor, in his attempt to cover up whatever was going on in the Pine Barrens, was instead shining a spotlight on it by insisting his men shadow them. Government intelligence at its finest.

Derek turned to Mitchell, having seemingly made up his mind. "Mitch, could you..."

"Already got them." Without missing a beat, Mitchell spun in his chair and produced a stack of paperwork from the briefcase by his side.

Derek smiled as he took them. "I must be getting predictable in my old age."

"You could use some new material."

Derek turned to Arthur. "Take a seat, kid. There's some stuff you have to fill out. Non-negotiable I'm afraid."

"I already signed the waivers that Dr. Reingold..."

"These are a bit more far reaching than a typical NDA. And they have more teeth, too. Trust me on this. Oh, and don't lie in the section about social media accounts. Everyone tries to be cute about that these days, and we always find out."

"I'm not authorizing this," Eric barked.

"And I'm not asking," Derek replied, clearly annoyed. "Your boss might have some pull, but he's not here. And if you want to test that, I have friends of my own who would be very happy to make your life difficult."

Danni was amused to see Zeist shut his trap and back up a step. The guy was nothing more than a bully, but her team was a slightly different animal than what he normally dealt with. No matter how powerful someone's friends were, the concept of messing with the feds tended to give people pause. She was less amused, however, to see that Arthur had gotten dragged into this, courtesy of her picking the wrong moment to return with him.

There was at least one upside, however. It would mean she'd have to watch her tongue a lot less around him. He seemed like a nice guy, and giving him bullshit story after bullshit story didn't feel right.

Arthur, for his part, looked utterly confused. "What's this about? Am I in trouble for something?"

"Not at all," Mitchell said. "If anything, this just means you can help out more."

Derek reached into his back pocket. His eyes met Danni's again, and she could see the twinkle in them. He always liked this part. Claimed it made him feel like a little kid playing cops and robbers, except his badge was real.

He handed it over to Arthur who took a quick look.

"U.S. Forest Service, Department of Cryptid Containment? You're kidding, right?"

"There's a joke here, all right, and it's..."

Derek cut the security director off with a glare. "Feel free to call and verify my badge number or any of my team's. You'll find we're quite legit."

Arthur turned toward Danni. She nodded back at him.

To her surprise, he actually smiled in return, albeit there was still a confused aspect to it. "And that paperwork?"

"Affidavits ensuring your cooperation and confidentiality. Don't worry, nothing onerous so long as you realize that anything discussed with us from here on in should be considered classified."

"Classified," he repeated. "As in legal penalties?"

"Precisely," Derek replied, clapping Arthur on the shoulder. "Welcome to the conspiracy, kid."

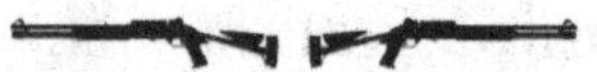

The next few hours were busy ones. Mitchell brought Arthur up to speed on what they were really testing and where the lab's systems were actually VPN'd to. The boy was skeptical at first – not surprisingly – but Mitchell had a way of taking the fantastical and making it sound plausible. However, Derek suspected the presence of government personnel, people not known for being great practical jokers, helped impart their seriousness to the boy.

While this was going on, the rest of the team busied themselves with discussing strategy and next steps. Following a brief, but heated, call with Governor Yarlberg, Derek agreed to cooperate with Eric and his men on the condition that the governor's people observe but not interfere.

As it turned out, another police report had been filed, a few days prior to their arrival, by the parents of some teenagers who'd gone missing. According to the teens' friends, the couple had been planning an illicit rendezvous out on Swamp Forge Road, a claustrophobic stretch of asphalt not far from the route Derek and Francis had taken earlier in the day.

The missing count now up to seven, the added pressure on the governor had put him in a mood far more suited to negotiating – especially after Derek pointed out that his team was almost guaranteed to work faster if they were allowed to actually do their jobs.

After coordinating with Donald Krychech's office, it was decided that Shilough made sense as the expedition's kickoff point. From there, they would head into the forest, using their ATVs to connect with the same trail the AEP's doomed expedition had used to get deep into the woods. The plan was to pick a spot close to where John Guiterrez's truck had been found and establish a base camp. Rather than a multi-day hunt, though, the plan was to pack light.

Assuming their first night was unremarkable, as Derek fully expected it to be, they'd take a detour to Leeds Point the next day. He didn't expect that to pan out, but Yarlberg's press conference had made it a necessary evil. It would give them a confirmed public sighting for any fans in the area in a safe place, far from the scene of the actual disappearances.

Derek wasn't happy that they'd already been tailed once by that reporter. He didn't want it happening again and risk someone getting shot by accident.

Their plan set, they were finally able to turn to other topics.

"Any luck with that snot?" Derek asked.

Mitchell shook his head. "Still waiting on it. Probably going to be several more hours at the least."

"Any initial theories?"

"It definitely came from something living, which I suppose is better than them handing me a canister of industrial waste. I don't think you're too far off, though. If I had to guess, I'd say it's mucus, maybe pus. From what? No clue on that one."

"Pus, eh?" Francis commented. "Just so long as you don't share the wealth with the rest of us."

"Oh please. I've seen some of the shit you eat."

Derek tried to steer them back on track. "So how do

you want to play this one, Mitch? I think we can handle it out in the field if you want to…"

"No chance," the medic replied. "I didn't like leaving you to your own devices up in Alaska, but those people needed help. There's no reason to sit here and babysit a monitor."

"What about Arthur?" Danni asked, pointing his way. He was almost finished signing the small mountain of paperwork that had been thrown into his lap. "He can keep an eye on things."

Mitchell shrugged. "That'll work. If anything of note pops up, he can phone it in."

"All right," Francis said, clapping his hands. "Let's gear up and get back to the vacation paradise that is Shilough."

"Oh?" Mitchell asked. "That bad?"

"I think Derek's afraid his new girlfriend will still be there waiting for us."

Derek chuckled. "I was more thinking that guy at the museum."

"Exactly. Who did you think I was talking about?"

That elicited a few laughs at the table until Mitchell asked, "So, what about the museum guy?"

"It's hard to say," Derek replied. "I just got a weird vibe off of him."

Francis leaned back and put his feet up on the table. "That's selling it short. Guy was a certified creep."

"It wasn't just that. Well, okay, it was mostly that, but some of the stuff he told us. I don't know, but it's been gnawing at me for some reason."

"Like what?" Danni asked.

"Hard to say. Something about that family photo Lesterfield showed us. I don't know. Maybe the guy just rubbed me the wrong way."

Danni leaned forward. "Lesterfield? Isn't that…?"

"That guy you looked up? Yeah. Turns out they're

related. Great-grandson or something like that. I just wish he'd have let us film in there. Then maybe I could point my finger to it."

Francis stood up. "Ask and ye shall receive."

"What?"

"Let me go get my camera."

"I thought he made you turn it off."

"No," Francis replied with a grin. "He made me *pretend* to turn it off. I kept it recording at my side the entire time. Figured maybe we could use some of it for the show. Amazing how useful a piece of electrical tape over the recording light can be."

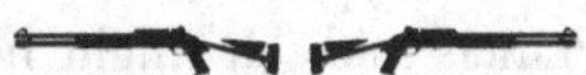

Derek could have kissed his cameraman, but instead settled for the big man fetching his gear. They commandeered a meeting room with a TV and played it back. Most of it wasn't watchable, being shot from the hip and all, but the audio was good and Francis had positioned the lens to get decent shots of some of the more prominent displays.

"The Leeds legend, the Kallikak family, the Philadelphia hoax," Ezekiel Lesterfield said on the screen.

"Stop it there," Derek said. "Something about that is ringing a bell."

"The Philadelphia one?" Francis asked.

"No. That was garbage. Pretty much a PT Barnum type scam. The Kallikak family. I think I've heard of them, but where?"

"Oh, that one is easy," Mitchell said. "Another urban legend or scam, depending on how you look at it."

"What does it have to do with the Jersey Devil?" Danni asked.

"Nothing. It was a famous case from around the turn

of the century. That's probably why it sounds familiar. The Kallikaks were supposedly this inbred family who lived deep in the Pine Barrens. There were whole books written about their mental and physical deformities from years of inbreeding."

"So what came of it?" Derek asked.

"Nothing. Turned out to be a hoax. All the reports were falsified – photos retouched, et cetera. It was all bullshit. But things like that die hard. Ever since then, Pineys, as they're called, have had a reputation for being sister-marrying hillbillies."

"Because that's what the world needs," Danni replied with a sigh. "More stereotypes."

"Hold on," Francis said. "It might not be too far off the mark. I mean, hell, you saw that family photo, Derek. You can't tell me that Lesterfield doesn't have some kissing cousins in his family tree."

"That's not nice, Frank."

"Screw nice," the big man said. "See for yourself." He touched the controls on the camera and the image fast-forwarded to Lesterfield telling them about his ancestor's exorcism. "Come on, I know I got it." The camera swayed back and forth trying to center on a picture hanging on the wall. It was hard to see much, but then it came into focus and, for a brief moment, the image was clearly captured on the screen. "There!" He backed up a second or two and hit pause. "I present to you the Lesterfields, a family for whom high definition is not particularly kind."

Before Derek could say anything, Danni leaned forward. "Whoa. And I thought Jedediah was kind of ugly."

"Apparently his kids took after his side of the family."

"I'm not sure that's the case." Danni pointed out the woman standing next to the reverend. "Those two could be fraternal twins."

"That's Sarah," Francis said.

"Doing your homework, Frank?" Mitchell replied with a grin. "And here I thought you were allergic to research."

The cameraman flipped him off. "Easy to remember, trust me on this."

Derek turned to the others and nodded. "Yeah. They definitely seem to have a thing for that name."

16

Despite Francis's foresight, there were no immediate answers to whatever had been nagging Derek.

Sadly, they didn't have a great deal of time to mull it over. Mitchell requested a printout of the screen capture so they could look it over again when they had a few moments to spare. However, daylight was burning and they needed to get out into the woods.

It was agreed that Eric and two of his men would come along. So as to avoid any further issues, Derek agreed to let them ride in the team's SUVs. However, once in Shilough, the security director and his people would remain with the vehicles while Derek's team rode into the woods and set up their base camp, keeping in touch via long range walkie-talkies.

The drive to Shilough was slow going at first, but once they got off Route 206, traffic lightened considerably. Though they hadn't seen too many people during their first visit to the small town, that didn't mean they hadn't been noticed. As a result, just to be on the safe side, Derek ordered their vehicles stopped and the ATVs unloaded

126

before they reached the town proper. There was no point in attracting more attention than their two hulking black SUVs already would. He just had to hope that Eric would behave himself and not do anything that would cause a scene.

There wasn't much he could do about that once they were off on the hunt, though, assuming it even *was* a hunt. Derek still wasn't convinced they would find anything more interesting than mud and trees by the end of the night.

Mitchell gave a quick call back to the lab, confirmed with Arthur that the results from their samples were still pending, then they loaded up and headed out.

They backtracked about a quarter of a mile until they found the turn-off for Swamp Forge Road. They followed it for another mile before coming upon a small trail that their GPS told them matched the one that the AEP team had followed while searching for John and Sophie Guiterrez.

The difference now, though, was that the majority of their gear was far less friendly to any rogue creatures that happened to cross their paths.

Once the forest and surrounding bog land began to get too thick for even the ATVs, Derek ordered his team to look for a suitable clearing. Roughly an hour later, they finished setting up their gear, including trail cams and trip-wired sensors that would serve as an early warning should anything breach their perimeter.

Camp set, guns loaded, and radios checked, the group set out into the ever-darkening woods. The hunt was on.

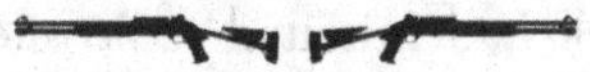

"Anything?" Derek asked, although from his tone, it was obvious what he expected the answer to be.

"Pretty sure it's a bear. Small one at that," Danni said, examining the tracks in the mud. "Half-grown cub probably."

"Oh no, not that," Francis replied with mock horror.

Mitchell let out a laugh. "Dickhead."

Francis turned to him and held out his arms. "Hold me."

"All right, calm down," Derek said. "If there actually is anything out there, we're going to send it running for the hills with all the noise we're making."

"If," Danni echoed.

"We all knew what we were signing up for."

She nodded and continued to lead the way slowly forward.

"Anything on the thermal, Mitch?"

"I think I might see a few squirrels."

"I'll take that as a no."

It was nearing midnight. The group had been covering an ever-widening circle from the spot where John and Sophie Guiterrez had supposedly disappeared. Unfortunately, they'd found precious little so far that was out of the ordinary.

There was no doubt the woods were very active. They found signs and spoor from multiple species, just no monsters. Derek tried reassuring the group that the trail was simply cold and that they needed to put in their due diligence regardless, but discipline had been waning the last hour or so. They were wet and muddy, and their mood wasn't helped by Eric Zeist's constant interruptions, demanding continual progress updates as if that would make their search go faster.

Finally, Derek had initiated radio silence, telling Eric that they had maybe spotted something interesting and were going to investigate.

It had bought them a small period of peace, but the

damage was done. His team was already debating where they should grab breakfast rather than staying focused. Even he had to admit that keeping them on task was more out of habit than any sense of urgency. He felt bad for Julia, but more and more began to wonder if perhaps some other, more easily explained, accident had befallen her sister and brother-in-law. "Hey, Mitch."

"Yeah?"

"What do you think about asking whether we can get a look at John Guiterrez's remains?"

"You thinking what I am? Maybe we can figure out what happened to him without traipsing around in these woods until the good governor decides he's had enough of us?"

"Pretty much."

"They might already have a coroner's report that we can look at."

"Good idea. Assuming, that is, Yarlberg didn't force them to list the cause of death as old age." Mitchell chuckled softly, then Derek added, "Okay, sounds like maybe we finally have a task for our friends back in Shilough."

Derek slid his earpiece in and activated the radio by his side. "Eric, are you there? This is Derek, over."

Silence greeted him.

"Asshole probably fell asleep," Danni said, standing up from where she'd been checking some more tracks.

"Eric are you there? Over," Derek repeated, wondering whether Danni was right. If so, he wasn't sure whether to be relieved or ticked off.

"Bob Hernandez here," one of Zeist's men answered.

"Where's Eric?"

"He's taking a piss."

"Thanks for the info. When he finishes, please have him radio me."

"Will do. Out."

"Sounds like a plan to me," Francis said. "Time to water the bushes." He shouldered his rifle and stepped off into the trees.

"Watch your footing," Derek called after him. "I don't want to have to pull your ass out of a bog." He heard a chuffing sound from somewhere behind him. "Gesundheit."

"Huh?" Mitchell asked.

Just then, the radio squawked to life in Derek's ear. "Zeist here. Did you find anything?"

Derek turned off his earpiece and lifted up the radio so Mitchell could listen in. "Not yet."

"Then why...?"

"A request," Derek interrupted. "We need access to John Guiterrez's body, or at least the medical report."

"John who?" Eric asked, sounding perturbed.

"The empathy on that one is astounding," Mitchell whispered.

Derek waved him silent, then explained, "He's that AEP worker who went missing. The one that Donald Krychech's men found."

"Oh, the stiff?"

Derek and Mitchell shared a glance, and then he replied through gritted teeth, "Yes, the man who was found."

"I don't think there is one."

"What?"

"A report, I mean. The governor ordered his remains cremated. I can ask, but I haven't heard of any..."

Derek switched off the radio. "Son of a bitch!"

"Took the words right out of my mouth," Mitchell said. "How the fuck can he do that to this poor guy's family?"

Derek didn't try to disguise the disgust in his voice.

"Wasn't there a paper published a while back that said sociopaths tended to gravitate toward positions of power, like politics?"

"If there wasn't, there should be."

Derek double-checked to make sure the radio was off, then said, "That reporter from yesterday, remember her?"

"The one who tracked you guys down?"

"Yeah. Turns out she's Guiterrez's sister-in-law. Guess who I think is going to get an anonymous tip when this is all over?"

Mitchell smiled. "It won't be about environmental damage, so I think we're free and clear there." He turned his head. "What do you think of all this shit, Dan...?" Before she could reply, he reached into his pocket. "Hold on, getting a call." He pulled out his cell phone and answered it. After a moment, he said to the others, "It's Arthur, back at the lab."

"What's up?"

"Hold on, I'm trying to find out." Mitchell returned his attention to the phone. "What's that? I couldn't hear you. Say it..." He pulled the phone away and looked down at the screen. "Damnit."

A few moments later, it began to vibrate again. Mitchell once more answered. "Hey, can you hear me? I'll call you back. I said, I'll call you back. I'm getting no..." Finally, he pocketed the device. "I lost him. No bars."

Derek looked around at the trees with mock concern on his face. "Mind blower, isn't it?"

"Very funny."

"So what's going on?" Danni asked, rising from some broken branches she'd been inspecting.

Derek was proud at how seriously she took her job, even if whatever she'd been examining probably wasn't a lead worth pursuing.

"Results are in at the lab, but I couldn't understand

what he was saying," Mitchell replied, before turning to Derek. "How long do you think we're going to be out here playing hide and go seek?"

Derek looked at his watch. "Too early to call it a night, at least without having Yarlberg crawl up our asses about it."

"Okay. Why don't I head back to camp and take one of the ATVs to Shilough? I should be able to get a signal there, see if our sample was anything other than a blob of bear puke."

Derek considered this. He didn't like splitting up the group during a hunt, but so far this night had been a bust. They hadn't seen anything more threatening than a chipmunk. "We could radio Eric, have him call Arthur."

"Do you really want those goose-steppers to be the first ones to get their hands on anything? Especially if it's something important?"

"Good point."

"Don't worry about me," Mitchell added, "I'll be fine."

After a moment, Derek replied, "Okay. Just keep your radio on and your eyes peeled."

"Trust me. I don't want to have to hear about it from Frank for the rest of my life." Mitchell checked their position, got his bearings, then unshouldered his rifle and walked off.

"Radio in when you get there and let us know what you learn," Derek called after him.

"Got it!" Mitchell replied back, before disappearing from sight.

Derek's radio beeped about an hour later. It was Mitchell, letting them know he'd made it out of the woods and back to Shilough.

"Any issues?"

"None on the trip itself. Although the company out here could be a bit better."

"You know, I can hear you, right?" Eric's voice cut in over the radio.

Derek let out a laugh, then said, "Let us know what you find out. Over."

"Can't say I envy him," Francis said. "I think I'd sooner be out here with the boogeyman."

"I know what you mean. Let's catch up to Danni."

They didn't have to go far. She was maybe twenty yards ahead, busy studying something on the ground.

"Find anything?"

"Huh?" she asked, hunched over.

Derek walked closer. "What have you got there?"

"I think these are footprints, but it's kind of weird."

"From what?"

"That's the problem. I'm not sure. Whatever it is, it's pretty messed up." She pointed to a large print in the mud that was more defined than the others. "See this? That looks like a fairly well-defined toe. But then here, that's a claw mark. And this bump here, maybe an old break."

"Or a deformity," Derek said.

"Maybe. Whatever it is, it's big and heavy. Look how far down that print goes. I'd say two-fifty, probably closer to three-hundred."

Francis joined them in peering down at the strange tracks. "It's on the low end, but still within squatch range. Juvenile, maybe? Could've had something wrong with it and was driven out of the clan."

"Not usually their style," Derek said.

Danni pointed to other parts of the print. "I don't think so. Look at this indentation in the back. Could be a dew claw. Never seen a bigfoot with one of those, deformity or not."

Derek leaned over and studied it as well. She was right. It did look like a dew claw, but more reptilian than anything. The rear of the foot was similar to the prints of a megalania, a giant monitor lizard thought to be extinct. They'd tracked one in New Zealand about three years back, but this print was far smaller. Definitely not a twenty foot dinosaur throwback. It was as if this print was cobbled together from different unrelated species ... which probably meant it was. "A fake?"

Danni stood up and wiped her hands on the seat of her jeans. "Could be. I mean, the way the ground is depressed looks like this came from a real foot, but then there's the shape. If it is a fake, then whoever carved this was either really good at what they do or really lousy."

"Oh, man!"

Derek and Danni turned toward Francis, but the big man didn't appear to be in any danger.

"Sorry, guys. Leaned against a tree and put my hand in something nasty."

"It's a bog," Danni replied. "Pretty much everything here is nasty."

"You're telling me."

Derek started to laugh, but was interrupted by the sound of his radio beeping.

He motioned the others over and raised the volume so they could listen. "Derek here. Tell me you got something, Mitch. Over."

"Something is an apt description."

"Come again?"

"I called Arthur. The results were in. I had him read them to me over the phone. Then I had him read them again."

"I take it they were interesting."

"That's just it," Mitchell replied over the radio. "I'm

not really sure what to make of it. I asked him to rerun the sequence to make sure it's not a glitch."

"What did they come back with?"

"Human," Mitchell replied.

The three hunters shared a glance, as if they'd suspected all along.

"Kinda, anyway."

"Wait, hold on," Derek said. "Define 'kinda.'"

"That's exactly it. Normally I'd expect high eighties or nineties, even with a contaminated sample. This came back as a sixty-three percent match with *Homo sapiens*."

"That's not very high at all."

"No, it's not. Problem is, the rest of the results are all over the map, and that's not even including the non-organic material in the sample."

"Non-organic?" Francis asked. "So what you're saying is the samples were fucked."

"Maybe." Derek could hear the frustration in Mitchell's voice. "I don't know. From what Arthur read to me, it sounds more degraded than contaminated, which doesn't make sense either. When you guys are finished chasing ghosts out there, I need to get back to the lab and read it myself."

"Not so sure about ghosts. Danni found some prints."

"From what?"

"Hate to throw this one back at you, Mitch, but we're not sure. They're either faked or whatever made them is some god-awful mess that I don't even want to imagine."

"What do you want to do?"

"Start wrapping up on your end. We'll head back, regroup, and double check those results. If it looks even remotely possible that we're dealing with human DNA, then I think we hand this off to the cops where it belongs."

"Roger that."

"We'll see you in a while. Over."

"So we're calling this turd hunt?" Francis asked.

"Yeah. I'm not seeing much reason to do otherwise. It's a shit show out here. Let's head in before we end up covered in leeches or something."

"What about those prints?" Danni asked. "There's one other thing we haven't considered about them."

"What?"

"If they are fake, then why bother making them all the way out here where nobody is likely to see them?"

Derek had to admit that was a good question, but he didn't have a good answer to go along with it ... at least not yet. Still, she was right. In their line of work, one didn't so easily dismiss potential evidence, even if later it turned out to be faker than a three-dollar bill. "Take casts of the best. We'll take a look at them in the lab. Maybe in better light something will stand out."

Danni nodded. "On it."

She turned back toward the prints, while Francis took off his pack and began rooting inside of it. He knew the big man would be fishing out his handheld camera so as to get some footage on the way in. That way the journey wouldn't be a complete loss.

He was about to turn away to ask Danni if she needed any help when he heard Francis zip up his pack, loud in the quiet woods.

Too loud.

It took Derek a moment, but then he realized the forest had gone completely silent around them.

17

"F rank?"

"I hear it," Francis replied. "Or more like don't hear it."

Derek glanced over his shoulder and found Danni had likewise abandoned the plaster kit in favor of her gun.

The silence of the woods was telling. Something was near, and it wasn't them.

Derek held up a fist, signaling his group to be alert but not move. His instincts were telling him that something had snuck up on them – not a situation his group usually found themselves in.

Then again, they usually took their hunts more seriously than this one. Just now, they'd forgone communication via earpiece to blare out Mitchell's report, giving their position away to everything within hundreds of yards.

Derek scanned the surrounding woods with both his eyes and ears, although focusing more on the latter. This late, in woods this dense, seeing wasn't necessarily believing.

There was nothing but the quiet around them at first, but then Derek caught a noise, halfway between a cough and a wheeze, off to their left. A moment later, he heard a branch break.

"What the hell?"

"Get the thermal, Frank," Derek whispered back at him. He turned and found Danni rooted to her spot, sweeping the surrounding bushes with her rifle. He caught her attention and motioned her over.

"Nice and quiet," he said, in as low a tone as he thought he could use and still be heard. "Let's not scare it off."

Francis gave him a raised eyebrow in return, but he ignored it.

He wasn't sure what was out there, but it didn't sound particularly dangerous. More like an asthmatic kid stumbling around in the dark, which was ridiculous, but a far cry from the growl or snarl he'd been expecting.

He almost laughed out loud at that. The truth was, they had no idea what to expect. It wasn't like the government archives contained much more than scattered reports on this creature, most of which contradicted themselves.

There came the sound of another branch breaking. Whatever was out there was moving ... none too stealthily, by the sound of things. That was odd in itself. Ambush predators that couldn't sneak up on their prey wouldn't last long. However, an injured predator, mad with hunger, would have gone for broke by now.

Foliage snapped again, followed by another wheezing chuff.

Derek's eyes narrowed as he tried to determine what path their stalker was taking. It seemed to be circling them, but purposely staying just out of sight.

He turned and whistled briefly, catching Danni's attention. He inclined his head, indicating she should close ranks with him and Francis. When she moved to join them, it was far quieter than whatever ... or whoever was out there.

That thought stuck with Derek. Was this some joke by Zeist and his buddies? Maybe some more of Yarlberg's minions were out here playing with them for some reason. He hoped that wasn't the case. You didn't joke around with people who were armed and more than ready to use their weapons.

"Are we being played?" Francis whispered, no doubt thinking the same thing.

Derek shrugged, then did something he'd only had to do a few times before during a hunt. He'd learned long ago that if something sounded fake, it probably was fake. He raised his voice and called out, "If there's anyone out there, identify yourselves now."

The others relaxed their stances ever so slightly. If someone did show themselves, they didn't want to accidentally shoot them. If they fled instead, it would be a waste of ammo to fire after it without a proper visual. In that case, they'd check for tracks and determine if it made sense to pursue.

The silence stretched out for a few more seconds, then there came a small sound from somewhere behind Derek – something striking a tree trunk, then tumbling to the ground.

"Did someone just throw a couple of pebbles to distract us, like they do in the movies?" Danni asked, her voice low but incredulous.

Derek lowered his gun and sighed. He wasn't sure if it was teenagers or Zeist having some fun with them but, whoever it was, they were going to get his foot up their...

Something charged out of the bushes to Derek's right. He had just enough time to sense its movement when he was bowled over by something big and heavy.

He rolled with the blow and came up to one knee. In

the space of a second he saw that his two allies had been taken down as well. Francis lay on the ground holding his head. As for Danni...

He turned and saw her down in the grass looking up at something looming over her. She tried to raise her gun, but it was pulled from her hands.

Derek raised his weapon and switched on the attached flashlight, illuminating the scene before him.

He'd seen many a strange creature in his time. Most had been extant survivors, small pockets of an otherwise extinct species that had somehow thrived where others had not. He'd seen prehistoric hominids, birds, giant eels, serpentine whales, and more. What he saw in front of him, though, wasn't like anything that should have ever existed.

What the hell?!

The creature was large, roughly seven feet, but grotesquely deformed. Several cyst-like growths protruded from its back, which probably kept it from ever fully standing upright. Amid these were boney protrusions which jutted out in strange non-symmetrical patterns. Its skin was brownish in color, if it could even be called skin. It was rough, almost scale-like in places.

Whatever it was, it turned toward Derek, gave a chuffing hiss, then took off into the bushes. He'd gotten, at best, a second's look at it, but it was enough for him to recognize its alien strangeness, its wrongness.

Then he was back on his feet, cursing himself for not taking the shot. The truth, however, was that he'd been shaken – not only from being ambushed, but from what he'd seen. Besides, his teammate's well-being was more important than pursuit at the moment.

Danni was already pulling herself up, a bit stunned but otherwise unharmed. She joined Derek at Francis's side, but fortunately he, too, was already rising.

"You okay?" Derek asked them, even as he heard the creature retreating through the woods.

"Clonked my head good, but I'll live," Francis replied. There was a thin stream of blood dripping down the side of his face, but that seemed to be the extent of his injuries.

"Danni?"

"Bruised and scratched up a bit." She held out her hands. In the glare from his flashlight, Derek could see long, thin scratches on her arms where the creature had grabbed her. "Where's my rifle?"

Francis switched on his light as well and they took a brief look around.

Derek wasn't surprised to not find the weapon. He hadn't seen the creature drop it before it ran off. "I think whatever that was took it."

"What the fuck was that thing?" Francis asked. "I only got a brief glimpse before it tackled me."

Danni had already retrieved her sidearm, a Glock 22, and was busy keeping an eye in the direction the thing had disappeared in. "No clue. Derek?"

"Same here," he replied.

"Did you get a good look at it?"

"Just enough to know it was more like something out of the X-Files than nature." He took a few moments to explain what he'd seen, allowing them all to recover from the shock of the attack. When he was done, Danni offered a few additional details she'd noticed from her angle.

"Clawed hands and definitely a male," she added, her eyes still wide. "A male what, though? Remember what you were saying earlier, about it being a disfigured squatch?"

"Sure as hell snuck up on us like one," Francis replied, scanning the surrounding brush as they talked.

"Doubt it," Derek said. "When it turned to look at

me, there was no eyeshine. It didn't remotely look or move like one either."

Danni nodded. "Yeah, I thought so. I caught a hint of scales. Devolved reptoid maybe?"

"Again with the eyes," Derek replied. "They were definitely mammalian."

"So what does that leave us with?" Francis asked, to which Derek smiled in response. "No. Don't say it."

"Yep," he replied. "I'm afraid so. Ladies and gentlemen, I believe that was the Jersey Devil."

As to what the devil actually was, Derek didn't care to speculate further.

At least not until they tracked it down again.

18

The creature left a trail that was easy to follow. Danni didn't need to even check for prints. It ran straight and true, not bothering to mask its passage. They took it slow, however, to ensure it didn't get a chance to double back and sneak up on them again.

She had seen the strange and bizarre before. Hell, she'd almost been killed by crazed sasquatches, their minds eaten away by rabies. This was the first creature she'd seen, though, that she could honestly describe as *wrong*. She'd gotten, at best, a quick glimpse as it ripped the gun out of her hands then stood there, almost leering down at her. It had been enough. She wasn't going to forget it anytime soon – the asymmetrical body; the strange, leathery skin. Its eyes were perhaps the worst of all, because they bespoke of intelligence.

However, intelligence didn't necessarily mean gentle or curious. She'd gotten no sense of that. Though she knew it was foolish to attribute human emotions to an animal, there'd been a malicious gleam in its eye. If she hadn't known better, she might have also said avarice.

Whatever the case, all of her doubts about being out

there had been thoroughly erased. They'd been on the verge of packing it in, but that had been a rare wrong call on Derek's part. She couldn't blame him, though. Even after finding the footprints, she'd been ready to blow the whole thing off as a hoax. But it wasn't.

There was actually something out there, some abomination of nature these woods had vomited up. And, while she couldn't be certain, she had no trouble believing that such a thing could be responsible for all of those disappearances. If Derek hadn't frightened it off, who knows what might have happened?

Danni mentally chided herself. Taken down and disarmed so easily. It was pathetic on her part. Her instructors would have been ashamed. She owed them better, owed her brother better.

She waved the others on after stopping again to make sure they were on the right path. They were deeper in the marshlands now, and the wetter vegetation left a less clear trail of broken branches and disturbed passage. Where that failed, though, the muddy ground was ideal. She looked past a pool of water in their path and easily spotted them.

Hard to miss such mismatched feet.

How this thing could exist was beyond her. It was so alien compared to what they normally dealt with, almost like something out of a horror movie. *Maybe alien is the right term*, she mused. Perhaps this thing wasn't of their world. Though her team's access primarily concerned cryptids with terrestrial explanations, she'd heard a few rumors in her year of service. Enough to know that the government had more secrets in their pocket than just bigfoot.

The team remained silent as they followed, standard protocol for when they were in pursuit. Eyes and ears needed to be focused on their surroundings, especially since they'd already gotten jumped by it once.

Danni wondered how much stamina this thing had.

They'd once chased a rogue squatch for miles through mountainous terrain. Had it not eventually taken shelter in a cave, she was fairly certain they'd still be running after it.

The muddy ground was starting to take its toll on their pace. Nearly every step they took was accompanied by a wet *schlup* sound as if the marsh was reluctant to let them continue.

They had just reached more solid footing when Danni thought she heard someone stumble behind her. She glanced back and saw Francis extracting his boot from a particularly deep patch of mud. She spared a smile his way, then turned and stepped forward.

The moment her foot touched the ground, it was as if something grabbed her around the ankle. Before she could look down to see what she'd gotten caught on, her legs were pulled out from under her. She hit the wet mud with her backside for a brief moment, enough to elicit a whoop of surprise, then was painfully yanked up into the air by her leg, dropping her pistol in the process as she found herself suspended upside down.

"Shit!" Derek hissed, stepping toward her before stopping and scanning the ground.

"A little help here," Danni said, after the shock had worn off.

Francis strode forward. "Coming."

"Hold on, Frank." Derek held up a hand and pointed. "There's another snare right over there. Might be more."

"Please tell me this thing isn't smart enough to set traps," Danni replied, beginning to sway back and forth.

Francis cautiously stepped forward, reaching for the knife at his side – an old navy Ka-Bar that his grandfather had bequeathed him. "Let's hope not."

"Doubt it," Derek replied. "Remember what Mitch was saying about Pineys. This place is kind of the north-east's answer to the bayous of Louisiana, or used to be anyway."

"Great," the big man said. "Not only do we have to deal with some murdering monster, but you're saying we need to keep an eye out for swamp hicks, too?"

"Who's to say? All we know is that someone still hunts out here. No telling if they're close by or not."

"Or if that thing got them."

"Exactly."

"This is all fascinating," Danni replied, "but maybe we could have this discussion once I'm down."

Francis laughed. "Hold your horses. We need to make sure your head doesn't wind up buried in a mud puddle. Although, you can bet if that happens, it's definitely going on the show."

"Remind me to call Shakti and ask her about how big of a house she wants."

"Enough, you two," Derek said. "Just cut her down and let's get a move on. I want to wrap this..."

A chuffing sound interrupted their banter, almost as if something took a halting, wheezing breath.

"Shit," Francis whispered, suddenly very loud as the bog around them once more fell silent.

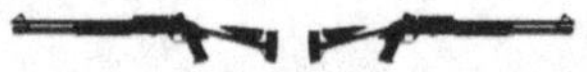

Derek pointed toward a stand of high swamp grass where the sound had seemingly originated. He glanced back, debating what to do. The smart thing would be to let Francis finish cutting Danni down. Problem was, if they didn't do something quickly, this thing stood a good chance of getting away.

Leaving their tracker behind to swing in the wind wasn't an option, though.

Something about this hunt was starting to leave a very bad taste in his mouth. He'd dismissed aloud the idea that this thing was smart enough to set traps, but now wondered if he was wrong. If not, might it have been intelligent enough to lead them here in the hopes that they would become entangled? It wasn't outside the realm of reason with some of the cryptids they'd encountered. Sasquatches, for example, could be very smart, on the order of bonobos or higher.

He backed up, being mindful to steer clear of the other snare he'd spotted. His foot came down and Derek felt a tug against his ankle, as if he'd just tripped a...

A crackle of branches snapping from on high caught his attention and he looked up to see a log swinging toward him suspended by ropes. Derek didn't have time to think. He dove for the ground and pinned himself flat in the mud as the trap swung over him, feeling the breeze as it passed. He quickly rolled out of the way to avoid getting slammed by it on the back swing.

"Holy shit!" Francis cried.

This went way beyond someone setting traps for deer. Whoever had put that there meant business. The problem was, there was no telling what other surprises were in store for them.

That did it, as far as Derek was concerned. They were getting out of there. There was only so much he was willing to risk on a hunt, and this situation was getting out of hand. It wasn't the first time they'd run into manmade obstacles. Plenty of forests were full of moonshiners and poachers. However, they had no idea what they were dealing with here.

"Cut me down," Danni repeated.

Derek rolled onto his back and sat up just as Francis moved to help her. The big man stepped toward Danni, his hand again reaching for the knife at his side, when something large launched itself toward him from out of the bushes.

The flat of Danni's rifle stock smacked into Francis's face, sending him sprawling. The creature that had ambushed them earlier lurched forward, swinging the weapon like a club.

Damnit! It had somehow gotten the better of them twice now.

Danni, still upside down, tried to reach up to free her ankle, but the devil slammed her own gun into her backside, eliciting a cry of pain from her before once again turning toward Francis.

Derek, however, was already lining up a shot. He'd had the sense to hold onto his weapon when he'd fallen flat. Now to only hope the barrel wasn't clogged with dirt.

Problem was, the creature was in a less than ideal spot for a clean kill. If he missed to either side, he'd end up hitting one of his teammates. Fortunately, their attacker was large and not overly graceful. As it bent down to attack his cameraman, he saw his opening.

He fired and saw skin erased, followed by a small flash of white from one of the ungainly protrusions sticking from the creature's back.

Fuck! From the look of things, he'd hit solid bone, meaning he'd probably done jack shit in the way of actual damage.

The creature howled in pain and staggered back, away from Francis, finally dropping Danni's weapon from its misshapen hands. It grasped behind its malformed body but couldn't quite reach the wound on its back.

The distraction was enough for Francis to draw his own sidearm and fire up at the beast, sending a spray of blood from its side that elicited a keening wail of agony from the monster.

It backed away, turned toward the bog, and took a few steps before sinking to its knees and whimpering.

Derek stood, covering the creature with his rifle while Francis pulled himself to his feet. "You two okay?"

Francis nodded, although he was breathing hard from the pummeling he'd just taken.

"Danni?"

"I'm fine," she replied. "Just hanging around."

"Cute," Derek said. "Cut her down, Frank. I've got this."

"You ... sure, boss?"

Derek focused on the thing that had attacked them. It was still alive, but most of the fight appeared to have gone out of it. Still, he wasn't about to take any chances. He kept his rifle trained on the creature, which still huddled in the shallow bog waters.

He took a moment to think about the shot he needed to line up. The creature's bizarre morphology meant he couldn't be certain he wouldn't just hit another bony patch. This thing needed to be put down, but he wasn't a cruel man. He didn't believe in letting an animal suffer needlessly.

Though it wasn't normally considered a sound idea, he aimed for the back of the beast's head, hoping to put it out of its misery quickly and cleanly. Afterward, he'd radio Mitchell to come back and join them for an impromptu autopsy.

Standing about twenty feet away, he sighted the monstrosity's head through his crosshairs just as it turned to look at him.

He'd begun to squeeze the trigger when it held up its hands and uttered in a guttural, barely understandable voice, "*Nooo. Don't s-shoot.*"

19

Derek almost shot the thing out of sheer surprise alone. Surely he hadn't heard what he just thought he had. He quickly rationalized that it must have been some cry that only mimicked speech, kind of like how some people taught their dogs to bark in a way that sounded like they were telling their owners they loved them.

"*Please!*"

Or maybe not.

This time there was no mistaking it. Derek lowered his rifle and backed up, not quite believing what he was hearing.

Behind him, he heard the thud of Danni finally being cut down.

A moment later, Francis was by his side. "Am I hearing things, or did the Jersey Devil just talk to us?"

Derek had no immediate reply to that. They'd faced some intelligent prey before, but none that had actually spoken to them.

He didn't quite dare lower his gun, not yet. This thing had attacked them, after all. More importantly, it was believed responsible for multiple deaths and disappearances. It was possibly a simple territorial response, but if this thing was smart enough to speak, then that went beyond mere instinct. "Do you understand me?"

The creature nodded.

Derek glanced back at his two companions. Francis merely shrugged, a wide-eyed look on his face. Danni was down on one knee massaging the leg that had been caught in the snare. She looked up at him and shook her head, the meaning clear. She had no idea what to do with this one.

Neither did he. This was way outside of his normal jurisdiction, leaving him and his team in a very bad spot. Doing their job would now potentially be tantamount to an execution, something he most certainly wasn't okay with. Bringing the creature back with them, however, opened up a whole other can of worms. Their job was to disavow, not confirm.

Then there was Yarlberg to consider. There was no telling what he'd do. He might order the thing put down regardless, or he might call another goddamned press conference and throw it in front of the cameras. And if this creature wasn't unique, what would that mean for others of its species? Dragging it back with them could easily spiral out of control, leading to the eradication of an intelligent race ... *genocide*, in other words.

What choice did that leave him with? Could he simply ask it to stop, to try to avoid people?

Would that even work?

Derek wasn't certain, but as leader of his team, he knew he had to make a decision, and quickly.

Danni was unnerved. She'd sensed this creature was more than it appeared when it first attacked her, running off with her gun like a trophy. Being proven right, however, wasn't quite the win she'd hoped it would be.

She could tell Derek was warring with the same emotions. Francis almost certainly had opinions, too, but he was a team player to the end. He'd go along with whatever Derek decided, trusting in their leader. Danni realized she should, too, but this thing actually speaking to them in English had shaken her. When she got back up, she didn't even bother to retrieve her weapons. She just stood there, staring.

Now, dead center as it was in the beam of Derek's light, she got a good long look at it. It truly was like nothing she'd ever seen before. She'd read up on the legends of various cultures in the year since she'd joined the team. Several had tales of chimeras, creatures said to combine the traits of two or more other animals. That was the word that sprung to mind. The Jersey Devil didn't look like any mythological devil so much as several different creatures thrown into a blender and mixed together: the bipedal gait of a human; skin that seemed to fluctuate between reptilian scales and rhino hide; bony plates on its back; tufts of wiry hair on its head; and more. One of its hands ended in what appeared to be stubby fingers with an opposable thumb. The other lacked the thumb, but had pronounced claws like something you'd expect to see on a dinosaur.

In short, it was hard for her to think of this creature as anything other than an *it*, despite obvious male genitalia that was vaguely human in appearance.

Almost as if reading her mind, it turned toward her and looked her in the eye, one half of its mouth opening in a mockery of a smile ... or snarl, it was hard to tell which. The teeth within were chipped, cracked, and sharp looking.

The creature coughed, then spat up a wad of viscous phlegm. It was impossible to tell for certain without proper examination, but she had a feeling it was the same gunk Mitchell had been analyzing.

It wiped the back of its hand across its mouth as a thought struck her. Predators were sometimes known to hunt people when they'd been injured. She seemed to recall that was one of the theories behind the infamous Tsavo man-eaters, a pair of lions that killed dozens of railroad workers around the turn of the twentieth century. Supposedly, one had an injured tooth which didn't allow it to hunt its natural prey.

Was that the case here? If so, that didn't bring her much comfort. They'd hunted man-eaters before, but never one intelligent enough to rationalize with.

"Derek?" she asked tentatively. "What are we going to do?"

"I'm weighing our options," he replied over his shoulder. His gun was still trained on the creature, but his posture seemed to lack his normal resolve. "You'll forgive me if I say this one has me a bit flummoxed."

"No shit," Francis replied.

"Danni, I want you to get on the horn with Mitch. See if you can get him to distance himself from Zeist, but in a way that doesn't raise suspicions. I think we need him to weigh in on this."

She reached up to tap the Bluetooth earpiece she wore, but then added, "We ... we can't shoot it. This isn't what we signed up for."

To her surprise, the creature turned her way again, its mouth once more opening in a gesture that resembled something between a grimace and smile.

"T-thank you, Sssarah."

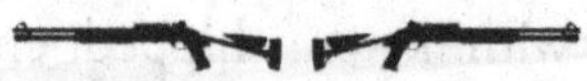

"Wait, what did you say?" Danni asked. "I didn't understand that."

Derek had, though, and his eyes opened wide. There was no knowing whether the creature was slurring something else – its speech sounded rudimentary at best – but he couldn't help but notice the name it had used. It was disturbingly similar to one he'd heard quite recently.

He glanced away from the devil and toward Francis. The big man met his eyes and in them Derek saw he was thinking the same thing.

"*A fine name for a woman*," the host of the devil museum had told them.

"Gotta be a coincidence," Francis said. "It's just gotta..."

The so-called devil hissed at them, as if its vocal chords were equally in tune with a snake's as well as a human's. Derek raised his gun again as it took a step back. "Don't do it," he warned.

"Derek..."

"Get Mitch on the horn, Danni. We need full team input on this one."

There was a momentary pause, but then she said, "Roger that. I'll let him..."

"I'm afraid I cannot allow our darling Sarah to do that."

Derek tried to keep his gun trained on their target while he craned his head toward the sound of the voice, hauntingly familiar despite them being deep in the woods.

Ezekiel Lesterfield stepped out from behind a tree, making so little noise that he probably could have walked up and tapped Derek on the shoulder before being noticed. His clothing was decidedly different than what he'd worn at the museum earlier in the day. He was dressed for the outdoors.

Before Derek could make sense of his sudden appearance, however, Francis asked, "What the fuck are *you* doing here?"

"My family has walked these woods for centuries, long before even old Jedediah and his brood. He was our patriarch in those days, you see. Generations of us have hunted these lands, fished these streams, been born here, died here. Taking that into account, I'm sure you could see why I might be far more justified to ask that question of you gentlemen."

"Sir," Derek said, "I'm not sure what you're doing out here, but I must ask that you leave."

"Oh, I think not, Mr. Jenner."

Derek didn't like the man's tone. There was something aggressive, almost predatory in his cadence. "I will ask again that you leave," he warned. "This is an official investigation and we are duly appointed deputies of the..."

"Official? Well, that is interesting. Fascinating, even. However, I am forced to focus on matters more near and dear to my heart."

"Derek?" Danni asked.

He glanced at her. "Escort Mr. Lesterfield from the area, please. We'll discuss this with him later."

She took a step toward him, but Ezekiel held up a hand. "As I said, I can't allow you to do that, Sarah."

"Why do you keep calling me that?"

He ignored her, turning his attention back to Derek. "The same way I cannot allow you to continue threatening my dear nephew Noah."

"Noah?" Francis asked. "The fuck are you talking about?"

Derek, however, was starting to piece the puzzle

together. "This..." He motioned with his head toward the creature, now standing knee-deep in the bog. "...is Noah?"

"Yes. He's a spirited child, but blood is thicker than water, I'm afraid. Now kindly lower your weapons."

Francis let out a laugh. "Like hell we will."

"That was not a request."

At Ezekiel's words, several hulking figures, almost a dozen in all, stepped out from the surrounding foliage, moving as quietly as he'd been. All of them were misshapen, disfigured in some way – sloping brows, discolored skin, mangled appendages, and more.

Danni let out a gasp, although Derek wasn't sure if it was the sight of these newcomers or the fact that every single one of them was armed, their weapons all pointed at his team.

Within seconds, they were surrounded. Derek quickly realized there was little chance of reaching cover before being gunned down. He still wasn't sure what was going on, but it was painfully obvious they'd somehow walked straight into an ambush.

He saw Francis tense and quickly threw him a shake of his head.

"Shit," the bigger man spat.

Derek lowered his gun and turned to face Ezekiel. "What do you want?"

"For starters," Ezekiel said, "I would ask that you kindly drop your weapons."

"Ask?"

Ezekiel turned toward Francis. "Let us not mince words, sir. My kin are not the type to tolerate fools."

Derek tossed his rifle to the ground, and Francis did the same.

"Radios, too, please."

The team did as told.

Derek still had his hunting holster and Ruger tucked

away beneath his jacket. It wasn't ideal against these odds, but he wasn't about to volunteer that information upfront. If they wanted it, let them search him.

Movement from behind caught his attention and he glanced over his shoulder to see the creature called Noah step past him with a huffing snarl.

The rest of the group circled around until Derek and his team's backs were to the bog. Most of the weapons pointed at them looked old. At least one appeared to be an actual blunderbuss. He wouldn't have been surprised to learn that half of them fired black powder cartridges. That didn't mean they wouldn't work, though. "What do you want with us?"

"With you?" one of the *men* asked, his voice slurred thanks to the hefty cleft in his upper and lower lips. He let out a laugh and several of the others joined in.

"I'm sorry to say," Ezekiel said after a few moments, "that we have no use for you and your friend here." He gestured toward Francis. "We do, however, have a powerful need for Sarah."

Several things happened at once.

Francis balled his fists. "Touch her and I'll bury my foot so far up your ass you'll be shitting toenails."

"Why do you keep calling me that?" Danni asked. "My name is..."

Before she could finish, one of the men stepped forward and clubbed her with the butt of his rifle, knocking her to the ground.

Francis took a single step toward her just as Derek saw fingers tightening on triggers. He spun toward his friend. "Frank, get..."

Any other words he had to say were lost against the sound of multiple gunshots.

20

For what felt like the thousandth time, Mitchell glanced down at his radio, as if trying to will it to come to life with some update from his friends.

At least when they'd split up at the Inuit village, he'd been kept busy with a steady stream of patients. His company now was far less friendly and didn't need any medical attention, aside from perhaps a few personality transplants.

Almost as if on cue, Zeist stalked over. "How the fuck long is this going to take?"

"As long as it takes," Mitchell replied irritably. "I don't know if you've ever gone hunting, but unlike what you see in the movies it's a game of patience and waiting."

"Why bother? Most everything I need is already at the supermarket."

"Yeah, well, the stuff we hunt usually can't be found in your local butcher's freezer section."

"Still sticking to that story, eh? That you hunt actual monsters."

Mitchell raised an eyebrow. "Your buddy the governor gave you the same information he has. Those are official

158

government files. Believe me, they don't have much of a sense of humor when it comes to anything."

"I get that part, but not the rest. Why hide any of this if it's real? Are they afraid North Korea is going to find out and start a weaponized sasquatch program?"

"I don't know, maybe." He wished he had a better answer, one that would shut this blowhard up, but the reality was he and the rest of the team had all asked that same question dozens of times.

"Whatever you say, Mr. Bigfoot Hunter." Eric looked down at his watch. "This is taking forever. Are they going to be out there all goddamned night? I thought they were heading back."

Me, too. "Not if they found something. Sorry to say, but usually the monsters don't come running right to us with a target hanging from their chests. Would be nice if they did, though."

Finally, Zeist walked away in a huff, leaving Mitchell to consider his next course of action. How he wished they still had their mobile lab. Sure, he had his laptop, complete with satellite uplink, but he couldn't lock himself inside it. Maybe when this assignment was finished and they'd smoothed over whatever feathers Yarlberg had ruffled, they could ask again for a replacement.

For now, it was sit and wait, both for Derek to return and for Arthur to send him the revised test results – albeit those weren't likely to be finished until much later.

He'd never seen such a bizarre mishmash of contradicting data before. It was as if someone had stuffed DNA samples from half a dozen species into the same bag. He'd heard of chromosome damage caused by outside factors, such as radiation, but this seemed to go way beyond that.

It was just plain weird.

Still, he was certain there was a reasonable answer. It was far more likely that a computer glitch was the cause than for the results to be from something that was actually alive.

Mitchell checked his radio again, considered heading back to their base camp, then dismissed that plan. That wasn't how they did things. Going rogue was a good way to get shot. It was an even better way to get yelled at. Though he'd never been in the military, he understood the chain of command and why it existed. Once the hunt was either concluded or Derek decided to give up for the night, they'd break radio silence and check in. That was the way things worked. So, for now, that meant waiting.

Mind you, it didn't mean he had to like it.

Surprise, pain, fear, confusion. All of these emotions were a jumble swirling in his mind. Everything hurt and his limbs felt numb, yet they weren't heavy. It was almost as if he were weightless, floating in the vastness of space.

No, not space. He took a breath, or tried to. Liquid entered his mouth, foul tasting and brackish. There was another taste buried within it, too, a familiar one ... coppery. It reminded him of...

Rational thought receded, replaced by panic as water filled his oxygen-starved lungs. Despite the pain, he somehow found the strength to flail about, albeit it didn't appear to do any good.

He forced his eyes open and saw nothing but infinite blackness – although whether it was the water or he was blinded, he couldn't tell. Nor would it matter if he couldn't fill his lungs with air soon.

The darkness seemed to almost be a living thing, reaching out, embracing him, invading his mind, and beginning to make it feel as numb as his arms.

His foot struck something, soft and yielding at first,

but then he gained purchase. With the little bit of strength left in him, he kicked off from it. It didn't matter where. This place was death. Staying here meant dying. Elsewhere might not be any better, but he had to try.

For a moment his leg stuck, as if grabbed hold by greedy fingers unwilling to let him go, but then he was free, still flailing, but moving in a different direction.

Long seconds later, an eternity of torment to his tortured body, he finally broke the surface, coughing out water to make way for life-giving air. Everything else was unimportant in that moment.

The cold water of the bog threatened to reclaim him, to suck him back under, so he continued to struggle despite his limbs refusing to obey all but the most rudimentary commands. He thrashed and kicked forward, seeing little, his eyes full of mud and silt, his hands not nearly coordinated enough to wipe it away and still keep him afloat. He continued to flail, his strength beginning to ebb, until he finally felt solidness beneath him again. It sloped upward, allowing him to feebly stand while the viscous water supported most of his weight.

At last, he clawed his way up onto the muddy embankment. Kicking against the thick mire, he pushed himself toward higher ground. Every inch was a struggle, the mud unwilling to release his arms and legs once it had a hold.

Eventually, he reached a point above the water line, the ground damp but solid. He turned over onto his back and breathed, unable to do much more except savor each hitching breath – certain that, with his injuries, any of them could very well be his last.

His eyes still shut against the muck encrusted onto his face, the water began to drain from his ears and, slowly, the sounds of the forest returned. Crickets chirped, frogs called to one another, and off in the distance, a coyote yipped.

Then a branch broke somewhere nearby, followed by another.

Something was walking through the underbrush and it was getting closer.

Panic, the same which had gripped him underwater, again flared up. Unfortunately, he found there was little left he could do with it. Cold, injured, and exhausted from the effort it had taken to get this far, there was nothing left to use against this new threat. All he could hope was that they'd pass him by, unseen. If not, then he prayed they'd make it quick. A gunshot to the head, a broken neck, anything but being thrown back into that dark hell and left to drown.

The footsteps came closer, faster now, and he was certain he'd been spotted. Hope began to fade as he sensed someone or something standing over him. He was helpless to do anything except wait for whatever came next.

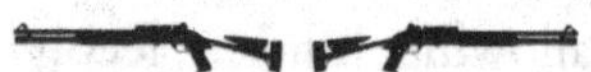

The sound of something being torn caught Danni's attention. Paper, maybe fabric. Whatever it was, it was alien to the place where she stood. It didn't belong and she wasn't immediately sure why.

But then realization hit. She was in a dream, albeit that didn't mean it was a welcome one. If anything, the strange sound echoing through the streets of Bonanza Creek was a near godsend. The alpha sasquatch, a massive beast the size of a house, had just finished killing both her brother and Derek. She'd been too late to save them, and now the beast was approaching her, seeking to ensure there were no survivors of its rampage.

The alpha's hands closed around her neck, but there

was no pressure, no sense of dying as her air was cut off. Instead, it became little more than a ghost to her as the strange noise reasserted itself, pulling her toward consciousness and away from the past that continued to haunt her.

More sounds of tearing came – definitely fabric – followed by the feel of something rough and coarse beneath her. Was she in a bed?

Wherever she was, she quickly became aware that she wasn't alone. Rough, calloused hands grabbed hold and turned her over. More fabric ripped and her body jerked with the sensation. She realized, with no small degree of horror, that it was the sound of her clothes being torn from her body.

Those hands touched her again – across her throat, lingering on her breasts, yanking at her pants, her underwear, all of it.

She reached up blindly, trying to fight them off, until a fist exploded against her cheek, sending her racing back toward the darkness where the doomed Colorado town awaited.

As the air around her again filled with the screams and cries of rabid monsters, she was afforded one brief moment of clarity in which she remembered what had happened and whose hands had likely been grabbing at her.

Suddenly, the nightmare of her past didn't seem so bad by comparison.

21

Derek felt something wet being pressed against his face and immediately jolted awake.

He tried to sit up and found himself only partially successful. His left arm didn't seem to want to cooperate, nor did the majority of his body. His right, however, was grabbed before it could move far and forced back down.

"It's okay, you're safe."

He cracked his eyes open, expecting to see nothing but blackness, certain he'd been blinded by whatever had befallen him. Instead, he saw dim light. It was still dark, but as he blinked, the world gradually came back into focus. He saw trees above him and, beyond them, the stars in the sky shining down.

"I can see," he croaked, his voice sounding cracked and weak.

"Now that the mud is out of your eyes you can."

He turned toward the voice, familiar, yet not one he immediately placed. The darkness was broken up by the flicker of a campfire. A stack of equipment lay next to it, equipment that he recognized.

"Hold on. Is this...?"

"Your camp?" Julia Wilhelm replied, leaning over him. "I assumed so."

"What are you? How did we...?"

"Shhh. Don't try to move. You're hurt. I'll explain as I work. Fortunately, someone left a pretty sizable first aid kit here."

He tried to sit up again, winced as pain bit him in multiple spots, then gave up and did as he was told. "How bad?"

"I ... have no idea. It's definitely not pretty." She poured some rubbing alcohol on a pad and proceeded to clean his left arm, pulling back when he hissed. "Sorry. Not really my specialty. Better than it could be, though. Fortunately for you, I ran an extended story on the local EMTs last summer. Rode along for a couple of nights and watched them in action."

"Lucky me."

"What happened to you?"

"Ambushed. Shot."

"Goddamn," she whispered before steeling her voice again. "Well, that explains a lot. Nearest I can tell, you got hit in at least half a dozen spots, mostly low caliber from the look of things. You're missing a strip of skin on your forehead where I'm thinking something grazed you. That or you're blessed with a thick skull." She chuckled, then continued her examination. "Hope you're a righty because it looks like a bullet punched clean through your left arm. All in all, though, I'd say you got really lucky."

"Doesn't feel that way," he wheezed.

"Believe me, you did." She held up a gun. It was the Ruger from his harness. There was a pronounced dent in the receiver. "Considering where you had this puppy strapped, I'd say a couple of your major organs owe it thanks. Otherwise, it could have been a lot worse."

"Still not great," Derek whispered.

"Not great is better than dead."

"Can't ... argue there."

"I'm going to tape you up as best I can. But we need to get you to a doctor. No way am I digging bullets out of your body by myself."

"Good thinking," he replied. "Only works in the movies. In real life, I'd probably bleed out if you tried." After a moment, he glanced around again, his eyes opening wide as remembrance of the ambush fully hit home. "Frank, Danni..."

He again tried to sit up, but Julia held him down. She was either stronger than she looked or he was a lot weaker. "You were the only one I found." Then, after a beat, as if she realized the significance of this, she added, "I'm sorry."

"Where?"

"You were at the edge of a bog. Pretty sure you crawled out yourself."

Derek nodded. After a moment, she produced a bottle of water, which she helped him sip from.

"Thank you," he said once he was finished. "What are you doing out here?"

She flashed him a guilty smile.

"You followed us again?"

"I had a hunch you'd be back. Besides, I told you to drive something less conspicuous. Not my fault you didn't listen."

"How...?"

"I found your camp a couple of hours ago. Almost scared the crap out of me. When I got close, a bunch of flood lights turned on."

"Trip wire sensors," Derek said. "Good thing we didn't set up the sentry guns, too."

Julia looked down at him, unblinking. "You're kidding, right? Never mind, I don't really want to know.

Anyway, I marked this place on GPS, then kept searching. I was lucky enough to be close by when I heard the gunshots." She held up his damaged Ruger again. "By the way, interesting camera you have."

"You shouldn't be out here. Too dangerous."

Julia put the damaged weapon down, opened a nearby backpack, and pulled out a semi-automatic Smith & Wesson. "I may be reckless, but I'm not stupid. And before you ask, yes, I know how to use it. I try to get out to the range a couple of times a month."

Derek debated how much to say, but quickly came to the conclusion that their situation didn't call for much discretion. He was too injured to fight and there was no telling whether those ... *people* were still lurking about. That they were having this conversation was promising, but they were still in a bad spot.

But he had teammates who were quite possibly far worse off.

He gritted his teeth, mentally envisioning how Norah – or Jacob, for that matter – would react upon learning that he'd brought a reporter into the fold. Though they didn't get along very well these days, he imagined this would be one area where they'd both see eye to eye in declaring him an idiot.

That's a chewing out for another day. Besides, it wasn't like she didn't already have her suspicions. "Listen, Julia. There are some things you need to know about my team and what we're really doing out here..."

"You need to put that thing away before you shoot someone, like me." Derek was sitting up in a foldable camp chair. His arm was splinted and Julia had done her best to sterilize and bandage the rest of his wounds.

He didn't feel particularly great, but it was the best he was going to get out here. With his radio gone and them out of range of reliable cell service, the immediate goal was survival. However, in order to survive, they needed to get out of there, which meant using the remaining ATV since he was certain there was little chance of him walking out in his current condition.

Julia had done an admirable job, but following his confession as to what had happened to him and his team, she'd been increasingly on edge, her gun never far from her hand.

"I thought I heard something," she said, scanning the surrounding trees.

"You did. It's a forest. Lots of things make noise."

"Not funny."

"I'm not trying to be." He took another sip of water, doing what he could to stay hydrated. "Listen. Those are all normal sounds. It's when everything goes quiet that you have to worry. So long as squirrels are chattering and birds are chirping, that means they aren't worried, and if they're not worried it means..."

"We shouldn't be?"

"Not necessarily, but it means we can probably stay one click shy of paranoid."

"Is it paranoid to want to shoot that thing in the balls and make it tell me where my sister and brother-in-law are? You said it could talk, right?"

"Nearest I can tell it's ... *he's* human, or some sort of human mutation. I don't know. He caught us by surprise and then his friends showed up while we were debating what to do."

"A group of mutant hillbillies?"

"You said it, I didn't."

She grew quiet as she continued to prep the ATV.

"What do you think those freaks did to my family? Do you think there's still a chance?"

Derek was silent for a moment. He'd told her a lot, but had stopped short of telling her about her brother-in-law. She deserved to know, but he was afraid what it would do to her, especially now when he needed her help. But then he remembered what Zeist had said about John Guiterrez's body. Grief could destroy a person, but anger could focus them. He hoped the latter was true for Julia. She seemed strong, but then, so had Kate Barrows.

"Listen, there's more..."

Derek needed to remind Julia several times that raising her voice was very much not in their best interest. To her credit, she didn't break down after hearing what he had to say, instead channeling everything she had toward seething rage.

"You knew this when I met you in Shilough and you didn't say anything?"

"It's not as simple as that."

"Because of fucking *government secrets*?" She held up her hands in quote marks.

"Yes. I know you're angry, but my team is under oath. We have to be very careful what we say, when we say it, and who we say it to. This isn't a 9 to 5 thing either. It's all the time."

"That doesn't make it right."

He nodded. "I know, but right and lawful are sometimes at odds."

She stared hard at him for several long seconds, then got onto the ATV and started the engine. For a moment, he was afraid she would hit the gas and take off, leaving him to his fate, but she turned and nodded for him to climb on behind her.

He got on and wrapped his good arm around her waist, even though he was certain he'd catch an elbow to the ribs for it. The rumbling of the engine even at idle was near torture for his wounds, but there was no other way about it. They needed to get out of the woods, get Mitch, and come back with a lot more firepower. He still had friends out there and, until he knew otherwise, he had to assume they were alive.

"Please be careful," he said as they started moving.

"You'll be lucky if I don't purposely aim for any rocks." Then, after a beat, she asked, "So what changed?"

"Huh?"

"You said you had oaths and shit like that. So why tell me now?"

Derek didn't consider himself the petty type, but he also wasn't particularly fond of his team being the fall guys either. He told her about John being cremated without the knowledge or blessing of his family.

She turned back and glared at him. "Are you shitting me?"

"Please pay attention to where you're going, and no, I'm not shitting you. Believe me, I was just as shocked to hear about it."

"I doubt that. I told you before that I was going to shoot that monster in the balls, but I think I'm going to save a bullet for the governor."

"You do know that's not going to work out for you ... *oof!*"

"Sorry." She steered back onto the trail and slowed them to a snail's pace. "Fine. Then let's see how he likes it when the six o'clock news runs a story on..."

Derek's grip on her tightened. "You can't run with this.

I'm sorry, but you're going to bring a world of hurt down on yourself if you do."

"What?"

"Think about it. What are you going to say? That the Jersey Devil killed your brother-in-law and the governor is covering it up? Even a tabloid rag would think twice before publishing that. And then there are my ... *associates*. It would be career suicide. You'd never work in journalism again."

"It would be worth it."

"For who? You'd be destroying your life. That's noble, but where does it leave you? With nothing but some conspiracy nuts believing your story, that's what. And that still doesn't help your sister."

Julia was quiet for several seconds, the rumble of the engine the only sound to be heard. "Do you think she's..."

"We don't know what to think. Those things, people, whatever ... I'm pretty sure they took my friends. It's quite possible they have your sister, too. We have to ... hold on to that."

She nodded, then took one hand off the handlebars to wipe her eyes. Seeing they were on a relatively level stretch, Derek carefully removed Julia's cell phone from the breast pocket of his jacket. She'd given it to him for the ride back. It took a couple of painful tries, but he finally got it out. It fluctuated between one and two bars of service. Hopefully good enough to call Mitch.

Before he could try, though, Julia spoke up again. "Okay. But even if we find her, are you saying Governor Yarlberg gets away with it? I thought you said you helped people. That you were the good guys."

"We are," Derek replied, dialing Mitchell's number. "But what we do isn't exactly black and white. And, I hate to admit it, but we live in a world where the good guys don't always win."

22

Danni jolted awake, the memory of rough hands violating her body far too fresh in her mind.

For perhaps the first time in months, her dreams hadn't bothered her, especially not once she realized she'd be waking up to a nightmare.

Opening her eyes, she saw a roof above her. Wherever she was, it was dimly lit – torchlight or maybe a low-wattage bulb. It was better than waking up in total darkness, if only marginally.

She gingerly sat up, taking it slow as a wave of vertigo passed. The memory of what had happened slowly filtered in to her waking mind, but it was cloudy, hazy, as if her brain was wrapped in cotton.

Once she was up in a sitting position, she swung her legs off the crude wooden cot she'd been placed on. Her bare feet landed upon packed dirt and she took a moment to look down at herself.

With a start, she realized she hadn't imagined the grabbing hands or the torn clothing. Gone was the outfit she'd worn into the woods – not just pieces or swatches ripped away, but all of it. She was clad in nothing but a filthy, oversized t-shirt. It was ripped and threadbare in places, barely providing even minimal coverage.

All at once it hit her, the grogginess finally fading away and leaving behind the stark terror of her situation. They'd been in control, the creature was surrounded, their guns covering him. Then, in a heartbeat, it had all changed.

Now all pretense of that control was gone. She'd been knocked out and kidnapped, but deep down she knew that was likely the least of her worries. They'd groped her with wild abandon, responding with violence when she made even the slightest protest. What else had they done to her?

Danni didn't want to even consider it. She'd never been victimized in such a way before, could barely even imagine it. The closest she'd ever come had been her high school prom date – he'd gotten a little grabby in the back-seat of the limo afterwards. But that had been nothing, easy to set straight. This...

Tears, unwanted yet seemingly unstoppable, began to well up in her eyes as she considered what might have happened to her.

Slowly, fearfully, she reached a hand beneath her meager clothing, trying at the same time to take in her surroundings – anything to distract her from the awfulness of what she was doing.

She was in a crude cell – small, barely six by eight. The walls were wooden planks. The bars of the cage were rusted and aged, but they also had the appearance of something that had stood the test of time. A small circular pit in one corner was the only amenity in sight.

Danni closed her eyes as she probed herself, sickened to her stomach to think that other hands, or worse, had touched her there.

No pain, soreness, or blood. She breathed a sigh of relief, although she knew that didn't necessarily mean much. There was little doubt she had enough adrenaline running through her system to stave off nearly anything. The fact that her jaw only dully ached as opposed to throbbing told her as much. Time would tell.

But, even if nothing had been done to her, that didn't mean it wouldn't be. Why bother to strip her otherwise, leave her with barely nothing on? If they were simply making sure she wasn't armed, they could have easily done so while she was unconscious. No. She had to assume the worst.

The others, the ones who'd surrounded them, they'd all been male – some of them more human-looking than others. What the hell were they? What was this place? When would they come for her again? And, perhaps most importantly, where were her friends?

Danni forced herself to stand, her legs still shaky beneath her. She approached the bars and took a look outside her cell. There wasn't much of a view to either side, but across from her were other cells of a similar crude nature. The dim light made it difficult to tell if they were occupied, but she thought she spied a figure curled up in the corner of the one opposite her.

She opened her mouth to speak, but for a moment, no words came out. Reminding herself of the murderous monsters she'd faced in the past, she took a deep breath and tried again. "Derek? Frank? Are you there?"

The words sounded louder than they were in the awful silence of the prison, the only other disturbance the drip of water somewhere close by. After a minute of waiting, she tried again.

Though her friends didn't respond, someone else did.

"Shhh. They'll hear you," came a low female voice from somewhere off to Danni's left. She couldn't see anyone, leading her to believe that maybe they were in a cell on her side of the hallway.

Detecting no threat in this newcomer's tone and not wishing to scare her off, Danni likewise lowered her voice. "Who's there?"

"My name is Sar..." Her voice trailed off into heavy, hitched breathing, as if terrified of saying more.

That alone told Danni far too much. The woman's tone spoke of hopelessness and despair, both feelings that threatened to overwhelm her, too. A part of her wanted to give in, to curl up into a ball and let the horror of her situation take over, but she refused. She fought back against it, remembering her training and the creatures she'd overcome.

Though she didn't feel particularly brave herself in that moment, she forced her voice to be strong for the other woman. "I want you to listen to me. It's going to be okay. I have friends. They're looking for me. They'll find us."

"Y-you don't know that," the woman replied after several seconds, her voice shaky but under control.

"And you don't know my friends. They're not the type who give up or get frightened easily."

"I-I can't..."

"I *can*," Danni replied, realizing the more she spoke, the more she believed her own words. Even if she was mostly talking to herself, she didn't want to stop and let the fear take hold again. "We're going to find a way out of this. I promise you that."

"W-who are you?"

"My name's Danni."

"I'm ... S..." Again the woman hesitated, as if fearful of speaking her name, but finally, after several seconds, she said, "I'm ... S-Sophie."

Sophie?! "Sophie Guiterrez?"

"What? H-how did you...?"

"We, my team that is, were looking for you." That wasn't entirely true. There hadn't been much faith that she was still living, but there was no need to share that information. She was alive. That was what mattered.

"John, too?"

Danni opened her mouth to reply but couldn't form the words.

"It's okay," Sophie said after a moment. "I know. I knew it when I ran away." Her voice began to waver. "I t-tried to fool myself that I was going for h-help, but the truth is I left him. I left my husband to die." She broke down into heavy sobs, loud in the claustrophobic confines of their prison.

Danni listened, tears forming in her eyes as she wanted nothing more than to join Sophie in her misery. But she realized that wouldn't solve anything. As much as she wanted to offer comfort, she waited until the other woman had gotten herself under control again before continuing.

"Sophie, I need you to listen carefully. We're going to get you out of this. That's what I want you to focus on. You and everyone else here." Danni glanced across the hall again, noting that the figure in the opposite cell had shifted a bit but still hadn't turned to face her. "First, I need you to tell me who else is in here with us. Can you do that?"

Sophie took several deep breaths before replying. When she spoke again, her voice was stronger, as if the crying had helped wash away some of her sorrow. "T-there were two other women here. Both Sarah. I mean, I'm not sure what their real names were."

"Were? Where are they?"

"One of them... Maybe a week ago. She didn't..."

"It's okay," Danni quickly replied, fighting against the horror of what she was hearing. "You don't have to say it. What about the other?"

"I don't know. They took her away a few hours ago. She's close."

"Close?"

"The one across from you is ... Abby. She's..."

"Don't call me that."

Danni turned to look across the hall. It had been the first sound the other prisoner had made. "What did you say?"

The occupant turned halfway and Danni saw she was a young woman close to her own age, off by no more than a few years. "I s-said, don't call me that. It's not my name."

"Abby..."

"Don't call me that! My name is Sarah. So is yours." She turned and pointed at Danni. "You, too."

"No. My name is..."

"IT IS!" the woman screamed. "Just shut up! I'm Sarah! I'm Sarah! I'm Sarah!" She beat her fists against the wall as she repeated herself, loud at first, but then growing softer until wracking sobs made the words nearly unintelligible. Yet still she repeated her mantra.

Danni's heart broke for the poor girl. She'd seen people, friends, whose minds had been pushed past their capacity to cope. Abby sounded that way now – broken – as she keened in her cage, rocking back and forth in an attempt to find some small measure of comfort where there was none to be had.

Both of these women, so terrified, so utterly hopeless. As scared as Danni was, the sight and sound of their anguish began to kindle a different emotion within her: anger. She latched onto it and used it to steel her resolve, pushing her own dread away and locking it up in a corner of her mind. She wouldn't be a victim and she wouldn't let these women down, not if she could help it.

Danni opened her mouth to say as much, but there came the screech of metal grating against metal, followed by a hollow boom. It sounded like a door being thrown open somewhere close by.

A few moments later, heavy footsteps approached and, despite her best efforts to keep the fear at bay, it returned nevertheless.

23

The approaching footsteps were accompanied by something Danni hoped to never hear again — the chuffing, labored breathing that told her the devil was near.

There came the clink of something being tapped against the bars of a cage, followed by a cruel chuckle that sounded far more human than the thing they'd cornered out in the bog. The devil wasn't alone.

Backing away from the bars, Danni was tempted to follow Abby's lead and curl up into as small of a ball as she could, but she also knew full well it was likely to only encourage her captors.

Holding on to the memories of all she'd done in the past year, she crossed her arms in front of her and did her best to look defiant.

A large, misshapen body stepped in front of her cage, looming over her. The dim light of her prison did nothing to make it ... him ... whatever this thing was any less repulsive than it had looked out in the woods. Not helping was the lopsided leer it wore upon its face or the fact that it was naked, aside from a few bandages covering the wounds it had sustained battling them.

It grasped hold of the bars with its clawed hand and she realized that was what had made the sound she'd heard. Leaning down, it peered in at her, giving her a chance to note that even its eyes didn't match. One was milky white, as if riddled with cataracts. The other was a clear blue, almost normal except for the vertical iris.

"*H...ullo, Sssarah*," it wheezed.

Danni forced herself to meet its gaze. "Where are my friends?" she asked in a voice that was as calm as it had been the prior day while she had walked the campus with Arthur. She'd almost felt like a normal girl in that moment, a stark contrast to the waking nightmare she now found herself in.

If the creature understood her, it didn't give any indication. "*You wanna be mine, Sssarah?*" The brute pressed himself up against the bars and Danni was horrified to see its erect manhood pushing through, pointing her way. "*I think, you'd l-like t-that.*"

The way it was talking, you'd have thought it was asking her out on a date. If she hadn't been nearly terrified out of her mind, she'd have thought it almost surreal.

"Put that thing away, Noah," another voice cackled. "You wouldn't know what to do with it anyway."

Noah? That man in the swamp had called it that, too, spoke of it like it was a person. And that's when it clicked. It was, or he was. But what could do this to a man? She knew about birth defects, but what stood before her was a far cry from even the case of Joseph Merrick, the so-called Elephant Man.

Someone else stepped into view besides Noah. He was smaller, but not by much. Both of his eyes were nearly black, like a dog's, and one side of his face was turned down in what appeared to be a perpetual frown. A large growth lay on his right shoulder, poking out through the overalls he wore. Though far more normal in appearance than Noah, he would have had a hard time walking down the street unnoticed.

He looked at her, avarice freely showing on his face as his dark eyes drank in her barely covered body. Danni suddenly found herself feeling far more naked than she was. She wondered if he was the one who'd undressed her while she lay semi-conscious. "This one's gonna be my wife." *Wife?!* "Don't that sound grand, Sarah?"

Danni realized she was right to be scared when she'd woken up. The way these things were looking at her was as if she was little more than a piece of meat.

"M ... my name is not Sarah," she replied, trying to keep herself together.

She expected to be screamed at. Perhaps the door to her cage opened and these things to launch themselves at her for her impudence.

Instead, the calm, almost jovial way the second man answered her was somehow far worse. "Of course it is. It's always been and it always will be. It's a good name. A good, God-fearing name."

The devil, Noah, turned and gave the smaller one a shove. "*Nuh uh, N-nathanial. She's mine. P-papa said so.*"

Nathanial laughed and pushed him back, albeit not moving him much. "You sure are stupid, you know that? He was having fun with you, that's all. You ain't never getting a Sarah of your own."

Noah hissed at the smaller man, then raised one of his hands as if to strike him.

"That will be more than enough!"

Danni turned in the direction of the voice. A third man stepped into view. She recognized him as Ezekiel, from Francis's video – the bastard who ran the museum and had been in charge of the ambush that brought her here.

Both Noah and Nathanial backed up several steps and lowered their heads as if they were little more than chastised children. Ezekiel spared one glance at her, then turned to address them. "You boys know the rules. Adam gets first go at them all. Nothing has changed. After that, he'll decide who Sarah will wed. Until then, you both keep your mitts off her."

Danni wasn't stupid. His declaration brought her little comfort. It was a small reprieve, nothing more, that bespoke of future horrors.

Though she knew it would be futile, she decided to confront her captors nevertheless. "Why are you doing this?"

"Why?" Ezekiel replied, smiling as if pleased she had asked. "He who finds a wife finds a good thing and obtains favor from the Lord. Proverbs 18:22. It's simply what we're meant to do."

"I don't understand."

"Of course you don't." He stepped close to the bars. For a moment, she was tempted to launch herself at him. She would have liked nothing better than to break his jaw. But where would that get her? She'd still be locked in, and she doubted the others would react kindly to any aggression on her end. "A woman is a simple creature, but she is good for one thing, and it is that which we need badly."

"What?"

"Children, of course."

Disgusted and horrified, Danni's mouth opened seemingly on its own. "But..."

"Female births have always been rare in our family and they're even rarer whenever a special child, like our dear Noah, is sent from Heaven to grace us. So we do what we must to continue the line. You should be honored. My family has lived in these parts since the American Revolution, and we'll continue to live here for so long as God wills it. You'll be a part of our clan, and your children will grow up to carry on the tradition."

"You can't ... I don't want..."

"It matters not, Sarah, what you want or what you don't want. We *need* you. My family needs you."

At that moment, realization hit. These things had a purpose for her, a terrible purpose she'd rather die than see come to fruition. But that same need they claimed to have for her wouldn't have been extended to... "Where are my friends?"

"Claimed by the bog, as it was also ordained. Don't feel sad, child. Their bodies will nurture the forest which in turn nurtures us. So, in a sense, they'll be here with you always."

Danni clamped a hand over her mouth and sank onto the hard pallet that served as her bed. Though she didn't want to cry in front of these monsters who masqueraded as men, she felt the tears begin to fall regardless. Derek, Francis – they'd both been so good to her, heroes to be admired. They didn't deserve this.

She looked up, blinking away the tears long enough to see Ezekiel smile at her once more before turning away, toward the cage across from hers.

Abby whispered, "Please, no more," as the three converged on her cell.

"Kindly collect my wife," Ezekiel said to the two others. "Sarah's ripe and ready for my seed."

He turned and began to walk away, but not before calling over his shoulder, "Be quick about it, boys. I'm in a sharing mood tonight."

24

Derek heard the sound of another engine approaching. Though he was groggy from blood loss and pretty certain he was on the verge of passing out again, the noise perked him up.

They had to be close to Shilough by now, even moving as slowly as they had been. He needed to get back, make a plan, and return in force – a concentrated effort by the police to comb these woods and weed out the Lesterfields, wherever they were holed up.

The sound of the approaching ATV grew closer and Julia applied the brakes, gently bringing them to a halt as they spied headlights closing in on them.

She was helping Derek to the ground when Mitchell parked and came racing over to them. "What the hell happened?"

"He's hurt," she replied.

"I can see that. And you are?"

"She's a friend, Mitch," Derek said, every part of him hurting. Pain was good, though. It was when everything went numb that he'd have to worry.

Mitchell unshouldered his pack and began to pull out

supplies. While doing so, he glanced back up at Julia. "Thank you for helping him."

"I did my best."

"That's all anyone can ever ask." Mitchell pulled back the gauze of the field dressings to inspect Derek's wounds. He grimaced as he examined them. "Call me crazy, but it looks like you were shot."

"Give that man a prize," Derek wheezed.

"You trip and fall on your own gun again?"

"Not quite."

"Is there anything I can do to help?" Julia asked.

"Yeah. Keep that flashlight on us."

"You got it." She did as asked, then added, "They were ambushed."

"Ambushed?" Mitchell turned toward her, eliciting a grunt of pain from his patient as his hand slipped. "Sorry about that."

Derek let out a tired sigh. "No problem."

"So who did this? I'm gonna go out on a limb and assume the devil was fake after all."

Derek shrugged. "Nope, he's real."

"You got ambushed by a monster with a gun?"

"More like ... his family."

"Okay, this is starting to get weird. Where's Danni and Frank?"

"Don't know." Mitchell moved to take something from his pack, but Derek grabbed him by the jacket. "We need to regroup."

"You need a hospital."

"That too."

Mitchell turned to Julia. "You're going to need to get him back. I'll go after the others."

"No," Derek said, putting as much authority into his voice as he could. "You don't get it. There's too many. Can't ... go alone."

"But…"

"You won't be helping them if they get you, too."

Mitchell looked torn. Derek completely understood the sentiment. He wanted nothing more than to rearm himself and go hunting these monstrosities, but he couldn't help anyone if he dropped dead of his injuries first.

"Fine," Mitchell said after several seconds, kneeling down and starting to work on bandaging Derek up again. "I'm going to give you something for the pain and you'll ride back with me. Don't die in the meantime."

"No promises, but I'll try."

"I won't lie and say it's going to be a comfortable trip, but we'll take it slow." He turned to Julia. "You got a name?"

"Julia Wilhelm," she replied.

Mitchell made a face as if he wanted to say something, but then apparently thought better of it. "You follow right behind us. Keep an eye on him from the rear."

She nodded.

Mitchell glanced at the ATVs, then back to Derek. "And you … next time I tell you we should ask for a couple of Side by Sides in the budget, I want you to remember this moment."

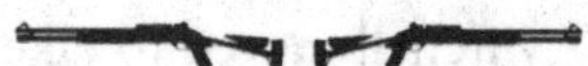

One eternity later, or at least it felt that way, the ATVs rolled out of the forest and into the outskirts of Shilough. Derek tensed up as they left the tree line. Ezekiel's museum was close by. There was no telling how many in this town were members of the Lesterfield family or whether they were driving into another ambush.

He couldn't help but envision worst-case scenarios:

returning to find Zeist's people dead, or their SUVs gone and them surrounded.

A few minutes later, though, found him nearly over-joyed to be proven wrong. Over Mitchell's shoulder he saw the lights from their small caravan of vehicles, right where they'd left them.

"Son of a bitch!" the medic cried.

"Huh? What?" Derek asked, suddenly wishing he had a gun in his hand.

Mitchell ignored him and continued onward until they saw Eric Zeist and his men waiting for them.

"I thought I told you to call 9-1-1," Mitchell said as he killed the engine.

"I alerted the governor. He said no ambulances."

"Are you a freaking...? No. Hold that thought." He pointed to two of Eric's men, then at the closest of the SUVs. "Clear the back of that one and put the seats down. We need to get him in there."

The men hesitated for a moment, but then their boss nodded and they got to work.

"Help me with him." Mitchell got off the ATV, careful to not dislodge Derek.

Eric, however, stepped past him toward Julia. "Who the hell are you, and what the hell do you think you're doing?"

She looked him defiantly in the eye. "If you're not going to call an ambulance, then I will."

"No, you're not." With a quick movement, he snatched the phone from her hand and tossed it away. "You're under arrest."

"What? You can't do that," she and Mitchell said simultaneously.

"Watch me." He dragged her off the ATV, leaving the medic to help Derek by himself.

"What should we do?" Mitchell asked in a low voice.

"Keep ... an eye ... on things," Derek whispered. "If he does ... anything but ... detain her, shoot him."

"I can't tell if you're kidding or not."

"Neither ... can I," Derek replied before promptly passing out.

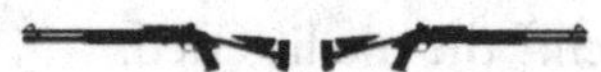

Derek awoke again when the SUV hit a pothole, stirring him from a troubled sleep in which he'd been surrounded by those things, helpless to save his friends.

His eyes opened and he saw Mitchell leaning over him, with Julia on the other side. She was holding a saline bag attached to an IV in his right arm.

"Why don't you try driving on the road," Mitchell growled at whoever was upfront.

"Sorry," Eric replied. "That's your New Jersey tax dollars at work."

"Wh-where...?" Derek asked.

"Don't talk," Mitchell ordered. "I'm doing what I can while we head back."

"Back?"

"To Rutgers," he said, a grimace of distaste on his face as he produced a large syringe. "Now hold still."

"What's that?"

"A cocktail of antibiotics designed to stave off flesh-eating bacteria. You aren't going to be much help if I have to saw your arms off."

"Lovely."

"It's not exactly FDA approved, so apologies if you start hallucinating ... or grow a second head."

Derek raised an eyebrow, then turned to Julia. "How ... are you doing?"

She glowered down at him. "These bastards are looking at the biggest lawsuit I can throw at them. I'm going to own the governor's mansion once this shit is finished."

Derek smiled, but said no more. He was too tired, not to mention he didn't have the heart to tell her there would be no lawsuit. Though he would have loved to see the governor try to explain his actions in court, he knew she'd be stifled by the same mountain of paperwork they had to give to everyone they rescued in the course of their jobs, the irony being that she'd been the one to rescue him. Regardless, his superiors weren't about to let a reporter shine a flashlight on this. If she tried, they'd do whatever they could to discredit her, whether it was true or not.

That was a concern for later, though. Once they got back and his body was no longer being bounced around like a basketball, he needed to call Norah and request backup. Try as Yarlberg might to keep a lid on this, there wasn't much he was going to be able to do once a unit of armed ATF agents were out in the woods.

The thought brought a smile to his lips as he once again closed his eyes and waited for them to reach their destination.

25

After a time the silence, broken only by the never-ending drip of water, became too oppressive. Danni stood and approached the bars, straining to see on either side of them. The way looked clear so far as she could tell, but that didn't mean anything. "Are you there, Sa...?" She hesitated, realizing she had almost said Sarah. "Sophie, can you hear me?"

After a few moments, the other woman replied, "Yes."

Though she didn't want to ask what she'd been thinking, she found the words forming on her lips regardless. "You said there was another woman here. That she was close. What did you mean by that?"

After several long seconds had passed, Danni feared she wouldn't answer. That she was perhaps reaching the same fugue state that Abby had been in, a place where a person became so damaged, so terrified, that they retreated deep into themselves, the only safe place left for them.

But then Sophie spoke up. "They took her away to give birth. She ... Sarah's been here longer than the rest of us."

"Don't call her that. It's not her name."

"It's the only name we have here," came the bleak reply.

"I told you. I have friends."

"And what good is that? My husband worked for the state." Sophie's voice broke. "Have they come looking? Have they found us?"

Danni considered her next words carefully, but then realized the truth probably didn't matter. What could they do to her? Punish her for saying it? They'd have to find her first. If so, she'd gladly welcome whatever they decided to do to her in retribution. "The state is why me and my friends are here. They called us in to search for you. We're a ... special team. We have guns."

"Didn't seem to help you much."

Danni wanted to punch the bars in frustration at her response, but she knew the other woman was right. "They caught us by surprise, an ambush. We were searching for one ... perpetrator. We didn't realize there were so many."

"And soon there's going to be even more," Sophie replied. "That's what they use us for. We're just livestock to them, bitches to be bred."

"I'm nobody's bitch."

"You say that now, but you can't fight them. They're too strong. Whatever it is that's been done to them, however it is they've been born, it makes them strong, tough. The one they call Noah, I fought him when they brought me here, fought with everything I had. Raked my nails across his face, figured I'd take a chunk out of him while I could. Nothing. I didn't even draw blood. We can't win. All we can do is ... hope they finish with us quickly."

By the end, Sophie's voice became devoid of everything, all emotion, all hope. It was like listening to a voice from beyond the grave, chilling Danni to her very bones.

Soon, all became quiet in the dingy prison again,

except for the dripping water and occasional low sob from Sophie's direction.

Unsure what to say, Danni looked across from her at the now empty cell. She hadn't dared ask what their captors had planned for Abby, mainly because she realized a part of her didn't want to know.

What she'd heard from them had been more than enough to turn her stomach. She could only hope that it was quick for the young woman and that they didn't hurt her – a sentiment which echoed Sophie's spoken despair.

That was little more than a pipe dream, though. These bastards had already hurt her, done far worse if her suspicions were correct. Danni had only spoken a few words to the girl, but it was enough to know she was broken, possibly beyond fixing. Whatever they were doing to her now, it obviously wasn't the first time she'd been taken from her cage to whatever torture they had in store for her.

Danni had never considered herself a particularly religious person. Nevertheless, she said a silent prayer to God – not for herself, but in the hope that he might show mercy to Abby, Sophie, and anyone else stuck in this hell.

"You must be the luckiest son of a bitch on the planet," Mitchell said. "No fragmentation, a couple of clean exit wounds, and the rest all small caliber ... or this." He held up what appeared to be a musket ball.

"And yet," Derek replied, lying on the conference table that currently served as a makeshift bed, "somehow I don't feel like it."

"Let the pain meds kick in, but don't expect to feel like a million bucks anytime soon. Hell, don't expect to feel like a buck-fifty either."

"I can live with the pain, but I can't live with…"

"Being a normal person and taking the next several weeks off? Yeah, I figured that."

"Hate to say it," Derek said, wincing as he gingerly sat up and swung his legs off the side of the table. "But the governor's yes-man might be doing us a favor. Pretty sure a hospital wouldn't be too keen on letting me walk out right now."

"And they'd be right. There's all sorts of complications that could happen between now and…"

"Hand me my shirt, please."

Mitchell did as asked. "I don't suppose I should waste my breath telling you to let the rest of us handle this."

"There isn't any rest of us," Derek replied. "At least until we get some backup."

"Then it's a good thing I stitched you up extra well. Gonna leave some scars, though."

"I don't have any beauty pageants on my calendar. Any word from Norah?"

"Not yet." Upon their arrival back at the campus, ushered in the back door so that as few people as possible saw them, Eric Zeist had tried to confiscate Mitchell's cell phone, but the medic had put a quick end to that. Zeist's men had grudgingly let Mitchell put in a call to their superiors but had been watching his group like hawks ever since.

"Dammit! We can't wait for her to comb through red tape. Danni and Frank need us now." Derek took a deep breath then indicated the door. "What's the word out there?"

"It's … a bit tense."

"Define tense."

"They've got Julia locked up in a conference room down the hall. Two of their gestapo buddies are guarding her."

"I bet she's pissed."

"A bit. Can't say I blame her. They dragged Arthur out of bed and brought him here before placing the building on lockdown."

"Why?"

"Containment. Seems our buddy Eric is acting on orders from the good governor."

"Great, just what we need." Derek stood and shuffled to the door. "Let's get out there and take control of the situation before this entire thing goes to hell."

Arthur stood up as Derek and Mitchell re-entered the room. "Are you all right?"

"I'm alive," Derek replied.

The college student walked toward them. "What happened to Danni? Nobody here will tell me anything."

"Sorry," Mitchell said. "I've been ... a little busy."

Arthur hooked a thumb toward Zeist's men. "I meant these guys."

"I'm not going to mince words," Derek replied. "She's in trouble, but we're going to do everything we can to save her."

"Trouble? Does it have anything to do with the samples we've been analyzing?"

"A lot to do with it."

"Because I've been looking over the results all night and have some ideas."

"That's enough," Eric barked, stomping over to them. "The kid doesn't need to know any more than he does."

Derek turned to him. "I'll be the judge of that."

"You can barely walk."

"That's more than enough to make a judgment call." Derek held his gaze. "So here's what you're going to do.

You're going to let our friend out of that closet you've got her in and bring her here. Then you're going to back off and let us do our jobs."

"The governor's on his way. He'll..."

Though the comment caught Derek by surprise, he didn't miss a beat. "But he's not here yet, is he? And until he is, this is my expedition and those are my team members out there. So you're either going to help or get out of my way. Those are your only two options."

The two men glared at each other for several seconds until Eric finally blinked. He turned to one of his men. "Go get the woman and bring her here, but don't let her even look in the direction of a phone."

"Better." Derek motioned Arthur over and took a seat. The small amount of time on his feet had been an effort, reminding him that overdoing it wasn't going to help anyone. Sadly, there didn't look to be much choice in the matter. "So let's talk about what you've got, kid."

Nervousness flashed across Arthur's face, as if he remembered he was a student intern talking to someone who was both a celebrity and a government agent. "Is this going to help her?"

"I won't lie. There's no way of knowing. But anything more than what we currently have is better than where we are now."

Arthur took a seat between Derek and Mitchell. "Those samples we found. At first I thought they were degraded because of contamination, but now I'm not so sure. I think they're actually human, but ... at the same time not. Almost an offshoot species, but more because of external factors, not evolution."

"Go on," Derek said.

"You're going to think this is crazy."

Mitchell chuckled. "Try us, kid."

"The toxins in the samples. At first, I thought they

were external, like maybe whatever DNA was in there got mixed in with something else, but I spent a little more time with it and now I think that sample was some sort of excretion."

"Like saliva?"

"More like pus or maybe phlegm. But whatever was in it originated from the source, not after the fact."

"So whatever this thing is, it has toxins in its body."

"Heavy metals, industrial waste, we're talking some serious shit." At that, Arthur looked embarrassed. "Sorry."

"Don't apologize," Derek replied. "I'm not your parent and you're not being graded. Speak frankly."

He adjusted his glasses, but smiled anyway. "Thanks. But yeah, that's what I'm thinking. I'm pretty sure this sample is from a human who's been badly affected by whatever is in their system, but at the same time, I don't think this is a freak occurrence. I've never seen anything like this, but my gut tells me you couldn't introduce this sort of damage to the human body all at once and have it survive."

"How then?"

"I think it's ... hereditary." Arthur paused, looking nervous as if he, too, felt his story was ridiculous, but then he nodded. "I know it sounds crazy, but..."

"Not as crazy as that thing opening its mouth and talking to us."

"What?!"

"Sit back. Let me bring you up to speed."

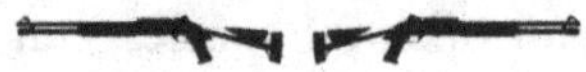

Derek's recounting of their ambush was interrupted by the sound of someone cursing up a storm in the hall. The door opened and Julia was led in, escorted by two of Zeist's men. She was busy chewing them out about civil liberties and freedom of the press. All were valid points as far as Derek was concerned, but not particularly helpful for her current situation, especially since he was certain his team wouldn't be allowed to back up her claims once this was over and done with.

Her sister was still out there somewhere, though, and he was certain she'd agree that was the far more pressing issue at the moment. "Miss Wilhelm, can you please join us over here?"

"Screw that! If this gorilla thinks he can..."

"Julia! It's about our friends and your sister."

As expected, that got through to her. She gave Eric and his men one last dirty look, then stalked over.

The security director, for his part, said, "Any of you tries to give her your phone and I'll smash it myself."

"Try it and I'll smash you in the..."

"That's enough, Mitch," Derek said before turning to Julia. "We're going over what we know, trying to piece together who or what it is we're up against."

"What do you mean 'what'? I thought you said it was a group of people."

"That's what we're discussing. Turns out, calling them people might be generous if what I'm hearing is true."

That caught her attention and she stopped complaining to listen in.

"What you said about this possibly being hereditary has got me thinking," Derek said, nodding toward Arthur. "Ezekiel Lesterfield."

"The museum proprietor?" Mitchell asked.

"One and the same. You saw him on the film. He's not what I would call a pleasant-looking fellow. At first, I didn't think much of it, but then he showed up in the swamp to save what we thought was the Jersey Devil. And he wasn't alone. The others who were with him, I didn't get much of a chance to examine them, but from what I could tell, Ezekiel and the devil represented two extremes."

"Extremes?" Julia asked. "I don't understand."

"That's okay, I'm just beginning to myself. According to what Ezekiel said, the devil is related to him. Called him Noah. It sounded like they're all family and kinda looked that way, too. There's Ezekiel, who looks normal enough to fit in with society, but at the other end of the spectrum is Noah. He's ... hard to explain, but it's like evolution decided to run in multiple different directions at the same time. Based on what he's presumably done to our own people and others, I'm not entirely shy about calling him a monster inside and out. As for the rest of the group who ambushed us, they were all somewhere in between – a veritable smorgasbord of birth defects and deformities, but apparently nothing so debilitating as to keep them from doing what they did. From that aspect, they were all hale and hearty."

"So ... a family of, what, freaks?" Mitchell asked.

"In a nutshell."

"I don't get it," Julia said. "Did a circus break down and the performers all decide to run away into the swamp? That doesn't make any sense."

Derek shook his head. "No, it doesn't, and I don't think that's the case anyway. According to Ezekiel, his family has been here for a long time, even before that crazy preacher grandpa of his."

"But I thought you said he and this Noah were related."

"Yes, and it's all starting to make sense now ... sorta anyway." Derek turned to Arthur. "What you said about it being hereditary, I think that might be the key here. The missing link, if you will."

The college student looked confused. "How so?"

"What if Jedediah Lesterfield's exorcism was less about god and religion and more about protecting his family?"

"You think this Noah guy is over a hundred years old?" Julia asked.

"Not at all. That would be crazy."

"And the rest isn't?"

Derek smiled at her. "Crazy is my line of work, but even I have limits."

26

"Before coming here, we did our due diligence on the legend of the Jersey Devil."

"I know a thing or two about it," Julia replied. "Mother Leeds and her thirteen children."

"The last one was born a devil and flew up through the chimney," Arthur said. Then, when he saw Derek staring at him, added, "I'm pretty sure anyone who lives here can tell you that much."

Derek nodded. "Not surprising. Stuff like this brings a bit of historical flavor to an area, but in a fun way. Still, it's nothing we didn't know. What we found interesting, and which led us to originally conclude there wasn't anything of note here, was the changing aspect of the creature."

"How so?"

"If you read about most cryptids, like sasquatch for instance, there's always going to be some variation depending on who's telling the story, but ultimately the vast majority of them add up to a giant hairy humanoid in the woods. They have that in common. Same with the Mokele Mbembe."

"The what?"

"A legend from the Congo," Mitchell clarified.

Derek nodded to him. "There's some difference in descriptions of skin texture and size, but almost all the eyewitness reports can be summed up as a sauropod dinosaur."

"That's pretty crazy," Julia said, leaning back in her chair.

Derek shrugged. "Regardless, there's a certain symmetry to the stories that gives them at least some potential for credibility. But that doesn't exist with the Jersey Devil. The reports of its appearance all vary wildly. Sometimes it has wings, sometimes hooves, sometimes a horse's head, sometimes it hops like a kangaroo, et cetera. When you read a history like that, it's easy to conclude that you're dealing with nothing more than a local tall tale."

"Or witnesses who are drunk enough to see pink elephants," Mitchell added.

"Also a factor in these things."

Julia folded her arms across her chest. "So what does this have to do with a hundred-year-old exorcism and the bastard who kidnapped my sister?"

"I'm getting to that. What if everything we assumed to be nothing more than a fabrication is actually fact? More importantly, what if it's all the same family?"

Julia looked confused, but Mitchell said, "I think I see where you're going with this. Same family, same fucked-up genetics, but different devils."

"Exactly." Derek slapped the table in front of him. "Ow! Need to not do that for a while. But essentially, yes. Say you have this family living out in the marshes, mostly isolated from the rest of society."

"New Jersey Hillbillies?" Arthur offered, his eyes wide as he apparently tried to process this.

"Yeah," Mitchell said. "But let's say the problem here is

twofold. First off, maybe they're inbreeding, keeping it all in the family."

Derek nodded. "Not unheard of for close-knit clans like this. Stories of inbreeding in the Pine Barrens aren't exactly new, so that seems a fair assumption."

"What's the second problem?" Julia asked.

"Part of the reason we were called in: toxic waste."

"Hey!" Eric cried.

Derek turned toward the security director. "Oops. Did I say that out loud?"

"You're playing with fire, Jenner."

"Sorry. I tend to forget myself when I'm full of bullet holes." He turned back to the group and rolled his eyes. "Pretend I didn't say that last part. But let's consider history. The Barrens used to be home to several industries that tried to make a go of it: steel, charcoal, glass. Let's assume – hypothetically speaking, of course – not all of those industries cleaned up their messes when they left."

Arthur leaned in. "So what you're saying is this inbred family probably lived, or still live, where a bunch of this stuff was dumped."

"Precisely. Both of those factors can contribute to birth defects, but now add them together. Brother and sister get married and raise a toast of lead and mercury at the reception ... and they do it over and over again, generation after generation."

Julia covered her mouth with her hand. "What would that do to them?"

"I think we met the answer to that question last night. This is a family that plays a hard and fast game of birth defect roulette. On the lucky side you end up with Ezekiel or Jedediah Lesterfield, people capable of fitting in with normal society. On the low end of things, you get someone who would be labeled a monster. Over hundreds of years and several generations, that's bound to happen at least a few times."

Mitchell smiled grimly. "Hence the different descriptions of the devil. Because it *was* different ... different members of this fucked-up family over the years."

"Yep, people far too deformed to do anything but live their lives in the woods, only occasionally being seen by outsiders."

"How tragic," Julia said.

"Tragic," Derek agreed, "except for when they decide to start killing or kidnapping people."

"But why?"

"That kind of genetic damage can't be good for one's state of mental health," Mitchell offered.

"I don't doubt it," Derek replied, "but I think it goes deeper than that. Ezekiel showed us a picture of his great grandad's family. There was over a dozen boys, but only one girl. He even specifically pointed it out. What if there simply aren't enough women in the family to go around?"

Arthur stood up and smiled. "The Y chromosome!" When the others turned toward him, he quickly sat back down, "Sorry about that."

"What did you mean?"

Arthur appeared to consider this for a moment, but then he locked eyes with Derek, the first time he'd seen the kid be self-assertive. "I didn't think anything of it when I was doing my original analysis, but the DNA results seemed to suggest an overly aggressive Y chromosome. Whatever it was that the sample came from, it was almost definitely male."

"What does that have to do with these things kidnapping my sister?" Julia asked.

"In nature, some species can change sex during times of need," Arthur explained. "If there are no females present, the males can spontaneously change their sex so as to allow for continuation of the species. But maybe, thanks to the damage introduced here, nature is kind of working in reverse. What if they're predetermined to be mostly male thanks to the screwed-up nature of their genes?"

Derek nodded. "I see where you're going with this. And what if there are some stretches of time where it's worse than others? Remember the Lesterfield exorcism? It was brought about because girls had gone missing in the area, presumably taken by the devil. Well, what if that was true? Maybe, out of desperation for their fucked-up way of life, that's exactly what happened."

"And Jedediah used the exorcism as a way to cover it up before people converged on the woods in force."

"That's exactly what I'm thinking, Mitch. What we're looking at here right now is history repeating itself."

"So those bastards kidnapped my sister to rape and impregnate her?" Julia cried, a look of horror upon her face.

"Danni, too," Derek said grimly, "as well as any others they've taken."

"But what about the guys?" Arthur asked. "I thought I read that a few men went missing, too."

Derek narrowed his eyes. "I'm not a betting man, but if I was I'd say they did to them the same thing they tried to do to Frank and me."

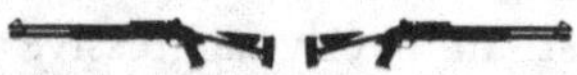

"He did what? B-but that's crazy."

"Is it any crazier than what we're going through?" Danni asked. "Or the things that kidnapped us?"

Bolstered by a need to do something, *anything*, to keep the oppressive weight of her situation at bay, Danni had started talking ... keeping at it until Sophie finally responded again. And, despite the pain of the memory, she could think of no better way to bolster her resolve than to once again face the horrors she'd already survived.

"And your brother actually tried to fight that thing?"

"We both did. But he was first, inspired me to keep going even after..."

"I'm so sorry," Sophie said.

Danni gritted her teeth. "I didn't tell you that story to make you feel sorry for me. I wanted you to hear it so that you understand there's no such thing as an unwinnable fight, an unkillable monster. These things are big, they're scary, and they're smart, but beneath it all, they're not much different than you and me. They can be beaten, but you can't give up. That's what they want."

"But how?"

"I ... don't know." Danni couldn't bring herself to lie to the poor woman. That would have been wrong. At the same time, she realized that so long as she could perhaps inspire a little hope in at least one other person here, she could keep that flame alive inside herself. "For now, all I know is this: we need to do whatever we can to keep ourselves safe and unhurt."

"Unhurt? But..."

"You don't have to say it." The truth was, she didn't want to hear it, was too afraid her own resolve would crumble. "Believe me, I know. I won't lie to you and say anything is going to be easy, but we have to try. None of that Stockholm Syndrome crap, no thinking we deserve this, no giving up. Always fight, even if it's only in your mind. No matter how long it takes. Let them get sloppy, complacent, make a mistake. And when they do..."

"What?"

"You do whatever you can to make them pay. *We* do whatever we can."

"I-I'm not sure I can. You don't understand what they've..."

"That's okay. Not knowing is fine, but it's a lot better than giving up. But please believe me when I say I won't stop fighting. And I swear on my brother's soul that I will find a way to..."

The sound of a door being thrown open immediately silenced both women.

"*But i-it's not f-fair!*"

"That will be enough, Noah." The voice of Ezekiel Lesterfield floated down the dank prison hallway toward Danni. He didn't sound pleased. "It's rightful retribution, that's all. I earned my place, my Sarah. It's only fair that I be compensated being that she hadn't taken to seed yet."

"*But Sssarah is mine.*"

"She belongs to whoever Adam says she belongs to. Unless, that is, you'd like to bring it up with the old man."

Silence followed, save for the fall of footsteps, one normal, the other heavy and plodding.

"I didn't think so. Now mind your manners and maybe you can have the next."

"*Liked this one.*"

"I can see that. There is a lot to like. It's rare to find a vixen in these woods so fresh-faced and unspoiled."

Danni could see them approaching. They passed by Sophie's cage. The woman stayed quiet, no doubt hoping to go unnoticed. Danni couldn't blame her, but at the same time, she had a bad feeling that she wasn't their target.

"*M-maybe you share her?*"

"Now now, dear Noah. Don't be greedy. Did I not try to be generous with you earlier, despite it coming at great personal cost to myself?"

"*Wasn't me,*" Noah replied in an almost sulking voice. "*Didn't even get a turn.*"

"I know that, child. Your cousin, on the other hand, had best steer clear of me for the foreseeable future."

Danni backed up as the grotesque form of Noah Lesterfield appeared in front of her cage. He leered down at her with barely concealed greed as Ezekiel stepped next to him.

"Good day to you, Sarah," he said cordially, removing his hat as if trying to be polite.

"My name's Danni."

"No, it isn't. But that's okay. You'll learn. All eventually do. Don't worry. I won't hold your initial reluctance against you."

"It's Daniella Kent, to be precise," she continued, ignoring him. "I want you both to remember that name. Danni Kent. Because I'm going to be responsible for you and your whole crazy family ending up behind bars."

Noah laughed a wheezing chuckle.

Ezekiel joined him. "I so do appreciate a sense of irony in a bride-to-be. I appreciate seeing it broken even more."

Danni looked past them, suddenly realizing they'd returned alone. "Where's Abby?"

"Who?"

"Abigail," Danni replied, refusing to play their game. "The girl you took earlier. If you've hurt her..."

"Ah, yes," Ezekiel replied, leering at her. "Alas, I am heartbroken to say that I have recently been widowed. My Sarah, she was a good lass, quite comely. I so did enjoy my time with her. Sadly, she was not cut out for the rigors of this life. But you, you have some fire in you, girl. Adam has agreed that you'll be my new Sarah to help ease my suffering."

She'd heard them say that name before. "Adam?"

"He's the patriarch of our dear family, Noah's father."

"*Sssupposed to be m-mine*," Noah complained.

Danni opened her eyes wide at their exchange but said nothing.

"But she's not," Ezekiel chided. "Your pappy has spoken and his word is law. If you have a problem with it, I suggest you take it up with him. Maybe he'll slap some manners into you."

That shut Noah up and he shrank away from the much smaller man like a whipped dog. Danni felt the slightest bit of empathy for his plight but quickly pushed it away. Her friends might very well be dead because of him. If he was looking for pity, he'd need to look elsewhere.

She shook that thought from her head as quickly as it came. Derek and Francis were both survivors. They'd pulled through worse. They had to be okay. And if they were okay, that meant they were coming for her. She had to hold on to that hope, do what she could to survive until then.

But if she got the chance to take out her frustrations on any of these fuckers in the meantime, so much the better. She sized up Ezekiel. He was thin and severe looking. She had little doubt that if push came to shove, she could take him.

He noticed her staring at him and stepped up to the cage smiling, revealing crooked teeth. "That's good. A woman should take a measure of her husband to be. You'll get to know the rest of me soon enough, but not quite yet."

A feeling of relief washed over Danni, but it was instantly quashed as he continued.

"Adam insists on getting to know every new Sarah first. Breaking them in, so to speak. And if his mighty seed should happen to germinate in your womanhood first, so be it. The clan will be that much stronger for it."

27

"All right, we've waited long enough," Derek said. "Mitch, head down and make sure we're loaded up. I'm going to call Norah back."

"You're in no shape to do this."

"Duly noted. I trust you have something in that bag of yours to help me compensate."

"Can I go on record as stating this is a stupid idea and that you should be in a hospital bed?" Mitchell asked with a frown.

"Of course."

"Good, because if you drop dead from a heart attack out there, I'd prefer to not be written up for it." He grabbed his backpack and began cataloging the various vials inside it. "And, just for the record, I have stuff in here that will not only keep the pain at bay, but it'll make you high as a fucking kite in the process."

"Keeping me on my feet will be good enough. Save the rest for when we end this."

"What about me?" Julia asked.

"Us," Arthur corrected. "I want to help, too."

"Absolutely not," Derek stated, borrowing Mitchell's cell.

"But you need backup," she said.

"Which is exactly what I'm calling for. No offense, but I need trained agents on this one, not someone with mean grammatical skills."

"I know how to use a gun," Julia said.

"Me too," Arthur added. "If you show me what to do, anyway. But seriously, I want to help you guys find Danni."

Derek turned to the younger man and put a hand on his shoulder. "You *are* helping her, son. The work you did for us has been immeasurable. We now at least have an idea what we're up against. We went in underestimating these ... *things* last time. We won't make that mistake again."

"You made a lot of mistakes you won't be making again, Jenner."

The group turned to see Jonas Yarlberg step in the door, with Eric Zeist and two uniformed police officers flanking him.

Derek stood up, wincing as he waited for the pain to pass, then strode over to him. "Governor Yarlberg," he said as way of greeting, forcing his voice to remain calm. "I don't know what you've been told, but..."

"You bastard!" Julia snarled, stalking past him. She raised a hand, no doubt intending to smack the smug grin off the governor's face. Derek managed to grab hold of her wrist before that could happen, just barely holding her off in his weakened condition.

"Let me go! This pig covered up John's death."

Mock concern replaced the grin and the governor replied, "Whatever do you mean, Ms. ... whatever your name is?" He turned to Derek. "By all means let her go." He glanced back at the two cops with him. "If she so much as raises her voice to me again, arrest her and have her charged with felony assault."

"Assault?" she cried.

"Oh, yes. It'll be your word against mine and my witnesses." Julia turned to Derek, to which the governor added, "I wouldn't count on Dr. Jenner's help or that of his friends." He stopped and looked around the room. "Friend, anyway. I think you'll find they have little to add to your defense in a court of law. Isn't that right, doctor?"

Derek refused to be baited by the man. Unfortunately, he was right. Doing what he and his team did required a certain amount of discretion, whether they liked it or not. "Julia, please go back and wait with the others."

"What?" She rounded on him, her green eyes wide and angry. "How can you just..."

"I'm not," Derek interrupted. "You'll just have to trust me. This isn't going to help anyone, including Sophie. We need to pick our battles, and this one is for another day. We don't have the time, and our friends certainly don't."

That seemed to get through to her. She nodded, however ruefully, then walked back to sit with Arthur and Mitchell, but not before flipping the governor off.

Eric looked like he wanted to say something, but the governor merely held up a hand. "Don't mind her. Just exercising her first amendment rights, nothing more."

"Enough with the games, governor," Derek said. "We need..."

"I one-hundred percent agree, Dr. Jenner. No more games, such as the cock-up I hear your people caused out there in the woods. I thought you were supposed to be professionals, yet in one day you've managed to potentially screw this up worse than my people have in months." He lowered his voice. "What the hell were you thinking? She's a reporter."

"She's also the only reason I'm still alive," Derek

replied, careful to keep his tone neutral. "You'll have to forgive me, but when I'm at death's door, I tend to forget to ask whether people have press credentials or not."

"You look pretty lively to me."

"I apparently don't have much choice in the matter."

The governor shrugged as if he wasn't concerned. "My apologies for that. I figured a celebrity, however minor, such as yourself would attract some undue attention in a public hospital. Such attention would bode ill for my administration, considering yesterday's press conference. I doubt we could convince everyone you were there for a simple case of food poisoning. Besides, it looks like your man did a fine job of patching you up."

It was all Derek could do to not deck Yarlberg, but he held himself in check. He didn't fancy being arrested, especially since he wasn't in any shape to do much damage anyway. Might as well save it for when he could at least dislocate the fat bastard's jaw.

The governor looked down and noticed the phone in Derek's hand. "I wouldn't bother if I were you."

"Oh?"

"Agent Caseman," the governor clarified. "I assume you've been trying to reach her. Don't waste your breath. I already had a chat with her superiors. There will be no backup coming."

"What?!" Mitchell stormed over, echoing what was going through Derek's head. "Are you out of your fucking mind?"

"Dr. Jenner, kindly keep your subordinate under control."

"Do you have any idea what happened out there?"

The governor faced Mitchell. "I only know what I've been told, as I believe is the case with you. Or did I hear incorrectly and you were out there, too, confronting this so-called Jersey Devil?"

Mitchell glared at him.

"I thought not, Mr. Harkness. Seems Dr. Jenner here is the only eyewitness. Awfully convenient, I'd say. And, considering his somewhat less than stellar condition, I'm not sure how any of us can be expected to believe his take on matters with one-hundred percent certainty."

Derek put a hand on Mitchell's shoulder. "If I'm not to be trusted, then where's the rest of my team? Are you implying that perhaps they ran off, maybe got a better deal from a competing channel?"

"Could be," the governor replied, all good humor gone from his beady eyes. "Or could be that you had an accident out there and are afraid to admit it. Or, maybe a falling out. These things have been known to happen."

"That's a serious accusation."

"Not an accusation at all. Merely speculation. But you'll forgive me if I find it a bit more believable than ... what was it you said, Mr. Zeist ... ah, yes. Toxic, inbred hillbillies."

Eric smirked and nodded toward his boss.

Derek turned to his teammate. "Knew we should have discussed that in the other room." After a moment, he faced the governor again. "Regardless of what you believe, the fact remains that my people are missing and I aim to find them and bring them home."

Yarlberg shook his head. "Out of the question. You've done enough damage out there and I, for one, won't stand by and let a small army of feds march into the preserve to play cowboys and Indians. The only thing you'll be doing is catching the next flight out of my state. I should have known better than to think you could fix this without making a mess of things."

"We're not leaving without our friends," Mitchell said.

"I don't recall giving you a choice."

"But..."

"Do I really need to point out," Yarlberg said, addressing both men, "that the door swings both ways when it comes to your service? I have lots of pull in Washington. Believe me, it would take all of one phone call to get an investigation launched. We're talking dereliction of duty at the very least, possibly even criminal negligence."

"Criminal negligence?"

"If you were to disobey, say, the jurisdiction of a publically elected official such as myself."

"That would never stick," Derek said.

"Maybe not, but you and your friend here would still have a chance to cool off nicely in a prison cell while awaiting trial." When neither Derek nor Mitchell said anything, he continued. "I'll assume my point is made then, gentlemen."

"You still haven't told us what you plan to do about..."

"Yes, yes, your friends. Don't worry. I'll, of course, do everything in my power to ensure their safe return."

"You'll forgive me for asking how you intend to do that," Derek replied.

"It's none of your concern anymore but, if it helps, we've decided to make it an internal matter. We'll cordon off the area, leak some story to the press about an endangered species being found."

"Cordon off the area?"

"Yes, to minimize any further casualties. Then, once the election is past, we can..."

"The election is four months away!" Julia cried.

"I'm warning you for the last time, Ms..."

Derek stepped in front of the governor. "My apologies. As you can probably guess, it's a stressful time for us all."

The governor's face turned a shade redder. "Stressful or not, I won't tolerate another outburst from her ... or you, for that matter. One more word and I'll see to it that your team is shipped off to the most remote part of the Alaskan tundra."

"Been there already," Derek replied grimly, but then held up his hands in a placating manner. "But I believe I get your drift, governor."

"Do you?" Eric asked.

Derek ignored him, continuing to face Yarlberg who he towered over by a full head. "I know how this game is played. So does my team. We know the risks involved, both in the field and out. And we also understand the consequences. So long as you can assure me that everything possible will be done, I'll take your word for it."

Yarlberg stared at him long and hard, their eyes locked until Derek looked away. That seemed to satisfy the governor. "I give you my full assurance."

Derek nodded and turned back toward Mitchell. "Start breaking everything down and packing up the equipment."

"But..."

"And get the paperwork ready for Julia."

"I'm afraid the reporter needs to come with..."

"And give her cause for both a criminal and civil lawsuit against your administration?" Derek asked, turning back to the governor. "Once she signs everything, I'll give you copies so you can make sure they're duly filed. You know as well as I do what'll happen if she tries to talk. Her word will be about as good as Monopoly money at a bank."

The governor thought that over for a moment, but seemed satisfied. "Mr. Zeist, please ensure Ms. ... uh..."

"Wilhelm," Eric offered.

"Yes, Ms. Wilhelm. Please ensure she doesn't leave until she signs everything Dr. Jenner requires of her. After that, she's free to go."

"You can go to hell if you think I'm signing squat!"

"Ms. Wilhelm," Derek replied in a placating manner. "Think about this. You want to help your sister, right? Well, you won't be able to do anything until you give us what we need. It's nothing onerous, just some affidavits swearing you to silence about this matter."

"And what? If I don't sign, some spook will shoot me in the head?"

"Hardly, but there will be consequences. At the very least, your career would most likely be over."

"So you're going to gag me?"

"I'm trying to ensure you're free to do your job and continue your search."

"And my sister and your friends can all rot while those things do God knows what to them?"

"The governor has assured me he'll do everything in his power. Officially, I'm inclined to believe him." He turned away from her before she could say anything further. "You're all set with us, Arthur. Same deal applies to you. After you help Mitchell wrap up..."

"And send copies of *everything* to my office," the governor interrupted. Derek raised an eyebrow, to which he added, "So that Mr. Krychech can continue this investigation from his end."

"Of course," Derek replied, before addressing Arthur again. "After that, you're free to return to your normal class schedule."

"But..."

"Where I *highly* recommend you forget about everything you've seen and learned here."

The younger man merely nodded, seeming to understand that he was well out of his league on this.

That seemed to finally mollify the governor. "Make sure that everything is handed over to Mr. Zeist's team within the hour. Then you're to be on your way, and by that I mean, I don't want to see your faces in my state ever again. Eric, kindly walk me out."

Eric did as told, but not before flashing the others a triumphant smile as he and the governor stepped from the room.

The second the door closed, Derek held up a hand for silence. He knew he was about to be bombarded with questions and accusations, but also realized they didn't have time for it.

"Let's go, people. You heard the man. We have an hour to get packed up and be gone. We wouldn't want to disappoint our esteemed host."

28

Noah more or less dragged Danni through the Lesterfields' *home*. Had it merely been Ezekiel, she was certain she could have fought him off, maybe found a way to escape. But, despite his seemingly endless deformities, the so-called Jersey Devil was far too strong.

She began to understand Sophie's dismay. One clawed hand was at the back of her neck, holding on just tightly enough to let her know that any false move would end badly for her. His other hand held onto her arm, occasionally letting go to readjust his grip and grope her in the process, something that made her want to vomit.

Danni tried to focus on the layout of the compound as well as any possible venues of escape. After a few minutes, it became obvious this was no mere shack in the woods. Wherever they were, it was both massive and very old – rusted girders visible through collapsed wall panels were a testament to that. She could see where rotted beams had been replaced with newer supports. Crumbling masonry made up the majority of the walls, although it still seemed pretty solid to her.

Whatever it once had been, the Lesterfields now claimed it. The various repairs that had been done suggested they'd been here for some time.

Most of it was dank and dirty, but she could see signs of habitation where members of this damnable family had set up home. A distant hum that seemed to be present everywhere outside of the prison suggested gas generators were used to power the place.

Unfortunately, she didn't have much chance to gawk. Every time she saw something of potential interest, Noah would give her a shove from behind, often punctuated by an excited grunt. Though still wearing the threadbare shirt they'd given her, Danni had never felt more naked.

"Come along, Sarah," Ezekiel said with eerie calmness from up ahead. "Adam shouldn't be kept waiting."

She'd almost given up trying to correct him. It was like talking to a wall. Her own family had always been close, but nothing compared to the cult-like mindset here. It wasn't even that her objections were met with violence – just a continual chiding that her name was Sarah now. Danni could understand how someone could break under that constant reinforcement, day in and day out. It was a form of brainwashing, infesting their victim's mind a little at a time until their will was imposed.

"Danni," she said defiantly, feeling Noah's hand momentarily tighten its grip on her neck.

"You will soon be dissuaded of that notion," Ezekiel replied. "All are. You may think you're different, but you're not. Just another Sarah to be welcomed into our family and loved as one of our own."

"Loved? Is that what you call it?"

"Of course. You'll want for nothing here, I can assure you."

"Except my freedom."

"Freedom is irrelevant when one is in tune with God.

For it was written, 'Wives, submit yourselves to your own husbands as you do to the Lord.' We are your freedom now. In our family you should put your trust and in me in particular … just as soon as Adam gives us his blessing."

"I can't wait."

He stopped and turned toward her, his eyes intense in the dim light of the hallway, although it seemed to go beyond mere lust. "Neither can I, for I had very much hoped my previous dear Sarah would conceive. We've had but one viable birth in the last three years. You are our hope for the future, my new, darling Sarah."

"What about that girl you took before I got here?"

Ezekiel shook his head. "Ah, Ezra's wife. Much like my Sarah, she was weak, not fit breeding stock. I am sad to say the child lived for an hour, no more, before being taken back to God's flock. Ezra was beside himself with grief. His reaction to his dear wife was … unfortunate. Poor boy. It'll be some time before Adam deems him worthy to wed again."

She didn't need to be told more. Danni wasn't a particularly religious girl, but she recalled that some parts of the Bible were perfectly fine with men disciplining their wives as if they were little more than cattle.

Just try that with me, asshole.

The threat was half-hearted, however, even inside her own mind. The mounting panic of what was coming, knowing she was being led to an unspeakable horror, was starting to take hold. Each step was harder than the last and, despite her best efforts, she began to tremble with fear.

Then, finally, Ezekiel spoke the words she'd been dreading ever since being dragged from her cell. "Ah, here we are."

They stopped in front of a closed door. Though it was

inlaid into the same ancient masonry as the rest of the structure, it looked much newer.

"Our patriarch appreciates his privacy," Ezekiel said, almost as if reading her thoughts.

"*Don't k-know why,*" Noah replied. "*I l-like it when they ssscream.*"

"Now, now, child," the older man chided him, "there's no need to scare my blushing bride. This should be a joyous time for her." He turned to Danni, smiling at her with crooked teeth. "Soon, Adam's seed shall be planted within you. You'll be one of us. You'll be my Sarah. And if it's God's will that his seed takes hold, then I shall rejoice just as if it were my own."

He knocked on the door, producing a hollow boom that echoed ominously in the long hallway in which they stood – almost as if it were a gong summoning an ancient horror from a dark place that humanity was never meant to know about.

After a moment, the doorknob turned and was pulled open. The figure standing within was silhouetted by the light coming from behind it, but Danni could see enough to know she was right to be afraid.

"*Pa, we brought Sssarah to you, just l-like you said.*"

"I can see that, boy," Adam replied in a gruff voice, his large frame filling the doorway. After a moment, he stepped forward and Danni was able to see him fully, though she wished she hadn't.

He was a big man, six and a half feet tall, almost as large as Noah. His deformities weren't nearly as pronounced as his son's, but that somehow made it worse. It was as if he were half a devil, stuck in some awful in-between place that ensured there were few places outside of this accursed dwelling where he would fit in.

Yet one would never have guessed that by the surety with which he carried himself. He stepped forward, wearing a button-down shirt and stained overalls, and glared down at Danni with his one good eye – the other a fleshy ruined mass overgrown with scaly, discolored skin.

He had a thick grey beard, making it difficult to see the rest of his facial features, although Danni caught a glimpse of a pug mouth and bent nose. When he smiled, he showed off teeth very similar to his son's – long and sharp, more fitting for a predatory animal than a man.

"I like this one," he said after a moment, still leering at her. He lifted a misshapen hand to caress Danni's cheek, two thick calloused fingers more reminiscent of a lobster claw.

She backed away, but Ezekiel was there to shove her toward the big man. "She's a feisty one, my Sarah."

"Not your Sarah yet."

"Of course not, Adam. It is, as usual, my sincerest hope that you properly break her in. And if it pleases you afterward, to bless me with her as my wife, so as to ease my aching heart."

"I got other aching parts that need tending to first," Adam said with a snicker, before turning his head and hocking a wad of discolored phlegm at Noah's feet.

"*I l-like h-her too, papa,*" Noah said in a small voice.

"I already told you, she ain't yours. There's too much work to do, keeping folks out of our woods. Can't be having you distracted by her womanly charms."

"*But when?*"

"When I say so, boy." He raised his claw hand in Noah's direction, and the devil actually flinched.

Rather than smack him, Adam placed the hand on Noah's shoulder in an almost affectionate way. "You're a good boy. And you will be rewarded for your diligence. But for now, there's work to do. You must have patience. Can you do that for me, boy?"

The devil nodded to his father and turned away, but not before giving Danni one last covetous glance. It lasted barely a second, but it was enough to make her skin crawl.

If she thought that was bad, though, she was quickly proven wrong as Adam latched his hand onto her arm and squeezed. He was dreadfully strong, and Danni had to bite her tongue to keep from crying out.

He pulled her close, his rancid breath making her gag.

Adam's one eye drank in the sight of her. Without turning to the other two, he said, "That's enough squawkin'. You both get out of here. Me and Sarah need some time alone to get to know each other, and I expect there to be no interruptions."

Noah grunted in affirmation while Ezekiel simply nodded once, a smile upon his face.

Then they were gone from her sight as she was dragged into Adam's room and the door slammed shut behind them.

29

Danni was shoved forward as Adam turned to lock the door to the bedroom. The action was deliberate on his part and sent her pinwheeling across the room, stopping only when she hit the edge of his bed.

At one point it had been a stately full-sized four poster bed, but that was seemingly long ago. She wouldn't have been surprised to find this had been pulled from a landfill somewhere. It sagged in the middle and only two of the four posts remained, both of those ending in jagged points where the tops had apparently been snapped off. Oddly enough, the mattress appeared to have a freshly washed sheet upon it, the discrepancy standing out like a sore thumb.

She had only a moment to get her bearings, noticing that the rest of the room had a similar odd cant to it. Everything within seemed old and beaten down, but it was neat in an almost fastidious way, as if the owner were trying to make the best of what they had to work with.

"You like it?" Adam asked from behind her. She heard him take a step closer as he continued. "Out here, me and my boys make do with what we can. I try to raise them right, give them an appreciation that we're men, not animals, but boys will be boys, as I'm sure you know."

Here, away from the others, he sounded different, almost thoughtful. For a moment, Danni hoped that perhaps this was someone who could be reasoned with. She turned to face him, but before she could say anything, he grasped hold of the front of her shirt with his normal hand.

"But girls will be girls, too," he said, grinning. "And right now, we have a powerful need for them."

Danni's eyes widened as he bunched his hand in the fabric, straining it against her skin. Her moment of hope evaporated in an instant and all she felt was fear – a primal, paralyzing terror as this mockery of a man leered at her.

"You have to understand," the big man said, stepping forward and forcing Danni back until her legs hit the bed again, "we don't do this because we want to. I prefer my boys to win their wives the old-fashioned way. That isn't an option for all of us, but so be it. The Lord will do as He will. But the clan must continue. It simply isn't an option for me to let our bloodline end. I will not stand by and watch my family die out."

The hand tightened again and Danni felt something give as the frayed fabric of the shirt began to tear.

"I only do what I have to." Adam grinned down at her and yanked, ripping the shirt from her body in one quick move, exposing her to him. "But that doesn't mean I can't enjoy myself in the process."

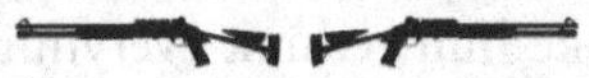

"Are we ready to go?"

"Mostly," Mitchell replied. "We're just missing the bulletproof vests."

"We don't have bulletproof vests," Derek pointed out.

"I know that. But maybe we should requisition a few."

"You do realize the things we hunt usually don't fire back at us, right?"

The medic shrugged. "Yeah, but if nine-hundred and ninety-nine monsters aren't carrying guns, that still doesn't make me feel much better about the one that is."

"If the next squatch clan we encounter is packing you can say 'I told you so,' but for now, let's hope these guys are an anomaly."

"An interesting way of putting it," Mitchell said, strapping on his sidearm. "By the way, you almost had me worried for a second there."

"Come on, man. How long have we worked together? You really think I'm going to bail on our own because some blowhard gets a bug up his ass?"

"No, but you've got a hell of a poker face when you want. Once this is over, maybe we should hit the tables at Caesars ... assuming we're not all being fitted for orange jumpsuits at Leavenworth."

Derek chuckled for a moment before he broke down into a coughing fit. His injuries were quick to remind him that, as necessary as this rescue was, it was still a stupid idea. Sadly, they were out of options. If this was going to happen, it needed to be now, before Zeist returned. Any attempt after that might be thwarted, not to mention he was certain the clock was ticking on Danni and Francis.

He was well aware of how petty some of the players in Washington could be, but to see Yarlberg actually choose his own public image over human lives was unsettling, enough so to make him rethink everything he was doing. As much good as his team did, the thought of being beholden to people like the governor was enough to make him question his life's choices.

Derek considered that it might not entirely be a bad

thing if the plug was pulled on their operation. It would stink, but at least his conscience would be clear. If something like this happened once, there was nothing to say it wouldn't happen again. Politics was a game of take and take some more. If someone else got wind of this and it served their political needs, he had little doubt they'd end up over the same barrel again. Precedent was a powerful thing in the law, and it held equal sway behind closed doors. Rolling over and playing dead for the governor was morally the wrong thing to do, but it would also send a signal to others that he and his team were up for grabs as scapegoats.

He took a deep breath and pushed those thoughts away. It was pointless to think about it now anyway. He had friends in need and it was time to get his head in the game.

"Which of those peashooters is mine?"

Derek sighed before turning to face the reporter. "Listen, Julia…"

She held up one hand and held out her other. "Save it. That's my sister out there. I'm going even if you slam the door in my face and drive off without me. What else can I do? Sit around and wait for Yarlberg's goons to arrest me the second they realize you're missing? At least this way I can do some good before I flush my life down the toilet."

"And if something goes wrong?"

"Then I'll die doing the right thing." She smiled. "But don't go shoveling dirt over my corpse just yet. Besides, you need the help and you know it. Two isn't going to cut it, not if what you said was true."

"It's not that simple…"

"I'd just like to say," Mitchell interrupted, "I'd very much prefer to not drag civilians into our shit, but you remember as well as I do who the deciding factor at Bonanza Creek was, and it wasn't us. Besides, she's right. If there's a small army of these freaks out there, I wouldn't mind an extra finger on the trigger."

Derek considered arguing, but nodded instead. Standing here and fighting was pointless – he knew that the second they stepped out of the building – but he had to try. It would have been the height of negligence if he hadn't. He was well aware that Julia knew the risks, but it still had to be said.

But now that it had and those concerns had been subsequently dismissed, he didn't see the point in continuing. Time wasn't on their side.

He turned, pulled a handgun from the rack in the SUV, and put it in her hand. "How do you feel about a Glock 23, .40 caliber?"

Adam pushed Danni backwards onto the bed. He grabbed hold of her legs by the ankles and shoved them apart before releasing her to work on his overalls.

The second she was free, she pulled back and kicked out, catching the big man right in his prodigious gut. She might as well have been kicking a brick wall. Adam grunted and backed up a step, but that was all the effect she had.

"Got a little fire, do ya, Sarah?" He grinned, showing off his sharp teeth, then unbuckled his overalls and let them fall to the floor. "That's okay. I'll quench that real quick, make sure you understand your place before I give you to Ezekiel."

Danni wasn't sure what was worse – his casual tone or the sight of his lower half. The patriarch of the Lesterfield clan wore nothing beneath his overalls, exposing the lumpy, alligator-like skin that covered his stomach and thighs. No wonder her kick hadn't done anything.

But it was the sight of his manhood, fully erect, that terrified her most – large, misshapen, and only human in the most bastardized sense of the word. For a moment she could only stare in mute horror, which seemed to make him grin even wider. It was the look on his face, the sickening lust in his eyes, that finally spurred her from her shock.

Danni rose from the bed quickly, hoping to use her smaller size and greater agility to her advantage. Sadly, the room wasn't large enough for her to sidestep out of his reach.

He lashed out with his clawed appendage, backhanding her across the face hard enough to see stars. She fell, fighting to shake off the daze even as she hit the floor, forcing herself to remember she'd fought creatures larger and stronger.

Noticing that his feet were still entangled in his discarded overalls, she rolled and scissored her legs around his, lashing out and kicking at the back of his knees with her heel.

Large and grotesque as Adam was, even he was not immune to such an attack. He stumbled and fell. She'd been hoping to maybe get lucky and for him to crack his head on the dresser or floor, ending this quickly. However, he merely pitched forward onto the bed. The springs squeaked in protest, but he was otherwise unharmed.

Wasting no time, Danni rolled to her feet and quickly scanned the room for a weapon, anything that might give her the advantage. There was a chair and a lamp, but the former appeared too heavy for her to wield properly and the latter looked likely to shatter the moment she touched it.

There was no time to second guess her odds against this man. With no hope of victory in sight, she stepped to the door, willing to take her chances running rather than stay here and face what he had in store for her. All at once she understood why Abby had retreated into herself. Her reality had been one of terror in which she was at the mercy of this bastard and his family. Though Danni didn't know what the poor girl had been like before her capture, she was certain her final days had been spent as little more than a shell of her former self.

It was a fate she desperately didn't want to share.

She grasped the doorknob and tried to turn it. It didn't budge, and that's when she noticed the keyhole on this side of the door.

There came a jingle from behind her and she turned to find Adam standing again, a pair of keys dangling from his hand.

"You think you're the first to get past me?" he said with a chortle. "I know damn well I'm getting old and slow, but I ain't stupid." He tossed the keys onto the nearby dresser and took a step forward. "And I ain't weak."

Danni thought of Abigail's fate, but then refocused instead on Sophie. She was still alive. That meant there was hope for her – a chance, however slim. She wouldn't let that hope die, not if she could help it.

Biting down on that anger and refusing to let it go, she readied herself as Adam crossed the room, sizing him up as he approached. He was large, strong, and even more thick-skinned than the saying allowed for. But he had one major weakness so far as she could tell. He had one eye, effectively leaving him blind on his left side.

He reached for her with his grotesque claw hand, but she ducked and sidestepped. His midsection was too tough for her to take him down that way. No matter what some action movies proclaimed, size and strength *did* matter. But crippling an opponent's extremities was always a good way to equalize a fight.

Kicking out low, she tried to drive her heel into the

side of Adam's knee, but he shifted at the last moment and she merely hit his calf muscle instead. Still, it knocked him slightly off balance, enough for her to stay out of his line of sight.

She knew that dodging and weaving wasn't going to win this fight, especially in these cramped confines. Were they out in the open, she could have eventually worn him down. But here? It was only a matter of time before he cornered her and it was all over. Once he forced her down with his bulk atop her, there would be little she could do to stop him.

She had to take the fight to him as best she could.

Danni stepped in and grabbed hold of his wrist. Before he could pull free, she hit his elbow with an open-hand aikido strike, hard enough to have broken a smaller man's arm.

Sadly, his meaty bulk was too much. She barely straightened his arm with the blow, eliciting an annoyed grunt from him as opposed to the cry of pain she'd been hoping for.

He spun, using his mass against her, and shoved her away, sending her stumbling back to the corner near the foot of the bed.

"Fucking bitch. Time to teach you some manners."

Adam was upon her before she could recover. His claw hand grabbed her throat and forced her back against the wall hard enough to knock the wind out of her. He pressed the rest of his body up against hers – his normal hand groping her breasts while he crushed her against the wall hard enough that she could barely breathe, much less move.

He bent his head down to hers and ran his tongue, a discolored elongated abomination, over her cheek. "Think I want a better taste," he whispered in her ear, spinning and practically tossing her onto the bed.

Danni managed to get one foot up before he could climb atop her, but he was too strong to push away. Desperate, she tried to use his momentum against him, hoping to throw him over her body. She grabbed hold of his wrists and lifted with her leg.

Come on ... just a little more.

Unfortunately, he was too heavy and the give of the mattress worked against her leverage.

She almost had him when his weight became too much and her leg gave out, sending his bulk crashing down atop her and driving the breath from her body.

30

Derek was far from happy. The circumstances of the past day were more than enough to put him in the foulest of moods. He had two missing teammates, had been shot, and was probably well on his way to becoming a fugitive. Now he could add being blackmailed to the growing list.

He glanced in the rearview mirror at Arthur, who was sitting in the back of the SUV with Mitch and being given a quick primer on proper handgun use.

That thing had better be empty.

Following their dressing down by Yarlberg, Derek had dismissed the lab assistant. That part hadn't been an act. Let the kid think him a monster, but he had no intention of putting a college student in danger. He'd known his chances of ditching Julia to be slim to none, but she was an adult. The choice was ultimately hers to make.

Offering Danni a place on the team had been an exception, done under extraordinary circumstances. Her competence and bravery had warranted it, but that didn't mean he planned to make it a habit of putting people not even old enough to drink in danger.

Yet, that seemed to be his fate.

They'd finished packing their gear and were just about to pull out when Arthur reappeared, stepping in front of their SUV and demanding to go with them.

He didn't believe it for a second when Derek had told him they were headed to the airport, the fact that they were all armed probably not helping his story. When Derek had finally relented and admitted that he planned to rescue his people, the kid had insisted on coming along, ultimately playing the ace up his sleeve: threatening to tell the governor's men if they left him behind.

Derek knew Eric and his goons would figure it out eventually, but the longer that took, the better chance he, Mitch, and Julia would be too deep in the woods for them to track down and stop. Though he doubted the kid would have actually ratted them out, he couldn't take that chance.

In the end, Julia had taken the shotgun seat while Mitch rode in the back with Arthur, giving him the Cliff's Notes version of gun safety so he didn't shoot the rest of his new teammates in the back by accident.

This is a one-time only thing, Derek told himself. *They're not part of the team. Once this is over and done with, they can go back to their lives.*

Problem was, it was difficult for some to go back once their eyes were open, but that wasn't his problem. Let them go out into the woods afterwards if they felt like playing recorded gorilla screams and waiting to see if anything responded. He couldn't stop that.

Derek noted that they were almost to the turn-off that led toward Shilough and the accursed woods beyond.

"Best get to the final exam, Mitch. It's almost show time."

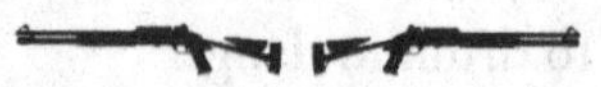

"So let me get this straight, Bob," Eric said to his underling. "You let them leave without an escort and now you don't have any idea where they are?"

"They said they were just packing up. I figured they'd be back for the rest of this ... stuff," Bob Hernandez replied, pointing to a heavy stack of printouts.

"And you believed them?"

"Loading a car isn't illegal. It usually doesn't require an armed guard. Hell, they didn't even hitch up their ATVs. How the fuck was I supposed to know they'd bolt?"

Eric took a deep breath. He knew Bob was right. Jenner's team weren't prisoners or wanted criminals. That alone limited his security detail's powers in what they could and couldn't legally do. Being handed what was essentially babysitting duty wasn't exactly a prime motivator for the men on his team to be at their most diligent.

That knowledge didn't make him feel any better, though. He knew that if the governor found out, he'd go through the roof. It would be yet another in a long string of tantrums. Though he strove to put forth an aura of complete loyalty to his employer, deep down, he felt that oftentimes his assignment was akin to being the personal assistant to a spoiled child. Yarlberg was petty, jealous, spiteful, and none too bright, if you asked him. But the fat bastard could schmooze like a pro, buttering up constituents with promises made of nothing but bullshit and getting them to swallow it whole.

Though he personally wouldn't have wept at seeing his boss eat a bullet, his job was to prevent such things, amongst myriad other duties that Yarlberg seemingly thought up at random. His position as head of the governor's personal security team was both prestigious and well-paying. It wasn't something one walked away from lightly. That the governor's golden tongue would likely garner him a successful Senate run, not to mention a potential future shot at the White House, told Eric where his bread was buttered.

Even if the governor's plans came to fruition and Eric's position was eventually supplanted by the Secret Service, that would still leave him in a good spot. Dismissed amicably after years of loyal service, he could transition that to protecting other high profile clients, preferably ones that weren't as fucking needy.

The immediate problem was avoiding the governor's wrath. Though Jenner might be nothing in the grand scheme of things, Yarlberg was currently worked up. If word got back to him that Eric's group had been ditched or, worse, if Jenner caused a major fuck-up in the Pine Barrens that the press got a hold of, the governor would almost certainly take it out on the person tasked with keeping that from happening. If so, Eric would be lucky to find a job working guard duty at a construction site, much less anything better.

This situation needed to be contained, at least in a way that Yarlberg's anger would be focused elsewhere. Eric didn't have anything against Jenner personally. Despite his gruff attitude toward the reality show host, he'd gotten the impression that the guy was competent, even if his story about mutants in the Pine Barrens was two steps over the border to Batshit County, USA. Still, if he was forced to choose between himself and a group of C-list actors masquerading as federal agents, it was an easy choice to make.

"Bob, get Vasquez and bring the car around. Then call up Muellenberg, Hopper, and Sullivan. We're heading to Shilough."

"We really need that many for these idiots?"

Eric nodded, even though Bob was right. Bringing half a dozen men, the majority of the team, was overkill. Jenner didn't strike him as a violent man, but he was definitely a stubborn son of a bitch. Confronting him with an overwhelming show of strength, though, would probably be enough to convince him that they weren't dicking around.

"You sure that's where he's headed, Eric?"

"Yeah. Even if he's not going there directly, he'll be heading into the forest near there." Eric looked at his watch and considered how much of a head start their quarry had. "Tell the boys to bring their hiking shoes. I have a feeling our feet are going to get muddy before this one is over."

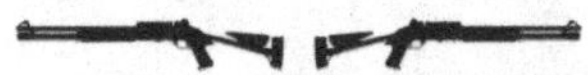

Danni was certain she'd smother as the rough skin on Adam's stomach pressed down on her face.

A moment later, feeling another part of him pressing into her midsection, she realized that perhaps smothering was the preferable fate to what would happen next.

She turned her head to the side and managed to draw in a breath as she waited for the inevitable.

The patriarch of the Lesterfield clan sighed atop her, a breathy moan. He twitched several times in what she was sure was perverse excitement on his part. Danni wanted to vomit, but wasn't certain her constricted airway would allow it, pinned beneath his bulk as she was.

However, rather than readjust himself and do the vile deed he'd set out to do, Adam Lesterfield settled atop her and became still.

After several moments, she realized something was off.

Did the bastard die of a heart attack?

She shifted beneath him, using what little leverage she had to free her arms. He didn't try to stop her. Struggling to keep the gorge in her stomach from rising, she slowly began to wiggle out from underneath him – the fear and exertion causing her to sweat, which slowly made it easier.

She eventually pulled her upper body free and found herself teetering off the edge of the bed, her legs still stuck beneath the leader of this loathsome family. She angled her head up, expecting to see Adam grinning back at her, this having been some sick game on his part to allow her some final hope before defiling her.

Instead, she saw the opened mouth grimace on his face, the last expression he'd ever make. Danni had been certain she'd failed in her desperate gambit to escape, but she now realized that she'd managed to catapult him back far enough.

He'd been impaled through the eye on one of the broken bedposts. In the end, his massive frame, the thing he'd no doubt used to dominate whomever he pleased, had been his downfall.

Bloody gore dripped down the ruined wooden post, and his head gave one final twitch as if to acknowledge his fate, but it was obvious that he was no longer a threat. The bastard had claimed his last Sarah.

Danni allowed herself a momentary reprieve, but no more. Stopping to think about what had almost happened threatened to bring with it tears. If she started crying now, she knew it wouldn't stop for a good long time, and she couldn't risk that. Adam Lesterfield had ordered his family to leave them alone so as to give him time to violate her at his leisure, but she knew she'd be a fool to test how long they'd wait before checking on him.

And once that happened, then what? Locked or not, they'd eventually break down the door and seek revenge for their fallen leader. But she'd also seen the lust in their eyes. There was no way they'd grant her an easy death, not before they...

No! She was far from out of danger, far from being

free. Sitting there and waiting, ruminating over what had almost happened, would only make things worse.

Taking a deep breath and steadying herself, she worked her legs out from beneath Adam's bulk until she was finally freed. She got to her feet and looked down at him, partially to make sure he wasn't playing possum. But he wasn't. His body had ceased its post-mortem spasms and lay still. With the exception of the blood and the strange angle his head lay at, he could have been deep asleep, but she knew better. In a few hours, rigor mortis would set in, but she needed to be elsewhere long before that happened.

Danni didn't have much time to spare, but she took a moment nevertheless to spit upon Adam's corpse – if not for her, then for all of the girls who hadn't been so lucky. There was no telling how many had come before her. Between unreported disappearances and those who wouldn't be missed, perhaps it would never be known, but it was enough for her that this bastard would claim no more.

Her one small indulgence finished, she put the keys on the dresser so as to not lose them, then set about finding anything in the room that she could use to aid in her escape.

31

Come on! Move it. Go grab a bite to eat. Take a piss. Do something!

Danni knew she couldn't afford to sit and wait. She'd already gotten far luckier than she had any right to.

She hadn't wasted any time in looting Adam's room. Though he was far larger than she, she'd manage to cobble together a soiled t-shirt and pair of shorts that she was able to cinch up enough to keep from falling off her lean frame. Wearing his shoes was out of the question, but she'd put on a triple layer of old socks so as to protect her feet from any sharp rocks on the ground.

Clothed as best as she was going to get, she'd nearly left before giving the room one final sweep. Though she didn't want to get anywhere near his body, she forced herself to look under the bed ... keeping as far away from him as she could. Despite him being unquestionably dead, she couldn't shake the irrational fear that he'd pop back to life and continue what she'd only barely managed to stop the first time.

Biting down her fear had paid off better than she

could have ever hoped. Far back against the wall she'd spotted a long plastic case, lying in the blood still dripping from Adam's ruined eye socket. Not wanting to, but knowing she needed to, Danni had scooted under the bed as quickly as she could and retrieved it.

Though the case was locked, its key was among those on the dresser. Danni had almost wept with joy when she'd opened it and discovered a gleaming Remington 12 gauge shotgun, along with several shells full of buckshot. As leader of the clan, he was no doubt allowed his pick of the spoils, and this was one treasure she was happy he'd hoarded.

It was that discovery which had finally emboldened her to unlock the door and venture forth. Though she didn't fool herself into thinking she had enough weaponry to fight her way out if need be, feeling anything other than helpless was enough by itself.

Danni briefly considered making her way back to the cells to free Sophie and anyone else she might have missed, but ruefully dismissed the idea. There was no telling if she could even find her way back, not to mention whether they were in any condition to make a run for it. Though Danni hated herself for doing so, she concluded that their best bet for rescue was her leading the rest of the team back here, preferably with plenty of reinforcements.

Her mind made up, she'd relocked the door behind her so as to hopefully buy as much time as possible, then moved quietly and purposely while sticking to the shadows – something not entirely difficult in the dank passageways.

Danni continued forward, turning randomly down hallways and backtracking when she came to any rubble-strewn dead ends. A few times she passed rooms occupied by others of the Lesterfield clan, but managed to slip by unseen. At last, just as she was beginning to conclude she was hopelessly lost and would likely never find her way out, she found a set of stairs leading up. Hoping that she wasn't going to strand herself on a rooftop, she decided to take them.

At the top she found what she'd been hoping for. She emerged into a room with actual windows, although the glass appeared to be long gone. From the look of things, she was on the second floor of the structure and it was nighttime, the thick vegetation beyond the windows dark and foreboding. Thanks to the aged masonry of the outside wall, it was a minor matter for her to find enough handholds to climb to the ground some fifteen feet below.

It was there, outside and with freedom practically beckoning, that she finally found her way blocked.

The building, an old factory perhaps, was surrounded by a fence. Old as the rest of this place appeared, the fence itself had been greatly fortified with rusted rebar, wood, and barbed wire. Rather than risk injury by trying to climb over, she explored further, hoping to find a gate leading out.

That's when she spied the light from up ahead – a lone lantern hanging above an opening in the fence. Unfortunately, standing between her and freedom, bathed in the light of the lamp, was another of those malformed bastards.

It was too good of an opportunity to disregard, though, so Danni quietly crept forward as far as she dared.

The man standing in the exit was armed, that much was obvious. The closer she got, the more details she was able to make out. Though she couldn't be certain from her vantage point, he looked familiar, likely one of the trio who'd taunted her when she'd first woken up here ... Nathanial, if she recalled correctly. For all of his big talk earlier, he'd apparently drawn nothing more prestigious than guard duty.

Danni had hoped to wait him out. Certainly fatigue, hunger, or boredom would take its toll, leaving her with an opening. But it hadn't. In her fear, she was certain she was over-exaggerating the amount of time that had passed, but it seemed an eternity in which he did nothing but stand near the opening, facing out toward the dark forest beyond. The only hint of movement from him was the occasional turn of his head as he surveyed the tree line.

Sadly, she had no frame of reference for how long Adam typically kept his victims locked up with him, but realized it was best to err on the side of caution – to assume that, even now, his family members might be breaking down the door to investigate the terrible silence within.

Danni made to move from her hiding spot, but then hesitated. If she was wrong, she could potentially give herself away.

There was also the problem of what to do once she was out. She knew from firsthand experience that these monsters had booby-trapped the surrounding woods. No matter which direction she headed, she would need to keep it slow. She'd stepped into that snare while she'd still had her flashlight on her. In the dark, she'd need to be that much more cautious.

Danni looked up at the sky. The view above was obscured by trees, but it was better than it would be once she was outside the fence. She located the North Star and got her bearings. She knew their base camp had been west of Shilough but had no idea how far off course she'd been taken after being captured. However, it seemed logical to head east. Eventually she had to come across something – a road if she was lucky.

Shilough itself was another potential issue. Ezekiel was from there. It was more than possible some of the other Lesterfields, the less grotesque among them, lived there, too. Even if she made it, she'd have to keep moving rather than risk knocking on the wrong door.

Danni silently cursed at her continued inaction. She knew what she was doing, trying to think through every possible scenario in the hopes of staying in her small hiding spot a few moments longer. But her current safety was nothing more than a ruse, a temporary balm. So long as she stayed where she was, she wasn't truly safe, and neither were any of the women left inside.

Bracing herself, she stepped from her cover and took a quick look around. There was no one in sight other than Nathanial, not that she could see very far. It was a risk she would have to take.

Though fear made her want to bolt, she'd been trained better than that. Holding the image of her brother in her mind, she crept up behind Nathanial until she was standing just outside the circle of light the oil lantern was throwing off. She was certain she hadn't made any noise in her approach, but he somehow picked that moment to turn around.

Surprise registered in his eyes as he spied not only her but the shotgun she was pointing his way. He threw a quick glance down at his own gun, an old rifle hanging from his right hand.

"Don't try it," she warned.

"Hello, Sarah." He grinned, revealing blackened teeth. "What are you doing out here at night? It isn't safe."

"You assholes have a strange idea of safe. Now drop that gun and step aside and maybe I'll let you live."

"I can't do that, girl. It would be a sin to let you walk out on your God-given husband."

"God didn't give me a husband, you bastards did. And you're not going to get a second warning." She'd loaded the gun before leaving and had a slug already in the chamber.

"Women should not touch their husband's belongings without permission," he said, continuing to smile. "A little lady like you is liable to hurt herself with a big, nasty old gun like that. Why don't you hand it over?"

She ignored him, focusing on his hands and eyes – the former in case he tried to raise his weapon, the latter as it would tell her if reinforcements were coming up behind her.

"I knew Adam should have made you my wife. Ezekiel is too soft from living in that town. Me, I'd learn you some manners real quick." The grin widened.

Danni realized he was stalling for time. Every second he stole from her was another in which those inside might realize their leader was lying dead in his room. She tightened her finger on the trigger.

"Ain't gonna work, dear Sarah."

"And why's that?"

"You left the safety on."

You've gotta be kidding me. That was his trump card? Did he actually expect her to fall for such a pathetic ruse?

When she didn't blink, the smile fell off his face, replaced with an ugly snarl. He quickly raised his gun in the hopes of calling what he no doubt thought was a bluff.

It wasn't.

Danni let out a breath and squeezed the trigger, the thunderous report shattering the silence of the compound. Nathanial's chest blew apart in a shower of blood and grizzle.

There was no time for regret that she'd just gunned down a man in cold blood. That would have to wait for later. There was absolutely no chance that blast hadn't been heard by the others.

Steeling herself, Danni strode forward to where Nathanial lay in the grass. He wasn't dead yet, but his respiration came in broken, choked wheezes and his eyes were already glazing over. There was nothing that could be done for him. It was only a matter of time.

She quickly checked him for a sidearm. Then, not finding one, she picked up his discarded weapon. It was a battered single-shot rifle. Not the best she could have hoped for, but she grabbed it anyway.

It was one less gun to use against her.

Danni briefly considered taking the lantern, but as much comfort as its light would give, it would also serve to let her enemies pinpoint her all that quicker.

She grabbed it off the hook, stepped through the gate, and then threw it onto the ground, where it shattered and ignited the grass beneath.

It wouldn't slow them down for long, if at all, but every second counted, and she'd already wasted enough of those.

The pitch black forest of the Pine Barrens lay in front of her. After a moment, she strode forward into it, praying that luck remained on her side for a little bit longer.

32

"We should have brought the ATVs."

"There wasn't time," Derek said, already breathing hard. "Besides ... it's a nice night for a walk."

"Ow!"

Derek turned back to find that Arthur had stumbled over something. "You okay?"

"Yeah," he replied, looking more embarrassed than hurt.

Derek had been tempted to order him to stay behind and guard the SUV, but he didn't like the idea of leaving the kid alone, even at the edge of these woods. That, and he wouldn't have put it past him to follow anyway and end up hopelessly lost or worse.

"Any chance we can turn these things to, y'know, normal light?" Arthur asked, pointing to the red beam of his head lamp. "I can't see shit."

"Sorry," Mitchell replied. "The red won't screw up our night vision, which, trust me, we're going to need if the shit hits the fan. Also, anything brighter is going to make us way too easy to spot out here." He turned to Derek. "Is it safe to say we don't want that?"

"Been there once. It didn't work out too well."

Julia stepped up to him and put a hand on his shoulder. "We'll find them."

He nodded. "I thought I was the one who was supposed to be offering you comfort."

"I think we could all use some. How are you holding up?"

"I'll make do. Mitch has some pretty powerful voodoo in that pack of his."

"Just don't go putting the lime in the coconut," the medic replied with a huff. "Mixing cocktails might not be a great idea in your condition."

"Noted."

Derek checked his GPS. They still had a ways to go before they reached where he guessed the Lesterfields' territory to be, but there was no point in being sloppy. They were up against a foe who knew these woods much better than they did and who didn't have any moral compunctions against defending it. That alone made them dangerous.

Fortunately, that door swung both ways. Due to the nature of their work, they had access to high-powered weaponry designed to take down nearly any terrestrial foe they encountered. "All the party favors one needs for a rainy day," Francis had once declared.

It sure is pouring now, buddy, Derek thought. *When we find you, I owe you far more than just a drink.*

Well-armed didn't mean much if they were stupid about it, though. Case in point: the Mossberg 12 gauge they'd handed to Arthur. Mitch was walking with the kid, making sure he didn't open fire at any shadows. Even though they'd double-checked that the chamber was empty prior to setting out, Derek didn't allow himself to relax. Panic could easily lead to friendly fire.

The real problem was the Jersey Devil and the men who'd come to its rescue. He'd tried his best to prepare Julia and Arthur for what lay ahead, but telling and seeing were two different things. That knowledge frightened him almost as much as what they were hunting.

"They're not here."

"I can see that," Eric said from the passenger seat. "Park anyway."

"But..."

"These guys aren't idiots. I didn't expect them to come back to the exact same spot. They're probably out there somewhere, parked on the side of the road just far enough back to not be seen."

"So what do we do?"

"You two get your shit in gear while I see how close Hopper and the others are with those ATVs."

Eric stepped out of the car and slammed the door. Chris Hopper owned a pickup with a trailer hitch. Though it wasn't an official vehicle, Eric had instructed him to stop by the campus and pick up Jenner's ATVs. He figured they might as well use them to their advantage since they'd been left behind. There were only two, but it would give them a chance to cover more ground faster.

He checked the GPS on his phone. Eric knew where Jenner's base camp had been and had a general idea of the direction he'd gone when whatever fuckery had befallen his people.

That story about mutated inbreds living deep in the Pine Barrens still struck him as nothing more than bullshit, but he had to admit Jenner's actions didn't fit Yarlberg's theory about friendly fire. If the guy knew his friends were dead, why bother with this charade? For that matter, why drag two civilians – one of whom was a loud-mouthed reporter – into it?

Was it possible they were both in league, trying to discredit his boss out of petty spite? But then what about that college kid? He'd come across as merely a nerd, not some hippie on a quest for eco-justice.

Maybe Jenner and that reporter are planning for him to have an accident, too.

The thing was, he didn't buy that either.

Eric shook his head and looked down at his cell phone. Ultimately it wasn't his concern. For all he knew, they'd simply gone out into the woods to fuck beneath the stars. All that mattered was making sure his boss stayed happy. Anything else was of secondary importance.

He glanced at the dark street around him, noting lights coming on in the few houses in sight. No doubt the occupants were curious as to who was parking in their shit-water town after dark.

Take a picture, assholes. It lasts longer.

He dialed Hopper's number without a second thought on the subject.

"Hey, it's Eric. How far out are you guys?"

Danni liked neither the pace she kept nor the noise she made as she walked, sweeping the barrel of Nathanial's rifle ahead of her as if she were blind and it was a walking cane. But it was better than stumbling into any hidden traps.

She was making frighteningly slow progress, but it was almost pitch-black, the stars only visible whenever the trees would allow it, which wasn't often. It was just barely enough for her to get her bearings and avoid walking in a circle.

Truth be told, she was terrified. She wanted to cry out at every cricket that chirped or branch she stepped on. Danni had to keep actively reminding herself that she wasn't helpless. Even before joining Derek's team, the woods had nearly been a second home to her. Since then, she'd learned a lot more about following trails, tracking prey, and survival.

She latched onto that training like a life preserver. Panic was the enemy. It wouldn't do anything except get her caught or worse. Forcing the fear down, she focused on her other senses. Her eyes were mostly useless out in the dark woods, but she could still hear, smell, and touch.

At the moment, all she smelled was the brackish water that seemed to be pooling everywhere. She hadn't seen any dogs during her imprisonment, but that didn't mean there weren't any. To be on the safe side, she crossed through several of those pools to obscure her scent trail, using the rifle's barrel to gauge depth and make sure she didn't accidentally step into any sinkholes.

That would be a hell of a shitty way for me to end up...

Just as she was stepping onto drier ground, the rifle caught on the edge of something. Danni stopped dead in her tracks. It was probably nothing more than a vine, but she bent down and felt ahead with her hands to make sure.

She touched the rough contours of a braided rope. *Definitely not a vine.*

Her hands explored further. It was a snare. No doubt about it. She'd reached the section of forest that the Lesterfields had booby-trapped to either keep unwelcome visitors out or entrap potential victims.

She had no way of knowing how close she was from where she and the others had been ambushed or how far this minefield stretched, but knowing she'd entered it was enough for now.

Danni lay down, placed her ear onto the ground, and listened. It was fairly well known that sound carried far in the woods at night. Less common was the knowledge that so, too, did vibrations. It wasn't entirely unlike putting one's ear to a railroad track to hear how far off an incoming train was. She covered her other ear so as to blot out the sounds of the forest. At first, all was still, a small relief to her, but then she heard a distant thump. She focused her attention and it came again, then another.

Danni didn't consider herself paranoid, but either a herd of deer were trampling through the woods somewhere close by or she was being pursued. Her money was on the latter.

She was tempted to get back to her feet and bolt, much like the aforementioned deer, but that would be a stupid move. Their knowledge of the surrounding forest as well as their greater numbers gave the Lesterfields the edge. Her only advantage was they didn't know where she was yet, something she'd certainly give away if she went tearing through the woods like a scared rabbit.

No. She needed to familiarize herself with the immediate area, make note of other traps to avoid, and then find a spot she could hide or, if it came down to it, defend.

Danni started to rise, but then remembered the snare again. The Lesterfields would almost certainly know where they'd placed their own traps. But what if some of those traps were moved, even if just slightly?

It was a long shot – resituating a snare without tripping it and then properly resetting its pin in the dark – but it gave her something to focus on rather than the fear.

If, in doing so, she managed to take even one of those bastards out of the equation, all the better.

33

Things could not have gone better for Ezekiel Lesterfield had he planned them himself.

He'd been the one to snap his kin out of their wailing grief once they'd discovered not just Adam's body, but Nathanial's as well. He'd done so under the pretense of being strong, of wanting to see justice done before they could be allowed to properly mourn.

But the truth was, he felt no remorse. With his half-brother dead, that left him in prime position to take over as clan patriarch. Adam had been both strong and crafty, a combination that ensured he'd be calling the shots until such time as he keeled over dead, something none of them had expected to happen anytime soon.

Not crafty enough, you old buzzard.

How the girl had managed to do it, he didn't know. It must have been stupid luck on her part. Perhaps the old man's lust had gotten the better of him and he'd simply tripped and killed his own fool self. That was the likeliest explanation.

It was the gunshot outside which had alerted them that something was amiss. They'd found Nathanial just as he drew his last breath. Where Ezekiel had been somewhat neutral regarding their former patriarch, it had been an effort to not smile at Nathanial's corpse. The boy had been a bully and a fool – a useless one, too. Wasn't fit for anything but guard duty, and he'd managed to screw that up, too.

That was the only part that worried Ezekiel slightly. Adam's death was easy to write off as a freak accident, but Nathanial's had been deliberate. Though his rational mind insisted the girl would be easily found and subdued, he found himself wondering.

She was a part of that stupid show, true – nothing more than whorish eye-candy waiting to be made into an honest woman. But when they'd found her and her companions, they hadn't been sporting cameras and microphones. They'd been outfitted for a hunt, with good, well-cared for equipment. That in itself was strange, but at the time it was easily dismissed in light of the new guns and fine wife they'd captured.

Now he was forced to consider whether the girl herself was more than meets the eye. If there was even the remote possibility that she could be dangerous, then it wouldn't do for him to take her as his bride. Ezekiel wasn't a stupid man. His relatively benign appearance allowed him to be accepted in the outside world, giving him experience far beyond his less conventional-looking family members.

From a young age, he'd known he wasn't their match physically, being thin and frail where they were brutish and strong. He'd made up for it by becoming book smart. It wasn't always an advantage in their ancestral home, but it usually allowed him to think several steps ahead of the others.

That was exactly what he needed right then. The girl's unsuitableness as his wife gave him an idea. Claiming the role of patriarch was risky. Some of the more aggressive members of the clan might object and he stood little chance of standing up to them. But if he had strong support backing him up, then his claim would be all the more solid.

"Jonathan!" he called out, playing the role of the authority figure for both his future standing and to make sure the others didn't run off into the forest half-cocked, opening fire at every shadow they saw in their quest for vengeance.

His second cousin came loping over, looking at him questionably. Half of his face was permanently swollen, the eye on that side nearly twice the size of the other and possessed of an odd greenish tint. Though it made him seem as if he were always glaring, the advantage was that it gave him unquestionably good night vision, making him easily the best tracker in the family. Alas, he was also a mute, having been born with no vocal chords.

"Any sign of our dear lost Sarah?" Ezekiel asked.

The others swore oaths at the mention of her name, their anger palpable even in the gloom. Jonathan merely nodded, though.

Over the years, he'd formed a crude version of sign language so as to communicate with the rest of the family. He used it to indicate that he'd found a likely trail, one that led to the southeast.

"Running, just like a scared rabbit," his brother Ezra said.

Ezekiel nodded. "So it would seem. Jonathan, take the point. The rest of you, spread out no more than twenty feet apart. I don't want anyone running off on their own. And turn those lanterns down for now. We don't want to mess with Jonathan's God-given gifts."

"The hell with that. All we need to do is flush her out..."

"You mind my words," Ezekiel snapped at his cousin

Lemuel. "That girl is armed. You saw what she did to Nathanial. Do you want to join him in meeting the good Lord? Any of you?"

The collective response was silence. That was good. The longer it took any of them to get their dander up about him giving orders, the more solid his position would be. Now to add a little foundation to shore up things.

"That's better. Let's get going. Keep your weapons up and your eyes open." The family began to spread out, but before they could fully disperse, he turned to his nephew. "Noah, my boy, walk with me for a moment longer, please."

Noah did as told, looming over him in the dark. He was impressive as always, Ezekiel noted, if a little naïve. It was that naivety he was counting on.

"*W-want to find her. Avenge Pa.*"

"And we *will* find her," Ezekiel replied, lowering his voice. "But you shouldn't have your heart set to vengeance."

"*But...*"

"What's done is done. Her blood won't bring back your dear papa, nor Nathanial, both taken before their time. What we need now is to focus on the future. We're two men short and we lost a mere babe today. Sad as that is, it's God's will. But it's also God's will that our family continue. In order to do that we must welcome Sarah, and others like her, back into the fold with open arms."

Noah opened his mouth and hissed, low and angry.

Ezekiel was tempted to back up a step, but he held his ground. Noah was part of his plan, but that plan wouldn't work if the boy thought he was afraid of him. "None of that now. We must put aside our anger and focus on the family."

Noah stopped hissing, changing from menacing to petulant in the space of a few seconds.

"You thought that girl was pretty, right?"

"*Y-yes.*"

"Wanted her for yourself?"

"*Pa p-promised me.*"

"Yes he did, but then changed his mind as was his wont as leader." He scanned the woods ahead of him, then picked up his pace. He didn't want them to be left behind. "Keep up with me, boy."

Noah walked with him, his hitched breathing becoming louder in the dark woods.

Now it was time for Ezekiel to spring his trap, the one that would ensure that, when the time came, Noah would stand at his side. The boy was by far the strongest of the clan, even stronger than Adam had been. Gifts as extensive as his hadn't been seen in generations. He was a thing of beauty despite others labeling him a devil. Ignorant fools and their beliefs, nothing more. "I've been thinking. I'm not a strong man, not like your pa, but I have a vision for our family. I want to see us not only survive, but thrive. All of us. I see now that Adam might have been wrong in his judgment. Sarah, she ain't right for me."

"*N-nuh?*"

"No. I don't believe she is. That one is wild. She needs a firmer hand than mine to control her, nurture her. How would you like her as your wife?"

"*Sssarah mine?*"

"Yes, son. I think that would be best. You may need to discipline her, sternly I'd say, for her actions. But I believe that once she is properly broken in, she'll make a fine wife, and I can think of no finer husband for her than you."

"*Really?*" Noah's tone was hopeful but reserved, as if he was afraid his prize would once again be snatched away. That was just fine by Ezekiel.

"I mean it. I foresee many sons in your future by her."

Noah's breathing became more urgent, and Ezekiel

could tell he was getting excited at the prospect of making those sons.

"And there'd be no need to share. I relinquish my claim to her. She'll be yours and yours alone. There will be no question that when she gives birth, it shall be by your seed."

"*Y-yes*," Noah hissed.

"But, I need your help, Noah."

"*Help?*"

"Yes. I can make this happen for you if I take your father's place. My word will be law and the others will have to respect that, even if they don't like it. But I don't know if they will accept me. Some of them might think they'd make better leaders. If that happens, they might decide to keep Sarah for themselves – your Sarah. I would be powerless to stop them."

"*No*," Noah said, followed by a low growl. "*She's m-mine. Mine.*"

"I wholeheartedly agree, but in order for her to be yours, you have to convince them that my claim is legitimate. Otherwise I can't help you."

Noah rose to his full height, looking down at Ezekiel with his sharp teeth bared. "*T-the family is yours*," he said at last. "*Sssarah is m-mine.*"

"Yes she is," Ezekiel replied with a grin. "Now let's go find her before she slips away."

34

"**S**low down, boss!"

As much as he wanted to ignore the advice and keep barreling ahead, Eric knew it would be foolish to become separated.

The ATVs allowed two riders – one in the front to drive, and one in the back to sweep the woods with the high-powered LED lamps they'd liberated from the storage boxes of each.

I should remember to thank Jenner for those after we arrest his ass.

That left two of his men on foot, greatly negating the advantage the ATVs gave them in the first place. Eric had been tempted to leave them behind with the cars, but that would have screwed up his plans for convincing their quarry to surrender via way of their superior numbers.

As much as he despised the idea of walking in these godforsaken woods, the plan was to ditch the ATVs once they found the camp site – after making sure they couldn't be reclaimed by their targets in case they doubled back.

Damned things have to have a distributor cap or something.

Nice as they were to ride on, he didn't want Jenner's team to hear them coming. There was also the swampy terrain to take into account. The ground had been getting increasingly muddier the further in they went. With his luck, they'd end up sinking in a bog.

He'd been hoping to end this quickly – catch them and make sure their asses got on a plane headed anywhere but here. But now it looked like this was going to be a long slog. Though Eric preferred to end this in a peaceful manner, the longer he was forced to be out in the woods, the less inclined he was to care whether Jenner and his medic were tossed onto a plane with a few extra bruises to make up for the trouble they caused.

They had just entered a small clearing when Sullivan called from the other ATV, "What's that?"

At first, Eric thought it was just a large pile of leaves and was tempted to dismiss it, but then he took a second look and realized it was actually camouflaged fabric – the side of a tent. They'd found the base camp.

Thank goodness for small favors.

Eric ordered his men to disembark. They secured the ATVs – fortunately, Hopper seemed to have some insight into that – then checked the camp site to make sure there was no sign of recent habitation. Everything was in good order, having been set up only the day prior, but there wasn't any sign of a freshly lit fire or that anyone had visited since then.

"Some decent stuff here," Bob said after checking things out.

"Trash it."

"What? But I just said..."

"I know what you said," Eric snapped. "I'm not about to let them circle behind us, grab what they can, and then make a run for it. Take anything useful you find. Scatter the rest."

"What about this?" Muellenberg asked, stepping from the storage tent holding something heavy.

Eric shined his light and saw it was a professional-grade camera. He didn't consider himself a petty man, but the bastards had already seen to it that he'd be robbed of a night's sleep in a warm bed. He decided to indulge in a whim. "Let me see that."

Muellenberg handed the camera over and Eric threw it into the side of a tree with a satisfying crunch of plastic and metal.

He turned back to his men. "Like I said, trash it all."

"Was that a tree knock?" Mitchell asked as a distant sound carried to them.

Derek stopped and listened. Usually knocks came in multiple strikes. After several seconds, he shook his head. "Doesn't seem like it."

"A tree knock?" Julia asked.

Arthur stepped forward, an uncertain look on his face. "You mean like Sasquatch is supposed to make?"

"Danni said you watched the show," Derek remarked with a grin. "But no. I don't think that was one. Didn't have the right cadence or duration."

Julia let out a nervous laugh. "Don't jinx us. The last thing we need is for bigfoot to crash this party."

Mitchell smirked at her. "Sorry, but you're a little late for that."

"What do you mean?"

"There's definitely one in the area," Derek said, his tone nonchalant. "Maybe more."

"One what?"

"A squatch." He started walking again. They were

closing in on the area where he and his team had been ambushed. Just a little bit further.

He glanced back and saw Julia and Arthur both staring at him.

"You're kidding, aren't you?" Julia asked.

"Not at all. Mitch?"

"He's right," Mitchell replied. "There was a fresh set of prints about half an hour back. Big fella. Probably male. At least five hundred pounds. Think I heard him skulking about a few times. Pretty sure he's been keeping tabs on us."

"W-what?! We need to…"

"Relax," Derek said to the younger man. "It's not mating season and there haven't been any reports of aggression from this area. He's not going to bother us if we don't bother him. Probably just curious as to why people are tromping around out here after dark."

"Are you sure?" Julia asked.

"Positive. Just don't accidentally shoot at any big shadows you see. The last thing we want to do is piss it off and give it a reason to choose sides."

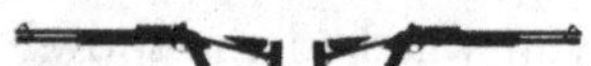

Danni put her ear to the ground again. She thought she'd spotted lights in the distance, but also realized her mind, combined with the surrounding marsh, could be playing tricks on her.

Her heart leapt in her throat when she heard the faint thud of footsteps. Again, hard to tell how far off, but she was convinced they were louder this time, and that meant they were closer.

Though it was hard to tell in the oppressive darkness, the area she was in felt similar to where they'd been ambushed. She'd found several more snares and trip wires since encountering the first one, drawing a mental map of where they were in relation to her.

If she was right in her assumption, that meant her team's base camp was less than an hour away. She longed to run to it, lock herself up in the supply tent, and pretend she was safe, but that was the plan of a scared child hiding from monsters under the bed. The truth was the camp, without her friends there waiting for her, offered neither shelter nor succor from the creatures chasing her down.

She needed to find a secure place that would give her enough cover to hide or – if discovered – stand and fight. It was time to act.

Danni had noticed a bog close by that would suit her needs. She leaned her weapons against a tree, regretting putting them down for even a few moments, but it had to be done. Tearing off a section of her shirt, she emptied the shells from her pockets, wrapped them up, and placed them at the foot of the tree where the weapons lay.

That finished, she turned toward the bog, the waters glimmering beneath the faint starlight shining down from above.

This is going to suck.

She stepped to the edge of the water, feeling her feet starting to stick in the thick mud. Then she lay down and rolled in the unpleasant muck – trying to coat every inch of herself. It was cold and vile to the extreme but in a pinch, nature provided the very best camouflage one could hope for ... so long as one didn't succumb to hypothermia first.

She coated her skin, her clothes, her hair, every part that could potentially stand out from the darkness of the surrounding woods, until she was certain that only the whites of her eyes could potentially give her away.

Finally, her teeth chattering from the cold mud

touching her everywhere, she clawed her way back to her feet and made to step away from the brackish water.

A bit of dirt fell into her eyes, obscuring her vision. As she tried to blink it away, her feet caught on something sticking out of the mud and she tripped over it, burying her face into even more of the muck.

She pushed herself up, silently cursing her clumsiness, and coughed the mud out of her mouth and nostrils.

All my training and I still trip over a log.

Except, it hadn't felt like a log. There'd been some give to it, a fact testified by her lack of stubbed toes. She was about to dismiss it as nothing more than a mound of mud, but could still feel the protrusion beneath her legs and it definitely felt more solid than just a lump of dirt.

Taking a few moments she didn't have, Danni began to feel around, expecting to find nothing more interesting than maybe a mound of rotting vegetation.

But then her hand closed upon something and she froze. Praying she was wrong, she felt further and confirmed it. Beneath the muck and grime lay what she was certain was the toe of a leather boot.

Momentarily forgetting the danger she was in, she began to dig with her fingers, using the feeble light from above as best she could. After several seconds, there was no denying she'd uncovered a pair of human legs at the edge of the water. The top half of the body was partially submerged in the bog.

Danni grabbed hold and pulled with everything she had. It was slow going, the mud as cold and slippery as ice, but she managed to drag the corpse from the water.

Please no, please no, please no!

She began to feel along the body with her hands, wiping away the muck as best she could, praying that she felt some deformity, anything that would tell her this wasn't one of her friends.

Pants, a waterlogged shirt... There was something around its waist – a belt with a knife scabbard. The weapon was still in its sheath. She drew it and held it up, the blade glinting in the meager starlight. It looked like a World War 2 Ka-Bar ... the same kind that Francis wore, a gift from his grandfather who had fought in the Pacific Theater.

"Oh God, no!"

Though it was too dark to know for certain, she had to be sure. She reached up until she found the body's face. Though muck-encrusted, the man's heavy beard was easily identified by touch.

She'd found one of her missing friends.

35

Grief, anger, shock, all of it fought for dominance inside of Danni's mind at the discovery of Francis's remains.

Sadly, he was beyond help, his body well in the grip of rigor mortis. Those murdering monsters had done this — killed him and taken her as little more than cattle.

Danni was tempted to scour the area for signs of Derek. As much as she didn't want to admit it, he'd likely met the same fate. Sadly, she also knew it was stupid. Trying to search the shore and surrounding bog in the dark was pointless. The only reason she'd found Francis was dumb luck. She could have easily walked past him and never seen him at all.

Searching for Derek would also leave her vulnerable, something none of her teammates would've wanted.

Still, it was hard for her to leave her friend's side. Derek might have been a sort of father figure since she'd joined the team but, if so, Francis had been a big brother to her. He and his wife had welcomed her into their lives with open arms as if they'd known her for years.

Her heart broke even further as she thought of Shakti.

Though different as two people could be, she and Francis had been dearly in love. The dead were beyond pain, but for the living, it would be just beginning. And the hurt would last for a long time. She knew that pain all too well, knew how long the wounds from her brother's death had remained raw and open.

She vowed to be there for her. But first she had to survive. There was no doubt in her mind that's what her teammates would want for her, even if she was the lone member to make it out of this.

And she had to wonder about that. With Francis and Derek gone, she realized just how alone she was. There was no telling if Mitch was out there somewhere searching for her or if he'd already tried, only to meet the same fate. Unfortunately, speculating either way was a bad idea, as it would inevitably lead her mind to dark places.

Though she knew her people wouldn't ever give up on her, she couldn't say the same for those who'd summoned them to this godforsaken state. The governor and his men were a joke, seeking to do nothing but cover this up. With them as her only *backup*, there was little doubt that she was on her own.

And that meant Sophie, still back at the compound, had no one but her to rely on.

Survival should have been the only thing on her mind, but the more she thought of her friends, Sophie, and any others still held prisoner, the more anger began to take the place of grief and fear.

Those sons of bitches. How many lives had they destroyed over the years? Tens, dozens, more?

Danni blinked away her tears just as something from off in the distance caught her eye – the briefest of illuminations through the trees. A trick of the light? Swamp gas?

She kept her eyes peeled in the direction it had come

from, the same she'd fled from. As she kept watch, her soiled lips pulled back from her teeth in a snarl.

There! This time it was unmistakable. The dim light from a lantern. They were coming.

She remembered back to Bonanza Creek, the feeling of being hunted – of being helpless as monsters pursued her. And now it was happening all over again.

No! Not this time.

In the space of a second, Danni made up her mind.

She took the knife and scabbard from Francis's body and strapped it to the belt she'd purloined from Adam's room. It wasn't long before all thoughts of survival were pushed to the side in favor of revenge.

They were getting close, he could feel it. Noah just hoped that Sarah had gotten tripped up on a snare again. If so, this would be easy. She'd be his and there wouldn't be any question about it this time. He'd take her home and make her his wife proper. But what if it wasn't a snare? If she'd run afoul of any of the other traps – set in a bid to keep strangers out of their lands – that would be bad. He'd likely be robbed of his rightful prize.

No matter. There was that other Sarah back at the compound, Though wed to Samuel, Noah's older cousin, his pa had taken a shine to her and she'd been brought to his bed more than once. But Pa was dead now. As for Samuel, he wasn't anything Noah couldn't handle. If his Sarah was stolen from him, he'd take his cousin's instead.

In fact, maybe he'd take them both.

Why not?

Noah glanced at Ezekiel in the darkness. His uncle thought he was stupid. Thought that because Noah was big and couldn't speak very well that he was a dullard. But there was nothing wrong with Noah's mind. In his head he spoke eloquently, but the gifts he'd been given were more for hunting and fighting than for giving a sermon.

It was a pity, because he used to listen with great aplomb to his father's stories about their ancestor and how he'd fooled the townspeople into leaving his kin alone through the use of his golden tongue alone. That was the type of power he truly wished for – to motivate men with nothing more than his words. But it wasn't to be.

He'd been blessed, as had others before him, with a form better suited to protecting their home and the woods surrounding it. He was strong, swift, and tough. But, despite all of that, he was already breathing heavily, his respiration thick and loud in the otherwise quiet woods. It was his one weakness – a lack of stamina – the lone cross the good Lord had burdened him with.

Though he'd never been to an actual doctor's office, on some level he was aware of the malformed lungs he'd been born with – too small to properly aerate his large body. That was the real reason he stayed at Ezekiel's side, not the older man's delusions of leading the clan.

No, only someone strong could lead the family. Noah wasn't stupid. He was well aware that he was the strongest, had been for some time. His pa had been strong too but, perhaps more importantly, the others respected him. It was that respect which had stayed Noah's hand. But now he was gone. The others respected Ezekiel too, but only as an elder, not a leader.

Once they found Sarah and brought her back home, he'd make his move. He'd show his kin, *all of them*, that he was the rightful heir to the family. If his uncle accepted that, so be it. If not, then Noah would snap his spine without a second thought as a warning to the rest.

Though it hurt his chest to do so, he quickened his pace, but then realized the others had slowed down up ahead. They'd reached the edge of their property, the hidden maze of surprises meant to trap or maim intruders. Though each of them had studied the map made each season as snares were moved and old traps replaced, it was still foolish to barrel through in the dark. But if it slowed them down, it would certainly slow Sarah even more so.

Noah coughed up a thick wad of phlegm, spat it out, then smiled.

His new bride was near. He could feel it. Near, alive, and ready to receive his seed so as to give birth to a new generation of his family.

Derek held up his hand for the others to stop as he leaned against a tree and tried to catch his breath. The exertion was taking its toll on him. He was either sweating more than usual or he'd reopened some of his wounds. It was hard to tell. But there was no turning back now. Even if it took his dying breath, he vowed to bring his people back safe ... if he was able to.

Mitch joined him after telling Julia and Arthur to hold their position and keep an eye out. "You okay?" he whispered.

"Peachy."

"I could give you a stimulant. That is, if you're in the mood to risk a heart attack."

"Is that the upside?"

"Not really. The upside is you could probably land-scape this entire forest before you dropped dead."

"Save it. We might need new careers after this is over."

"Seriously, are you all right?"

"Just waiting for my second wind," Derek replied, "but that's not the only reason I stopped. Check it out." He bent low and gestured for Mitchell to do the same. The red light of his headlamp illuminated a rope lying at ankle height across the path.

"Trip wire?"

"Not exactly military grade, but it doesn't need to be. Someone just hiking along would never see it, especially in the dark."

"Is this the spot where they ambushed you guys?"

"No. Pretty sure we're still a bit south."

They took a few moments to study the trap. Tripping over it would release a branch under tension, one with several sharpened stakes tied to it. It would be a nasty surprise to anyone unlucky enough to set it off.

Mitchell let out a low whistle. "These guys must have a lot of time on their hands to…"

"Hey, what's the holdup?"

Derek turned toward Julia. "We're getting close. From here on in, we go silent. No talking unless absolutely necessary. Headsets on, and nobody try to be a hero. That's a good way to die out here."

The oppressive darkness around them gave greater weight to the seriousness in Derek's voice. Neither she nor Arthur questioned him. As for the kid, he looked wide-eyed, the reality of the situation obviously starting to sink in, but so far, he was holding it together.

"Switch to channel 3, privacy code 19." Derek adjusted his radio and then turned on his Bluetooth ear piece. The rest all followed suit at his instruction. "I think we just passed the border into the Lesterfields' territory. From here on in, shit gets real. Last chance to back out."

"I think there's a new episode of *Game of Thrones* on tonight."

Derek narrowed his eyes at Mitchell, who smiled and held up his hands. "I'm just saying."

"I'm not leaving without my sister," Julia said.

The iron in her voice heartened Derek, but also worried him. "Rescue first, revenge later."

She didn't answer him, opting instead to check her gun again.

Arthur went to chamber a round in his weapon, but before he could pull the pump, Derek shook his head. "Not yet. Save it for when there's something to shoot at, and only if you need to. This isn't a video game."

The kid didn't look like he appreciated being talked down to but, rather than argue, he simply asked, "How do you know this is the place?"

"Everyone back up a bit." Derek stepped to the side and kicked out, triggering the trap.

The branch flew free, striking the area he and Mitchell had been standing in moments earlier.

Audible gasps escaped from their new teammates' lips at what could have befallen them.

"Any questions?" he asked into the stunned silence. Okay, good. Julia, you're right behind me. Then Arthur. Mitch, take up the rear. Oh, and everyone ... make sure to watch your step."

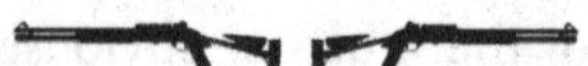

"Watch your fucking step!" Eric hissed as Bob stumbled into him, almost causing him to lose his footing on the muddy ground.

"Sorry, boss. I think I stepped in a gopher hole or something."

"Well, watch it. Last thing I want is you tripping and shooting me in the back."

"We should've brought the ATVs," Muellenberg griped from a few paces off to his right.

"I already told you," Eric replied, "they'd hear the engines coming from a mile off. Sound carries in the woods. Same with voices, so keep yours down and your lights pointed low. I don't want us giving away our position because we were too busy falling over our own fucking feet."

There were muttered acknowledgments all around. Eric had to admit, he was starting to rethink this plan. It was ridiculously easy to take a few steps in any direction and lose one's bearings in this shit show.

The professional in him had assumed this would be easy, no different than walking through a dark backyard. Hell, he'd watched enough survival shows on TV to think he had it all figured out. But the reality was proving to be different.

Even with their lights, it was oppressively dark. And that was only the start of it. The shadows played tricks with one's mind. More than once, a member of his group had pulled their sidearm and aimed it at what turned out to be nothing more than a tree.

Hell, even Eric wasn't immune. About fifteen minutes earlier, he'd turned his head and glimpsed what he could have sworn was a massive fur-covered figure staring at them from behind some tall bushes. It had taken every ounce of self-control he had to not scream. But when he looked again it was gone – nothing more than a figment of his imagination, or so he hoped.

They were all getting jumpy. He had to continually remind his men that they were there to find Jenner's crew and escort them the fuck out of the state, not blow them away on sight. That would be just his luck – for someone to shoot first, all because they were spooked of boogeymen lurking in the woods.

He couldn't entirely blame them, though. The urge to draw his gun and turn off the safety was almost overwhelming.

Eric took a moment to check the GPS on his phone.

No signal, but thankfully it was still triangulating via satellite. They were almost there, or at least he thought they were. He was giving it his best guesstimate. Either way, he hoped they were close.

The more they walked through this dark, damp hell, the angrier he got. Though Eric intended to do his job, he wouldn't have minded if that wannabe celebrity gave him enough shit to justify decking him across the jaw. Something like that would be extremely satisfying.

It was that thought which kept him going long after he wanted to call it a night and deal with the consequences tomorrow.

He was right in the middle of imagining pistol whipping the bastard upside the head for resisting arrest when Bob tripped into him again. This time, his foot caught on something and he lost his balance, falling forward and landing flat on his face.

Before he could right himself, he felt more than saw movement through the air immediately above him. There came a dull thud of something smacking into something else.

Barely a second later, the silence of the woods was torn asunder.

36

Danni's head spun at the sound. Someone was screaming, either in pain or surprise. The high pitch of the voice, however, made it difficult to tell whether it was male or female.

It wasn't far away, but the cries cut off quickly.

At first, she hoped one of the Lesterfields had stumbled into a trap she'd reset. There was just one problem with that; the scream had come from the opposite direction she expected.

Had they circled around her somehow? It was possible. But why bother? If they figured out how to get past her so as to cut her off, then they could have easily caught up to her by now. Also, she hadn't moved any traps in that direction.

Was it an owl or some other animal? It was easy to misidentify some cries as a human voice, but her gut was telling her that wasn't the case here.

Perhaps there were others out in the woods with her. But who? Was it a search party, or just some unlucky campers?

Danni was split. A part of her wanted to wait and see

if the Lesterfields decided to chase after the source of the screams, then make a run for it. But she couldn't get Sophie's or Abigail's faces out of her head, nor the utter horror of the place from where she'd just barely escaped.

If whoever was out there was male, they'd no doubt share the same fate as her friends, but for any women in the group ... what was waiting for them in these woods was worse than death.

That made up her mind. Much as she didn't want to leave the hiding spot she'd taken refuge in, she couldn't allow someone else to fall victim to these bastards.

However, before she could move, the decision was taken out of her hands as the sound of movement caught her attention. Branches cracked, followed by low voices. She couldn't make out the words, but it was definitely someone speaking, and they were coming from the direction she'd escaped from.

A moment later, she caught sight of light coming through the trees.

There was no way to get to the newcomers and remain unseen by the Lesterfields. Whichever of their awful clan it was, they seemed to be moving at a good clip, perhaps mistaking the cry in the woods for hers and thinking their quarry was near.

Danni huddled down in the hollow of the rotted-out tree she'd found close to the bog, hoping the mud covering her was enough to make her invisible in the darkness.

She held onto Francis's knife as she waited, the loaded shotgun also within reach. If they passed her by, she'd make her move. If not, she'd make certain her last stand was one they didn't soon forget.

"Hear that?" Ezekiel whispered. "Let's go."

The cry had come from somewhere up ahead. It hadn't lasted long, but he was certain that Sarah had run afoul of one of their traps. The only question now was what condition they'd find her in. Alive was good, but dead would at least sate his family's anger.

"Keep your eyes peeled," he told Jonathan.

The mute signed back at Ezekiel. He indicated the snares ahead and signaled that perhaps they should slow down.

Ezekiel waved him off, though. "Watch your footing, boys, but stay sharp. She's close, and we ain't letting her get away this time. You all with me?"

There came nods and grunts of approval from all around.

He turned back to where Noah stood, his head up as if he were sniffing the air. "How about you?"

"Want Sssarah."

"I think we all do," Ezekiel replied, barely concealed glee in his voice. None of the others were questioning him. That was good. "We move fast. Anyone gets tripped up, they can catch up."

Chuckles came from the clan members.

"Keep your weapons at the ready, but don't shoot unless you have to. She ain't getting out of this that easy."

There came more assent, louder this time, but he held up a hand. He didn't want them giving away their position prematurely if they didn't have to.

"Save it for when we find her. We have proper mourning to do, but that don't mean we can't have a party right afterwards."

Ezekiel heard Noah hiss from behind him, but turned and gave what he hoped was a reassuring glance back. Hopefully the boy had the brainpan to understand that he was just saying what was needed to motivate the rest.

They set out again, moving faster this time. Speed was

more important now, in case Sarah had merely been caught in a snare. She was a clever girl. He doubted she'd be kept hanging around for long.

Even if it didn't slow her down much, though, the odds were still heavily in their favor. These were his family's woods. They'd grown up here, hunted here, lived here. Even he, with a house in Shilough, could find his way back home practically blindfolded if need be.

He stepped high, knowing there was a trip wire close by, then sidestepped past where a bear trap had been laid.

Off to either side he watched as his family members likewise moved quickly and with purpose, their muscle memory taking over where their eyes failed...

Then there came a hiss of anger from behind him, followed by a heavy thump. Ezekiel spun on his heels, careful not to lose his step, and shined his lantern back the way they'd come.

What in God's name?

He wasn't sure whether he should laugh or be angry, but somehow Noah had managed to step in a snare. He was too heavy to be pulled into the air, but it had dragged his feet out from beneath him. The others weren't so generous. Hearty guffaws could be heard from all around him.

Ezekiel debated whether to go back and cut him down, but then remembered his words only moments earlier. Giving an order and then immediately countermanding it was likely to hurt the respect he was trying to instill for himself.

"Cut yourself loose and catch up," Ezekiel ordered. "And be more careful. You should know this place better than any of us." He turned without another word and followed the others. It was unlike Noah to be this sloppy. Of all the family, he'd been designated the protector of their lands. He should have been intimately familiar with every inch of these woods.

Ezekiel sighed and considered things. The boy was probably just over-excited by the prize which had been dangled in front of him.

But now he'd best get his head in the game. Perhaps this was just the motivation he needed to do that.

"What the..."

Derek turned and silenced Julia with a quick glance. He held her gaze, hoping to impart that discipline was absolutely necessary in what they were doing.

After a few more seconds she nodded, then silently mouthed, "Sorry."

The scream hadn't lasted long. Whoever it had come from had either been smart enough to know to shut their trap ... or had been killed quickly.

Mitchell stepped up, keeping his light low. "Pretty sure that came from east of here," he whispered.

Derek nodded. "That's what I was thinking, too. Close to where our base camp was."

"Think it's a coincidence?"

"Here, now? I doubt it."

"You think those idiots were actually stupid enough to come into the woods after us?"

"Never discount the power of politics. I'm more interested in whether they stumbled over something, or whether something stumbled into them."

They held position for a few more minutes, waiting to see if there came more cries, but all was quiet again.

"Do we go that way?" Arthur asked in a low voice before immediately shutting up again.

Derek thought hard about that. It was possible

someone was in trouble, but it was also just as likely they'd walk right smack dab into the people who were probably looking for them. He didn't think things would devolve into a gunfight, but he also wasn't about to surrender either – not after coming this far, and not with the fate of his friends still unknown.

Their objective, the place they'd been ambushed, lay north of their current location. After that, it was up in the air. He was hoping to find tracks, anything to give them a clue as to where the Lesterfields might be holed up.

Of course, his team's tracker was among the missing, which didn't help matters. Fortunately, he and Mitch had done this long enough that they'd picked up a few things via osmosis.

"No," he said after a few seconds of deliberation. "We have a mission to complete. We stick to that. If we don't find anything, then we can go and see who else is traipsing out here with us. Now quiet down and keep your ears open. I mean it this time. No giving away our position unless we find someone we're looking for."

Left unsaid was the possibility of finding *something* that was looking for them instead.

37

Fortunately, Hopper was on the ball. He stepped in before Eric could even get off the ground and clamped a hand over Bob's mouth, silencing the man's cries before every fucking squirrel in this forest knew where they were, much less Jenner's crew.

Bob was quietly whimpering by the time Eric stood up and shined his light on them. Muellenberg and Vasquez kept watch, guns drawn and flashlights scanning the forest while Hopper and Sullivan tended to the injured man.

The fuck?! Something had speared Bob. Thankfully, it hadn't been dead center, otherwise he'd probably be too busy nursing a sucking chest wound to cry out. Eric saw a wooden spike buried in the man's arm. It was secured to the branch which had apparently just missed him when he'd fallen.

There was no way this was an accident. He played his light out over the trap. Definitely manmade. A trip wire of some kind, like out of some fucking Vietnam war movie.

What the hell? Had Jenner set these up? Was he actively trying to kill them?

"It's in there pretty deep," Sullivan said after a few moments.

"Huh?"

"I said it's in there deep," he repeated.

"Can you patch him up?" Eric asked.

"With what?"

"What about that shit back at the camp?"

"You mean the stuff you ordered us to trash?" Hopper replied.

Eric was tempted to round on the man, but that wouldn't do any good. How were any of them to know this would happen? "Goddamn it! Can't believe those fuckers did this to us."

Bob had calmed down enough for Hopper to let him go. He was obviously still in a lot of pain, but was at least holding it together for now.

Hopper shone his light on the trap. "I don't know, Eric. This looks like it's been here for a while. Besides, why bother to stop and set it?"

"Because that son of a bitch is smart. He knew we'd come looking."

Hopper appeared as if he wanted to argue the point, but he simply nodded. "So what do we do about Bob?"

"Pretty sure he needs a doctor," Sullivan said. "I can tear off a sleeve and wrap that around it, but I don't know what else we can do. I'm no medic, but I'm fairly certain he could bleed out."

Eric turned and kicked at the rope which had been set across their path, now hanging limp on the ground. "Fuck!"

In one fell swoop, his grand plan had gone totally FUBAR. He was sorely tempted to call it a night, head back, and hand this off to the state troopers. Let them handle this shit. They'd eventually corral Jenner, but that still wouldn't save him from being chewed a new asshole by the governor. And now, with a man injured, that would give Yarlberg extra incentive to keep on chewing.

Going back emptyhanded was looking like a grim prospect, but an injured man was better than a dead one. He turned to Bob. "Camp's back that way. Think you can make it on your own?"

The wide-eyed look on the man's face told Eric what he thought of that idea.

Double fuck!

"I can take him if you want," Vasquez said. "Pretty sure I can find the way."

Eric's first instinct was to lay into him for being the first to puss out, but he stopped himself. Vasquez was right. Someone needed to keep an eye on Bob, get those ATVs up and running again, and get him to a hospital. Losing two men erased his numbers advantage, but maybe it wasn't as bad as he was making it out to be. Jenner's reinforcements were a college kid and a reporter. He'd be surprised to find them anything other than useless. No idea why Jenner had even brought them along, but that wasn't his concern.

He still had three trained men with him, all of whom knew how to shoot and at least one, Hopper, who seemed to have half a clue about being out in the woods. This could still work.

He turned to Vasquez. "Fine. Go with him. There's a hospital in Pomona. Call ahead and see if they can send an ambulance out to meet you."

"Gotcha. Should I go with him?"

Eric considered this. "No. You make sure he's okay, but then you haul ass back to the campsite and wait for us there. If Jenner and his crew show up, arrest their asses. If not, hold down the fort until you hear from us."

"Maybe we shouldn't have destroyed everything."

"And maybe you should have gone into a different line

of work. What's done is done. Bob, hand over your flashlight and extra ammo."

The injured man didn't seem overly pleased with that, but he did as told once Sullivan had bandaged him up as best he could. It wasn't pretty, but hopefully it would keep him alive until Vasquez could get him to the EMTs.

They handed over the parts for the ATVs and Eric wished them luck as they set off back the way they'd come, watching until the light from their lone flashlight disappeared from sight.

Hopefully the dumb bastards won't get lost.

He turned to the rest. "Let's keep moving. Eyes peeled for any more tricks. Shit just got real, boys. If he is trying to kill us, we're not going to give him the satisfaction of dying."

"What if he is?" Hopper asked.

"Then we teach him the error of his ways."

Eric turned back toward the dark woods ahead of them.

"Let's go get this bastard."

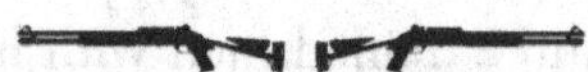

Jonas Yarlberg slammed down his phone. "Where the hell is everyone?"

It was after hours and most of his staff would be home by now. But he dialed his assistant Myra from the back of his car and commanded her to keep trying to reach Eric or anyone on his team, whatever their names were.

Myra insisted she'd do just that, although he was certain she was merely yessing him to death to get off the phone. That was the problem with the help these days — you couldn't trust anyone to do their job without looking over their shoulder.

This whole mess with Jenner was turning into far more

trouble than it was worth. Why the hell had he brought the man and his team in to begin with? Sure, the girl was a piece of ass, but she had a mouth on her. The rest were worthless so far as he could tell. That he'd actually thought for one minute there was an unexplained creature in the woods they needed *specialists* to deal with. He must have been losing his mind.

Jonas opened up the dry bar, pulled out a glass and a bottle of bourbon, then poured himself a generous splash.

He ordered the driver to take him home, but via the scenic route. Hopefully his wife and kids would be long asleep by the time he got there. He was in no mood to deal with them either.

Eric's job had been a simple one: make sure those assholes got out of his state. How hard was that to follow? Yet, for some reason, none of them were answering his calls. He'd sent a police cruiser back to the university to check on them, but there was no sign of his people, Jenner, or any of them, for that matter.

Jonas supposed it was possible they were doing their job and escorting the so-called Crypto-Hunter back to whatever fucking rock he'd crawled out from under. But why the radio silence, and to him of all people?

It made no sense unless something had gotten fucked up and Eric was trying to clean up a mess without his knowing.

Stupid son of a bitch. He's not paid to think!

Jonas considered his options. He could get out in front of this and order a press conference, but that was likely to lead to several uncomfortable questions, especially since he'd welcomed Jenner as a celebrity guest just a few days ago.

The press would likewise get wind of any APBs put out.

He knew he should probably trust his men to do their job, but the current silence was enough to drive him nuts.

Jonas poured another drink and tried to convince himself that all of this was nothing. What could a second-rate TV star do to him, even one with connections in Washington? There was that reporter, but she'd already been warned. He had no problem stepping on her if she made even the slightest peep in his direction.

It was probably nothing to worry about. Definitely nothing that could hurt him or his chances for reelection. It was a minor blip on his radar. Something to distract him from the bigger issues plaguing the state, nothing more.

But, try as he might, something in the back of his head worried him about this situation.

Much as he hated to admit it, he found himself hoping that the silence continued indefinitely. That nothing was ever heard again of either party, but especially from Jenner and his team. If they went missing without a trace, it would simply be one more unsolved mystery – something for the next cable TV show to do an episode on, but nothing that could hurt him.

Yes, he considered, downing a hearty slug of bourbon. Such an outcome wouldn't bother him in the least.

It was all Danni could do to not grab the shotgun and immediately open fire when the first of the Lesterfields stepped into view. A voice in her head screamed that, after everything she'd been through, taking down even one of them before they could converge on her would be a victory.

She managed to ignore it, remembering her team's last hunt and how she'd almost been mauled by the Thunderbird – all because she'd acted rashly. She'd gotten lucky and her teammates had been there to pull her ass out of the fire, but now she had only herself. One stupid move and this would be all over.

The worst part was perhaps the fact that getting killed didn't frighten her nearly as much as being taken prisoner again. There was no doubt in her mind she'd used up whatever bit of luck fate had granted her. The Lesterfields were unlikely to give her a second chance. They'd broken the spirits of those they'd captured, but that didn't mean they couldn't do worse if they were angered enough.

Danni forced herself to stay her hand. She closed her eyes to the barest of slits and remained still. The hunch-backed man who'd emerged from the woods was a good thirty feet away, his lantern making him stand out like a beacon. But just because she could see him didn't mean the opposite was true. Let him make the first move, prove he saw where she was hiding. Then she'd act.

For now, she remained unmoving – no matter how much the mud made her skin crawl, no matter how great the desire to run.

The man stepped closer and Danni readied herself. If he got close enough without spotting her, she'd use the knife then dump his body into the brackish water. Let his family wonder what happened to him just as she'd been forced to wonder about her friends before learning the awful truth.

Twenty feet away, then fifteen. Danni was certain he saw her. How could he not? But she knew that was her mind playing tricks on her. She'd learned as much during her training. It was little more than transference, assuming that since she knew where she was, everyone else did, too. But she understood all too well that one could practically step on a properly camouflaged opponent and not realize it. Unfortunately, it was an easier lesson to heed on a training exercise than when one was being hunted by mutated monstrosities intent on rape or worse.

The hunchbacked man turned her way and seemed to be staring right at her, although she couldn't tell for certain. His face was in shadow now, thanks to the lantern he held up.

Danni held her breath, praying that she was right, yet her hand tightened its grip on the knife nevertheless.

The hunchback started to take another step toward her when a sound further out in the woods startled him.

He spun, weapon raised, but then blew out a breath as someone else stepped from the bushes carrying a gun but no light source. The hunchback's lantern was old and dim, but it was enough to see that the newcomer was disfigured every bit as badly, maybe even worse. Half his face was overgrown and misshapen. An exaggerated eye peered out from it, open and staring, seeming to almost glow with a light of its own.

"Goddamnit, Jonathan!" the first snapped, spitting onto the ground at the newcomer's feet. "I almost blew your idiot brains out."

The second man, Jonathan apparently, pointed off in the direction Danni had heard the scream originate from. He then gestured in some way she didn't quite understand.

"Yeah, I know. You don't have to tell me. Don't wander off. Gonna be a hell of a show for you all if I need to squat and take a shit."

Jonathan again pointed and the hunchback sighed in disgust. "Okay, I got it. Don't be a prick. Last I checked, you ain't running the show."

The first man stalked off into the woods, walking past Danni's spot. She could hear his footsteps fading as he headed east.

Come on. Get going!

As if defying her thoughts, Jonathan stood where he was and surveyed the area with his strange, bulging eye.

Danni's guts compacted and she froze, becoming as still as she could. Though she couldn't be sure, the deliberate way this bastard was examining the area gave Danni the impression he could see with far greater clarity than the one with the lantern could.

Despite the unlikeliness of his oversized eye giving him some sort of superior night vision, it seemed prudent to pretend that the boogeymen under the bed were real. Her lungs began to ache from holding her breath, but she forced herself to remain still, willing herself to be nothing more than a lump of mud beneath a rotted-out tree.

Please leave.

Rather than do as she hoped, Jonathan turned toward her – his eye, still visible despite the lack of a light source, wide and staring. It was like being stalked by some mythical cyclops. Danni's heart froze as he took a step toward her.

He came closer and she began to fear that he'd see her before stepping into striking range. If that happened, he'd have her dead to rights. There was no way she'd be able to retrieve the shotgun before he opened fire.

Just as her nerve was about to break, he turned and cocked his head to the side.

He abruptly changed direction, walking toward the edge of the bog where Francis lay. That was apparently what he'd spotted. Jonathan looked down at the body which Danni had cleaned off as best as she could. It had been a mere show of respect on her part, but it seemed now that perhaps it allowed her friend to save her one last time.

Jonathan kicked at the body once. Then it was Danni's turn to open her eyes wide, this time in rage, as he slung his rifle over his shoulder and unbuttoned his pants. A moment later, the bastard began to urinate on her friend's remains.

Danni would have been happy to let him walk away before this, but what he was doing infuriated her. It was bad enough they'd killed poor Francis, but to show the utter disdain of defiling his body was too much for her.

Knife in hand, she crept out of her hiding spot before she was even fully aware she was doing it. The Lesterfields might have the advantage in numbers, but this one was alone, separated from the pack. She crept quickly but quietly behind Jonathan as he continued to relieve himself.

Sadly, the ground near Francis was little more than thick muck. Silent as she tried to be, she couldn't completely mask the sucking noise her foot made when she misstepped and came down on a semi-solid patch of ground that was more mud than dirt.

Jonathan Lesterfield's head perked up at the sound and he spun to meet her challenge.

38

Chris Hopper was doing all he could to mask his glee at watching Eric's slow disintegration.

The guy was a tool, completely unfit to lead a security detail, much less this midnight jaunt through the woods. It was a near miracle that Bob hadn't been killed outright when their idiot boss had stepped on that trip wire.

That right there should have ended this farce. Sometimes you just had to suck it up and admit you'd been duped. Mind you, the duping was already an exercise in incompetence – letting Jenner and his team slip away from right under their noses.

He didn't like Yarlberg anymore than the rest of his teammates, but knew there was a good chance there would be some turnover when this was done. As the next most senior member, he could claim he'd done what he could, but by the time he'd been called in the situation had already been beyond help. Best of all, it was the truth. No sugar-coating needed. If pressed, he was pretty sure the others would back him up.

At the end of the day, Eric had no tact whatsoever.

That was fine for a lone gig as a bodyguard, but for a state official's security detail, it was intolerable. The man had made an enemy of Jenner and his people roughly thirty seconds after they'd met. It should have surprised exactly no one when he ran.

But instead they were out here, tromping through the dark woods with pretty close to zero chance of finding anyone who didn't want to be found...

Or maybe not.

"I think there's someone up ahead," Eric called out in a harsh whisper. "Lights down and spread out. Let's surround these fuckers and get out of here."

Hopper spat in disgust. The moron was getting desperate. Probably heard a deer and suddenly got delusions of grandeur. Chances were they'd spread out and then have to spend the next hour finding each other again.

But that wasn't his problem. Let his boss dig his own grave.

Hopper did as told, fanning out. He kept his light low, more to make sure he didn't stumble over anything like his boss had, but his weapon remained holstered. No way was he going to be held responsible for accidentally shooting one of his own people. He intended to keep his nose clean for this one. When Eric inevitably returned empty-handed, Hopper was hoping the governor would see the wisdom in changing the guard.

And there would definitely be changes made under his leadership. No more acting like macho assholes just for the sake of it. He'd make sure they picked their battles like adults, not like testosterone-fueled teenagers.

He was still mentally rehearsing what he'd say in the private audience he planned to request with the governor, so was caught off guard when he heard what sounded like someone walking up ahead.

Idiots already got themselves turned around.

"That you, Sullivan?" he asked with no real sense of worry. Even if it wasn't, what would happen? Despite the bullshit theories the governor had put forth, he didn't think Jenner was out here playing government assassin. Of course, he didn't buy the other man's excuse of what had happened either.

Chances were the truth was somewhere in between: a bad accident or someone had screwed up. And now Jenner was out here trying to retrieve his friends' bodies before the local wildlife picked them clean.

That made the most sense. It was unlikely that anything else...

"You ain't Sarah."

Hopper spun toward the voice, raising his flashlight. He caught a brief glimpse of a misshapen face – puffy, discolored, and with a massive overbite – before the light was yanked out of his hands.

He reached for his gun, but his shock had slowed him. Before he could unstrap the weapon at his side, a powerful hand reached out and covered his mouth. Hopper was forced back against a tree, as a knife – sharp as a razor – slid into his belly and emptied his guts onto the ground.

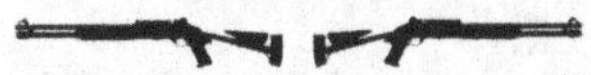

Derek sensed something was wrong long before he saw it. It wasn't so much what he heard as what he didn't. The forest, loud and alive before now, had gone dead silent. No crickets, no birds. It was as if everything had retreated into hiding, hoping to remain unnoticed by whatever was occurring up ahead.

He held up a hand and this time, no one said anything. They'd probably all realized something was off on some level or another in the sudden oppressive silence.

No, not entirely silent.

He heard something from up ahead – the crackle of a branch, the crunch of leaves. There wasn't enough of a breeze to be doing it. He immediately discounted any wildlife, as they seemingly had enough sense to lay low.

More movement, this time from a different location – even accounting for any sound distortion playing tricks with his senses. Derek hunkered down low, motioning for the rest to stay where they were. Then, as quietly as he could, he sucked up the pain from his injuries and slowly crawled past some bushes to get a better look ahead.

He was on a small rise, affording him a slightly better view through the trees than he might otherwise have – or it would have if it wasn't so dark. He was about to look through his rifle's night scope when he spotted several lights among the trees ahead. They were all held low, but Derek got the impression of two opposing lines converging on each other.

He raised the scope to his eye for a better look and began to scan for signs of movement.

It was only a few seconds before a head appeared above the bushes. Whoever they were, they weren't dressed for the outdoors. Between the distance and the foliage, it was hard to tell, but he could have sworn he saw a tie hanging from the man's neck.

Shit! Did that idiot Zeist actually follow us out here?

Derek wasn't able to ID the man, but there didn't seem to be any other explanation. Who else would be out here dressed in a fucking suit of all things? Zeist must have come looking for them upon noticing them missing. He hadn't even bothered to stop and let his people properly outfit themselves first.

It was the height of stupidity, but then, the guy's boss wasn't exactly a paragon of logic and practicality. He sincerely doubted the governor possessed the patience for a proper manhunt.

Derek realized he should have been grateful for that. With him slowed due to his injuries, that left Mitch as the sole member of the team who was both fully mobile and capable. Had Yarlberg sent experienced men after them, they would have had little trouble catching up.

It was fairly easy to surmise that Zeist was probably tracking them via the GPS coordinates that had been previously shared. Reasonably smart, but easily anticipated.

He was just about to lower his scope and return to the others when more movement caught his eye – something in the bushes just north of the man's position.

Heeding his gut, he zoomed in on that spot, hoping it was nothing more than an animal. But then Derek saw a large man step from the bushes, a rifle slung behind his back and a machete in hand. The arm wielding the blade was lumpy and misshapen, as was the rest of the man's body. There was no doubt in Derek's mind. It was one of the Lesterfields and he was trying to flank Zeist's man.

No, not trying. The security agent appeared to have no clue he was being stalked. Derek watched in mute horror as the agent's would-be murderer came up behind him, moving deliberately but quietly as well.

The misshapen man's profile was to Derek. He lined up the side of his head in his crosshairs, but then hesitated. Shooting him would save the life of one of Zeist's men, but it would give his team's position away, and he doubted this was the only member of the Lesterfield clan out in the dark woods this night.

But why?

He could understand Zeist and his people being out here, but why the Lesterfields? Surely their booby traps could dissuade a group of unwary trespassers. Was this typical behavior of them, patrolling their territory after dark?

Derek considered the two lines of lights converging on each other. There was a deliberateness to it. Had the Lesterfields been aware of the incursion, much as they'd been when Derek and his team had first gone in? Or were they out here for a different reason?

Was it possible that his friends were not only alive, but one or both had managed to give those bastards the slip?

It seemed too much to hope for.

But if so, then it would be in Derek's best interest to remain unseen, so as to slip past both groups and search the surrounding woods for Danni and Francis.

The mutated son of a bitch was nearly upon Zeist's man. Another few seconds and it would be all over. If done right, the victim wouldn't even have a chance to scream and alert his teammates.

But then Derek remembered his hesitation to pull the trigger when the devil had spoken to them. It had resulted in them being caught unawares. In showing mercy, he'd potentially doomed his friends, and in doing so again, he'd likewise be responsible for the death of another man. Zeist was an asshole so far as he was concerned, but that didn't mean his people should die.

That settled it. Derek centered his shot, let out a breath, and squeezed the trigger ... unleashing death into the surrounding woods, as well as the chaos that would follow.

39

Noah Lesterfield was trying to catch up to his family when he saw Jonathan veer off in another direction. There was a bog that way, the same one where they'd ambushed those strangers and captured his Sarah.

But there was nothing there now save for perhaps the bodies of the two males – useless to the clan for anything except target practice.

He heard a muffled curse coming from the direction Jonathan had gone, impossible as the man was a mute. Noah hissed and prepared to charge, but then his cousin Samuel stepped from the bushes ahead and turned east. A false alarm. The dimwitted fool had probably just wandered off to take a dump or something.

Noah swallowed a heavy gulp of air and prepared to follow. He didn't fancy his kin finding Sarah first. If their anger was still burning hot enough, they'd kill her. If their dander was up, they might instead decide to throw her down into the dirt and take turns with her. Neither would make him happy. She was to be his and his alone.

He'd only had a woman once before – a lumpy,

unpleasant-looking thing who his father decided to share with him out of pity. The others had gathered around to watch, but in his nervousness, he couldn't finish. Then there'd been the laughter. Bad enough from his family, but she had spit in his face once he climbed off her in defeat. Such disrespect wasn't tolerated among his clan. That particular Sarah hadn't lasted long, not even long enough to take seed.

But he didn't want that fate for *his* Sarah. He planned to enjoy her in the privacy of his own den – take his time, get to know her right. And he didn't fancy the idea of the others getting to her first.

He began to follow after his cousin, but then stopped.

Where was Jonathan? He should have been hot on Samuel's trail. There was no reason for him to still be at the bog – unless he knew something the others didn't, saw something the rest of them had missed, and wanted to keep it for himself.

Noah growled deep within his chest.

If he found Jonathan with Sarah, *his* Sarah, they were going to be burying three family members this night. It didn't matter. More would be born to take their place. His father had taught him that much. It had always been that way, ever since his family laid claim to the abandoned paper mill they'd called home for generations.

Yes, that was the way of his family, now and for...

A booming *crack* of sound ripped through the woods – a gunshot, from the direction Samuel had headed in. Too high-pitched to be the shotgun Sarah had stolen from his pa. It was someone else firing at something, or *someone*.

Sarah!

Noah glanced toward where Jonathan disappeared, considered things for a moment, then turned toward the direction of the shot. If they hurt his Sarah before he'd gotten his rightful taste of her, there was going to be hell to pay.

Marcus Sullivan felt the warm, wet splatter against the back of his head before he heard the gunshot. He practically jumped out of his skin, spinning so fast he almost tripped over his own two feet. The sight that met his flashlight upon turning was nearly enough to make him piss himself.

He wasn't sure what was worse – that someone had appeared behind him as if out of thin air or that half that person's head was missing. Marcus stepped robotically toward the still-twitching body and realized he was wrong. The *worst* part was the man's appearance, if he even was a man. Even discounting the fatal head wound, he looked wrong. His body jutted out at all sorts of crazy angles, and his skin looked more like a tumorous mass gone wild than actual flesh.

An old rifle was slung across the intruder's back, but it was what lay in the man's grasp that caused Marcus's bladder to finally let go – a rusty machete.

Was that meant for me? There couldn't be any other explanation. Why sneak up on him otherwise?

Realization began to dawn as he continued to study the body. Over six feet tall and heavily disfigured, a true monstrosity of a man.

Holy shit. Jenner was right.

Too late he heard the sound of branches snapping. He spun, bringing up his weapon just as a bright light was shined in his face. "Stop, or I'll..."

"Jesus Christ, it's me, you idiot!"

"Eric?"

"Who else?"

Eric lowered his light, and Marcus blinked the spots from his eyes. He didn't think he'd ever been so glad to see his boss. "Thanks, man! You saved my ass from ... whatever the fuck this thing is."

Eric frowned from over his flashlight. "That wasn't me. I thought one of you guys was shooting at shadows or something. I ... what the fuck is that?"

Both men stared down at the corpse for several long seconds. Finally Eric asked, "Is that what I think it is?"

"The Jersey Devil? No idea, but whatever it is, I'm pretty sure hell puked it up."

For several seconds Eric was silent, something that was entirely out of character for him. "I'm not a praying man, Sullivan, but I might have to agree with you there."

"You know what this means, right?"

His boss nodded. "I guess Jenner wasn't full of shit." After a moment, he straightened up. "Still doesn't change our job. We need to find him and his yahoos and get their asses out of Dodge. The governor can decide if he wants to rethink his stance once he sees ... *this*."

"You think one of the others got him? Maybe Hopper?"

Eric shook his head. "If they did, then why haven't they come and checked? Hell, I heard that shot and my first thought was to hit the deck and open fire myself. You're just lucky I saw your light first."

"Then who took the shot? Do you think it was...?"

"Probably. They're the only other idiots stupid enough to be out here with us. I'm betting our invisible benefactor is feeling pretty smug about himself right now."

"He saved my ass."

"You think I don't know that? We still have a job to do."

Marcus watched his boss cup his hands around his mouth, probably readying to shout for Jenner to come out and surrender. But then he remembered what else they'd dismissed as nothing more than a bullshit story.

He grabbed his boss's hands and pulled them down before the man could speak.

"What the hell, Sullivan?"

"Don't forget the rest of what Jenner told us."

"Listen, Mark. I know you're shook up. I think we all are. Trust me, I'm probably going to be checking under my bed for the next month, but don't go all..."

"It's not that," Marcus hissed, his eyes opening wide. "Remember what else he said ... that whatever attacked him, it wasn't alone."

Eric glared at him hard, but before he could say anything further, the forest came alive with the sound of leaves crunching, twigs snapping, and – perhaps most terrifying – footsteps headed their way.

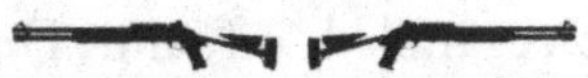

"So much for subtle."

Derek shot Mitchell a look before motioning for the rest to follow him as he cut a perpendicular path through the trees, hoping to throw off anyone trying to triangulate where his shot had come from.

He was moving slowly but purposefully, partially to keep an eye out for more traps, but mostly because he wasn't able to move much faster. The kick from the high-powered rifle hadn't been kind to his existing injuries.

Julia caught up with him after a few minutes.

"Not now."

"Yes, now," she whispered. "What happened?"

"I saw one of the things that ambushed us."

"So you decided to pick it off, just like that?"

"He was going after one of Eric's men."

"And you didn't let it?" Derek threw her a glare to

which she quickly replied, "I'm kidding, okay? Well, mostly, anyway. Those guys are bastards."

"Bastards who've bitten off far more than they can chew. That still doesn't mean we should be feeding them to the lions."

"They'll arrest us if they get half a chance."

"Maybe, but the enemy of my enemy is my friend ... and right now, I'd trust the devil I know versus the one who took my friends."

Julia appeared as if she wanted to say more, but she simply nodded and fell back to Mitchell's position. Derek heard her ask, "This just got more complicated, didn't it?"

"Pretty much par for the course in this job," Mitchell replied. "Thinking on your feet is kinda the number one job requirement ... that and shooting straight. Speaking of which, Arthur, make sure you don't have that gun aimed at my..."

Mitchell's voice trailed off and Derek instinctively slowed down. He knew that tone. Had heard it before.

"Arthur?" Derek stopped and turned. Mitchell had already fallen back a few steps. "Hey, kid?"

Son of a bitch!

Derek backtracked to where his teammate now stood. "Where'd he go?" Then he held up a hand. "Yeah, I know, if you knew that, you wouldn't be calling for him."

"He was just here."

"Do you think someone grabbed him?"

"Doubt it. I didn't hear a thing. I was sure he was right behind me. Hold on a sec." Mitchell tapped his Bluetooth earpiece. "Arthur, are you there? Come in." He tried a few more times, but no answer came. "The hell?"

Derek considered things. Heading back was stupid. He had little doubt someone — be they Lesterfield or government security — would soon be converging on their previous location. He'd used up the advantage of surprise. The only thing they had going for them was that their quarry didn't know how many of them there were or how well-armed.

Problem was, even with all of their firepower, Derek knew they'd be outgunned if the Lesterfields were out in force.

The smarter course was to continue on their way, hopefully flank the Lesterfields and trace their trail back to wherever they'd likely taken his friends.

Assuming they've taken them anywhere.

Derek pushed that thought from his mind. It wasn't helping. Besides, there was still the burning question left from what he'd seen a few minutes earlier. Were those bastards out here hunting Zeist and his crew, or was there another reason?

He chose to believe the latter. If there was anyone who could have escaped from their clutches and given them a run for their money, it was one of his team.

Of course, finding them was still the issue ... a veritable needle in this haystack of a forest.

Make that two needles.

Yeah, the smarter option was to continue on their current path, hope the kid got lucky and stayed off everyone's radar, and try to find him afterwards. Smart, but not right.

"What do we do?" Julia asked.

Derek looked at the others. "We find him, of course. Lights low and keep your voices down. We're likely going to be targets enough without drawing more attention to ourselves."

Mitchell and Julia both nodded grimly in the darkness.

As a team, they turned and headed back in the direction they'd come.

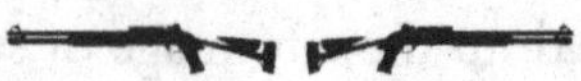

Arthur could have kicked himself. He'd just wanted to take a look, see one of those things with his own eyes. The data that had come back on those secretions had been utterly insane. From the amount of toxins that the samples had shown, there should have been no way for these people – a term best applied loosely – to have survived infancy. Yet somehow, they had. It wasn't pretty – if what Dr. Jenner said was true – but this family had not only survived but thrived, even if they'd become walking monstrosities in the process.

The thing was, they were medical marvels, too, a testament to the adaptability of the human species in a hostile environment. Once this was over, he'd be buried under a mountain of paperwork, forced to keep his mouth shut. Even if not, who was going to believe a crazy story about toxic inbred mutations? That was B-movie material at best. He kind of wished he'd made copies of the genetic screen when he'd had the chance. Not that it would've helped his cause much. People would just think he'd falsified the results and, with little more than his personal testimony to back him up, he'd be a laughing stock, finished in his field before he even got a chance to truly start in it.

But still, he'd wanted to see for himself if only to know the truth. So when Derek had led the others away, he'd taken a moment to fall back so as to try to take a quick peek. Arthur slung the shotgun off of his shoulder, momentarily getting the strap caught up on the items clipped to his belt. He gave it a yank to free it, then raised the night scope to his eye.

There was definitely movement somewhere up ahead, but he was neither experienced enough with the equipment nor patient enough to focus and wait. Instead, he used the scope to quickly scan the surrounding area, only realizing he'd turned himself around – losing his bearings in the process – once he'd finished.

He had no idea where the others were or how far they'd gotten. Unfortunately, for him at least, Dr. Jenner knew what he was doing. So there was no sound of their movement through the forest for him to home in on. There was barely any sound at all, except maybe what he was making.

Arthur briefly considered shouting for help, but even a newb such as him knew that would be the height of stupidity. They weren't alone out there. The last thing he wanted to do was make himself a sitting duck for unfriendly company.

Truth be told, Arthur wasn't a fan of the outdoors. He barely liked going outside to use the swimming pool at his parents' home. But that didn't mean he was an idiot. He'd watched enough TV to know that the smartest thing to do in a situation like this was to stay where he was and wait for rescue. Problem was, that assumed nothing bad was looking for whoever was lost.

He realized he didn't have that luxury.

Though he desperately wanted to see the creatures these Lesterfields had *evolved* into, he was far more interested in making sure Danni was safe. When he'd met her, she'd been little more than a personal crush of his – perky, charismatic, and so freaking hot. However, he'd been amazed to find out she was an awesomely cool person in real life. They'd gotten along – kind of hit it off, even. Arthur wasn't delusional that anything would come of it, but he was hopeful that he'd made a new friend. She kind of struck him as a person who could have used one.

Of course, nothing was going to come out of it if he got caught standing out here with his thumb up his ass.

Arthur considered things. He had little clue how to survive in the woods, much less track anyone. But he wasn't in any danger from the elements and had a full canteen of water with him. And, perhaps best of all, he was armed and had been given just enough training to know how to use the weapons he had. He could defend himself if need be.

That settled it. He took a guess on the direction that Dr. Jenner and the others had gone and set off that way, hoping that he didn't come across anything of a less friendly nature first.

Soon, all became silent once more, save for the small voice calling Arthur's name from the radio he'd accidentally dislodged from his belt.

40

Ezekiel Lesterfield wasn't entirely sure what was going on, and that bothered him. They'd been following what he was certain was Sarah's trail, expecting to find and capture her in short order.

Then they'd heard the scream and spotted lights through the trees up ahead. They weren't alone. More intruders were invading their territory – most likely a group of unwary campers. He doubted it was a search party. They'd have called it quits before it got dark. Besides, from the look of things, it was too few people and too haphazard.

No matter the case, they wouldn't be allowed to leave. Not if there was a chance that Sarah could get to them, too.

He'd sent a few of the boys ahead to scout out these trespassers and deal with them if the opportunity presented itself. Any females would be kept, added to their flock. The rest, well, their bodies would never be found.

It was a distraction from hunting Sarah, but a necessary one.

Then he heard the gunshot. They all did. The thing

was, it hadn't come from the intruders up ahead but from somewhere south of their location. For a moment, he feared they'd somehow walked into a trap in their own backyard, but how was that even possible?

The only explanation that made sense was Sarah. She'd seen these newcomers, too, but rather than run to them, she'd set an ambush.

That thought chilled Ezekiel to his bones. It bespoke of a cold-bloodedness he would never have expected from her. But perhaps he should have. She had, after all, already murdered two of his kin this night. One was luck, easy enough to dismiss. Two was desperation. But three? Those weren't the actions of some two-bit bikini hussy from the TV. Sarah was acting like a killer, one who knew what she was doing.

Ezekiel began to wonder whether it was all worth it. No matter how badly Noah wanted her, she might be too much trouble. At the very least, they'd need to hobble her arms and legs, make sure the rest of her days were spent as a cripple. He couldn't recall ever having to do that before with another of the clan's wives. Noah almost certainly wouldn't be pleased, but that was his cross to bear.

Though he was unsure how to handle this latest development, he also knew inaction wasn't an option, not with the others following his lead. Whatever happened, he couldn't let the intruders ahead of them escape. There was no doubt they'd heard the gunshot, too. If they had a lick of sense between them, they'd be turning tail and running as fast as they could back the way they'd come.

Ezekiel quickly and quietly rallied the clan members still near him. He sent half of them up ahead – no waiting, no caution – to hit these trespassers hard and with finality.

The rest he sent after Sarah. Let them flush her out and deal with her as they would. If they killed her, then that would be on them, not him.

Within moments, he found himself standing alone. Though he knew these woods well, he wasn't used to the feeling of being watched. Knowing that Sarah was out there somewhere, armed and with no qualms about fighting back, frightened him.

Ezekiel was neither the bravest nor strongest of the Lesterfield clan. Fear wasn't unknown to him. But from a woman?

He pulled his revolver from his side, backed up against the trunk of a nearby white cedar, and crouched down low so as to not present an easy target. The only thing to do now was wait.

Let the others take care of this. He was their new leader and as such wasn't about to put himself at undue risk.

Danni twisted the knife in Jonathan Lesterfield's back. She knew it was unnecessary. The movements he made were all involuntary, the last twitches of his nerves as they shut down. But she did it again anyway, unwilling to give this monster any quarter or leave any doubt that he was dead.

He'd spun toward her as she'd come up from behind, but the same mud which had given away her position proved to be his undoing. He had lost his footing on the slick muck. It was for the barest of instants, but more than enough for her to strike.

Danni had been on him before he'd even hit the ground. Oddly, he made no sound, gave no protest, as she'd plunged the knife into his body, again and again, his struggles quickly turning into nothing more than a death rattle.

All she could picture was Francis's face and how this

bastard had tried to defile his body – as if what they'd done to him hadn't been bad enough.

She pulled the knife out and prepared to bring it down once more, just to be safe, when she heard the gunshot.

Spooked as Danni already was, she immediately threw herself into the space between the two bodies. Several seconds later, she slowly lifted her head, certain it would be blown off, but no more gunfire came.

Were the Lesterfields shooting at shadows? Or had they found whoever had been screaming earlier?

She didn't dare to hope that someone was out there looking for her, but that hope bloomed nevertheless. It was a dangerous thought at a time like this, bringing with it the potential to make her do something stupid.

It was also possible that it was all little more than a trap by the Lesterfields, something to draw her out while they waited to ambush her. If so, it wasn't going to work. The only way she was going to get out of this was if she kept her wits about her, and that meant playing this game by her rules.

But that didn't mean she wasn't still scared out of her mind. Though knowing it was pointless and overkill, she turned over Jonathan Lesterfield's corpse, preparing to drive the Ka-Bar through his throat if he so much as twitched.

There came no movement, though. His oversized, misshapen eye stared sightlessly up at the stars, that odd glow gone from it – no more threatening than a doll's eye.

Danni rooted through his pockets but found nothing of use except a few spare bullets. His gun looked to be slightly newer than the one she'd taken from Nathanial, but it was now completely caked with muck. She had neither the time nor inclination to clean it out. However, it was foolish to leave it for his family to find. She sunk the old rifle in the bog, then rolled Jonathan's body into the thick, muddy water. Rotting in a marsh was better than he deserved, so far as she was concerned.

There were now three less of this accursed clan to terrorize these woods, but in taking Jonathan down, she realized she'd most likely used up all the protection this location offered her. If they came back looking for their missing member, there was enough evidence left for an experienced woodsman to piece together what had happened.

She needed to get moving again.

The Lesterfields were ahead of her now, so the smart thing would have been to head back to the compound to free Sophie and anyone else held prisoner. Yet the thought of returning there alone, of being caught and caged again, terrified her to the point of inaction.

Much as Danni hated herself for it, Sophie would have to wait.

The rest of these bastards had their backs to her now. It was a mistake they'd regret.

Another shot rang out in the distance, different in pitch to the last. A pistol, maybe?

Mere moments later, the silence of the forest was shattered with the sound of gunfire. Multiple shots rang out, all seeming to come from different directions.

It was an impossible dream, but the more Danni listened, the more she became convinced that there was a gunfight going on. She wasn't alone out there after all. Even if they weren't specifically searching for her, they couldn't be worse than the devil she knew.

The problem was the Lesterfields still held home field advantage. She needed to reach whoever was out there before it was all over, because she had a sinking sensation about which side would eventually prevail otherwise.

41

Eric was well aware that he could be rash and overly temperamental, but he didn't consider himself a stupid man.

A part of him still refused to believe there was a family of monsters out in these woods, monsters who thought like men. The problem with that theory was the dead body lying at their feet.

"Boss?" Sullivan asked from beside him, his sidearm out and ready.

Eric briefly considered the rifle slung over his back, liberated from Jenner's SUV. He knew it was more powerful, especially out here where there was no shortage of obstructions, but he was a lot more familiar with his 9mm semi-automatic. Knew it like the back of his hand. It was quick, reliable, and fast to reload. In a shit situation, like the one rapidly headed their way, he'd sooner rely on it than risk fucking things up while he fumbled with a rifle sight.

It was possibly just Hopper and Muellenberg returning. But whatever was approaching their position sounded like more than two men.

Eric drew his pistol and fired a shot into the air. "Only warning you're going to get," he cried out. "Stand down!"

His voice was steady, belying the fact that he was afraid, something that almost never happened in his day to day job. The urban jungle was his territory, not this shit. All at once, it hit home what a bad idea it had been to come out here.

Silence descended upon the forest immediately following his warning. The movement around them ceased and all became still. For a moment, he thought perhaps he'd been successful. But then, when no acknowledgement of surrender was announced from the surrounding brush, he realized it was the exact opposite.

In firing a warning shot, he'd told whoever was out there exactly where he was.

Shit!

Eric grabbed Sullivan and dragged him to the ground a mere moment before the forest around them erupted in thunder and the smell of spent gunpowder.

It sounded like all hell had broken loose up ahead. Unfortunately, Derek didn't give Zeist's team much chance of winning. They were badly outnumbered and trying to fight a war in the Jersey Devil's backyard, of all places.

Fuck me sideways.

Much as he wanted to go and help them, though, tough decisions needed to be made. By saving one of Zeist's men, he'd alerted them to the danger, given them a fighting chance. How they used it was up to them now.

Finding Arthur before he could get too far off base was their top priority, especially once they'd found his radio lying on the ground.

Derek felt a hand tap his shoulder. He stopped and

turned, hoping he wouldn't see a face from a nightmare staring back at him.

"Let me take the lead," Mitchell said.

"I'm…"

"You're wheezing so loud I can practically hear it over the shit storm going on out there. Need I remind you that if you drop dead the network is unlikely to renew my contract?"

Derek let out a quick snort of laughter that quickly turned into a cough. *Damnit!* Mitch was right. He should be sidelined, not running around out here. He prided himself on being the best leader that he could be, but one of the tenets of good leadership was knowing when to let someone else take the reins for a while.

After a moment, he simply nodded.

"Good," Mitchell replied. "Show me what we're dealing with."

Derek flashed his light down at the ground directly in front of him. There were footprints plainly visible in the dirt. Mitchell was the weakest tracker on the team, but Arthur had left a clear trail.

"Could follow this with my eyes closed."

Derek clapped him on the shoulder. "Looks like the kid got curious, then got turned around. Easy mistake to make."

"Easy if this was a hiking trip," Mitchell said. "Stupid when we're out here…"

"Um, guys," Julia warned.

Both men stopped, realizing there was a commotion up ahead, and it was coming their way.

Derek leveled his rifle, trying to force himself to remain calm. It was probably just Arthur backtracking, he told himself. Even if it wasn't, he couldn't afford to lose his cool. He…

A figure broke from the bushes ahead of them.

Whoever it was, it definitely wasn't Arthur. Derek's finger tightened on the trigger, but then Mitchell grabbed the barrel of his gun and forced it down before he could fire.

The medic's light came up, illuminating the newcomer – neither Arthur nor one of the Lesterfields.

Despite convincing himself his head was in the game, Derek realized he'd almost shot the man. Unfortunately for them, the newcomer was apparently of the same mindset.

He raised his sidearm in a panic, before Julia cried out, "Do it and die!" from immediately behind them. She stepped up, gun at the ready.

The man, dressed in a suit jacket and tie of all things, was quick to lower his weapon. "Don't shoot, please."

Derek realized he looked familiar. "You with Zeist?"

A look of relief flashed across the man's face. He composed himself and nodded. "Is that you, Jenner?"

"In the flesh."

"Um, you and your men are under arrest for..."

"Are you sure I can't shoot this asshole?" Julia interrupted.

More shots were fired from somewhere up ahead and the man flinched.

"I'm going to assume you're smart enough to realize that's not us," Mitchell said once the barrage subsided.

"I don't know what the fuck is going on out here."

"Well, I'd say you have a choice," Derek replied. "You can head back out and see for yourself, or you can drop the shit and stick with us."

The newcomer blinked a few times, then holstered his weapon.

"Good choice. So what do we call you?"

"Oh, sorry. Kyle, Kyle Muellenberg."

"Pleasure to meet you, Kyle," Derek said. "Now kindly

do as you're told and maybe we'll all have a shot of getting out of this alive."

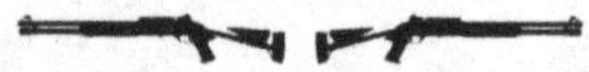

Arthur didn't really know what he was doing, but heading away from the gunfire sounded like a smart idea.

That wasn't what he'd signed up for. He was here to rescue Danni, not get into a gunfight he couldn't win against foes he couldn't even see. Hell, knowing his luck, he'd end up getting shot by the very people he was trying to find again.

Arthur didn't consider himself a coward. He wouldn't have come to begin with if that had been the case. He was a realist, though, and the reality was he was almost certainly the least qualified person out in the woods this night.

However, that didn't mean he hadn't been paying attention. He remembered everything Derek and Mitchell had told him and, while it didn't even remotely make him a woodsman, it would hopefully keep him alive.

Case in point, he stopped as his light illuminated something in front of him. He removed the headlamp and held it out to get a better look, spying a circle of leaves on the ground – a little too perfectly shaped. Arthur followed its outline and caught a glimpse of the wire that made up the snare trap.

Close one.

He stepped over it, being careful to watch for more.

That was the ticket. Be smart, keep his eyes open, and try not to do anything stupid ... or anything *else* stupid.

The gunfire petered off, which either meant one side had won or they were all reloading. It seemed to be coming from off to his right, so he turned left. Derek had been certain the Lesterfields had a home or compound out here somewhere. If there were traps scattered on the ground, then it seemed logical such a place couldn't be too far off.

He decided to pick a direction and search for it. At least that way he'd be doing his part.

If he found it then ... well, he wasn't sure. Losing his radio was possibly the stupidest thing he could have done. He still had his phone, but it wasn't worth dick out here. If he found the compound, he'd need to figure out a way to mark it, then make his way back until such time as he got a signal. It seemed as good of a plan as he was likely to come up with.

Arthur spotted a break in the trees up ahead. A moment later, he stepped into a clearing, thankful to have found a momentary reprieve from the oppressive closeness of the forest.

He almost jumped out of his skin when a voice called out, "Noah, that you, boy?"

Noah?

A tall figure stepped from around a tree.

Arthur flashed his light at the man and, for a moment, was relieved that it was apparently just some hiker or camper who was unlucky enough to ... but then he took note of the man's face in the red glow of his lamp – the bent nose, the heavy brow, the strange shape of his jaw – and his heart leapt into his throat.

He'd found one of the Lesterfields. Surprise shone in the other man's eyes for a moment then, much to Arthur's horror, he started to raise the pistol in his hand.

"Don't," Arthur warned. He brought his own gun up to bear, dropping the headlamp in the process. That was okay. He could still see the man, and he needed both hands on his weapon to hold it steady.

"There's no need for that, son," the man said in a smooth voice. "We're just two strangers out here enjoying the woods on a fine evening."

"Y-you have Danni."

"I don't know any Danni and, as you can see, I'm all alone."

Arthur did his best to keep his voice steady as he concentrated on what Mitchell had showed him about the shotgun. He steadied it against his shoulder and aimed at the man's center mass. "Don't bullshit me. You're one of them, the Lesterfields. Dr. Jenner told me all about you."

The man's eyes opened wide in both surprise and recognition. That alone cemented his guilt in Arthur's book. "You're going to take me to her, or I swear to God I'm going to…"

"That won't be necessary," the man replied. He held his gun out in front of him and dropped it to the ground. "I think you're confused, son, but I'm not the type to agitate a situation."

"I'm not your son," Arthur said, the steel in his voice real this time. This bastard was definitely one of them. He'd recognized Dr. Jenner's name. That meant he knew where the others were. "Come over here, nice and slow. I want you to pick up my light."

The man stepped forward slowly, his hands raised. "Happy to oblige." He bent at the knees and lowered his hands toward the red light shining up from the grass.

"Okay, now you're going to…"

A wheezing breath came from somewhere off to the left, heavy and wet as if someone with a bad cold had just stepped near.

Arthur turned his head toward it at the wrong moment, just as Ezekiel Lesterfield charged at him.

Noah was sorely tempted to let the trespasser take Ezekiel. Would serve the cowardly fool right. The others were somewhere up ahead and here his uncle was, trying to stay safe while the rest of the family got their hands dirty.

He wasn't fit to lead the clan. His pa would never have done something like that.

But Ezekiel was still family, and they'd already lost two that night. If the intruders up ahead were armed, it was possible they'd lose more. He couldn't remember a time in his life when so much tragedy had befallen his kin in a single day. There hadn't been anything like this since the days of his ancestors.

It needed to end now.

But that still didn't mean he was going to do his uncle's work for him.

He might not be fit to lead, but maybe he'd prove he was fit to live.

Noah closed in on the trespasser's location – a mere boy from the look of things, perhaps not much older than Noah himself. None of that mattered to him. He didn't care to make friends with outsiders. He'd learned that lesson at an early age, remembered the horror in his own mother's eyes ... at least before she'd managed to displease Pa once too many times.

He made his presence known, ready to act if this boy turned out to be more adept than his shaking form seemed to indicate.

Much to his amazement, Ezekiel didn't hesitate, throwing himself at the trespasser before he could recover and pull the trigger.

Maybe he did deserve to live after all, but that was in his and God's hands now.

Noah took a deep breath, turned, and walked away as his uncle fought for his life.

Sarah was still out there somewhere, and there was nothing more important than finding her.

42

Danni was well aware that there were few things stupider than trying to sneak into a firefight. One stray shot was all it would take.

But it was an opportunity to turn the tables. She well remembered the slaughter at Bonanza Creek. Hiding, waiting for help, none of it had quelled the bloodlust of the rabid beasts. It only ended once they stopped running and fought back.

It was foolish to think it might be different now. She was outnumbered and against a persistent foe in woodlands they knew far better than she did. Her only advantage was that she was armed and the Lesterfields were currently distracted by some unknown third party.

From the sound of things, the response from that other group was desperate and scattered. They wouldn't last long. But the thunderous reports as the Lesterfields peppered their location with gunfire were the perfect cover for Danni to make her move.

Keeping low, she spotted something through the trees ahead. At first she thought it was nothing more than a trick of her eyes, but then it raised a weapon and fired into the darkness beyond.

Danni leaned the single-shot rifle against a tree then crept forward. It was definitely one of those monsters. Not even the cover of night could completely hide that fact.

He never stood a chance. Between the shots he fired and those coming from elsewhere around them, he didn't notice her sneak up from behind. She leveled her shotgun at his back and pulled the trigger – no words, no snarky comments, nothing but vengeful judgment against this family who so casually assumed they could do whatever they pleased to those they deemed weaker than themselves.

Danni took no pleasure in ending this mockery of a man, but she felt no pity either. Her mind kept going back to two things: Adam pushing her onto the bed, and Abigail's shrunken form hiding away in her cell – no more than a shell of a person.

She was on the move again before the body even hit the forest floor, cutting a hard right through some bushes and heading toward another member of this inhuman family, one too occupied with trying to kill his intended target to know that death was coming for him instead.

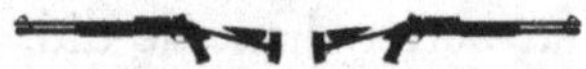

They were fucked and Eric knew it. He and Sullivan were pinned as bullets flew everywhere. Worse, they were unable to get a clear bead on anything, doing little more than firing randomly into the brush.

At least Sullivan had the good sense to douse their lights the moment they hit the dirt. Otherwise this would have been a very short, extremely lopsided gun battle. As it was, it seemed their only hope was to return fire blindly, so as to keep their assailants from charging in and gunning them down, but it was doubtful that would be a viable defense for long.

It was hard to tell how many were out there, but they were definitely outnumbered if his ringing ears were any indication.

Where the fuck are Hopper and Muellenberg?

For that matter, where was Jenner? Much as he hated to admit it, the man had saved their asses once. Eric wasn't so stubborn that he wouldn't take a second assist.

Probably still thinks I'm gonna arrest him. Well, screw that. At this point the governor could go fuck himself. Eric didn't care about bringing Jenner in so much as he wished he'd turned back with Bob and Vasquez.

Unfortunately, wishes weren't horses, and waiting for a cavalry that most likely wasn't coming was a surefire way to make sure they'd be nothing but corpses come morning.

He reached over and tapped Sullivan on the arm, almost causing the other man to turn his gun on him in surprise. Eric wasn't entirely unsympathetic to the concept of panic at that moment, but that didn't mean he wouldn't bitch him out later, if there was a later. "We need to get out of here!"

Sullivan nodded and started to get up, but Eric pulled him back down. "Crawl, you idiot!"

Eric loaded a fresh magazine into his gun and began to fire while the other man took the lead, fanning his aim through the foliage and hoping to provide enough cover to buy them a few minutes. He then rolled onto his belly and followed Sullivan, praying their luck held.

Sullivan disappeared through a small stand of bushes and Eric followed, moving as fast as his prone position would allow. He just had to hope Marcus didn't panic and open fire directly into his face the moment he was through.

Up ahead, Eric spotted Sullivan's feet and legs working

their way through the bushes. If they could reach something – a hollow, the trunk of a large tree, anything that could provide some cover – they'd have a fighting chance. They could more properly return fire and potentially cover each other's retreat.

Sullivan continued to crawl forward, putting a little more speed into his movements.

There came a lull in the gunfire, their unseen foes probably reloading for another volley, and then Eric heard a strange noise from up ahead. There came the snap of a stick, then a strangled gasp, followed by the sound of leaves being disturbed. He watched as Sullivan's feet were suddenly dragged forward and out of the bushes.

What the fuck?!

Ignoring the danger all around him, Eric pushed himself up enough to get a clear view and found that Sullivan had triggered another trap, this one a snare. Except, rather than his leg, it had closed around his neck.

Sullivan's feet hung about two feet off the ground while his hands desperately clawed at the rope strangling him.

"Shit," Eric hissed.

He began to clamber to his feet when a light was shined in their direction, illuminating his struggling teammate. Their pursuers immediately opened fire again. Sullivan's body jerked as multiple rounds hit home. His arms fell slack to his side even as he continued to be peppered with bullets.

Marcus was dead and, Eric realized with even greater horror, their attackers now knew where he was.

He was trapped like a rat against enemies he couldn't possibly hope to overcome.

Eric glanced back in the direction he'd come from. He could see lanterns shining through the brush, coming his way. Whoops of unearthly laughter could be heard between the shots that continued to hit the body of his teammate.

All at once, Eric understood why the others hadn't come to his aid. They were, in all likelihood, already dead.

He was truly alone.

But not for long.

Someone, or *something*, pushed through the bushes to Eric's right and held up its lantern to Sullivan's body. In the dim illumination Eric could see the leering grin, the leathery skin, and the three-fingered hand which held its light source.

Though he'd seen one of those things' corpses, it had seemed almost surreal at the time, lifeless as it was. But here now, seeing this creature in the flesh prodding his teammate's body with the butt of its rifle, the true horror of the situation finally dawned on Eric.

He aimed and opened fire, emptying the magazine into the creature before it turned and noticed him.

It went down as the last of the bullets left his gun, but he wasn't fooled. More were coming. He could hear their cries of outrage and anger even as they opened fire again.

They knew this forest better than he. Even if he managed to run, they'd find him. What then? He glanced once more at Sullivan, his mind awash with whatever horrors these things might have in store for him.

Suddenly, everything else – his job, the governor, all of it – seemed so insignificant compared to escaping this nightmare in any way he could.

Eric ejected the magazine and loaded a fresh one, his last.

That was okay, though. He just needed to be careful with his count. Depending on how the next few minutes went, he would have to make certain he kept one bullet in reserve.

"We need to get back, report this."

"No," Derek replied. "You need to shut up and do what you're told. I'm not playing your boss's game anymore. I'm here to find my people and I don't give one flying shit about the governor, politics, or the goddamned law. Either suck it up, or you're free to find your own way back."

"I'd think hard on that one," Julia said, pushing past Kyle. "The woods are not a friendly place tonight, and they're going to be even less friendly for anyone standing between me and my sister."

Kyle Muellenberg wasn't sure what he'd gotten himself into. This crap definitely wasn't in his job description. A part of him wished he'd ignored his cell phone earlier when Bob had called him in, but he needed the overtime. The divorce had drained him financially, leaving him in no position to be choosy.

Broke was better than dead, though. More and more, that latter choice seemed the most likely outcome of this ill-fated outing. He'd been half-certain he was going to be shot when he first came across Jenner's crew, at least based on the bile Eric had been spewing. He'd instead been conscripted. On the upside, they appeared to be far more adept at being out here than Eric and the others were. The downside was they didn't seem inclined to leave.

The only question now was how to spin this once it was all over so that he didn't get fired, but that was definitely a worry for later. For now, staying alive was at the top of his list. Finding his teammates was secondary, but that seemed to be more in the hands of fate than in...

"Jesus!"

Kyle had fallen a bit behind in his wool gathering, but the cry from up ahead jolted him out of his reverie.

He raced to catch up and stepped into a small clearing, finding his new, and quite temporary, teammates standing there stunned at what was before them.

It took Kyle's mind a moment to wrap around what he was seeing. Two men, one straddling the other, his hands around his throat. The one on the bottom lay limp and unmoving. The one on the top ... there was something *off* about his face.

The impasse was broken a mere second later as the man with the strange face leapt to his feet and bolted into the woods, just as Julia raised her gun.

"Son of a bitch!" She fired, the noise deafeningly loud this close, although he doubted she hit anything.

That seemed to spur the others to action.

The one in the lead, the medic, ran to the downed man. The leader, Jenner, turned to him and the reporter. "You, help Mitch. Do whatever he tells you to. Julia, you're with..."

He was too late. She was already speeding off in pursuit.

Kyle, still trying to process what was happening, said, "Are you sure it's a good idea to split..."

But Jenner had already disappeared into the forest after her, leaving him behind.

Ezekiel winced as he pulled his hand away from his side, feeling the wetness seeping through his shirt. It was too dark to see, but he knew it was blood. Thankfully, it only seemed to be a scratch – painful, but not enough to slow him down as he ran for his life.

He still wasn't sure what had happened. One moment he was certain he'd heard Noah close by. The boy had clearly heard it, too. He'd used the distraction to rush him, thinking his kin would step in to end their scuffle quick and clean. But that hadn't happened.

Instead, Ezekiel had wrestled with the boy, each clambering for purchase with neither finding it. The young man had been no fighter, that much was obvious, but then neither was he. His strength had always lay in his mind as opposed to his arms, but he'd been in more than one scrape in his life and at least knew how to take a punch.

His opponent was sloppy, unsure of himself, and ultimately stupid.

The boy had broken free at one point and made a mad dash for his gun. That was his undoing. Ezekiel wasn't particularly strong, but he was a survivor – smart enough to know you didn't turn your back on an enemy who still had his wits about him.

He'd tackled the boy to the ground, managed to pin his arms, and then wrapped his hands around the young man's throat. He'd squeezed with everything he had, pressing his thumbs into the intruder's windpipe until his hands went numb. By then it was all but over. The young man's eyes had rolled up into his head and his struggles had become little more than errant twitches.

He'd won, proven his will to survive was superior, but there'd been no time to celebrate his victory. Just as he was about to let go and claim the boy's weapon as his own, more trespassers had stepped into the clearing.

That wasn't the worst of it, though. Far from it. The worst was that one of them had been a ghost. Though their lights had been in his eyes, he'd seen well enough. One didn't easily forget the face of a man sentenced to death. It was impossible – he'd seen the TV host and his companion both die.

Alas, it had seemed a poor time to stick around and ask questions. He'd bolted but one of them had opened fire first, managing to nick him in the side.

Now he raced through the woods as quick as he could, relying on his memory more than his sight – thinking of nothing except putting distance between himself and them. He needed to find the rest of the family and direct them back the way he'd come. The intruders would think twice once they were faced with the full might of his kin.

Even better, he'd caught a glimpse of long hair just before he'd fled. That meant the possibility of welcoming a new Sarah into the fold. That would make up for things. One for Noah and one for the rest to share.

Speaking of his nephew, though, he planned to have words with him. Where the hell had he gotten himself off to?

The gunfire up ahead had fallen silent. That meant his kin had made the kill, were probably even now divvying up the spoils of war. That was good. Less trespassers to divide their atten... "UGH!"

A dark shape leapt from the trees ahead and slammed into him. In the gloom of the night, it was little more than a shadow, a shade, and for a moment Ezekiel was certain that God's reaper himself had come for him.

But then a fist, cold and wet, struck his jaw, momentarily stunning him.

He staggered back, dazed, and the shadow fell upon him, tackling him to the ground. He looked up and found the stars above blacked out by a mass of darkness. The only thing visible were two eyes, devoid of mercy, that stared down at him.

"Remember me, asshole?" Sarah's voice asked him, seemingly dredged in hatred itself. "Here's your wedding gift."

Before Ezekiel could so much as open his mouth to question why God had sent this angel of death to him, seven inches of cold steel was plunged into his chest, making it all a moot point.

43

Danni wasn't entirely sure how to feel about killing Ezekiel. She was sick to her stomach from her actions, but knowing he'd never victimize anyone ever again gave her grim satisfaction nevertheless.

What that said about her, she didn't care to know. Had she crossed a line tonight? Her team hunted monsters, not for sport, but because they endangered people. Did that change once the monsters turned out to be human? Or were human monsters even worse because they knew what they were doing?

The thought haunted her even as she pulled the knife out of Ezekiel's body, wiped the blood off, and sheathed it. If she could go back in time a year, what would her old self say? She'd lost some of the carefree spirit that had once defined her life, but in its place had apparently arisen a willingness to do whatever it took to survive. That knowledge frightened her, or it should have, but that was a luxury for another time and place.

Out here, now, it was hard to question. There was little doubt in her mind that it was kill or be killed with these sons of bitches. They acted more like a sick cult than anything, unable to be reasoned with in their single-minded pursuit of preserving their twisted line.

But what about the future? What would happen if she found herself in a similar situation, but one where help was within reach – walking down a city street, or in the suburbs? Before, it had seemed such an easy decision. But now, given her experiences with the Adam and Ezekiel Lesterfields of the world, she was forced to wonder.

Danni gave her head a shake, sending small globs of mud flying. She'd need to think good and hard on that once this was over. But first she needed to make sure this ended, one way or the other.

Pushing those and all other thoughts, save survival, from her head, she crept back into the surrounding brush, retrieved her weapons, and disappeared once more into the darkness of the forest.

Noah crouched over the body of his uncle Ezra. At first, coming across his crumpled form on the ground, Noah assumed he'd simply been a casualty of the firefight that had ensued just minutes earlier. But it soon became clear that wasn't the case. Ezra had been shot in the back at close range.

He dropped to all fours, a position almost as natural to him as walking upright, and studied the ground around the kill – taking his time on the gloom-enshrouded floor of the forest. There! A track, much smaller than Ezra's. Not a shoe – more like a sock or slipper.

It was his Sarah. He was certain of it. They'd thought they were hunting her, driving her forward, but in the confusion she somehow doubled back on them. Then, while his family was dealing with these new trespassers, whoever they were, she'd turned the tables.

Such a thing should have worried him. All the Sarahs he'd ever known were cowed, timid creatures, just as the Good Book said they should be. They were breeding stock, cattle, nothing more. That one could potentially do something like this was nearly unthinkable.

Yet it only excited him. All Noah could think about were the fierce children she'd bear for him. The family, under his lead, would need strong offspring to survive. More importantly, they'd need wives durable enough for child rearing for many years to come because they would also need to be more careful about choosing them. Noah was far more clever than the others realized. He was well aware of the concept of search parties, knew that those who went missing in the woods would be looked for. He also knew that the more they took, the more danger they'd be in, something even his father seemed to not care much about.

His Sarah would be the first and together they'd live a long life with many offspring, God willing. Their children would grow strong and...

A gunshot sounded from somewhere behind him. It was followed by voices which carried on the wind. He couldn't make out the words, but was certain they weren't from anyone in his family.

Noah turned. He would find his Sarah, hunt her down, conquer her, and make her his. But first, he had more trespassers to deal with.

"Let's get him," Elijah Lesterfield growled from the side of his mouth. The lips on the other side of his face were fused shut thanks to the tumorous growths covering his upper body.

He let out a whoop of laughter as he glimpsed the

intruder's body dangling from a snare, hanging like a pig left out to dry. The stranger was almost certainly dead, especially following the peppering they'd given him, but they needed to make certain.

"It only takes a second to gut a man, so best be sure," his daddy used to tell him. Wise words indeed.

He'd offered those same words up the day before, after they'd ambushed that trio of trespassers and captured their newest bride, but had been ignored. At the time, it hadn't seemed like an issue. But now, with Ezekiel calling the shots, he wondered if such wisdom would be thrown to the wind.

Adam Jr., one of the youngest of the clan, stepped past him.

"Be careful, boy." Elijah grabbed hold of his arm, but the arrogant teen just scoffed.

"What's the matter? Afraid of the dead?" Adam Jr. pulled free and continued on through the bushes ahead.

Almost as soon as he reached the hanging man, gunshots erupted from the woods.

Damnit! They'd miscounted. Elijah was certain the hanged man was the last of them, as the forest had gone quiet up ahead. But now he realized there was at least one more lying in wait.

Elijah raised his gun and yelled for the younger Adam to pull back, but the teen dropped to his knees, his good hand clawing at his throat.

More gunshots answered the first volley, his kin returning fire from their places in the surrounding bushes.

"Get down, you fool!" he cried, raising up his own rifle and shooting in the direction he thought the attack had come from.

Adam Jr. fell prone and gunfire rang out for several more seconds. One of the trespasser's bullets came dangerously close, nicking the tree next to Elijah.

He fired once more, then was forced to pull back to reload. Elijah was dismayed to find his pockets almost empty. Only two shells left. More than likely the same was true of the others. They'd come out here in search of one runaway girl, not aiming to hunt down armed intruders.

Elijah was forced to consider how best to proceed. With only two bullets left, he wanted to make sure he didn't waste them firing at trees.

"Fuck you, you fucking freaks!"

The cry had come from up ahead. Stupid. The fool of a trespasser had just given away his...

A single gunshot sounded from the intruder's location. Elijah ducked back behind cover and waited, but only silence followed.

After several seconds had passed, his kin returned the salvo, but their shots were staggered, more deliberate. He was right. They were all running low.

When silence once again had descended on the woods, Elijah let out a bird call, a sign to let his family know to keep their eyes peeled but hold fire. He got down on all fours and slowly crawled to where Adam still lay prone.

"Come on," he whispered, copious drool dripping from the side of his mouth. "I think he's out. Get moving."

He shook the lad, then did it again. Finally, he grabbed hold of him from the side and turned him over. Even in the darkness, Elijah could tell the eyes that stared back at him were glossed over and unseeing. The boy had been shot in the throat and bled out.

"Goddamn it all!" he muttered, the curse escaping his lips before he could think better of it. Lashing himself for his sinful words would have to wait, though. He needed to avenge the boy and send this intruder to whatever hell awaited those who stepped foot where they didn't belong.

Silence continued to reign. Elijah listened hard for any

sign of movement from the stranger's location, but none came. Either the bastard was damn good or he was standing his ground, hoping for them to make a mistake. Elijah didn't get a sense of the former. These interloping sons of whores had acted like fools from the get-go. No reason to think they'd smartened up since.

He picked up a rock and threw it, listening as it knocked against a tree and fell to the ground with a thud.

Still nothing.

Elijah whistled again, letting the others know to keep holding their positions, and then crept forward.

The quiet was just beginning to unnerve him when he heard a shot from somewhere further back the way they'd come. He flattened himself on the ground and waited to see if there was more, but that was all he heard.

What the?

Had the others found that bitch Sarah? Or maybe they'd flushed out whatever bastard had shot Lemuel earlier.

He couldn't worry about that now, though. He had to trust in his family and God to protect them.

Elijah Lesterfield continued to creep forward, inching past bushes and pushing through undergrowth toward where he thought he'd heard the intruder last. He said a silent prayer as he moved, begging the Good Lord to watch over him.

He was just about to mentally add an "Amen" when he slid some branches out of his way and found a pair of eyes staring back at him.

Elijah cried out in surprise, pulled his rifle up, and fired it point blank into the intruder's face.

Three more shots answered from somewhere behind him – his family. He heard them strike the trees around him while he ducked down and hoped for the best.

"It's me, you idiots!" he cried out once the echoes from the gunfire died down.

He stood up, covering the trespasser with his rifle just in case he was playing possum. It was the space of a second, no more, to see that wasn't the case. His own bullet had struck true, nearly splitting the man's forehead open. Fatal as it was, though, it hadn't mattered because the stupid son of a bitch's brains were already splattered on the ground beside him.

The intruder's final shot suddenly made sense. The crazy bastard had blown his own head off rather than let them catch him.

Elijah gave the man's body a savage kick, then another. *Son of a bitch!*

He put his hands together and gave a crow caw, the signal for all clear. Soon enough, Samuel and Matthew stepped out, guns at the ready, and joined him.

"Where's Adam?" Samuel asked.

Elijah shook his head. "Bastard got him. Where the hell are the others?"

"I saw Jonathan back near the bog. No idea where he wandered off to after."

"I thought Zacharias was with us," Matthew said.

Elijah opened his mouth to shout for their missing family members but then remembered there were still more trespassers in the woods.

"You don't think..."

Elijah rounded on his brother. "I don't think anything. We're not through here yet. We ain't found Sarah, and there's no telling whether our kin found whoever shot Lemuel. Let's go find the others."

"What if they've already been got?" Samuel asked.

"Then we'll find those who laid them low and do the same to them. God smiles upon us just as he has done for centuries. Now is not the time for us to lose faith."

44

Derek bent down to examine the body, then was forced to close his eyes for several seconds as his guts cramped up.

"You okay?"

"Yeah, I'm fine" he lied. His meds were wearing off fast and his head was swimming from the pain and exertion, but he needed to focus. They couldn't give up, especially not now.

Derek didn't often care to indulge in false hope, but the reality was they'd found Ezekiel Lesterfield's body and the cause of his death was somewhat unexpected.

At first he thought perhaps Julia's shot had hit home and the man had simply collapsed. But a cursory examination proved that to be untrue. There was a gaping knife wound in Ezekiel's chest. Someone had stuck a blade in him. Pretty darn deep, too, by the look of things.

"Think Arthur did this?" Julia asked, holding her light steady over the body.

"Doubt it. This isn't something you get up and run away from. Pretty sure whoever did this not only punctured one of his lungs, but outright shredded it. No way was he sprinting through the woods after that. Also, look at his face."

"You're right. He was an ugly bastard."

"Not that. Look at this bruising. Something hit him in the jaw. Can't tell for certain in these conditions, but I'd be willing to bet someone ambushed and then killed him, probably before he even realized what was going on."

"Couldn't happen to a nicer asshole."

"Not arguing that one," Derek replied. "But I'm more interested in who our avenging angel is. Shine the light over there, please."

Julia did as asked. "I don't see anything interesting. Trampled grass, some mud, blood splatter."

"Exactly." Derek dropped to one knee. He put a hand on the ground, hoping it looked like he was examining the crime scene, but in actuality it was to keep from toppling over. After a moment more, he caught his breath again. "Why is there mud splattered here? This ground is dry? And look. Tracks."

"From who?"

"I don't know, but whoever they are, they're on our side, which means we need to find ... ugh." Derek rose, staggered, then leaned against a tree to keep himself from falling.

"Fine my ass," Julia said. "What we need to do is get back, see how Arthur is, and have that friend of yours pump you full of whatever it was that was keeping you on your feet."

"I'm..."

"Oh, shut up." She took his rifle from him without much protest, then offered her shoulder for him to lean on.

"I'm okay, really, Julia. I can..."

"You can make it, I know. But I'm *making sure* you

can. Because if you keel over, I doubt I'll be able to drag your ass all the way back."

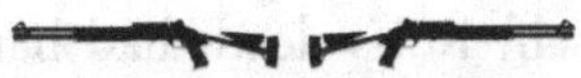

"Hold the goddamned light steady," Mitchell ordered.

"I'm trying. Jesus Christ, what are you doing to him?"

"Emergency tracheotomy," the medic replied, unfolding his pen knife.

Mitchell had feared they were too late when they'd come across that bastard atop Arthur. Those fears had been confirmed when he'd found the kid wasn't breathing and had no pulse.

From the look of things, he'd been strangled. Mitchell had hoped for the best – that Arthur's windpipe hadn't been completely crushed – and had immediately started CPR, having the new guy stand guard.

A few breaths were enough to tell him that Arthur's airway was definitely obstructed. It was likely already too late for the poor kid, but Mitchell refused to give up. Unfortunately, there was no chance of opening an airway if he couldn't see what the fuck he was doing.

"Good. Now keep it there. This is only going to take a moment."

"Oh, God! I think I'm gonna puke."

"Then look at a tree or something," Mitchell snapped, trying to insert the hollowed tube into the incision he'd made.

"Okay, I'll try."

Mitchell forced himself to concentrate. He couldn't afford to babysit the other man, not when he was racing against the clock here. Memories came back to him, unbidden, of another kid of similar age. His name had been Rob and he, too, hadn't deserved what had happened to him.

It had been over quickly, his body broken beyond repair by a monster driven mad by disease. There'd been no chance to save him. Though Mitchell often kept such thoughts to himself, Rob's death had haunted him. He'd invited the kid to help with his analysis, placing him in the very danger that had ended his life.

It was only now, working to save Arthur, that he realized he'd done almost the exact same thing again. That struck a chord deep within him and he redoubled his efforts. Once the kid's airway was open, he'd do his damnedest to get him breathing again, even if it meant working until he collapsed.

Mitchell taped the tube into place. He bent down to start CPR again when he heard a wheezing breath. His first thought was overwhelming joy. But then he heard it again and realized it wasn't coming from Arthur.

The flashlight beam was suddenly turned elsewhere, once more draping the medic and his patient in darkness.

"What the fuck?" Kyle asked, playing the light out into the surrounding tree line.

"Goddamn it, I told you to..."

The attack came before he could finish. Something massive launched itself from the surrounding brush between where the two men stood. Mitchell had only a moment to note the tough lumpy skin before he was back-handed away. He was knocked ass over teakettle, his head colliding with a tree trunk.

Mitchell slumped to the ground unconscious – the sound of screams following him down into the darkness until he heard no more.

Danni was tracking another of the Lesterfields when she heard shouting. Then came gunfire, followed by silence.

After a few more minutes, she'd spied lantern lights moving through the trees. She had a bad feeling that whoever had been fighting back had lost. But that didn't mean they couldn't be avenged.

She'd been closing in, trying to determine how many of the bastards were up ahead and whether she could pick them off one by one, when she'd heard the others.

First a cry of pain – short, brief, and easily missed had the forest not been dead silent. But then came the screams. Unmistakable, but also brief, as if whoever had made them had been silenced quickly.

It was that last thought that stuck with her. The gunshots up ahead, followed by the Lesterfields moving off, told a story, one with a likely unhappy ending for whoever had been their victim.

But if there was even a chance she could save someone else, she had to take it. As much as she wanted to hurt these monsters for what they'd done, she was relieved to find she didn't want to live with herself knowing she could have saved someone and chosen vengeance instead.

She once more unslung the single-shot rifle from over her shoulder and held it out to guide her way as she turned in the direction the cries had come from. Though she wanted desperately to escape this forest, there wouldn't be much she could do if she fell victim to one of the many traps littering the area.

As Danni moved away, she failed to notice the lantern lights she'd been tracking speeding up, as if in pursuit.

45

"Don't move," Derek whispered into Julia's ear. "Not a muscle. If you pull back, you could set it off just as surely as stepping forward."

His breath tickled her ear, but there was nothing funny about what was happening. She'd been helping him walk back when they heard cries coming from the direction where they'd left Mitch to work on Arthur. In her haste to hurry up, she'd forgotten about the pitfalls of this place.

She felt guilty about leaving the poor kid, but the opportunity to wring some information about Sophie from these bastards had seized hold of her. Unfortunately, Ezekiel Lesterfield had already been dead by the time they found him, something that gave her no small amount of satisfaction, but ultimately didn't do much to help her sister.

Now here she was, her leg pressed against a trip wire, afraid to so much as breathe lest she trigger it.

"Hold steady." Derek slowly disengaged from her grasp, doing whatever he could to keep her from shifting her weight.

She could feel the heat radiating off him, saw droplets of sweat dripping down his face. He was probably running a fever, the result of pushing himself too far too soon.

He was trying to mask how hard he was breathing – probably his way of reassuring her – but was doing a poor job at it. Nevertheless, she appreciated the effort.

It felt as if her heart skipped a beat as he finally untangled himself from her. He reached up to tap his earpiece. "Mitch, come in. Do you read me, over?" A second later, he tried again. "Just give me a ping, that's all I need. Over." The expression on his face said it all. "Shit!"

For a moment, she was worried he'd race off to help his friend, leaving her alone and trapped in the woods, but then Derek dropped to his knees next to her. A new fear instantly took hold – that he was going to pass out right there – but, fortunately, it appeared to be purposeful. He slowly crept forward to investigate the wire her ankle was pushing against.

He moved off into the bushes to the right, barely making a sound as he did whatever the hell he was doing. It didn't matter so long as the end result wasn't her being impaled or worse.

A few seconds passed, then Derek whispered in a barely audible tone, "Your light. Kill it. *Now!*"

She was tempted to ask if he was crazy, but the urgency in his voice said otherwise. Praying that she wasn't about to condemn herself to a death she wouldn't see coming, she reached up and flipped her headlamp off.

A moment later, she heard it. The barest rustle of leaves, a small twig snapping. She held her breath and realized Derek was doing the same. Well, either that, or he was unconscious, although she really hoped that wasn't the case.

Up ahead, moving parallel to the way they'd been going, she thought she spotted movement. Not much, just the sway of a branch a couple yards away. It was hard to tell in the darkness, even with her eyes adjusted to the gloom. More than once this night she'd jumped at what she thought to be something moving in the dark, only to realize it was her eyes playing tricks on her.

Julia didn't think that was the case now. Derek had apparently heard it, too, even before she had. She did her best to become little more than a dead spot in the woods, silently praying things didn't get worse.

Again she thought she heard something, this time further on. It was slight, just barely there. Whoever or whatever it was, they were definitely heading in the direction she and Derek had been going – back toward Mitch, Arthur, and that guy who worked for Zeist.

Damn it all!

Sadly, there wasn't much she could do about it, not with her life perhaps a pound of pressure away from being snuffed out. Even if she could draw her gun and fire without setting off the trap – a dubious proposition – there was little chance of hitting anything through the trees. So she remained as still as she could, hoping that their friends were okay, even if she didn't believe that to be the case.

Julia was just about to call out to Derek again when she heard something else. More movement, this time coming from behind them.

What the hell?!

Whatever Derek was doing, he continued to remain silent, and again she couldn't help but fear that he'd succumbed to his injuries, leaving her trapped and alone.

Julia risked turning her head and realized it was definitely not her imagination. She saw a trio of lights in her periphery, and they appeared to be headed her way.

"Derek," she whispered as low as she could and still be heard. There was no response. With her light off, she couldn't see where he was, although he couldn't have been more than a few feet away. She certainly hadn't heard him move off. At least she hoped he hadn't.

As the lights – lanterns from the look of it – drew ever closer, she debated her course of action. There was little doubt in her mind that whoever was out there was unfriendly, be they mutant freaks or the governor's men. The difference was, that latter group would just arrest her. The others, she didn't really want to think about it. Julia desperately wanted to learn what had happened to her sister, but this wasn't the way she hoped to do it.

She was rooted in place, neither able to move nor adequately defend herself.

Whatever she was going to do needed to be done quickly. Two of the lanterns appeared to be fanning back and forth, as if searching, but one of them steadied and pointed in her direction. She'd been spotted.

"Don't shoot!" she cried out, raising her hands above her head. "Please!"

If the others hadn't noticed her before, they certainly had now.

A gunshot rang out in the darkness. She saw a muzzle flash and heard wood splinter from a tree only a few feet away. Julia almost dove for cover out of instinct alone, but managed to hold her ground at the last possible second.

"Don't move," a rough voice cried out. "Only warning you get."

Julia stayed as still as she could, sweat pouring down her face despite the cool night air. She silently prayed for Eric Zeist or one of his men to step from the forest. Right at that moment, a jail cell didn't sound too bad.

The three figures who stepped from the brush were shrouded in shadow, but when they held up their lanterns, Julia saw enough to know that, whoever they were, they didn't work for the governor.

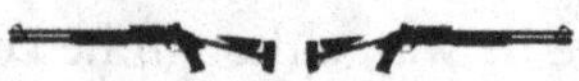

The faint sound of movement caught Noah's ears just as he removed his teeth from the trespasser's ruined throat. He coughed out a thick wad of blood and eyed his handiwork with a smile.

Someone was coming and their timing was perfect.

He didn't spy any lights approaching through the trees. Not that it meant anything.

Crouching down to all fours, Noah slipped beneath a felled trunk and began to work his way around the clearing, slow and steady, but keeping close so he could see who emerged. Once in place, he took several deep gulps of air so as to get his breathing under control, his respiration sounding like halted chuffs. He'd been over-exerting himself, first searching for Sarah and then dealing with these intruders. His injuries from the day before, minor yet still painful, weren't helping matters. His chest was starting to hurt. If he didn't calm down a bit, they'd hear him the second they moved into the clearing, and he didn't want that.

A moment later, a dark shape stepped from the tree line. Noah crouched low, preparing to engage this newcomer, but then there came a shout from off in the distance. It was a bit distorted, but he could have sworn he heard a female voice cry out, "Don't shoot! Please!"

My Sarah!

Before he could react, a gunshot rang out ... a rifle, from the sound of it.

Whoever had stepped into the clearing halted in their tracks and turned back as if listening for more.

A male voice followed, one Noah recognized. Elijah perhaps, and he was saying something about a warning shot. That was good. If any of his kin dared to hurt Sarah, they'd have to pry his teeth out of their throat next.

That assumed it actually was his Sarah. He'd only heard her for a moment. Definitely female, but he wasn't entirely certain the voice was hers.

The trespasser before him held their ground, probably debating what to do. Then they turned back toward the clearing and surveyed it before muttering a quiet, "Oh no."

Noah's eyes opened wide. The figure was dark, despite his eyes being well attuned to the night, almost a void against the blackness of the forest. But the voice that had come from it was unmistakable. *His Sarah* was here, no more than twenty feet away.

His kin could keep whoever they'd found. In fact, with any luck, she'd keep them busy for a while so he could...

He was about to move from his spot, but then she pulled something from her back – a rifle judging by the brief glint of starlight the barrel caught. She leaned it against a tree at the edge of the clearing and moved in.

But why? Why disarm herself if she was going to...

His question was answered a moment later as she pulled a second weapon from her shoulder. This one she kept hold of.

Noah began to understand. When they'd found Nathanial, he'd been without his weapon. There'd been that empty gun case in Pa's room as well. Then there was Ezra's body, shot in the back. His Sarah was smart, far smarter than Ezekiel had given her credit for. She was hunting them and taking their weapons as her own – as trophies.

A woman like her was truly a force to be reckoned with, and she would soon be all his.

He continued to watch from the shadows as she first checked the body of the trespasser he'd just finished. A smile crossed his face, knowing what she would find. She'd examine the others next, putting her back to him. Then he would strike.

As much as he liked that idea – the thought of getting his hands on her – he was forced to acknowledge it was still risky. If she knew what she was doing, as he now believed she did, rushing her from across the clearing was potentially dangerous.

He needed to play this game as smart as she was.

Noah didn't normally hunt with weapons. It was rare that he needed them, his body tough and resilient as it was. But he wasn't bulletproof. That much he knew. The grimy bandages still covering his wounds were testament to that.

As good as his claws were for rending flesh, they wouldn't be much help if he was caught at a distance.

He turned to where she'd discarded the first weapon and decided on his course of action.

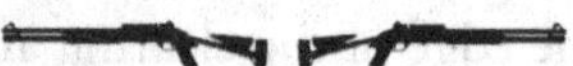

"What have we got here?" the one in the middle asked from the side of his misshapen face.

The two others, equally as grotesque, chuckled as they advanced upon her, weapons raised.

"Nice night for a walk, ain't it, Sarah?" the leftmost one said.

Julia wasn't sure whether he'd mistaken her for someone else, but realized that keeping them talking was her best course of action. By then, she was certain Derek had passed out, or worse. Rescue seemed little more than a fantasy. It was all up to her now. "I'm ... looking for my sister Sophie."

"Sophie?" the middle one replied. "Don't know anyone by that name. I do know a Sarah, though. More than one, as a matter of fact. How about this? You take off that rifle you're wearing, nice and slow. Sidearm and pack, too. Toss them to us, and we'll take you to meet them. Would you like that?"

The crooked smile he wore terrified Julia to her very core. They were passing looks back and forth between each other as if they were cats who'd just caught a mouse. Worse, they had her dead to rights. There was no way they'd miss if she tried anything, not with three against one and her barely able to move.

She carefully slid the rifle strap off her shoulder, then her backpack, making it a point to not move her leg. She tossed them behind her, toward them, then did the same with the Glock at her side.

"That's mighty considerate of you," Crooked Smile, the one seemingly in charge of this threesome, said. "Now, why don't you tell us whether there are any more of you out here?"

"They're dead," Julia replied, craning her neck to keep them in sight. "You bastards killed them."

"Maybe we did and maybe we didn't. But if you're lying to us, believe me, we'll know."

He stepped forward and retrieved her weapons, taking a moment to look them over. "Nice. Fine prizes for all our troubles tonight." He shoved her pistol into his belt, then shouldered his own rifle and held on to hers.

The leader nodded to his two buddies and together, they approached her. The nearer they got, the more clearly she could see them and the less she liked it. Derek hadn't been kidding. It was a whole family of monstrosities – their asymmetrical bodies all displaying numerous deformities, but nothing that seemed to hinder them in any way that might help her.

Crooked Smile reached a hand up to her cheek and grinned. "There's plenty enough here to share, boys."

Right before his fingers could touch her skin, though, Julia's legs were kicked out from beneath her.

She fell with a cry of surprise and landed hard on the ground. A strong arm grabbed her by the shoulder and pulled her flat.

"Stay down!"

Julia turned her head just in time to see Derek let go of the trip wire he'd been holding onto.

46

Danni didn't recognize the body. Whoever he was, he'd been mangled badly – throat torn open and one of his arms ripped from its socket. He was beyond help.

Her heart went out to him, but she couldn't spare herself the luxury of sympathy, not with the woods still full of enemies. Danni didn't fool herself into thinking she'd gotten them all. Even if they caught her now, though, she'd taken a hell of a chunk out of their numbers – hopefully enough to make them think twice about grabbing anyone ever again.

She once more glanced down at the body. *Is he wearing a tie?*

Strange, but a mystery for another time. She had more important things to worry about, such as the fact that of all the Lesterfields she'd encountered since escaping, she hadn't seen hide nor hair of the one who terrified her the most – Noah, the so-called Jersey Devil. With any luck he was lying in a ditch, a victim of the earlier firefight.

She hated to think of him escaping, remaining free to

351

haunt these woods and anyone unlucky enough to cross his path.

Danni pushed that thought away and moved across the clearing to where she spied two more prone figures in the dim starlight. She didn't detect any movement, which probably didn't bode well for them, but needed to check anyway. If they were merely unconscious, she couldn't just abandon them.

She reached the first body and dropped to one knee, digging the butt of the shotgun into the ground for purchase. Her breath caught in her throat as she leaned in and recognized a familiar face.

"Arthur? Oh my God!"

It was like Colorado all over again and, for a second, the memory halted her in her tracks. Tears dripped from her eyes at the sight of him, creating tiny furrows in the mud that still caked her face. She gave his shoulder a nudge to try and wake him, but there was no response.

In a near panic, she wiped one hand clean against the grass and pressed two fingers to the side of his neck, praying that she wasn't too late, but then feeling the sticky blood coating his throat.

No!

Several seconds passed and she felt nothing. She leaned down and pressed her ear to his lips to no avail. There was no pulse, no sign that he was breathing. He was likely gone, another victim of these soulless monsters.

Danni wasn't about to give up that easily, though. She hadn't known him long, but in the short time since they'd met, he'd reminded her what it was to be a normal girl again – giving her back a little piece of the life she'd walked away from.

And those bastards killed him for it.

She bent down and began chest compressions.

What is he even doing out here?

She didn't try to fool herself as to the reason. She'd seen the looks he'd given her when he didn't think she was looking. He came out here to save her, and that somehow made the hurt even worse.

Danni wiped away the tears, smearing the grime on her face. *Was he out here on his own? How the hell did he even know how to find...*

She glanced up and noticed something lying next to Arthur that she'd missed in her horror at finding him – a large side-satchel pack. Even in the gloom, it was instantly recognizable.

Danni reached for it, but then she heard a sound, a low groan from somewhere nearby. Acting on pure instinct, she shouldered her shotgun and spun to meet this new challenge.

Derek wasn't trying to scare Julia, but there hadn't been any other way to go about it. His injuries were catching up to him, and his reaction time was likely not up to the task of a firefight against three armed opponents. That Julia was holding his rifle while he was on the ground likewise severely limited his options.

He'd heard them approaching just as he realized what kind of trap she'd almost triggered, hoping the thick bushes which obscured the trip wire were enough to hide him from their view as well.

Of course, none of that would have mattered had Julia panicked and set it off, but he had to hand it to her. She'd kept her cool. It was more than admirable considering what they were up against.

He'd used the time as best he could – working quickly and quietly to brace the trigger mechanism so that she wouldn't accidentally set it off. Not that he was in any position to let her know that.

Fortunately for them, their *guests* – three, if he heard correctly – hadn't immediately opened fire. Then again, perhaps it shouldn't have been all that surprising. Julia was a woman, an attractive one at that if he allowed himself the conceit. It was the reason these monsters had taken Danni and all the others before her, the reason they'd left Julia's brother-in-law behind to rot in the woods.

Derek hadn't intended to use her as bait, but sometimes one had to think on the fly. Truth be told, they were both in a bad spot, not helped by the fact that he wanted nothing more than to pass out for the next several days.

He reached a hand to his hunting holster. His Ruger had given its life saving his, but fortunately, he had a backup in the form of an old .357 Colt Python. It didn't have the punch of the other weapon, but it was more than enough for these assholes.

Derek hesitated just as his fingers brushed against the release, realizing that unsnapping the button would make a sound, however slight. In these conditions anything could potentially set off their foes, who were likely already on edge.

No. He couldn't risk it, not until the time was right. Even then he'd have to hope that his reflexes were still quick enough to make it count.

The Lesterfields ordered Julia to disarm, then stepped in.

Come on, just a little more.

The one in the middle moved close enough to touch her, the others barely a step behind. It was now or never.

Hoping the reporter was in a forgiving mood, he kicked out at the back of her knee, toppling her over.

She hit the ground and he released the trigger. With

any luck, the Lesterfields had put their all into this particular trap.

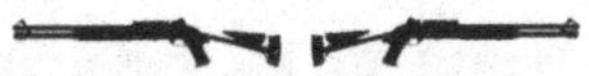

Julia felt a *whoosh* of air above her, then heard a meaty thud as something heavy collided with the trio who'd been accosting her.

She rolled over and saw a heavy log swing back over her. Wooden spikes jutted out of it and dark, viscous liquid dripped from their tips. Considering the nasty look of those spikes, she didn't have to guess too hard as to what it was.

"Go!" Derek shouted from next to her. She didn't need to be told twice, even if she did plan on kicking his ass when this was all over.

For now, the priority was making sure they were the last two standing in this skirmish, something made more difficult by the fact that she'd thrown away their weapons.

Or maybe not. She rolled clear of the death pendulum's backswing and saw Derek's rifle lying on the ground several feet away, illuminated by the discarded lantern lying next to it.

Two of their assailants lay unmoving in the grass close by. It was hard to tell at this distance, but she was fairly certain the one with the lopsided smile wouldn't be getting up again. Good riddance to bad rubbish.

She bent low and retrieved the gun, but before she could bring it up, movement registered from her flank. Julia turned in time to see the third member of her would-be kidnappers rush toward her. The lantern light revealed a wicked-looking knife in his hand and a snarl of pure hatred on his face.

Julia's eyes opened wide and she braced herself as best as she could.

In the moment before he reached her, Derek launched himself into the misshapen man's side, knocking both of them to the ground where they began to wrestle for purchase.

"Go help the others!" Derek cried out, driving a punch into his foe that appeared to do little to dissuade him.

Julia raised her gun but didn't have a clear shot as the two men continued to grapple.

Come on! Get out of the damned way!

There came a moan from behind her and she dared a glance over her shoulder. Sure enough, another of the Lesterfields was slowly pulling himself up to a sitting position. She knew Derek was barely in any condition to go one on one with a toddler, much less a murderous mutation. If another managed to join the brawl, then all hope was lost.

She weighed the odds and trusted that he could keep fighting long enough for her to make sure this didn't become a tag-team match.

Julia turned and stepped toward where the man-thing was trying to get up. He hadn't caught the full brunt of the trap like his buddy, but he was pretty badly injured. A pair of nasty gashes bloodied his torso and his left arm hung uselessly at his side.

She raised the gun and pointed it at him. "Don't move."

"You a-ain't got the sand, S-sarah." He spat out a wad of blood. "Put down that peashooter and I'll tell the others you submitted like a good girl."

Julia wanted nothing more than to put a bullet right between his eyes, but he was right. Self-defense was one thing, but outright murdering someone — even one of them — was something she wasn't prepared to do.

He grinned, apparently sensing this.

Besides, if they're all dead, then there won't be any of these bastards left to tell me what they did with Sophie.

A smile of her own creased her face. She quickly shifted her grip on the gun and had just enough time to register his look of triumph turn to one of surprise as she slammed the butt of the rifle into the side of his head.

Broken teeth flew from his mouth and he fell to the ground, motionless.

Julia allowed herself a moment to savor her victory, then she remembered the fight going on behind her.

She spun back to find that the tide had shifted against Derek. He was on his back desperately trying to hold the other man's knife at bay. It was a losing battle. He was too weakened by his injuries and his opponent had the advantage of leverage.

Time seemed to slow down as she spun the rifle around and tried to bring it to bear once more, knowing she was going to be too late. The hunchbacked man atop Derek pulled back, yanking his arm free from his opponent's grasp.

He raised the knife high for a killing blow.

Julia aimed the rifle from her hip, praying her aim was true.

She pulled the trigger just as the knife came down.

47

"Mitch! Are you okay?" Danni lowered her gun, relieved beyond belief that she hadn't pulled the trigger. "Come on, wake up. I need your help. Arthur's..."

A wheezing cough came from behind her. "*D-don't worry 'bout them, Sssarah.*"

She froze in place, one knee on the ground and with her weapon in a bad position. There was no mistaking that voice. Slowly, so as to not provoke him, she glanced over her shoulder.

Noah Lesterfield, the Jersey Devil himself, and a monster far worse than any urban legend, stood no more than ten feet away. His misshapen bulk was terrifying enough, but she saw that he was now armed, holding the stolen rifle she'd left behind while she checked on things. It lay awkwardly in his inhuman hands, but there was little doubt he had her right where he wanted her.

He let out the breath he'd no doubt been holding so as to sneak up on her. It came out in a wet cough. But despite the thick gasps which escaped his body, he held the gun true, offering her no quarter with which to open fire before he got off a shot.

"*T-throw it away and ssstep back,*" he said, in between sucking greedy gulps of air. "*Over there.*"

"My friend..."

"*Ain't no helping the dead. Now do as I say.*"

Danni stood up. Noah growled and tightened his grip on the rifle. Rather than tempt fate, she threw the shotgun into the bushes and raised her hands in surrender, risking a glance down at where her teammate still lay unmoving.

As much as it killed her to admit it, Arthur was most likely beyond help thanks to this son of a bitch and his family, but Mitchell wasn't. Though she wasn't sure she'd ever forgive herself for making this choice, she realized neither of her friends would survive if she couldn't keep Noah's attention firmly locked on her. *I'm so sorry.*

The devil opened his mouth in a grotesque semblance of a smile, coughed again, and then spat out a mouthful of viscous phlegm. "*M-my Sssarah.*"

"I'm not your anything."

A sliver of drool fell from his scaly lips and again he took a large, shuddering gulp of air. "*Yes, y-you are.* "*G-god's gift to me. My wife.*"

Danni lowered her arms and took a step to the side, away from Mitchell. "No."

"*You'll bear fine ch-children.*"

She took another step. "I'd sooner die."

Noah let loose with a wheezing chuckle. "*You k-killed my kin. Need to m-make more. The c-clan must continue.*"

"No," she repeated, her hand coming to rest on the hilt of Francis's knife, still sheathed at her side. "It's time for you and your clan to die out. To join the myths and legends of this forest. Nothing more."

He tensed. "*D-don't. N-nowhere to run. Nowhere to hide.*"

"I beg to differ," she said with a grimace. "I don't think you're going to do it. And I know these woods now. Maybe not as well as you, but enough to get away."

"*No.*"

"Get away and never see your disgusting face again."

"*N-no,*" he sputtered. His breath was coming hard now, making his words difficult to understand.

A volley of gunshots sounded from somewhere close by – back in the direction where she'd left Ezekiel to rot, if she had her bearings straight. She had no way of knowing who was firing or what they were shooting at, other than that neither she nor Noah appeared to be the target.

Noah spared a quick glance that way, then focused on her again. "*My kin are coming.*"

"You don't know that." She took another step.

"*D-don't matter. You're mine. SSSTOP!*"

"You won't..."

"*D-don't need to kill you.*" Noah smiled, more thick drool dripping from his mouth. "*D-don't need to chase you either.*"

He shifted his aim lower and pulled the trigger.

The barrel of the rifle exploded and Noah cried out as he dropped the weapon and clutched his face.

Now it was Danni's turn to smile. She'd been using that old rifle all night as a walking stick, to look for traps and for testing the depth of any bogs she came across. The barrel had become good and clogged by a combination of dirt and drying mud.

Not as useless as I thought.

That was all the time she allowed herself to celebrate. Though in pain from the shrapnel of the backfire, she didn't fool herself into thinking Noah was injured enough to no longer be a threat.

Drawing Francis's knife, she raced at him, looking to change that status quo once and for all.

Julia wasn't sure what had just happened. She knew the second she pulled the trigger that her shot had gone wide. The knife had come down and she'd heard the sickening sound of it striking flesh. But then, before she could fire again, three more deafening gunshots rang out from close range.

Her breath caught in her throat, certain for a moment that more of the Lesterfields had found them, but instead the one straddling Derek fell slack atop him. She approached and saw three ragged exit wounds in the man's hunched back.

"A ... little help ... here."

Derek's voice was weak and ragged, but he was alive.

Julia quickly stepped in and realized his attacker, on the other hand, was quite dead.

She spared a glance back at the one she'd knocked out, still on the ground where she'd left him. He could wait. Julia grabbed hold of the dead man and shoved with everything she had. He was a lot heavier than he looked and even in death seemed reluctant to release his prey.

"Come on!" With one more heave, she pushed him off.

Her breath caught as she laid eyes on Derek. He was holding a large revolver in his right hand, one with a very short muzzle. But drawing it had come at a cost. The hunchback's knife was buried deep in his other arm. "Oh my God!"

"Don't," Derek warned when she moved to grab it.

"But you're bleeding."

"I'm ... going to be ... bleeding a lot worse ... if you pull it out." He threw her a weak smile. "Not to mention, I think ... it's stuck in the bone."

Julia looked down at him, feeling helpless. "What do we do?"

"I just need a breather."

"A breather?!"

"We're not ... done yet." He fumbled with his gun before finally getting it back in its holster.

"You are."

"Not yet," Derek replied tiredly before slowly sitting up. He glanced past her. "The other two?"

"One dead, one not going anywhere."

He pointed. "Help me over to that tree and then go get your backpack. There's rope in there. Tie up the survivor, then go find Mitch."

"What about you?"

"It's a nice night for guard duty."

"Oh?" she asked with a laugh. "So you get the easy..."

She was interrupted by a loud report from the direction they'd been headed. It sounded to her like a muffled gunshot. "What the?"

"Crap," Derek growled. "Forgot all about whatever passed us earlier. Change ... of plans." He held out his good hand so Julia could help him up. "Let's go."

"You're in no shape to..."

"That wasn't a request."

She was tempted to clock him upside the head with her rifle, but instead asked, "Can you make it?"

"No idea, but ... going to try."

Julia saw there was no arguing with the man, and doing so was just wasting time anyway. She helped him up, offering her shoulder for him to lean on.

"Thanks."

"Save it, you stubborn bastard," she replied. "You ready?"

"Yeah. Just do me a favor?"

"What now?"

Derek glanced down at the knife sticking out of his arm. "Try not to brush up against anything. Oh, and watch your step this time."

Danni changed tactics at the last moment. In her rage, she'd raced right at the devil, intent on tackling him and burying her knife as deeply into his chest as she could. She realized mid-stride though, that strategy was little more than suicide. Even if she managed to gravely wound him, he was still much larger, stronger, and durable than she. There was little chance of winning that way without Noah taking her with him. If anything, she'd just end up dying badly, leaving this bastard to finish off Mitch and then return to his compound to start the cycle anew.

Her advantage was in her smaller size and agility. She needed to use that.

She veered hard left and raced past him as he continued to claw at his face, ducking low and raking the blade across his thigh.

As she feared, his skin was tough, as if he were more alligator than man, but Francis had kept his knife razor sharp. It drew a furrow of blood before she stepped out of his reach.

Noah, still breathing hard, snarled and dropped his hands so as to follow where Danni was circling him. It was hard to tell in the dim light, but she was pretty sure his face was scraped to hell from the gun blowback. He shook his head, blinked, and wiped at his eyes once more before facing her again.

He was in pain and likely at least partially blinded. That was good. Served the fucker right and also gave her a fighting chance, however slim. She knew her best bet was to double back, find her gun, and use it to blow some proper holes in this abomination. But that would leave her flank vulnerable, and she didn't trust in her ability to do so without him closing the distance.

"*G-gonna, learn you good ... Sssarah.*" He put his hands on his knees and bent over to cough.

A possible course of action began to form in her mind. "Wrong on both counts!"

She stepped in slashing with the knife, but he countered with his claws. Bone clinked off metal and she almost lost her grip on the weapon from the sheer strength of his attack.

He lunged for her, faster than she was expecting, but the mud covering her body made her too slippery for him to easily grab hold of. She pulled away and backed off, sporting three wicked furrows on her arm for her troubles.

Danni drew in a sharp breath of pain and backpedaled. Noah was quicker than she gave him credit for. She couldn't afford to be sloppy like that again. No. She had to fight this battle smarter than that. "Your dad died badly – choking on his own blood with his pants around his ankles."

A thick snarl escaped Noah's lips and he leapt at her.

She sidestepped and threw a punch to the side of his head, immediately regretting it. It was like hitting a wall. Danni considered herself to be in good shape, but she might as well have smacked him with a flyswatter.

What she lost in actual damage, though, she made up for in angering this monster who called himself a man. Noah let loose with another angry growl which again dissolved into thick coughs.

It gave her a chance to step around to his flank where she raised the knife high and brought it down into his back with everything she had.

It wasn't nearly enough.

He shifted at the last possible second and, in her haste

to strike a killing blow, she instead hit one of the many protrusions covering his torso. Despite putting her all into the blow, the blade sank in less than an inch, becoming stuck tight in his thick hide.

Before she could pull the weapon free, Noah spun, throwing a wild backhand that caught Danni in the side and sent her flying.

She tried to roll with the blow but was too dazed and went tumbling end over end ... finally skidding to a halt at the edge of the clearing.

Sadly, there were no timeouts in this duel against the devil. She'd barely stopped moving when she heard him coming for her again.

Danni pushed herself to her knees, doing her best to ignore the stinging pain in her side. It would be a near miracle if she didn't have at least a couple cracked ribs.

Praying she didn't immediately collapse onto the ground in agony, she gritted her teeth, pushed off with her foot, and sprinted into the darkness of the forest, moving as fast as her injuries would allow.

If this son of a bitch wanted her, he'd have to catch her first – even if deep down she feared this was a race she couldn't win.

48

It took an agonizingly long time to return to the clearing where they'd left Mitch to care for Arthur.

Fortunately, they weren't too far away when they'd gotten waylaid by the Lesterfields. Derek just hoped it was close enough. Something else had passed them in the woods before they'd been forced to battle the trio of mutants. What that something else was, he wasn't sure. Likewise, he had no way of knowing if it was friendly, but it seemed a smart precaution to assume it wasn't.

Still, whoever or whatever it was hadn't turned back and tried to flank them when the first warning shot was fired, something near impossible to miss in the stifling darkness.

Derek supposed it could have been an animal looking to escape the battlefield, but it hadn't sounded like one to him. There had been purpose to its steps, not blind panic.

One of Zeist's men maybe? It was possible. But if so, who had fired the weapon?

Since that single shot, the woods had seemingly grown quiet again. Not that he could tell much of anything the

366

way his head was swimming. Between blood loss and his other injuries, Derek felt like a deflated balloon.

Truth be told, he was done. It was a near miracle he was still on his feet, even with Julia's help.

Unfortunately, their mission wasn't finished, so that meant he couldn't afford to be either. Not yet anyway. They still had to find Danni and Frank and then get out of this place alive. Quite the daunting tasks for a man as tired as he was.

The Colt felt heavy in his hand, but he refused to holster it as Julia helped him forward. They might well stumble into another ambush, but whoever lay in wait for them would at least learn they were anything but easy prey.

There, at last, the clearing they'd been seeking loomed ahead through a break in the trees.

"Just a little more," Julia whispered to him.

"Promises, promises," he wheezed back, surprised by how weak his voice sounded.

They stepped through the tree line and into the clearing.

Almost immediately, a dark shape rose up near the other side, seemingly in challenge to their presence, and called out in a groggy voice, "Whoever's out there, that's far enough."

As it turned out, those were apt words indeed, for when Derek pulled away from Julia, to raise his weapon in response, he promptly passed out before his finger could even touch the trigger.

Danni coughed, tasting copper in the back of her mouth, but she continued onward despite the pain. Behind her, she could hear him coming. He'd given up all pretense of stealth, seemingly intent on running her down instead, his labored breathing giving his position away as surely as the crackle of branches breaking in his wake. At least she'd succeeded in pissing him off.

The only thing that kept her going was what he'd do to her once he caught up. By this point, Danni was no longer afraid of death. If Noah killed her, so be it. There would be no shame to such an end. It was what would happen if she didn't die that terrified her.

The pain in her side was intensifying, but it paled in comparison to the fear of being dragged back to the compound as his *wife*.

Danni wasn't stupid enough to think she could run forever in her shape, but from the sounds Noah was making behind her, hopefully she wouldn't need to. She abruptly turned right, hoping that in her race to keep ahead of him she hadn't lost her bearings.

She knew she was risking a lot, running all out through a potential minefield of traps – that at any moment she could step wrong and that would be it.

"*Sssarah!*" The wheezing cry came from close behind her, too close.

Danni spared a glance over her shoulder. Though she couldn't see him gaining in the dark, she could definitely hear him.

The pain, combined with the exhaustion at having been on the go for hours, was slowing her down. Had she been fresh, she was certain she could have outpaced her pursuer, but it felt like someone had poured gasoline on her insides and made her swallow a match. As it was now, she would be overtaken within seconds.

Unless she changed the rules of the chase.

Listening to the wet, heavy breathing coming up behind her, she got an idea how she might do that, but there was little time to properly plan. She had to act and hope she got lucky.

Danni burst through a heavy bramble of bushes, scraping herself up in the process, then slid to the side and dropped prone. It was an amateurish trick at best, something one might expect of a grade schooler, and it made her side scream in protest, but it was all she had to work with.

She was counting on the fact that Noah was too pissed off to risk losing her.

Sure enough, he came plowing through the same bushes she'd just emerged from. Danni kicked out and caught one of his legs with her own. It was like striking a concrete piling and, for a moment, she was certain she'd hear the sound of her own leg shattering like a matchstick, but the brute went tumbling face-first onto the forest floor instead.

Danni spied the knife, still stuck in his back, and was sorely tempted to try to wrench it free, but she abandoned that idea almost immediately. One fall wasn't going to do much more than slow her pursuer down for a second or two. If she truly wanted to win this, she had to keep up the pressure.

Noah pushed himself to his knees and coughed several times, but Danni was already back on her feet. She took a moment to look up at the stars and check her direction, then she was off again, moving at a running limp that was barely able to classify as a jog. Danni again realized she needed to be smarter. In her bid to escape, she was doing more damage to herself than him. Not a winning strategy in the long run.

"*SSSSARAH!*"

The cry dissolved into a wheezing, hacking cough that echoed behind her. Unfortunately, her hopes that maybe he'd had enough were dashed when she again heard him barreling through the woods. He was getting more reckless, charging full steam ahead, whereas she was slowing down with each potshot she took at him.

Almost as if in response, a sharp stab of pain rose up from her side, reminding her that another blow like that would almost certainly be lethal.

Though Noah sounded like he was breathing through a snorkel filled with mud, he moved like a freight train on legs. She began to fear that she'd run out of options long before he ran out of steam.

If that happened, she'd...

Danni's foot caught on the edge of something and all thoughts dissolved as she pinwheeled her arms and toppled forward.

She managed to barely break the fall with her hands, but the shock of landing rippled through her body, causing her to cry out in agony.

There was no time to waste on pain, though. She quickly sat up and looked to see what she'd tripped over, despite knowing that she'd erased whatever lead she had.

As bad as it was, she saw that it could have been much worse. Her foot had caught on the edge of a spiked pit trap. Another inch or so and she'd have gotten her leg stuck fast, with little chance of freeing herself in time.

Danni rolled to her feet and started to turn again, but then the bushes parted as a massive form seemingly exploded through them, headed toward her.

Come on, step in it.

Sadly, luck wasn't on her side. Noah's foot came down on the far side of the trap and before she could take much more than a step away from him, his hand wrapped around her arm and spun her back toward him.

He grinned maniacally down at her. "*M-my Sssar...*"

His words dissolved into a strangled cry as Danni, acting on pure instinct alone, brought her knee up. Large, powerful, and possessing skin more suited to a dinosaur, the Jersey Devil was apparently quite human when it came to a kick in the balls.

He let go of her, his claws scraping furrows across her bicep, and dropped his hands to his crotch.

Danni saw a potential opening, stepped in, and shoved him with everything she had. Off balance as he was, Noah backed up a few steps, a keening hiss of breath escaping his lips.

Come on!

She could have cried out in joy as he fell to one knee, his other leg disappearing into the spike trap. He took a desperate swipe at her, falling well short of the mark, but Danni jumped back anyway. Her side protested the movement with a wave of nausea, causing her to lose her balance in the process and fall onto her butt in the damp soil.

She lay there, unable to make any sound more audible than a whimper for a moment. However, she saw she wasn't the only one.

Noah opened his mouth, perhaps to scream out her name again, but all that escaped was a tiny wheeze of air. He took a great big, gulping breath, then another, before pounding on his chest with one fist.

He looked up at her, his eyes nearly bulging from their sockets. "*M-my, Sssarah,*"

Danni pulled herself to her feet, a task not nearly as easy as it should have been. Once she was up, she looked back and spat in his direction. "My name isn't ... Sarah, you dickless loser."

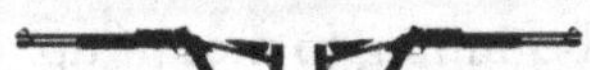

Noah gritted his teeth. The lightheadedness he felt was instantly forgotten at her words, spoken like an insolent strumpet with no respect for her betters. His father had warned him of jezebels like this. Whores of Babylon, he called them.

He finally began to understand that he would never truly make her his, not in the way he wanted. A woman like her might birth him a child, true, but she'd never be fit to raise one. Never be worthy to stand by his side. There would always be a need to keep one eye open around her.

There was still one other Sarah left at the compound, a properly cowed female. She'd do for now. As for this whore, he'd put her in her place. It would be the last painful lesson of her life.

Noah bent low, bracing his powerful arms against the ground, trying to ignore the dull ache that came from between his legs. He sucked in as much of a breath as he could, then pushed with everything he had.

The sharpened sticks in the trap bit into his leg, drawing blood, but not nearly as much as if his skin had been thin and weak. Still, it hurt like the dickens as he pulled, but finally he was rewarded with a crack of wood that told him the man-trap was giving way.

He glanced back at Sarah and smiled, spittle pouring from his lips as he freed himself. Her eyes were wide as saucers, fear showing nakedly in them despite the rest of her body being covered in the grime and muck of the forest.

It was fitting, that she die layered in filth, for that was what she was – filth, nothing more.

The false Sarah backed up, then turned to run, but she was moving much slower now. The bitch was tired, and her injuries were beginning to mount up.

Noah launched himself at her, but a searing pain erupted in his chest before he could close the distance. He doubled over, fighting for air. It was as if his lungs refused to fill up.

But he wouldn't quit, not now when he was so close to victory. He'd catch her and take her on the forest floor, then he'd wrap his hands around her throat and watch as the life left her eyes.

Afterwards, he'd go back and finish any intruders who were left, making sure their bodies were scattered for the animals to feast upon. These lands would once more belong to his clan which would rise anew from the ashes, like Lazarus reborn.

Noah pushed himself up and lurched after Sarah. Each breath was more difficult than the last, but he closed on her quickly thanks to his longer stride. She looked back and saw him coming, his excellent night vision allowing him to enjoy the fear etched on her face.

She turned away and redoubled her efforts, but it was a feeble attempt on her part. This race was all but over. She just refused to acknowledge it.

He watched as Sarah leapt over something up ahead. Her foot hit the ground, slipped, and then she fell forward with a pained cry. Noah considered this. There was no log or other obstacle in the path. That meant something else – another trap.

His hurt leg was already a testament to how sloppy he'd been, a situation he didn't care to repeat. He knew these woods and what lay in them. It was time to use his head.

Noah slowed down just as Sarah turned over onto her back to watch him approach. He could see by the look on her face that she was nearly spent, almost ready to accept her fate. But, rather than leap upon her and ravish her as he planned, he trod carefully, keeping his eyes on the forest floor in front of him.

He easily spotted the snare – one of Lemuel's, from the

look of it. Probably wouldn't have stopped her for long anyway. The damned fool was always sloppy with his work. Still, it would have held her long enough.

No matter. He'd have her either way.

Noah sucked in another breath, barely getting enough air to satisfy the burning need inside of him, then lifted his leg to step over the trap. Once he was past that, nothing would stand between him and Sarah.

Danni was done. She'd landed wrong and messed up her ankle on that last leap, slipping on the wet ground. It might still support her weight, but not for running. Worse, it was all for nothing. In trying to clear the snare, she'd telegraphed exactly where it was.

From the labored sound of his breathing, Noah appeared to be in almost as bad of shape as she was, but he apparently still had enough left to finish the job. If he got his hands on her, there would be nothing she could do except pray it was quick and...

Danni mentally chided herself as he moved toward the snare. She'd been raised better than that. To give up so easily ... it was an insult to who she was and why she'd joined Derek's team. It was a slap in the face to those she couldn't save, as well as those who still needed saving – whether today or in the future.

So long as she continued to draw breath, she couldn't give up.

As she watched the devil's misshapen foot cross the boundary where the rope loop lay, she realized there was still hope for her. If he wouldn't step into the trap, then she'd bring the trap to him.

Fighting against the fear and pain, Danni flung herself in Noah's direction. His head cocked in surprise at the sudden display of aggression, causing him to hesitate for the barest of instants. It was all she needed to slap her hand against the trap's trigger, manually setting it off and sending the snare rising up from the ground, where it wrapped around Noah's foot.

He cried out as his leg was yanked up. For one agonizing moment, Danni wanted to scream in triumph as he teetered off balance, but then there came a *crack* as the branch struggling against his weight snapped. It fell to the ground next to her, and the rope holding the devil's leg went slack.

No!

Noah stumbled back several steps, his hitched breath becoming a shrill whistle. Danni knew she should try to run again, but her body didn't seem to want to respond. She could only watch, horrified, as he regained his footing and then smiled as if to let her know her final effort against him had failed.

The devil opened his spittle-caked mouth, no doubt to gloat, but no sound came out. He tried again, but nothing but a weak choke of air escaped. For a moment, he stood there looking perplexed. Then he tried to draw a breath and the grin on his face was instantly replaced with another expression, one Danni had become intimately familiar with – fear.

Noah grabbed at his throat as he tried to suck in a breath, but to no avail. All that escaped his mouth was a rope of thick phlegm.

Danni subconsciously held her own breath as she watched. This was what she'd been hoping for. She'd known from the start she was no match for this man-beast, but his labored breathing had been hard to miss. She had wagered a desperate gamble when she led Noah from the clearing, that the devil's weakness lay not within his arms or legs, but within his lungs, and that pushing him hard enough might succeed where weapons failed.

He began to desperately pound on his own chest, the meaty impacts breaking the silence of the forest.

That's right! Suffocate, you bastard!

Noah hit himself again and stumbled against a tree, almost losing his footing, but he managed to pull himself back upright. Eyes bulging, he stood as straight as he could, arched his spine, and then slammed both fists into his ribcage.

There came the dull *crack* of his hands striking bone, followed by a small wheezing gasp that escaped his lips.

Oh, God, no!

Noah sucked in a greedy breath of air, then did so again. He took a step toward her then staggered, no doubt still woozy from lack of oxygen. Off balance he might be, but he was breathing again. It would be only a matter of seconds before he cleared his head and came for her. She was out of ideas and too weak to run. It was over...

Wait — off balance!

There was still a chance, however slim. Danni turned and spied the snare rope lying within reach, the end still looped around Noah's foot.

Summoning the last of her strength, she grabbed hold and pulled with everything she had, trying to drag his tree trunk of a leg out from under him. For a long moment, she was certain it wouldn't be enough — that she'd give herself a hernia long before she budged him — but he was standing on the same slick ground she'd slipped on. His foot slid on the wet dirt and, with one final yank, she dragged his leg out from beneath him.

Noah let out a yelp of surprise as he fell backward, landing with a heavy thud.

The cry became a snarl as the monstrosity that played at being a man scrambled to his feet. Spent, Danni could only watch, accepting that the end was upon her, but then the snarl turned into a pained gurgle and Noah's eyes opened wide in panic. He opened his mouth again, but any words he had to say were drowned in the gout of black blood he coughed out.

He spun and then reached around, clawing at his back. In the dim light shining down from above, Danni spied the barest glint of metal.

Francis's knife! It was now buried up to its handle in the devil's back. So grotesque were his deformities that he couldn't reach far enough to grab it. He doubled over, coughing out even more gore.

She suddenly understood what had happened. When he fell, his own weight had succeeded where her strength had failed, pushing the knife through his bumpy hide. Danni couldn't begin to guess at Noah's strange anatomy, but it seemed a fair assumption that Francis's blade had pierced one of his lungs.

A mix of sadness and triumph passed through her as Noah took one more step in her direction, then collapsed to his knees, slowly drowning in his own fluids. Her friend had saved her one last time, avenging himself in the process.

The devil reached out to her, his mouth moving but no sound escaping. Even faced with the near impossibility of reading his misshapen lips in the dark, she was certain of what he was trying to say.

Exhausted, injured, but alive, she looked him in the eye one last time before he collapsed in front of her.

"I told you. My name is Danni Kent, and I was never yours."

EPILOGUE

"Turn that up," Danni said, "I want to hear it."

"Can't imagine why." Mitchell let out a bitter laugh as he cranked up the volume in the small waiting room.

On the screen, the news was playing highlights from the previous night's gubernatorial debate, specifically a section where Governor Jonas Yarlberg – most likely soon to be ex-governor – was absolutely lambasted by his opponent for his role in attempting to cover up an ecological disaster in the Pine Barrens.

He was being blamed not only for the environmental impact, which had rapidly become a hotbed item in this year's election, but for covering up the disappearances of several people who'd gone missing in the area. He hadn't been formally charged yet and – according to what they'd heard – likely wouldn't be, but the damage to his reputation was almost certainly irreparable.

It was a small, bittersweet victory compared to all the other lives that had been lost, but it was a well-deserved one nevertheless.

In the end, upon escaping the forest, their show had actually been their saving grace. Despite the governor's best attempts to clamp a lid on things, their status as minor celebrities had prevailed – helped by the fact that the ambulance driver who'd responded to their 9-1-1 call was a fan. Unbeknownst to them at the time, he tweeted out their dire status almost immediately after dropping them off at the hospital.

Not even Yarlberg's myriad friendships had been able to stop the story from going viral. When rumor began to spread that the cast of *The Crypto Hunter* was not only badly injured but suffering from the effects of exposure to toxins too, the governor's house of cards began to collapse. Donald Krychech's abrupt resignation a few days later only served to fuel those rumors.

Though what had leaked was more than enough, the public would sadly never be allowed to know the whole truth. Despite his ties to Washington, Yarlberg was power-less to stop the ATF officials who descended upon the Wharton State Forest to clean up any evidence that Derek and his team had been there.

Samples were collected and bodies burned. Thanks to information Danni was able to provide, the Lesterfield compound – a derelict paper mill from the dawn of the industrial revolution – was found. Sophie Guiterrez was rescued, alive but in critical condition. Unfortunately, the bodies of several other victims – including Abigail – were also discovered.

No trace of survivors from the Lesterfield clan were found – including the one Derek and Julia had left lying unconscious in the woods. It was as if he, and any others who might have escaped, simply disappeared into the night, hopefully to never be seen again – a likely scenario since their former home was now the epicenter of a massive cleanup effort by the state's new head of environmental protection.

The governor was just sputtering out a response of "no comment" on the TV when Danni heard the door to the inner office open. Derek stepped out and closed it behind him. He'd been hospitalized since their return from the Pine Barrens, having only recently been released. However, he still had months of physical therapy ahead of him to regain full use of his left arm. Even now, he couldn't quite stop it from shaking slightly as he approached his teammates.

"Norah wanted a few minutes alone to speak with her. Last-minute paperwork, make sure she knows what she's getting into."

"And probably warn her to ignore all your bullshit," Mitchell said.

Derek smiled, then turned to Danni. "You sure you're okay with this?"

Danni nodded. "Nobody can replace Frank, but as you told me last year, the show must go on."

Derek reached up to wipe a tear from his eye. "So I did."

Danni put a hand on his shoulder as her own eyes misted up. They were the lucky ones. They'd lived to tell the tale. Others weren't so fortunate. Even less so were their families.

Arthur's parents were now stuck in the same boat as her own. He'd been gone by the time she limped back to the clearing, despite Mitchell's best efforts. Now his family was left to think his death was nothing more than a stupid accident. They couldn't be told the real reason why he'd ventured into the woods that day, nor of how brave he'd been.

Still, she wasn't sure which was worse: his parents believing a lie, or that Francis's wife knew the truth yet couldn't tell anyone. At least Shakti understood that her husband had been a hero to the end, but it would be a long time before she could take any comfort in that now that their future together had been stolen.

The team was there for her, but all of them were aware that it wasn't nearly enough, especially since their superiors had already handed them their next assignment. The *show* indeed had to go on and, in order to do that, they all had to be on board and with a full roster.

At first, Danni had been against Derek's suggestion of Julia joining the team, but she realized that was nothing more than her own anger and hurt speaking. She knew the others had likely felt a similar resentment toward her following Chuck's death, even if none of them had ever voiced it. The mission was bigger than any of them and they all understood that.

Julia had proven herself to them. And, sadly, though the governor's influence was shrinking by the day, he'd still been spiteful enough to pull what strings he could to ensure her career as a journalist was over. She needed them and they, interestingly enough, needed her. As it turned out, she'd started her career behind the camera before being promoted to the front of the screen.

"Any word on her sister?" Mitchell asked, wiping his eyes and changing the subject.

Derek shook his head. "Julia said she hasn't been returning any of her calls."

"Poor girl."

Derek nodded. "She lost her husband, suffered through God-knows-what, and can't even talk about it. She's going to need time."

"But Julia is her sister," Danni replied.

"I know, but we each have to heal in our own way."

"How's Julia taking it?"

"She's putting on a tough face, but you can tell she's hurting inside. Nevertheless, she's grateful her sister is alive. For now, that's good enough. Eventually she'll come around. And at least we'll be busy enough to not dwell on it much."

Mitchell let out a sigh that turned into a chuckle. "No rest for the wicked."

"None indeed. Norah told me that those squatches in Arkansas are acting up again. Sounds like a rogue male, maybe two. Then there's been complaints of chupacabra activity at some farm in New Mexico..."

"Call a dog catcher. Freaking coyotes with mange aren't our problem."

Danni patted the medic on the shoulder. "Don't knock an easy assignment when they give us one."

"Oh," Derek continued, "and there've also been reports of divers going missing off the coast of Bermuda. There was an abandoned fishing boat found with sucker marks six inches wide in its hull, which would indicate a..."

"Sold," Danni interrupted.

"Huh?"

"You could have stopped at Bermuda. I don't know about you, but I've about had it up to here with forests for a while."

Derek smiled sadly and nodded. "Yeah, me too."

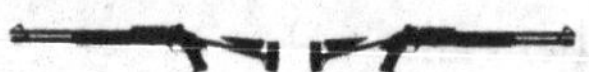

Sophie Guiterrez erased the messages on her machine — two from her mom, one from a concerned aunt, and three more from her sister. As she stepped away from the phone and into the kitchen, a spasm racked her stomach, nearly doubling her over.

She grabbed hold of the countertop to steady herself and squeezed her eyes shut until it passed. It was the same as always, but she'd begun to welcome the pain. Best yet, she was certain she'd felt a kick this time.

It was probably too early, but she knew what she felt and it made her proud. Her baby – *John's baby*. Despite everything that had happened, their child was alive and growing within her.

The doctors had all shown concern for her condition, specifically her blood tests. They wanted to monitor her progress, take steps to terminate it if necessary. She wouldn't allow that. After all she'd been through, they wouldn't take her baby away, too.

She made sure of that – checked herself out of the hospital, sequestered herself away, and kept the pregnancy a secret from her family. She was certain they'd understand, but at the same time, she didn't want to run the risk of them trying to talk her out of it.

Despite what those monsters had done to her, she knew – *knew* – the baby was John's, one last miracle from God before he'd taken her husband into his fold. It *had* to be. And, knowing that, she wouldn't let anyone take that away from her.

Sophie swallowed some vitamins, then washed them down with water. As she was leaving the kitchen, she felt another kick from inside, stronger than the first, and she winced at the force behind it.

Yes. Their child was going to be strong and healthy. She wouldn't let anyone tell her otherwise, no matter what.

THE END

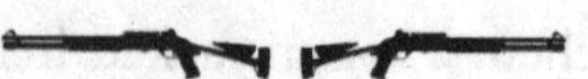

The Crypto-Hunter will return in
Kraken Hunters

If you enjoyed this story, I invite you to sign up for my newsletter. Not only will you be kept up to date on new releases, but you'll get awesome freebies, too. CLICK HERE to gain join today!

BONUS CHAPTER

KRAKEN HUNTERS
A Tale of the Crypto-Hunter

The leviathan lay upon the ocean floor, nearly perfectly camouflaged despite its bulk.

Fish of all sizes swam by it while innumerable crustaceans crawled close enough for it to easily ensnare, but it paid them no mind. It was a night hunter. For now, its hunger was sated and it merely slumbered, enjoying the current that washed over its massive form.

Soon enough it would rouse and when it did, the ocean would become a feeding frenzy of quick strikes followed by the tear of both flesh and carapace as its powerful beak crushed anything placed within. But for now it was content in its territorial waters.

Once, long ago, its species was more numerous, but a rapid growth rate, declining food sources, and aggressive competition had gradually whittled their numbers down. Now, no more than a handful remained in the depths, and encounters with others of its kind were rare as they were solitary creatures by nature. Those that survived and grew into great beasts, such as the leviathan, were often loathe to venture into the shallows. As a result, they were relatively unknown to the world above, where the sea gave way to air.

There came a slight shudder in the ground beneath the massive creature, causing it to stir slightly. A minor nuisance, nothing more, as I began to settle down again.

Mere moments later, though, a much larger tremor hit, shaking the silty ocean floor, stirring up debris, and clouding the normally clear waters.

The roar of a distant explosion came next, disturbing its sensitive ears, and bringing with it a torrent of swirling water. The resulting shockwave stunned all of the fish swimming nearby, but was ultimately little more than a minor discomfort to the leviathan.

Once it passed, the creature prepared to settle itself down again.

Thrum.

Something unseen jostled the beast. It was as if a wave of energy passed through its body, electrifying its brain and jolting it fully away.

Thrum.

Another invisible wave passed through it, causing it to recoil. Pain and discomfort registered in its mind and it lashed out with its tentacles causing the water around it to swirl in a maelstrom.

Again and again the invisible enemy struck, driving the creature into a near frenzy. However, it could neither see nor sense where its foe was. All it knew was that it was being attacked and whatever was doing so seemed to be both relentless and outside its reach.

More waves of energy passed through the mighty beast. Soon enough, misery and confusion gave way to rage. It struck out again with its tentacles, lashing at anything that moved. In short time the water was slick with the blood of any fish unlucky enough to be within the great beast's vast reach.

But still the thrumming continued, relentlessly tormenting the beast with its silent but inexorable power.

The leviathan began to scan the ocean floor, looking for something, *anything*, to attack that would stop the assault on its senses.

All surviving creatures within its immediate vicinity had fled following its initial fury. Finding nothing upon which to vent its anger. It began to swim, casting its mammoth form off the ocean floor and toward the surface.

Soon enough, it detected something worthy of its wrath. Killing this new thing would surely cease the torment.

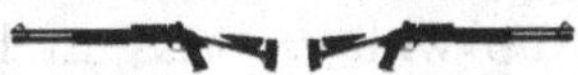

"Say that again, please. I was ... distracted."

Sydney Treco was bored. This assignment was bullshit and everyone aboard the San Cristóbal Tortuga knew it. They were out here for one reason and one reason only, to give the illusion that they were doing something worthwhile.

In fact, the only one who seemed excited was the geologist standing in front of him, a Dr. Rigel, or Regal ... some R-word Sydney couldn't be bothered to remember.

"The core samples we took yesterday," the scientist said, calling up a chart on his laptop. "They're very unusual."

"How so?" There was only one level of unusual that would have roused Sydney's interest and that was news that they'd found an unexpected pocket of oil or natural gas, the bigger the better.

"We're not certain yet."

"Come again?"

"We found traces of iridium along with the expected sediment, which in itself is highly unusual. But there was something mixed in with it, trace fragments of a metal of unknown origin."

"Unknown origin?" Sydney asked, perking up.

"Well, maybe unknown is a bit strong," the scientist said, pushing his glasses up on his nose, no doubt to emphasize his nerd credentials. "What I mean is we haven't identified it yet. We're still analyzing it, and there hasn't been time to carbon date it yet, but..."

"Oh." Sydney's interest dropped to near zero again. Why was this asshole bothering him, then? The guy was getting all worked up when even he admitted a full analysis hadn't been completed. Was he really that bored, too? The sad thing was, Sydney had seen this before, had gotten his hopes up with reports just like these. Then, invariably, when the results were double-checked there was almost always some excuse: contamination or machine error. Every *fucking* time. It seemed to be the story of his corporate life.

He official title on this mission was Offshore Installation Manager. He was in charge of this expedition, on paper anyway, by the ZarroGreen Oil Company, named after its founder Miguel Zarro, one of the richest men in all of South America.

The reality was he knew why he was actually there, and had been passed over for the far juicier Gulf expedition he'd been hoping for. He'd mouthed off to the wrong VP.

Now, as punishment, he was onboard this floating asylum. The fact that the weather had been beautiful up until now, only accentuated the fact that he was in the heart of the Caribbean yet unable to enjoy any of its splendors. Hell they were barely a hundred miles north of Turks and Caicos. A short helicopter ride could have him relaxing on a beach with a tropical drink in hand, but instead he was busy being bored to death.

"So, why are you bothering me with this then?" Sydney asked, interrupting some other nonsense chart the geologist was pontificating about. "Go finish your analysis."

"I thought you might want to know what…"

Sydney opened his mouth to correct the over-eager scientist when the cabin shuddered. He felt the ship lurch around them, and then the lights flickered for several seconds before stabilizing again.

"We're done here," he said with finality, before reaching for the com on his desk even as the geologist beat a hasty retreat. "Anybody there? What the hell was that?"

"I don't know," came the voice of the first mate. "But whatever it is, all of our equipment is going haywire: sonar, ship-to-shore, it's all glitching out."

"What the fuck?" Sydney asked, more to himself than the officer, "Get someone from the platform on the box."

A few moments later Eddie Gunch, the ship's drilling supervisor, got on. "We're working on it, Treco."

"Working on what?"

"I'm not sure. I think we might've hit a pocket of methane. We're checking the drill now."

"A pocket of methane wouldn't have disabled the entire bridge," the first mate complained.

Sydney didn't give a rat's ass about the bridge, the crew, or the whole damned ship for that matter. Well, that wasn't entirely true. He cared about it from a budgetary sense. It wouldn't have surprised anyone at headquarters if this operation turned out to be a bust. Hell, it was practically designed to be. But equipment damage was a whole other ball of wax. Shit like that would be dumped on his shoulders in a hot second.

"How's the drill?" he asked.

"Like I said, we're checking it out, but there may be some damage."

"Just fucking great."

"Might take some time to know for sure. The controls are..."

"Are what?"

"They're acting ... weird. Not responding like they should."

The first mate continued to bitch about the crap on the bridge, but that was his problem to deal with. Sydney wasn't captain of this rust bucket. It wasn't his job to do anything except make sure everyone else was doing theirs. He told the first mate as such just before signing off.

Fucking wonderful! Sydney stepped from the cabin, preparing to head for the drilling platform. It was just his luck. This entire operation had been pretty much designed to be a cluster-fuck from the start, but a necessary one. ZarroGreen wasn't about to let their hard-bought drilling rights expire via entropy. They'd lost most of their bids in the Gulf, minus the expedition Sydney had been jockeying for, but had made up for it by greasing pockets all over the Caribbean. But now, those rights were up for renewal, and if ZarroGreen didn't show at least some effort on their part they could very well lose them.

The problem was, they were on, at best, a fishing expedition as far as Sydney was concerned. The geological surveys of this area weren't exactly promising, but they were in too much of a rush to risk botching the areas that were likely to yield fruit.

The company's exploratory teams were currently too busy elsewhere, spread too thin. So when it was finally noticed that the clock was ticking for them here, they panicked and did what they could in the fastest – and cheapest in Sydney's opinion – method possible.

The Tortuga was one of ZarroGreen's oldest and

smallest drillships, due for decommission by year's end. It seemed the perfect solution to the higher ups: send an old ship that wouldn't be missed to make sure their rights didn't expire. If something was found, great. Newer and better equipment would be called in. Even if not, though, so long as the company could show evidence that they'd done their minimum due diligence, then ZarroGreen could continue to sit on their rights until they were ready to mount a more serious operation.

Unfortunately, the Tortuga wasn't exactly in prime maintenance condition. Everything about it was old, rusty, and unpleasant.

It wasn't a surprise to anyone aboard when something broke down. However, to seemingly have everything go haywire at once was not something that Sydney wanted to hear. The captain was off duty and, while they were anchored, Sydney was technically in charge anyway, so that meant it was his job to kick at least the drilling operation in the bulkhead until such time as it decided to play nice again.

As he climbed the stairs to the platform, he amused himself with a small fantasy in which this accursed ship sank beneath the waves, through no fault of his own of course. He envisioned himself sitting on a beach, a babe on his arm and a drink in his hand, watching it go down for the final time. Fuck *Titanic*, that was the movie he wanted to see.

A few roughnecks passed him as on the way, barking out greetings which he didn't return, being too busy stepping to the side so as to not get his button down shirt more dirty than it already was. That was perhaps what he hated most about going up to the platform. Everything, even the control room, felt like it was encrusted in a thin layer of grime.

That included the personnel.

Eddie met him halfway up. He stopped without offering the drilling supervisor a hand in greeting. "Please tell me you have good news."

Before Eddie could answer him, though, the ship lurched again, this time more violently than before.

"I thought you said the drill was off."

"It is," Eddie replied, looking around. "That wasn't the..."

The deck lurched beneath them, the ship visibly listing to one side.

"What the fuck," Sydney cried, as both men grabbed hold of the railing. "Did we hit a reef?"

"Way out here?" Eddie asked, holding on for dear life as both men were a good fifty feet above the main deck.

A rogue wave maybe? Sydney knew about those. But he'd had a clear view of the horizon just moments earlier. The sea had been calm, clear with nothing in...

"What the fuck?" Eddie cried, pointing.

Sydney turned his head. What he saw made him certain he must have passed out or had maybe started hallucinating on gas fumes.

Something was rising up past them, coming from the sea itself. It appeared to be an impossibly long fleshy mass, covered with massive suckers that scraped along the side of the ship as it continued to climb.

A memory played out in Sydney's mind, a movie he'd seen a few years back, something with Johnny Depp. Pirates! That's what it had been about, Sydney considered, as more monstrous tentacles rose from the deep.

One of them wrapped around the superstructure upon which Sydney and Eddie stood and began to deform it with a groan of tortured metal.

It was impossible, yet somehow happening anyway.

Sydney grabbed hold of the railing, holding on for dear life, but Eddie wasn't nearly so lucky. He tumbled past the offshore manager into the open air. For one surreal moment, the drill master reached out, as if hoping to be able to catch hold of something by sheer will alone, and then he was gone – falling toward the deck below.

The ship began to lurch more violently to the side, and Sydney felt the rig beginning to give way under the assault of the nightmare tentacles wrapped around it.

His feet slipped out beneath him as the ship listed again, and Sydney found himself hanging by his fingers over fifty feet above the surface of the water.

Screams and cries could be heard amidst the fatigue of metal being strained beyond its capacity, but nothing mattered to Sydney beyond his own predicament.

I knew this fucking mission was cursed.

Almost as if in answer to him, a great mass of orange-brown flesh emerged from the ocean beneath him. He had time to glimpse one massive eyeball which seemed to peer up at him and then his fingers slipped and he fell – desperately hoping he'd hit the water instead of the deck, but knowing that at this height it would be the equivalent of slamming into solid concrete.

Somehow, though, the thought of a quick death wasn't all that frightening right at that moment.

KRAKEN HUNTERS

AUTHOR'S NOTE

So ... this one might have been a wee bit late. Yeah, that's entirely my fault. But there's the old saying about better late than never.

Truth be told, I was beginning to worry that never might be the case. But, no matter how many times I put this story back into my digital drawer, the fact remained that I'd made a promise: both to my readers and myself that this story would see the light of day.

Now, don't get me wrong, this is less a tale of woe and more one of it simply not being the right time. The tale presented here is fairly unchanged from the outline I first created for it, so it was never a case of being unhappy with the story itself.

Devil Hunters had the unfortunate luck to be started right when two other things were happening – the muse had dropped an awesome story idea into my head, which would eventually become *The Necromancer's Wife* (by my nom de plume Cara Vance), and my other series *The Tome of Bill* was starting to gain in popularity.

Both events caused me to set this aside with that most vile of lies to myself: *I'll get right back to this.*

Needless to say, it took somewhat longer than expected and for that I sincerely apologize. That said, please do not think I enjoyed writing this any less as a result. I continue to be wildly passionate about cryptozoology as well as monster stories. As much as I might enjoy writing my comedic novels, there is something about a bloody monster rampage that is satisfyingly cathartic.

I hope you feel the same way and that you'll stick around for a while longer. We're not done with this world and its characters yet, not by a long shot.

Rick G.

ABOUT THE AUTHOR

Rick Gualtieri lives alone in central New Jersey with only his wife, three kids, and countless pets to both keep him company and constantly plot against him. When he's not busy monkey-clicking words, he can typically be found jealously guarding his collection of vintage Transformers from all who would seek to defile them.

Defilers beware!

Also by Rick Gualtieri
TALES OF THE CRYPTO-HUNTER
Bigfoot Hunters
Devil Hunters
Kraken Hunters
Boar War

HIGH MOON
The Girl Who Punches Werewolves
The Girl Who Fights Witches
The Girl Who Hunts Fairies
The Girl Who Defies Fate

THE TOME OF BILL UNIVERSE
THE TOME OF BILL
Bill the Vampire
Scary Dead Things
The Mourning Woods

Holier Than Thou
Sunset Strip
Goddamned Freaky Monsters
Half A Prayer
The Wicked Dead
Shining Fury
The Last Coven

BILL OF THE DEAD
Strange Days
Everyday Horrors
Carnage À Trois
The Liching Hour